"I read The Last Apostle by Dennis Brooke and loved it. My only regret is I finished it in one day and I want more! A fantastic story with an even better message."

-**Tom Ziglar**, Speaker and author of bestselling book *Born to Win*

"Emotionally compelling and extremely well written, The Last Apostle is a wonderful fable of hope, faith, and love that left me inspired and renewed in my faith."

-**Rob "Waldo" Waldman**, author of the national bestseller *Never Fly Solo*

"Skillfully plotted, paced and written, The Last Apostle is an engaging read that sets the hook hard and reels one in quickly. In truth, I cannot wait to read the sequel — and wish I would have conceived of the concept myself!"

-**Brannon Hollingsworth**, co-author of *H20, Skein of Shadows*, and *The Guestbook*; author of *The Truth Is Out There, Ambush, Nod, Robot Dad*, and *Sundered.*

"When Dennis Brooke first told me the idea for his novel, The Last Apostle I was intrigued. After reading it, I'm captivated. By weaving history with modern day allure, Brooke has created a fascinating, fresh perspective on the apostle Jesus loved. Can't wait to see where he takes the story from here."

-**James**

"Well-researched and beautifully written! Dennis Brooke weaves a complex tapestry of human emotion that flows across 2000 years in the life of one man. Imagine what you might learn and how you might engage the culture if you'd lived more than two hundred lifetimes. Brooke's unique concept for "The Last Apostle" and his excellent description of John's emotion as the oldest man alive makes me wonder... does Dennis know him? "The Last Apostle" will grab you from the start."

-**Austin Boyd**, Award-winning author of
Mars Hill Classified series and speaker

"With a weaving of current events and history, Brooke's novel provides a narrative drive that has plot surprises, moral challenges, and thought-provoking character dilemmas."

-**Dennis E. Hensley**, Ph.D., author of
Jesus in All Four Seasons

"In The Last Apostle, Dennis Brooke effortlessly blends past and present as he creates a world where Jesus' beloved disciple is still alive. Brooke gives readers a glimpse of daily life in the ancient Mediterranean and how the Gospel spread across the Roman Empire. He explores the burden of living a prolonged life, including the challenges of staying hidden in our shrinking modern world. Drama, romance, and humor all come together in a story that's both entertaining and edifying. The Last Apostle is a must-read for anyone who's wondered about the rumor mentioned in the book of John. It's for anyone who's ever thought What if the last living apostle was still alive?"

-**Kim Vandel,** author of *Into the Fire*

"A compelling premise, engaging characters, and a well-crafted plot make The Last Apostle a stunning speculative fiction debut. Dennis Brooke is a novelist to watch."

-**Janalyn Voigt**, author of
DawnSinger (Tales of Faeraven)

"I dare you to set this book down after the first chapter. The compelling premise that the apostle John could still be alive hooked me, but it was the well-crafted plot and strong characters that kept me reading. Put The Last Apostle at the top of your reading list!"

-**Lesley Ann McDaniel,** author of *Saving Grace*

"I didn't have to read far in Brooke's debut novel to realize this was going to be a captivating read. Strong characters, who are easy to relate to, and a compelling plot propel this story in a way that simply carries the reader from one page to the next. One for the keeper shelf!"

-**Lynnette Bonner**, author of Shepherd's Heart Series, Islands of Intrigue series and The Hearts of Hollywood series

"Every so often a novel comes along that blurs the lines of fact and fiction to such an extent that it draws the reader into a world where one questions if what they are reading is true. The Last Apostle does just that by setting an elaborate story of the Apostle John's never ending life as eluded to by Jesus in the Gospel of John. Dennis Brooke leads us on a mesmerizing journey filled with action, mystery, intrigue, and suspense. I just couldn't put it down. Like the main character, John Amato, you

will want this book to keep going and never stop. This is truly one of the great adventure novels of the 21st Century."

-**Buzz Leonard**, Missionary

"Dennis Brooke draws readers in and keeps them entertained with fast-paced action. Whether describing John's adventures in the first century or the twenty-first century in this work of speculative fiction, the author includes realistic descriptions accented by gentle humor. I found some scenes reminiscent of the Jesus in the 9 to 5 series by master storyteller Dr. Dennis E. Hensley. The Last Apostle is a page-turner for sure."

-**Diana Savage**, author of *52 Heart Lifters for Difficult Times,* Director, Northwest Christian Writers Renewal

THE LAST APOSTLE

THE LAST APOSTLE

DENNIS BROOKE

Made for Grace
PUBLISHING

Made For Grace Publishing
P.O. Box 1775 Issaquah, WA 98027
www.MadeForGrace.com

Distributed by Made For Grace Publishing
Cover Design by DeeDee Heathman
Interior Design by DeeDee Heathman

Library of Congress Cataloging-in-Publication data
Brooke, Dennis
The Last Apostle

p. cm.
ISBN: 9781613398395
LCCN: 2015945895

Printed in the United States of America

For further information contact Made For Grace Publishing
+14255266480 or email service@madeforsuccess.net

To Laurie, my partner in this adventure of life. It is an honor to be your husband.

To my parents, Ron and Jonie, who instilled love for reading in me.

To Jesus, the true Author of all.

Chapter One

Peter turned and saw that the disciple whom Jesus loved was following them.... When Peter saw him, he asked, "Lord, what about him?"
Jesus answered, "If I want him to remain alive until I return, what is that to you? You must follow me." Because of this, the rumor spread among the brothers that this disciple would not die. But Jesus did not say that he would not die; he only said, "If I want him to remain alive until I return, what is that to you?"

JOHN 21:20-23

JOHN AMATO WATCHED the man with salt and pepper hair run his hand through the long blonde tresses of the woman at his side. The man seemed much more interested in his companion than in listening to the lecture on *The Fate of the Apostles* by Professor Wes Cavanaugh. From his seat directly behind the pair John noted the weathered gold band on the man's ring finger and the gray accents in her locks. He watched them lean their heads into each other and share some whispered secret. The sense of longing in him flared.

At the front of the auditorium Cavanaugh cleared his throat. "Now, I'd like to pose a provocative question." John turned his attention to the professor. The couple did the same.

"Imagine that the last apostle to die—didn't." John dropped the heavy pen he had been twirling idly in his fingers. It clattered across the floor and rolled against the seat in front of him. He raised one eyebrow as the professor picked up the bottle of Perrier sitting on the table to his left and took a languid sip, seemingly calculated to let the audience ponder his incendiary statement.

Cavanaugh let his statement linger over the suddenly silent auditorium. "What if the only apostle reported to have expired of natural causes is actually living among us today?"

John ran his fingers through his curly, dark hair, and scratched his scalp. *Shut up. For the love of God, please shut up.*

Finally, the professor stepped out from behind his podium. "I can see from the expression on some of your faces that you're trying to think where you might find wood suitable for a bonfire so that you can burn me at the stake as a heretic." Some, but not all members of the audience chuckled.

"Now, I don't want you to think that I believe John, the Beloved Disciple, is still alive after two thousand years. I've just found it interesting to think, what if Jesus meant what he said when he told Peter in John 21:21, 'If I want him to remain alive until I return, what is that to you?'"

Cavanaugh stepped behind the podium, gripped both sides, and enunciated every word of his next sentence slowly, "What if Jesus meant exactly what he said—that John would remain alive until he returned?"

John shook his head.

"I am pleased to announce that this idea also intrigues a Hollywood producer. I am in negotiations for a television series based on a living apostle John." Cavanaugh grinned broadly. "And with that, I will take time to autograph a few books."

The noise from polite clapping in Pigott Auditorium at Seattle University was supplemented by the buzz around Cavanaugh's announcement. A young woman who had been sitting next to John during the lecture turned to him and flashed him a smile. "That's cool." John gave her a distracted nod. But his heart started racing as he thought, *The end times couldn't be triggered by a stupid TV show, could they?*

The man in front of John leaned over to his wife and whispered in a loud voice, "And maybe John rooms with Elvis." John grinned.

Most of the crowd, including the couple, headed to the exits to enjoy what was left of the summer evening. As John's eyes followed the pair to the back, he recognized a resident from the local men's mission. The scraggily bearded man snored softly in the back row, unaware that the lecture was over. John headed to the rear of the auditorium and patted him on the shoulder.

The homeless man woke with a start. "What the—"

John grinned down at him. "Show's over, Dave."

A look of recognition passed over his face. "Oh, it's you. I was just, uh…"

"No worries, buddy. The professor was a bit dry at times." John leaned toward Dave and asked in a conspiratorial voice, "But what do you think of Cavanaugh's idea of a movie with the Apostle Thomas as a superhero?"

"Oh, yeah." Dave nodded enthusiastically. "I thought that was cool."

He laughed and patted Dave on the shoulder. "You should catch the bus before it gets too late. Let's grab some coffee after breakfast tomorrow."

He left Dave and joined the line of autograph seekers up front. As he inched toward the book table, he could hear the supplicants ahead of him. Several asked the one-time celebrity expert about a fine point in his talk. Others seemed bent on impressing Cavanaugh with their own knowledge of New Testament history. Many were enthusiastic about his idea for a television show and asked questions about it.

As John stood in line, he compared the picture of Cavanaugh on the back of the book with the flesh and blood author sitting behind the table. From the few silver strands in the professor's dark hair and the crow's feet at the corners of his eyes John guessed he was in his mid to late forties. Cavanaugh looked more like a television newscaster than a New Testament scholar.

When John reached the head of the line, he pushed his worn copy of *The Fate of the Apostles* across the table for an autograph. John felt a deep, simmering anger and struggled to make his words civil. He leaned toward Cavanaugh and in a measured tone he asked, "Why a show around the myth that the apostle John is still alive? Why resurrect an idea that was debunked in the second century?"

Cavanaugh raised his left eyebrow and looked across the table at John. He scanned him up and down as if he was looking for a concealed weapon.

John gave him a wan smile. "It just seems that this idea is out of line with someone of your stature, professor. You have a reputation for defending the faith."

Cavanaugh seemed to relax. "I'm not attacking our faith, young man. I'm just using an old legend to entertain people. Entertain them in a way that makes our history live."

"So, what would the apostle be doing nowadays? Why wouldn't he reveal his identity and make millions of converts?"

The professor looked up and gave him a knowing smile. "You'll just have to wait and get the answers to those questions when my series airs." He opened the book in front of him and poised his pen over the title page. He looked up at John. "And your name?"

He hesitated for a moment. "John. John Amato."

"John, same as the Apostle."

"Wasn't his name actually Johanan?" John pronounced the name in ancient Aramaic. The word rolled out of the back of his throat, like he was trying to clear an obstruction.

Cavanaugh gave him a sly smile. "I see you know something about the subject." He turned back to the book to finish the inscription. "Are you a student here, John?"

John hesitated again. Finally, he said, "No, just interested in New Testament history. I teach a few classes on it myself at local churches."

"What do you do for a living?"

"Lots of things." He shot the professor a serious look. "Basically, whatever God asks me to do."

"Of course." Cavanaugh closed the book and pushed it back across the table to him, once again giving John a wary look. "Keep an eye out for the show and all your questions will be answered." He turned to a middle-aged woman in line behind John and beckoned.

John gritted his teeth and forced himself to walk out of the auditorium at a deliberate pace. As he passed through the atrium he glanced up at the tower of glass over the building exit. The fiery orange and yellow tendrils of the twenty-foot tall Dale Chihuly sculpture looked like a genetic experiment on squids gone awry. After a few moments John tore his gaze away.

He exited the hall and strode to the bike rack near the entrance. By the time he reached it, his anger had dissipated. As John strapped on his helmet, he looked skyward and concluded his internal conversation. *Just ignore Cavanaugh. It will blow over.*

He glanced at his watch. He had promised to meet Scott, his twenty-something neighbor, at Doyle's Public House on Queen Anne hill to catch the Sounders match. Should still be early in the game. Hopefully Scott had a table staked out.

He turned on his iPod and put the earbud in his right ear as he scanned the playlists: Arabic, Afrikaans, French, and a half dozen other languages. John selected the Hindi refresher course and strapped the player onto his arm. He turned on the rear blinker and headlamp and slung himself onto the seat of his bicycle. As he pushed off toward the pathway that passed by the chapel, he noticed the couple he had been watching earlier sitting on the edge of the reflecting pool next to the chapel.

They were holding hands. They were laughing. John stared for a moment, then finally turned his head, swallowed, and pumped hard on the pedals to take him away from the scene.

In moments, he reached the arterial that bordered the north side of the campus. John stopped to wait for the light to change and pressed the play button on the iPod. He followed the language lesson, quietly responding to the instructor.

When the light turned green he stroked the pedals hard to build up speed. He glanced around him, keeping an eye out for drivers oblivious to his presence. John kept his left ear open to listen for traffic noise. As he pedaled up hills on his route, cars moved gingerly around him. On the downhill parts he kept up with the moving vehicles.

He was heading up the street to Doyle's when motion in a narrow passageway between two buildings caught his attention. Two figures, but were they in an embrace—or a struggle? The evening light was fading so fast that in another five minutes he would have missed them entirely. He swung around for another look.

As he pulled up on the sidewalk, he could see the broad back of one of the figures. His head was covered in short, charcoal colored hair. He had the other figure in a grip. He could hear a woman pleading in heavily accented English. "Please, let me go. Don't hurt me." He placed the accent: Portuguese—Brazilian Portuguese.

The click, click, click of John's bike gears echoed in the passageway. The man jerked his head around. John realized that what he had mistaken for hair was really a dark ski mask pulled down over his head. His pale skin showed through the large holes for his eyes and mouth. "Go away," the man said. He flashed a large knife at John with his right hand. At a glance he could tell it was a standard military issue KA-BAR—the type of knife an amateur would pick up at a military surplus store.

His left hand firmly gripped the blouse of the woman. He shook her in warning. "Go away or I'll cut you and her up."

"Please, help," the woman said. Her voice quavered with fear.

John gently laid down his bike and pulled the earphone out of his ear.

He held out both hands at his side, palms forward, to show he was unarmed. In his most soothing voice he said, "Let her go and leave right now. Nobody gets hurt."

The man pulled the woman around in front of him and faced John. He pointed the knife at her throat. "Go away or I cut her up." She began to plead frantically—in Portuguese.

As John's vision adjusted to the dark, he could see heavy beads of sweat around the man's eyes. He was breathing rapidly through his nostrils.

John stepped slowly forward. "Easy friend. Just let her go."

In response, the man pulled the woman more tightly to his chest with his left hand. He held the blade against her throat. John noticed the corners of his eyebrows move up and together. His eyes opened wide. *The guy's terrified. He's no professional.* John looked at the woman. In Portuguese he calmly said, "Don't move. Be absolutely still. Close your eyes."

She looked at him in shock for a second, then nodded imperceptibly. She stiffened and squeezed her eyelids shut, as if she could make the scene go away. The man said, "What did you say to her? Stop that. I tell you—"

John stepped forward again. He stopped with his feet a shoulder's width apart. "Let me give you some money. Just let her go." He slowly reached back, pulled out his wallet, and extended it toward the man. The woman, eyes still tightly shut, began to whimper.

"I'm warning you, get out of here now," shouted the man. He moved the tip of the blade away from the woman's throat and pointed it at John.

"Here, take the money," With a flip of his wrist John sent the wallet up and over the robber's head. He kept his gaze locked on the eyes of the assailant and watched him track the arc of the billfold as it passed over his head.

Now! In one fluid motion John stepped forward and struck the man's wrist with the edge of his left hand. The man shrieked in pain and the knife flew out of his grasp and ricocheted off the wall. John grasped the assailant's wrist and pulled him forward.

The thug released the woman, who fell sideways and landed on her hands and knees. John pulled the man's arm behind his back and then swept his legs out from under him. As he collapsed, John pushed him face first onto the cement.

He put his knee in the small of the man's back and gripped his wrist tightly. He was trembling with anger. He took a few seconds to control his breathing before he leaned forward and said, "Don't move. Don't even think of it, or I *will* hurt you."

A voice came from behind. "Dude, that was awesome."

John looked over his shoulder. "Scott, what—"

"I was going into Doyle's and saw you turn into the alley. Man, you kicked his—"

"Scott, call 9-1-1."

"Oh. Yeah."

Scott pulled his phone out of his pocket and started to dial. "Where did you learn those moves?"

The masked man started to struggle. John grasped his wrist more tightly and pushed his arm higher up his back. The captive howled in pain. John let off some of the pressure and leaned over. "I told you, don't move."

John looked at the woman. She was sitting on the ground, face in her hands, sobbing. He asked in Portuguese: "Senhorita, are you okay?" She looked at him and nodded. "Senhorita, you should fix your blouse."

She looked down. Her blouse had been torn partly open in the struggle. She slowly buttoned it, then stood up, and started to brush herself off. She looked down at John who was still holding her assailant on the ground. "Obrigado—thank you. I was so afraid." She started to sob again and sat down on the ground. She buried her face in her hands.

John said, "It's okay. It will be all right now. It's all over."

The sound of a police siren split the evening. John could see Scott standing on the sidewalk, waving his arms. A squad car squealed to a stop at the entrance to the alley. Two officers jumped out and approached John, hands on the butt of their holstered weapons.

"Detective, this guy just tried to rob this young woman." He nodded at the man under his knee.

Scott chimed in. "You should have seen my buddy take him down. He was amazing."

The cop smiled as he pulled out a pair of handcuffs. "I'm no detective. I work for a living." He addressed the man on the ground. "Little warm for a stocking mask, don't you think?" He jerked it off his head. The second cop knelt down next to the young woman.

The captive moaned as the officer cuffed his right wrist. John released him and the cop finished cuffing him and then pulled the mugger firmly to his feet. The unmasked man howled with pain as the handcuff pulled at his knife hand.

"Dude, what happened to your ankle?" said Scott.

John looked at Scott, then down. A long cut on his left ankle, right above the sock, was bleeding into his shoe. He felt the warm blood pooling under his foot. John sat down and started to gently pull off the shoe. "The knife must have hit me when I knocked it free. Looks like it only cut the flesh."

"Man, we should call you an ambulance." Scott pulled out his phone.

"No need. Just get me the first aid kit off my bike." He pointed to a pouch on the handlebars. Scott rushed to retrieve it.

The second officer bent over John's ankle. "Does look like a nasty wound. The EMTs are on the way to take a look at the young lady."

John pulled a gauze pack out of his kit and wiped away the blood. The cut was deep, but the flow was already slowing. "That's alright. I can bandage it up myself." As John cleaned the wound and taped on a gauze compress, he gave the officer the basics about the attack.

The officer passed him a business card. "That's a good start, Mr. Amato. But we'd like to get an official statement. If you wouldn't mind coming down to the station."

John nodded as he laced up his bloody shoe. "I'll be there in an hour."

As John entered the lobby of the police station, his phone rang—Mozart—a ringtone that indicated it had been forwarded from a number still used by only a few people. He pulled it out of his pocket and looked at the display: *Greta Wallenberg.*

He answered with the gravelly voice of an old man with a noticeable, but not thick, German accent. "Ja?"

"Mr. Fischer?" The voice was familiar, even though he hadn't heard it for a decade.

"Yes. Is this Greta?"

"It is."

He chuckled, the friendly chuckle of a kindly old man. "Well then, you know to call me Johannes, or at least John."

Silence ensued. Finally she said, "Johannes. It's my father." She stifled a sob. "Franz is dead."

Chapter Two

No man has ever lived that had enough of children's gratitude or woman's love.

William Butler Yeats

I CAN'T BELIEVE HE'S dumping me with a text.

Nicole Logan glanced down at her phone as she hurried down the jetway. Dan wanted to take a break? Fine. Nicole stared at the screen and tried to believe it really was fine.

She shoved the phone into her laptop bag and glanced up in time to see the man in front of her had stopped. She stumbled, fell forward, and planted her face hard between his shoulder blades.

Nicole took a step back as she rubbed her nose. She blinked and looked up.

The deeply tanned man was looking over his shoulder at her. He scanned her up and down—his gaze lingered like a pastry chef critically assessing a cheesecake. Then he glanced down at her legs below the hem of her business skirt. Finally he looked back at her and smiled.

She flashed an embarrassed smile. "Should have watched where I'm going."

"No problem." He smiled again.

She broke her gaze and nodded at the passengers in front of him. "Looks like we're moving again." She glanced at his left hand, which was holding the shoulder strap on his laptop bag. No wedding ring—but there was a tan line where one would normally be.

He glanced forward. "Looks like." He turned back and gave her one last smile. "Bump into you later, I hope."

She smirked, smoothed her gray skirt and shuffled forward.

Nicole passed through the hatch of the Alaska Airlines 737, gave the flight attendant a perfunctory smile, and turned down the aisle. She frowned as she passed through the first class cabin. She had been number one on the standby list for a comfy seat up front but the whole section had checked in. Now she was dragging her gear to seat 29C, just ahead of the toilets.

The man she had bumped into stopped just behind first class. He stepped out of the aisle to let her pass. "Bye for now."

Nicole nodded but didn't respond.

She reached the back row and saw a man with dark, curly hair occupied the window seat. He was wearing a bright Hawaiian shirt that featured 1930's era seaplanes in tropical settings. He glanced up at her from his notebook computer and gave her a distracted smile. Nicole guessed he was in his early to mid-thirties, slightly older than she was. She dropped her laptop bag onto the seat and started to lift her rolling suitcase. "I can give you a hand," he said.

"No need. I'm used to hauling this around." As she grunted and pushed it into the overhead bin, she regretted having packed a full set of workout gear, extra baggage that had again gone unused. After she shoved it into place she put her laptop bag on the floor in front of her seat. Her companion had turned back to his computer and was scowling at it. She sat down, pulled her phone out of the bag, then pushed the case underneath the seat.

The text message still waited for her on the screen of the phone, like a taunt: *Nicole, I think it's best for us and the company if we take a break from our relationship.*

She gritted her teeth and squeezed the armrest with her free hand.

As she contemplated composing a pithy response to Dan's text, the man next to her banged his hand on the tray table next to his laptop and sucked air in through his teeth. She jerked her head to look over at him.

"Sorry," he said and gave her a sheepish grin. "I'm trying to read this financial report and it doesn't make sense to me."

She turned back to the text message on her phone, then looked over at her companion's screen. "Do you want me to take a look? I know a bit about finance."

His eyes grew wide with delight. "That would be great." He passed it over the empty middle seat onto her tray table.

She quickly scanned the report. "What are you trying to do?"

"I'm trying to decide if I should invest in this company. I used to have a friend who made decisions like that for me."

He seemed to have a slight accent she'd originally overlooked. Italian? Greek? She couldn't quite place it. She perused the figures and scrolled down. "Where's your friend now?" she asked absentmindedly.

"He passed on—several weeks ago. I'm on my way to visit his daughter."

She looked over at the man. "I'm sorry."

"Thanks. I'm going to miss him terribly, but he was in his eighties and happy and healthy to the end." He flashed her a smile. "He's truly home now."

Nicole gave him a wan smile. *One of them.*

He gestured at the notebook on her tray table. "But now I'm trying to figure out this stuff on my own."

Nicole turned back to the screen. She noticed the Dell was

well used. Some of the lettering on the keyboard was almost worn off and the upper right casing on the screen had been crushed and inexpertly glued back together.

"How did you come to know finances?"

She kept her eyes on the screen as she answered. "I work as a consultant on accounting software systems. We install them at mid-sized companies." She scanned through several pages of the report. "I'm also a partner in a firm I founded with a friend." She blinked rapidly to clear her eyes.

He whistled. "Looks like I found the right seat mate."

"How much do you have to invest?"

He hesitated before responding softly. "A lot."

"A lot?" She looked at him and raised an eyebrow.

He grinned like a mischievous kid who had been caught drinking milk directly out of the carton. "Miss, we've just met."

"Mister…."

"Amato. John Amato." He extended his hand. She shook it firmly. *If you're going to compete in the world of men, shake hands like a man* her dad had taught her.

"Nicole Logan." She dropped his hand and turned back to the screen. "So now that we know each other maybe you can tell me how much you have to invest."

He paused. She turned to look at him. For the first time she looked directly into his deep brown eyes. She felt like she was looking into a wise old soul rather than the eyes of a thirty something guy. He looked back as if he was trying to take a measure of her. Uncharacteristically flustered, she finally broke the gaze.

"You don't have to tell me if you don't want to, Mr. Amato."

"No, that's okay, Ms. Logan. But call me John. Even my father didn't go by Mr. Amato."

She glanced back and he flashed a grin.

A muffled announcement came through the intercom: "Ladies and gentlemen, we're almost ready to close the door and pull away from the gate. Please put away your electronic devices and make sure your seat belts are fastened and your tray tables and seats are upright and locked."

Nicole passed the notebook back to John. He closed it, slid it into a worn leather backpack, and shoved it underneath the seat in front of him.

As the plane started to back away from the gate, the flight attendants launched into their safety patter. Nicole turned back to John.

He asked, "What do you think? Good investment?"

She wrinkled her nose. "From what you showed me, not so much. Their sales figures for the last few years are flat. Most companies in that market are growing."

"Oh."

"So, again, how much do you have to invest?"

He looked into her eyes and with a sly smile said, "Millions. Tens of millions."

She laughed. "You have tens of millions of dollars, but a beat up computer, and you're sitting in the blue water row on a passenger jet?"

A puzzled look crossed his face. "Blue water row?"

With a jerk of her head she indicated the bulkhead behind them. "The row just ahead of the bathrooms." She wrinkled her nose. "For the blue disinfectant they use in the toilet system."

"I'll have to remember that one." He laughed.

She scowled at him. "I have to admit, 'I have tens of millions' is one of the more clever pickup lines anyone has ever tried on me."

He looked at her, eyes wide in surprise. "I would never do that. I really do have that kind of money to invest. But—it's actually not even mine. It really belongs to three very close friends. I'm just their agent."

"Can't they find another person with a little more—financial acumen?"

"People are my thing, not numbers. But I'm the one they trust.

She sat silent for a minute. "Seems like trust is so rare in this day and age."

He nodded. "I haven't always been the most reliable partner for them, but they've always been there for me."

"How long have you known them?"

"Since I was very young." He paused to look out the window as the plane turned onto the runway. "In many respects they're my family."

Their conversation paused while the engines spun up and the plane hurtled down the ribbon of concrete. The crescendo of engines, rattling tray tables, and tires on concrete climaxed when the plane lifted into the sky. In a few minutes it leveled off and the noise faded.

Finally Nicole looked back at John. "So what are you going to do with all this money?"

He grinned his broad grin again. "Change the world."

Her business radar triggered like a 747 had just popped up on her scope. "Do you have a company or something?"

"Nope. Just me and a couple of friends."

Her interest faded—more like a Cessna than a jumbo jet. Their conversation was broken up by the captain's announcement that the aircraft was passing through ten thousand feet and it was now safe to turn on electronic devices. Nicole reached under the seat in front of her and pulled out her own laptop bag.

"If you don't mind, I have to finish a status report before we land." She fired up her laptop and was soon immersed in her work. John pulled out his own notebook and left her in peace.

"Miss?" Nicole looked up at the flight attendant standing next to her. The sandy haired young man was holding a single serving sized bottle of wine with a plastic cup inverted over the top.

Nicole cocked her eyebrow. "Yes?"

"A gentleman sitting toward the front of the plane sent this back for you."

"How do you know it's for me?"

"He described a pretty woman with shoulder length, reddish brown hair in a stylish gray suit." He smiled. "He also said your nose would match a dent in the center of his back."

Nicole rubbed her nose. "That would be me." She looked at the offering in the attendant's hand. "Normally I wouldn't, but this has been a day." She moved her laptop to make space.

The flight attendant set down a paper napkin on Nicole's tray. As he reached for the cup on the top of the bottle, the plane bucked suddenly. He lost his balance and started to fall across Nicole's tray table. She jerked back to avoid a collision. John's hand shot across in front of her and clamped onto the attendant's forearm, stopping him in mid-fall. The bottle in his hand popped into the air. Nicole watched as if it were in slow motion. The cup flew off the top of the bottle and both sailed in an arc toward the window.

John reached up and snatched the bottle out of the air with his left hand. The cup bounced off the wall of the cabin, ricocheted off the window, and finally clattered to rest on his tray table.

The attendant regained his footing and John released his forearm. "I am so sorry," he said. He reached over and retrieved the cup.

"No worries," said John, passing him the wine. "At least the bottle wasn't open yet."

As the attendant removed the screw cap and poured, Nicole looked at John. "Are you some kind of athlete? That looked like something out of a superhero movie."

John grinned, sheepishly. "I like racquetball."

The attendant finished pouring and said, "Compliments of Mr. Barker."

"Tell him thank you—and sorry for the dent in his back."

"Of course." He turned back toward the front of the jetliner.

Nicole stared at the wine.

"Secret admirer?" John asked. She looked at him and frowned.

"No, just someone I ran into on the jetway." She rubbed her nose. "Ran into, *literally.*" She picked up the cup. "I guess this is his pickup line." She lifted it to her lips and savored a long sip.

"You mentioned it's been a day."

"I guess I did."

"I'm a good listener."

She looked at the seat back in front of her and placed the glass down on the table next to her laptop. "I hardly know you."

"Even better. What you tell me goes nowhere."

She looked over at him and found herself looking again into his inviting brown eyes. "Okay, Mr. Going to Change the World. My boyfriend dumped me—dumped me by text."

"Ouch."

She frowned. "He's also my boss, and my business partner."

"How long have you been dating?"

"Five years." She closed her eyes. "I thought he was the one."

I'm so sorry."

She opened her eyes and turned away. *Pull yourself together, Nicole.*

He gently touched her forearm.

At his touch she flinched. "Why am I telling you this? I barely know you."

"Like I said, I'm a good listener. I have that effect on people." His smile tugged at her soul but her will urged that she regain some semblance of cool.

"Are you a shrink or something?"

"I work as a counselor. That is, when I'm not trying to save the world."

She touched the sleeve of his Hawaiian shirt that sported the collection of seaplanes. "This is rather odd attire for a counselor. I picture them in button down shirts and ties. People who want to be taken seriously."

He glanced down at his sleeve and grinned. "Shirts like this help people relax. And think of something other than Seattle winters."

She laughed, dabbed her eyes with the napkin again, and gave into the urge to blow her nose. Finally she asked, "So, how are you planning to save the world?"

He gave her a knowing smile. "I barely know you."

She laughed again. "Fair enough."

"Do you want to tell me about your boyfriend?"

She hesitated, then with a wavering voice finally said, "We met when we were working for a large consulting firm. Four years ago we figured we could do it better and started our own company. We called it DANISoft for the initials of the four co-owners. My boyfriend—ex boyfriend—loves it because his name is Dan."

"So you're partners?"

"Me, Dan and two others. There are twenty of us at the company in total."

John waited.

"He's actually the president and majority owner. He raided his trust fund for most of our startup costs. Plus, he's a natural leader."

"Sounds like a good partner."

"He has been—up until recently."

"Recently?"

Nicole clenched her fists and looked at the seat back in front of her. "I've always felt like I was beneath him. He went to Stanford on a full ride daddy-and-mommy scholarship. I came from the wrong side of Oakland and had to work my way through a local business college as a waitress and through student loans—loans I repaid."

"School of hard knocks?"

She laughed. "Pretty much. But when I started at the consulting firm I managed to outwork all those silver spooners and earn a rep as the girl who makes things happen." She held up her hand like she was wearing a sock puppet and moved her thumb and fingers together. "Blah, blah, blah. I'm sure you've hear this sad story a hundred times before Mr. Counselor."

He shook his head. "Everyone has a unique story."

The beverage and snack cart arrived at their row. Both asked for club soda with lime. Nicole started to tuck the packaged cookie the flight attendant gave her into the seat pocket in front of her, then offered it to John.

He took it from her. "Not hungry?"

"Yeah, but when I'm on the road my diet is terrible."

He laughed. "Doesn't look to me like your diet is terrible."

"Boy, you really are a good counselor."

"Just an honest one." He started to unwrap the cookie and then held it between his fingers and mouthed a silent prayer.

Nicole watched him out of the corner of her eye. When he was done she said, "You say grace over an airline cookie?"

"There've been times when I would have been very grateful for a cookie. And thanks to you, I have two." He held his hand up like it was a sock puppet and moved his thumb and fingers together. "But blah, blah, blah. I'm sure you've heard that before."

"Bravo, counselor." She laughed.

John took a bite out of his cookie and chewed slowly. He swallowed and asked, "So, back to you and your boyfriend?"

She pursed her lips and picked up the remainder of the wine. She gave John a wry smile. "If he tries to get rid of me, he's dead meat. Half of our business depends on my reputation." She drained the plastic cup. Nicole pulled her laptop toward her. "I should get back to work. What do I owe you for my session in the blue water row?"

"What do I owe for the financial advice?"

"Good. We'll call it even." She turned to the screen and started to type furiously.

An hour later the captain announced their approach to San Francisco International Airport. Nicole tucked away her laptop and turned her attention to John. "So, you know all about my troubles. And I know you're visiting the daughter of your friend. Are you from Seattle?"

"Nope. I've been there about a year, but was in the city before."

"Are you from the Bay Area?"

"No, I came to this country from Kosovo, after the civil war."

"Oh, that explains the faint accent. But your English is excellent."

"Thanks. I learned to speak the language long before I moved here. But I work hard to speak like the locals."

"I lived in Germany for a few years when I was a kid. My dad was an Air Force security cop at a little air base south of Frankfurt. I should have learned more of the language than I did. Might have helped in a few business deals."

Another announcement from the cockpit interrupted their conversation. The aircraft started a precipitous descent, like the pilot was late for luxury suite tickets at a Giants game.

John glanced toward the cockpit, then turned back to Nicole. "So, if I need more financial advice, how do I reach you?"

She gave him a thoughtful look. She really didn't know him, despite how quickly she had warmed to him. "Why don't you give me your card and I'll call you when I need some counseling. Then we'll trade services."

He pulled a card out of a pocket on his leather backpack. It read "John Amato, Fisher of Men" JohnZAmato@gmail.com, and his phone number.

"John Z Amato? What's the Z for?"

He flashed a coy smile. "It's an old, hard to pronounce, family name."

She glanced back at the card. "I don't suppose you're on LinkedIn."

He shook his head. "No. Not into social media."

She wanted to ask him if he was in a witness protection program, but resisted the urge.

The plane touched down and five minutes later they were pulling up to the gate. As Nicole towed her suitcase up the jetway, she noticed the man she had bumped into earlier was standing just inside the terminal, cell phone to his ear, facing the line of passengers exiting the plane. She turned toward John. "Please, play along with me." She grabbed his arm and pulled him close, making sure they walked up the jetway side by side.

"What is this—"

She leaned into his shoulder. "Please, just play along."

As they walked into the terminal, Mr. Barker put away the phone and looked toward the line of disembarking passengers. When he caught Nicole's eye he smiled. Then he noticed John on her arm and frowned. As they walked past him Nicole winked and said, "Thanks for the drink. Bump into you later."

Nicole, John still firmly in tow, turned to the left toward the International Terminal and BART station. John started to look over his shoulder. "Did I just help you ditch that guy?"

"Quiet. He's probably right behind us." As she pulled him closer she could feel the muscles in his upper arm were firm, but not bulky. More like an endurance athlete than a body builder.

As it turned out, both of them were riding the same train; Nicole to her apartment, John to the home of his recently deceased friend. He got off several stops before Nicole. As he stepped off he pointed at her, "Don't forget our plan to trade services. I need your advice."

She smiled and nodded, expecting to never see the curly haired man from the Mediterranean again. Five minutes later, she was towing her suitcase up the hill from the Powell Street station toward her condo.

Despite the warm evening, she was hassled by only a few street people on her walk home. As she pulled her bag up the front sidewalk of the turn of the century Victorian turned into condos, she thought she should really sell and move out of the Tenderloin district to someplace more upscale and safer. She had thought her next move would be into Dan's place in Pacific Heights. But that dream was evidently dead.

As she unpacked, she considered her next step. Call Dan and have it out with him? Let him make the next move? She pulled her Nikes out of her suitcase and held them up in front of her. Better idea: take a run and cool off before she decided on a course of action.

She dressed, stretched, and was soon pushing up the hill toward Fisherman's Wharf. She passed the imposing Grace Cathedral, which looked to her like it had been transported directly from medieval Europe. The French Gothic style house of worship was beautiful inside, or so she had been told.

Thanks to a favorable wind, refreshing salt air occasionally brushed aside the acrid smell of auto exhaust. As she attacked her route with short but powerful strides, she considered what was wrong. Things had seemed to be going so well with Dan both at work and in their personal life. Why had things had gone sour in the last month, and ended with an abrupt text message this afternoon?

Her route passed several regular hangouts that were indelibly tied up with her life with Dan. The Peet's Coffee they met at most mornings. The little park they would walk to when the weather was sunny and they wanted a break from the office; the French bakery where she stopped to pick up pastries for Friday morning staff meetings. She had cherished these places. Now each one she passed reminded her that her life plan had been derailed.

As she pushed up toward the crest of the hill, sweat began to trickle down her back. Nicole leaned forward, pumped her arms, and reached the top. As she descended toward a cluster of restaurants, a pearl gray Lexus convertible, top down, approached from the street on the right. Dan? It turned down the street, heading away from her. From the passenger seat, long, blonde hair flowed in the gentle wind. Nicole glanced down at the license plate. Even from half a block away she could read it: DANISOFT. She slowed to a stop and stepped into the shadow of a phone pole as the Lexus pulled up to the curb and stopped in front of Chez Monique, a favorite special occasion hangout. Six weeks ago they had gone there together. That night she felt he was on the verge of popping the question. But Nicole had gone home without a rock on her finger.

The valet stepped to the curb and opened up the passenger door, bowing slightly and holding out his hand to assist the blonde. Out stepped a slender woman in a spaghetti strap cocktail dress. She flipped her head and gossamer hair cascaded over bare shoulders. Dan, dressed in his favorite Brooks Brothers suit—a suit Nicole had helped him select—walked around the back of the car and passed the keys to the valet. As the woman turned toward Dan and took his arm, everything fell into place.

Penny Walker. Penny Walker whose family had a stake in enough real estate and businesses in the Bay Area to influence every important local decision from behind the scenes. Penny Walker who had engaged DANISoft several months back to plan for a new accounting system for her family's holding company. Nicole had been the logical person to manage the project, but Dan had taken it on himself, saying they needed her to focus on the Neely Seafoods project in Seattle. Glamorous Penny Walker, from the right side of the tracks, who could advance Dan's career in ways Nicole never could.

Nicole leaned forward on her right foot, ready to sprint the half block down the hill to confront Dan there and then. As Penny and Dan stepped toward the door of Chez Monique, Nicole hesitated. No, she needed a better plan than that. She waited until they were inside and then continued on her route to the waterfront, fists clenched as she sprinted past the restaurant.

John ducked into the men's room at the BART station. The memory of his encounter with Nicole Logan on the flight down from Seattle lingered. Something about her air of confidence, bordering on cocky, fascinated him. Not to mention her polished good looks. The prospect that she might call him excited him. Then he caught himself. Even if she did call, it could never lead to anything.

He glanced around the men's room. The strong antiseptic smell stung his nostrils. The restroom was sparsely populated with only a few commuters doing their business. John scanned the row of stalls and selected the one on the far end.

After pulling the door behind him, he hung his backpack on a hook and pulled a small leather pouch out of his suitcase. He unzipped the pouch and hung it on the same hook. A small mirror was mounted on the inside top of the case. The bottom had a neat array of small combs and a costume beard and mustache. Several travel size shampoo and mouthwash containers were in the plastic bag that had gone through the TSA scanners and been tucked into his carry on. He pulled out the one that was labeled mouthwash and went to work.

Thirty minutes later a gray haired old man with a neatly trimmed white beard shuffled out of the stall. John's leather jacket had been replaced by a wrinkled blue blazer. The backpack had been stuffed into the suitcase. The disguise was completed with a set of bifocals and a collapsible cane. As John worked his way toward the exit, he glanced over at his image in the mirror.

The eyes were those of a young man, but the skin was that of a senior citizen.

He walked the twelve blocks to the home of his old friend, Franz, careful to maintain the pace of an octogenarian. When he reached the steps of the turn of the century Victorian he pulled the suitcase up behind him, step by step, like a climber on the last stage of a Himalayan peak. He affected a wheeze and pressed the doorbell.

It took only a few moments for Greta to open the door. She was slightly more plump and gray haired than the last time he'd seen her, but still sported the blonde hair and regal facial structure of her Teutonic ancestors. John found it hard to believe she had never married. If it had been possible, he would have married her himself.

Tears sprang into Greta's eyes. She hesitated, then stepped into his embrace. "Johannes. It's so good to see you."

For several hours John and Greta shared stories about her father—some new, many familiar. He finally ended with how the two had met on a train in Italy, six decades before. "We were an unlikely pair of young men: two survivors of Auschwitz. Me on a mission from God to make a pile of money and a Jewish banker unsure of his faith."

She smiled a wan smile. "Obviously it was meant to be. Without my father, you never would have become wealthy." She touched the sleeve of John's jacket. "And without you, he never would have followed Jeshua."

"We have been good for each other." He picked up a cup of tea from the side board. "I am so sorry I couldn't make it to his funeral."

She touched his forearm. "He would have understood. And it's difficult to travel at your age."

John grinned. "Young lady, are you disparaging my age? I still feel like a man of thirty three." He leaned over and coughed.

She passed him a tissue from the box on the coffee table. "No slight intended. You are certainly one of the more fit men in his 80's I know."

"You don't know the twentieth of it." He wiped his mouth with the tissue. "I still wish I could have been there to say goodbye to Franz."

Greta reached for the teapot. John waved her off. "I must be going to my hotel. I do need some rest."

"Of course. Let me pull the car around front and I'll give you a ride." As she stood she asked, "Who will manage your portfolio now? Can you do it yourself?"

He chuckled. "No, that's not for me. But don't worry, I will find someone." He leaned on his cane and pulled himself to his feet.

She grabbed her purse. "I'll get the car and meet you at the front door. Don't try to take those front stairs on your own. I know how stubborn you are." She raised an eyebrow. "Promise?"

He raised his hand like he was being sworn in as a witness. "I promise. No ending our visit with a tumble into the street."

She turned and headed toward the back exit and John made his way to stand just inside the front door. He looked around the modest home Greta had shared with Franz. His old friend had been the last critical connection to Johannes Fischer. Now it was time for that identity to fade into history like so many others.

He glanced down at the end table near the door. In the upper right corner on the cover of *Entertainment Weekly* was a picture of Professor Cavanaugh with a caption: Heresy or Just TV?

He picked up the magazine and quickly flipped to the article. A reporter had interviewed a number of church leaders and theologians about Cavanaugh's proposed television show. Several quotes stood out. One fundamentalist preacher with a large television ministry suggested the biblical record clearly showed John was dead and that anyone who disputed it would "...burn in hell when his time came." A University of Notre Dame historian remarked, "While the professor's premise for the show is fanciful, there is nothing in or outside of the Bible or the historical record that definitively describes the fate of the last apostle."

Cavanaugh himself had the closing remark: "Nobody on this earth really knows for sure now, do they?"

John snorted and tossed the magazine down on the table.

Chapter Three

Saints...die to the world only to rise to a more intense life.

Lynn M. Poland
100 AD

IT WAS A cool, spring night on the eastern shores of the Aegean Sea, near the town of Ephesus. Johanan bar Zebedee, the sole remaining apostle of Jesus Christ, was being carried from the shores of the azure waters to his hut. The withered arms of the century old man were draped around two of his own disciples.

They sat him in a chair padded with several blankets to protect his parchment thin skin. He leaned back and raised one wrinkled hand to shade his eyes from the setting sun. A young man grabbed a fan and shielded Johanan's eyes from the light. The old man lowered his hand to his lap and gazed toward the ocean, watching a small fleet of fishing boats come in from the labors of the day.

A dozen disciples sat on the ground next to the apostle's chair and peered out at the sunset as well. His aged eyes could only see blurry outlines of the boat hulls and sails.

He asked, "Does it look like they had a good day?"

"Yes, they're all riding low in the water," the man holding the fan said.

Others murmured in agreement.

The scene brought back fond memories of the days when a young Johanan fished with his father Zebedee's fleet, before he left all to follow Jesus.

Johanan turned his head to look in the room behind him. Several scribes had ceased their work of copying the gospel penned by Johanan, or one of his many letters, to enjoy the peaceful scene themselves.

He turned back to the scene on the sea. "Little children," Johanan said in a raspy voice, "as the sun sets so does my life."

Johanan paused to catch his breath. His exile to the marble quarry at Patmos, decades ago, had coated his lungs with a thin film of stone dust. The effort to speak cost him dearly.

"You must never forget what the Lord taught me. Love one another."

A young man at his feet turned to him. "Teacher, why do you always say the same thing? Why don't you tell us stories of the Christos?"

The apostle leaned over and put his hand on the shoulder of the young man. "It is the Lord's command, and if this alone be done, it is enough."

The young man nodded and turned his gaze back to the incoming fishing boats.

As Johanan leaned back, he thought that soon enough it would be time for him to go. The writings left by him, his fellow apostles, and other church leaders would have to carry the message. He had no energy to do it himself.

Johanan lay on a straw filled mattress set on the floor. Rolled up blankets elevated his head and upper torso to help him breathe. A small fire burned in a brazier near the window to keep away the chill of the night air. Moonlight showed through the partly open window shutter above the fire. On a short stool next to his bed sat a simple clay cup filled with wine. A drink before bed aided his sleep, and periodic sips throughout the night soothed his dry throat. An oil lamp, recently extinguished by one of his loyal companions, sat next to the cup. Several times during the night someone would come into his room to tend the fire in the brazier and make sure he was comfortable. Johanan suspected they were also checking to see if he was still alive.

As Johanan drifted into sleep, he became aware of a presence at his bedside, as if in a dream. He opened his eyes, and there stood Jesus, clothed in brilliant white, just as he'd seen him at his transfiguration seven decades before. The light filled the room as if it was daylight.

"My Lord and my God." His heart beat faster and his eyes watered with joy at the sight.

"Johanan, my beloved disciple. You have done well. But now I have a new commandment for you."

"My Lord, it is my time to go with you." He struggled to sit up, finally propping himself up on his elbow. "I have been waiting for this day for many, many years."

"No, my good and faithful servant. You will leave this community and travel the world. Many of my sheep have never heard my name. You must spread my message to all nations."

"My Lord, I am an old man. I am ready to come home with you." He wheezed as he struggled to catch his breath. "To live with you, and my brothers and sisters."

"No, Son of Thunder." Jesus leaned in and placed his hand firmly on Johanan's arm. Johanan felt a tingle where Jesus' hand touched his arm. In a moment, the sensation spread up his arm and throughout his body. Jesus withdrew his hand and smiled down at Johanan. "You will live as other men and show them my love through your life. But from this day forward you may never tell anyone who you are."

"But Lord, I am old..."

Jesus' visage became grim. "Know that many powers will oppose you because of what you do in my name. At times the trials you've been through until now will seem as nothing."

"But, how will I—"

"Johanan, my beloved disciple," Jesus said, "go down to the shore and you will find a boat with a man in it. He is there to help you start your new life. Remember: you may never tell anyone who you are. Never. And you must share the good news with all nations before we are reunited in the Kingdom of Heaven."

Jesus stood before him and smiled down on Johanan. The light grew in intensity, until Johanan finally had to close his eyes because of the brilliance. "Go now and know I am with you always."

He awoke and sat bolt upright from the dream, breathing hard, as if he had just finished a foot race. He continued to pant, in exhilaration from the vivid vision.

Wait. He was sitting up without pain, breathing hard—not wheezing.

He felt like a young man full of energy. Not like a centenarian looking forward to the peace of death. He looked over at the fire. He could clearly see the patterns of deep orange flame on the coals, rather than the dim glow he'd grown used to seeing through his failing eyes. He looked at the back of his hand in the moonlight and saw the skin of a young man, not the sallow flesh of his recent years.

He was confused and exhilarated. Then he remembered the command: "Go now."

Johanan pulled back his blankets and swung his feet over to the dirt floor. He jumped nimbly to his feet and moved slowly across the room. He gently eased the door open and stepped out into the night.

He could clearly see the brilliance of the individual stars above and hear the splashing of waves on the nearby shore. Johanan started walking toward the beach and then broke into a sprint, reveling in his newfound energy. He could feel the cool sand between his toes. As he pushed off with each step, he noted the absence of pain in the joints. He resisted the urge to burst into joyous laughter.

As Johanan approached the shore, his pace slowed. He walked gingerly over a band of rocks to the soft sand near the water. He now regretted he had left his sandals back in the hut. He waded into the surf in his bare feet, pulling up the hem of his nightshirt to keep it dry. Tears of excitement rolled down his face.

He remembered his instructions from Jesus, and looked up and down the shoreline. There, away from the houses, on the beach, he could see a short mast in the moonlight. He broke into a sprint as he ran toward the small boat.

As he came upon it he could see the bow was beached on the sand, but the stern was still in the water. It rocked gently in the waves. It was a small fishing vessel, more suitable for a lake than for the Aegean; big enough only for two, maybe three men. He looked into the boat. There, facedown, in water deep enough to cover his head, was the body of a man. Johanan turned him over and was surprised to see how old he was. The face was bruised and cut. Being soaked in salt water had swollen and distorted his features. Evidently he had fallen in the boat, injured himself, and died. Or maybe he had died first of natural causes, and then collapsed into the bottom of the hull.

Johanan placed his arms under the body. With his renewed strength, he lifted the man and carried him up onto the beach. He placed the corpse gently on the sand. In the moonlight he could see he was a frail old man about the size of Johanan. Looking more closely, he noticed the fisherman closely resembled him, or at least the Johanan who had gone to bed last night. They could have been brothers. The battering he had taken only served to hide any differences. This was clearly the man sent to help him start his new life.

As this man was dead, so must Johanan be. He quickly stripped off his nightshirt. As he did he marveled at the young flesh and firm muscles that had reappeared in his formerly withered body. He gently removed the clothes from the body of the fisherman. Johanan redressed him reverently in his own garment. He looked down at the ring on his own finger given to him by his own disciples a decade before. It was a simple bronze band with the inscription of the ichthys, or fish. This secret symbol of believers had gained popularity during recent decades. With a lump in his throat he removed the ring and placed it on the finger of his deceased companion. It fit, perfectly.

Johanan dressed himself in the wet clothes of the old man and then lifted the body in his arms. With no real plan in mind he started back up the beach, carrying the man who would take his place. He walked along the shoreline in the gentle surf where the beach was sandy. Johanan's heart was still pounding with adrenaline and the old man was so light that he easily carried him. When he reached the point opposite his hut, he stopped and turned. He started up across the sharp rocks toward the dwellings, and then stopped. He looked down at the face of the man and then back at the ocean.

Johanan hesitated. Then he backed into the water and walked up the beach in the surf to cover his tracks. He reached a stretch with sharp rocks just above the high tide line. He reverently laid the fisherman face down with the lower part of his body in the water. The tide was receding and the body would be left there for his companions to find. The cuts and distortions on his face caused by his journey in the bottom of the boat would hide most of the differences. They would not be expecting to find someone else in Johanan's clothing. He expected they would assume he had wandered out in the night, fallen, and then washed up on the beach. And if someone did notice he looked different than Johanan?

"Lord, you've made blind eyes see, now make seeing eyes blind."

He backed into the water again and said to the old fisherman, "Thank you for what you are doing for me."

Johanan turned and sprinted through the surf toward the boat. He reached it in moments but found the tide had receded and the vessel was farther up on the shore. He strained mightily to push it back. With strength he had not wielded for many decades, he finally managed to inch it over the sand until it floated free. Johanan pushed the boat into the surf until the water was up above his knees. Then he pushed off of the bottom and pulled himself up and over the side where he fell into the bottom of the small fishing vessel. He grabbed the oars, turned the boat around, and began to dig into the water. His years of earning his trade as a fisherman served him well, He handled the boat with ease and began to head out to sea. As he did, he could see all was quiet in the direction of the collection of dwellings where he had lived with his followers. Johanan began to stroke in a smooth rhythm, pulling steadily away from the community on the shore near Ephesus.

He looked in the direction of the body he had deposited on the beach and mouthed a quiet prayer of thanks. Then he looked toward the horizon. As he had watched the setting sun last evening, the horizon had seemed very near. Now, even in the dark, it seemed distant, very distant.

Johanan rowed steadily until the shore faded from sight. He raised the small sail and adjusted it to catch the wind blowing offshore. He grabbed the steering oar and steered the boat directly downwind to put as much distance between him and his Ephesian home as possible.

His rejuvenated body was exhilarating. In the light of the full moon he looked at the smooth skin on the back of his hand again. He turned it and noticed the deep scar on his palm was gone; a scar he'd had since a knife accident in his youth on his father's fishing boat. He looked up and down his arms and noticed other disfigurements from working the quarry on Patmos, from minor burns, or other incidents over his century of life were gone. The marks on his ankles from shackles he'd worn during various imprisonments were gone as well. He had the skin of a man reborn.

But the rejuvenation went deeper than his skin. He felt strength he'd been missing for many decades. He was used to being exhausted and having to conserve his energy. But now, he felt like a Roman catapult unleashed. He gazed up at the blanket of stars overhead. The clarity of each individual point of light amazed him. In recent years, he would have seen a milky cloud through his aged eyes. His vision dimmed as tears of joy filled his eyes.

Then he thought back to his encounter only an hour ago with the Messiah. It had been over seventy years since he had seen Him ascend bodily into heaven and years since he'd seen visions of Him he had recorded in the prophetic letter to the seven churches in Asia. Johanan thought back to the encounter earlier that evening and the words of Jesus.

He shook his head. He had expected to die and pass on to heaven any day. This situation was totally unexpected.

As the boat ran with the wind across the Aegean Sea, Johanan's mind raced as it hadn't for decades. He would need to find a place where he could blend in and start his new life. How was he going to share the love of the Christos if he couldn't tell people he was Johanan, the Beloved Disciple, the companion of the Christos? Frankly, he had enjoyed being the center of attention among the growing community of believers.

"Oh Lord." Tears ran down his cheeks, "Why couldn't you have just brought me home?"

Johanan looked up at the stars, this time with the eye of an experienced sailor. The boat was heading due west, toward the mainland of Greece. He could go to Corinth, the capital of the Achaean province. There was an active Christian community there. However, there were also many church elders in Corinth who remembered the younger Johanan. They might ask difficult questions.

Athens was also in that general direction. He knew of a church there and had heard the name of Strabo, their leader, though he didn't know any of their members personally. That might be a more suitable location for him to begin a new life. Far enough from Ephesus but close enough for this little vessel to reach within a space of a month, if the winds held.

He secured the steering oar and began to explore the vessel. Several clay jars stowed in a compartment up front contained fresh water. A leather bag contained dried fish and dates. One jar contained salt—enough to preserve a good sized catch. A clay pot contained charcoal for cooking. On top of it was a flint and steel along with a small bag of tinder. He found another leather bag underneath the one with the fish. This one had additional charcoal, wet from contact with the water in the bottom of the vessel. He placed the bag on top of the compartment so it would dry and continued his exploration. Worn nets were stowed on either side of the mast. An old wooden bowl floated in the water on the bottom of the boat. It looked like it was suitable for bailing; something that was desperately needed in this creaky, leaky vessel. He set to the task and soon had the bottom clear of all but a bit of water.

He then returned to the forward compartment and pulled a few pieces of fish out of the bag. He went back to the stern with the salted fish and a jar of water. Johanan looked up at the stars and adjusted his heading several times until he felt he was on the correct course. As Johanan chewed on the fish, he savored the sensation. Even his sense of taste was rejuvenated. The dried, salty fish contained flavors he hadn't experienced in years. He washed it down with a swig of the water. *Good Lord, it is wonderful to be young again*!

Stowed in a leather bag in the stern was a heavy, woolen cloak. It was soaked through and he did his best to wring water out of it before spreading it out to dry. In the pocket of the cloak he found a small pouch with several Roman coins. Not a fortune by any means; maybe enough to pay for a meal and a night at an inn. As he fingered them, the profile of the Emperor Domitian glared back at him from one of the older coins.

My tormentor, long gone. Now I may outlast you by many years.

He set the pouch aside and spread the cloak out so it could dry in the warm night breeze.

Johanan continued to chew the leathery fish and ponder his future. The evening before, as he had watched the setting sun, his fate had seemed so clear. Johanan would soon fade away, surrounded by his own beloved disciples, and then rejoin his Lord in the promised Kingdom. But now his whole world was turned upside down. He never considered when Jesus had said to Peter, "If it is my will that he remain until I return, what is that to you?" that he would remain alive. Especially in the body of his youth! And if he was going to be here until the Lord's return, how long would that be? Forty years? Maybe even a century? The church had anticipated the second coming of the Christos at any moment. Some rationalized the Lord's comment to Peter indicated He would return when Johanan's own life was running out. But this changed everything. He was a young man once again.

Johanan nodded in exhaustion. The excitement of making his escape, bailing out the boat, and thinking about his future were taking their toll. He looked around at the sea. The wind was steady and the waters fairly calm. He finished his meal, made another adjustment of the steering oar, and secured it with a rope. Then he pulled the damp cloak around him and with the experience of many nights and days spent napping on a boat, leaned back and dozed off.

Johanan slept for several hours before waking up. His initial thought was the whole experience had been a dream. Then he looked around at the boat and at the youthful flesh on his arm. He settled back in for another hour or so sleep. This time when he woke, the sun was rising at his back and water was lapping at his feet. Johanan bailed the boat out again. Then he made another adjustment of the steering oar and retrieved some of the dates in the leather bag.

As he ate his breakfast he considered what to do next. He could join the community of believers in Athens and find lodging among them. He could help teach and spread the truth about the Christos. Many churches needed guidance from teachers to keep them on the path and away from rising heresies. Maybe it would be made clear to him through visions how long he would be waiting. But, in Johanan's experience, visions were infrequent. He would have to depend on the teaching and guidance he had received so far, God's grace, and his own frequently imperfect judgment to make his way. The prospects were exciting, and daunting. He ran his fingers over his scalp and through the curly hair covering what had been a bald pate the night before. He even pulled back the cloak to his knees to look at previously withered calves. They were now smooth and muscular, with no trace of the bulging, purplish veins that had plagued his old age.

He sipped the water. There were only a few small pots. Not enough water to last to mainland Greece. He'd need to stop and refill his containers at one of the many islands along the way.

Enough worrying about the future; he had first been a fisherman. And, he had done some of his best thinking while plying his trade. He pulled out a set of the nets and began to inspect the rough fibers. As he found tears, he mended them with the eye of experience and the nimble fingers of a young man. In short order, the net was serviceable. Johanan watched the water off both the port and starboard side of the boat. He could see infrequent silver flashes off of either side. He cast the net over the side and retrieved it. Nothing. He cast again and this time several good sized fish came up with the net. He continued for several hours until he had filled the bottom of the boat with a modest catch. The weight of the fish made his vessel ride more deeply in the waves, giving it some stability. The sun was now high overhead and the wind gusted, still at his back, driving him toward the Greek mainland. The prevailing wind would usually oppose him as he headed west. God appeared to be blessing his journey.

Johanan pulled out the cooking brazier and replenished it with the now dry charcoal. He found a dull knife in the forward compartment along with a sharpening stone. The apostle worked the knife against the stone until it was sharp enough for cleaning a fish. He selected a good sized specimen and gutted it, throwing the entrails overboard. With a bit of work he managed to get a small fire going in the charcoal brazier with his cloak serving as protection from the wind. A small reed served as a spit for the fish and he held it over the coals, feeding in fresh pieces of charcoal as needed to keep the fire going. Johanan turned it, too frequently he soon found. He had grown in patience as he grew older but now it seemed the impetuousness of his youth had returned. He consciously forced himself to turn the spit less often. Soon it was done and he was eating his meal out of the bailing bowl using the tip of the knife.

In the late afternoon he spied a sandy shore on what appeared to be an uninhabited island. He beached his boat and secured it to a rock above the high tide line. The exertion of pulling the boat up onto the sand left him exhausted, but exhilarated. After a short rest he scouted the area and found a small creek where he refilled his water jugs. He built a small fire and slept near it, rolled up in his cloak.

Johanan spent the next several weeks working his way toward Athens. He knew various islands and the mainland blocked the direct route to the ancient Greek city and had turned to the southwest to bypass them. When the weather was clear and it looked like he was in an open stretch of water he would spend the night at sea, sleeping in short snatches and watching the stars to adjust his course. Other nights he would find an uninhabited coast with a creek to refill his water pots and spend the night ashore. He spent one stretch of several days ashore on a remote beach cleaning and drying a large catch of fish that he hoped to use for trade.

One evening, during what he expected was the midway point of his journey, Johanan bailed out the boat right before he settled in for a short nap. It had always needed regular bailing but it seemed like it was taking on water faster. He passed another night on the boat, sleeping in short stretches. When the sun finally rose, Johanan noticed his sandals were again in standing water. He bailed all the water out, and then cast his nets. In short order he had pulled in a good catch.

Soon he was up to his ankles in water. It seemed like more water than would normally be pulled in as part of his fishing. He started to inspect the hull, pushing aside fish to get a good look at the planking. Up toward the bow he found a discolored spot on the wood. He pressed gently on it. It was soft. *Wood worms!* Any attempt to repair it at sea might be disastrous. He could push through the soft planks and the sea would gush in, and his fragile vessel would slip beneath the waves. Could his new life end so soon?

He spent the rest of the morning and early afternoon looking for a suitable place to land. Finally, he saw an island to the left, near the horizon, and made a course toward it. As he got closer he could see several plumes of smoke. Soon Johanan saw a wide beach with several small vessels pulled up onto the sand. The shoreline stretched from the sea up to a dozen dwellings on higher ground. The buildings were made of stone and wood, and looked to be in good repair. Most had fish drying on racks on the roof or out front. As Johanan grew closer, several children playing on the shore spotted him and alerted the adults. He steered toward the beach and soon four men waded into the water to help pull him up onto the sand. They seemed friendly enough, but you could never tell. They might be getting ready to rob him and toss his body into the ocean for scavengers.

"Greetings, stranger," a gray bearded man said, in Greek. His sparking blue eyes looked straight into Johanan's, almost as if he was discerning his deepest secrets. He grasped Johanan's forearm and helped him out of the boat onto the shore. "What brings you to our island?"

Reassured by his manner Johanan said, "I'm traveling from the mainland to the east to Athens. I hoped I might be able to trade my catch for some repairs and supplies."

The men looked into the bottom of the boat at the silvery cargo, and then at each other. They nodded. "A very good catch," the graybeard said. "Stay awhile and tell us of your travels. We don't have many visitors to our island. You may stay in my home until you're ready to continue your journey."

Johanan and the men pulled his boat high up on the sand. Soon he was working alongside them to patch the other boats, using pitch collected from trees on the island and bitumen bought in trade. As the men worked, they talked of bits of news from Rome, Corinth, Alexandria and other cities. He learned the Romans didn't bother the island much. A tax collector would stop by occasionally, but they had never suffered an occupation or persecution at the hands of the empire. Johanan entertained them with stories and news brought by travelers to Ephesus, which was on a major Roman trade route.

As they worked, Johanan noticed he was drawing attention from the other villagers. As women, in the course of their daily work, passed the men on the beach, their glances at the stranger seemed to linger. Children playing in the vicinity seemed to congregate around Johanan. The graybeard finally shooed them away. It appeared visitors were a welcome novelty.

Johanan managed to determine from discussions about the island that he had strayed farther south than planned. This location was off the more direct route to Athens he thought he was steering.

When they turned to patch his boat the men admired it and started to ask questions.

"This is a fine vessel, but small for such a long voyage with one man," a tall villager said.

"Yes," Johanan said. "It is small, but I have many years of experience sailing."

"Many years?" the graybeard laughed. "You look to be only barely out of your twenties!"

Johanan hesitated. He was going to have to think before he spoke more. "Maybe it only seems like many years, Father. But I started young and learned at the feet of wise men like you."

A stocky man scowled at Johanan. The apostle noted that although the top of this man's head was bald, his facial hair was composed of curls so thick it reminded him of the snakes in the legend of Medusa. He half expected the beard to come to life. The man asked, "How did you come by such a boat?"

Johanan pondered the question briefly. "My master gave it to me. He has sent me on an errand."

"What kind of errand?"

The graybeard pounded the stocky man on the back. "Enough questions. Let him save some stories for tonight.

On the hull of Johanan's boat, they cut out two sections of planks infested with wood worms. The greybeard had his son fetch several pieces of wood to replace the section. He skillfully cut them to fit the gap and inserted them. A brace on the inside secured with wooden pegs made the patch permanent. A coating of pitch and bitumen completed the repair.

At that moment, a young man carrying a wooden bucket walked up to the boat. Water was dripping from his dark hair and beard. He held up the pail for their inspection. "Look what I caught for dinner tonight." Johanan peered into it. The contents of the water filled bucket, roiled. A mottled skin broke the surface. Two tentacles reached up and over the side.

The young man reached in and pulled out an octopus. He grasped it at the base of the slimy body. The tentacles thrashed in the air and entwined themselves around his forearm. He smiled broadly. "A special treat for dinner tonight, in honor of our guest." He dropped it back into the pail.

Johanan stepped back. His Jewish stomach wanted to wretch. He wanted to say it was one of the most disgusting things he had ever seen. Instead, he said, "I am honored, I think."

The graybeard laughed loudly, and pounded Johanan on the back. "Enough work. Time to eat."

That night the villagers put together an impromptu feast at the community fire pit near the beach. Johanan contributed a dozen fish from his catch, and they were soon cooking alongside a goat and a small pig. Despite being freed from the restrictions on pork in the early days of the church, the smell of the meat still made Johanan queasy.

The graybeard formally introduced himself as Tullius, the leader of the small community. He then presented his family. Thais, his wife, carried herself as if she were a benevolent queen, rather than the wife of the headman on an out of the way island. Silver strands accented her rich brown hair. Her kindly smile was accented by crinkles at the corners of her deep brown eyes. If you replaced her plain, but neat, tunic with a white toga, she would meld neatly with the Roman aristocracy.

Tullius' older son, Aprius, who appeared to be in his mid-twenties, had missed Johanan's arrival because he was out hunting. His youngest son, Marcus, looked to be in his late teens. He had helped Johanan patch his boat earlier on the beach. The sons of Tullius looked like they were cut out of the same cloth as their father. The three men had dark, curly hair. Aprius' beard was charcoal black and thick. Marcus beard was lighter, and still bare in patches. Neither of the fit young men sported the slight paunch their father wore.

The daughter, Anteia, was about two decades of age. She blushed when introduced to Johanan. She was a lovely girl with long, light brown hair, bleached almost blonde by the sun. She was of marrying age, even a few years beyond it. She displayed the regal look of her mother, and the bright blue eyes of her father. *A remarkable beauty,* thought Johanan.

Tullius escorted Johanan to a seat of honor at the head of the pavilion. Baskets of local fruits, vegetables, and hard breads were passed around. Johanan took samples of each, as several were unfamiliar. Platters of goat, pork and fish also made the rounds. Johanan hesitated at the pork. Tullius noticed his reluctance.

"You do not like pig?" he asked.

"I don't eat it often," he said. "It is not common among my people."

"Try some of this on it," Tullius said, as he passed a clay pot with a wooden spoon. "It is a special recipe of *garum*, passed down from my grandfather."

Johanan sniffed the garum, or fish sauce, that was a common condiment throughout the empire. This one didn't smell nearly as strong as ones he had tasted before. He ladled some of the dark, honey colored liquid onto his pork and took a bite.

"This is very good," he exclaimed. "The best garum I've ever tasted! I might even get to like pig flesh if I can have this on it."

Tullius laughed his hearty laugh. "Pass the pork back to Johanan."

The village leader was in a good mood and soon he had a large clay amphora containing wine brought out. Two men stuck the pointed bottom of the vessel into the sand. Tullius used a wooden dipper to fill several goblets and passed them out to the elder men of the village. Johanan noticed the goblets in the hands of the islanders ranged from plain wood or clay, to metal with intricate designs. Tullius turned over the wine steward duties to Aprius and brought Johanan a glass goblet.

"This is from Syria. It is made with a new process."

Johanan marveled at the wine glass. He had never seen anything like it. Usually drinking vessels like this were made of strands of glass laid on top of each other like a coiled rope. This looked almost as if it had been cast.

"The trader who sold it to me tells me it is made by blowing into the molten glass and twirling it. Be careful. It is very expensive."

He admired the container. "It is truly a privilege to be entrusted with such a rare object, and one of such beauty." Johanan sipped from the glass at first and then drank more deeply. The wine had a sweet taste and went down easily.

Then, a platter was set before Johanan. The young man who had caught the octopus smiled at him. "For our guest, a special treat." Johanan stared at the mix of roasted tentacles and flesh. The mottled pattern was still visible on the cooked carcass.

"My friend," Johanan hesitated. "You honor me, but I tell you, there is not enough garum on this whole island to make me eat that."

The islanders broke out in laughter. "Julius," said Tullius. "Pass it to me. I'll take Johanan's share." It only took a few moments for the crowd to clear the platter. Johanan had to turn his head. He couldn't imagine ever eating the thing he had seen reach its tentacles out of the bucket.

"And now, before our visitor tells us his story," Tullius said, "we will entertain him with our athletic feats. First, boys to the beach." He led a dozen boys in their early to mid-teens down to the beach. One of them drew a line perpendicular to the shore and they all gathered behind it.

"The first one around the tree on the point and back is the winner." He pointed to a gnarled old tree on a point of land far down the beach. They all nodded.

Johanan approached the group. "If I may," he said, "a prize for the winner?" He pulled out the smallest of the Roman coins in his pouch, held it up, and passed it to Tullius.

"Most generous," Tullius said as he turned the coin over. Then he held it aloft over the boys and said, "To the winner. But for such a prize the race will be two laps."

The boys lined up and began to chatter, each determined to take home honor, and the coin. At Tullius' signal, they begin the sprint down the beach to the tree, cheered on by their family and friends.

At the end of the first lap, a group of five in a tight pack led, the others trailing behind. Goaded on by the crowd, they made the turn and pushed themselves even harder. When they finally sprinted up the beach to the finish line, one of the oldest crossed the finish line only a few paces ahead of the runner up, with the others trailing well behind.

"Well done, Dagon," Tullius said, as he presented him with the worn coin. Dagon bowed to Johanan and then waded into the surf to cool himself off. He was soon joined by his fellow runners and their joyful chatter filled the evening air.

The rest of the villagers retired back to the community fire pit where Tullius soon called for the next round of entertainment. "Aprius, Proitos, in the ring." Proitos was a good-natured man who had labored alongside Johanan earlier that day. Both men were in their mid to early twenties, and in excellent shape from the hard work of survival on the island and the sea.

The pair grappled in the center of a hastily drawn ring in the sand. It was soon clear that although Proitos was bigger and more heavily muscled, Aprius was the more skilled at the art of wrestling. Proitos rushed Aprius several times and missed his target as the smaller man stepped aside and laughed. Proitos made mock threats veiled behind a smile. But his face was getting redder as he was frustrated by the skill of Aprius. Finally Aprius tired of toying with his opponent and took advantage of a charge by his bigger friend. In one swift move he hooked his arm under Proitos' armpit, leaned his back against the big man's abdomen, and flipped him up and over onto the sand.

"Well done, my son," Tullius said proudly. The villagers joined in the cheering as the victor grabbed the arm of the vanquished and helped him to his feet.

"Julius, Agon, your turn," and the next two men took their turn. Julius was the octopus catcher, Agon his younger brother. This pair were more evenly matched in skill and strength. Large young men, they grunted and groaned as they tried to best each other with brute strength. Finally Agon outlasted his older brother and threw him to the sand.

After a short rest period, the last match paired Aprius and Agon against each other. Agon was wary, and stayed just out of Aprius' reach. Finally, Aprius taunted him, "If you won't wrestle me, maybe your sister would represent your family in a match." Aprius gazed at a dark haired beauty, sitting next to his own sister, Anteia. He smiled broadly at her. The villagers hooted and hollered in appreciation.

With Aprius' attention on the young woman, Agon saw his chance. He stepped forward with his arms ready to encircle the smaller man. His gaze seemingly still on the young woman, Aprius sidestepped Agon's charge and grabbed the inside of his arm. He stepped back and jerked to pull him off balance, then pushed him on his back to the sand.

"I guess the match with your sister will have to wait." The villagers laughed and cheered Aprius' victory. He pulled Agon to his feet and they pounded each other on the shoulders.

Agon returned to his seat, but Aprius stood in the center of the ring. He looked at Johanan and said, "Would our friend care to take on the village champion?"

He caught himself as he almost said, "You would wrestle an old man?" Instead he slowly pulled himself to his feet, faced the fisherman and said, "I would be honored."

Johanan enjoyed physical activity but it had been many years since he had been able to do anything more strenuous than a short walk. He entered the ring and shuffled warily around Aprius. The two were about the same size and the contest seemed to be fair in terms of size and strength.

"Don't worry stranger—I won't hurt you," Aprius said. "We still need to hear your story."

Johanan grinned and said, "Are we here to talk or wrestle?" With that, he stepped in and grabbed Aprius around the waist. He had expected him to sidestep the move but the islander stood his ground as if he was testing Johanan's strength. They grappled and grunted much as the two brothers had done earlier. Johanan was reveling just in being able to physically exert himself in a contest again.

Finally, Aprius seemed to tire of the match and managed to flip Johanan over on his back with a swift side move. True to his word, he had been gentle.

"You are a worthy opponent," he said graciously as he helped him to his feet. Johanan knew otherwise, but nodded.

Tullius ordered up another round of wine as the villagers congratulated both wrestlers on a fine match. After a few minutes, the conversation died down. Almost as if on cue, they looked at Johanan.

Then Tullius asked, "So our new friend, what brings you to our island and takes you to Athens?"

Johanan sat up from his reclining position and sipped his wine to buy some time. Where to start? What to say?

Chapter Four

We are called to be fishers of men, not hunters of men.

Kevin Mather, President, Seattle Mariners

KER-POCK, KER-POCK. THE crescendo on the racquetball court rose to a climax as Scott and John battled for the point. The match stood at one game apiece. They had traded the lead five times in this final round. After several volleys, John blasted it past the lanky twenty-five-year-old for the point.

As he stood bouncing the ball, getting ready to serve, John asked, "So, where did you get the money for your fancy new Mustang?"

"Credit man, credit. But it will be worth it. You should see how the girls turn their heads when I pass by with the top down."

John grunted, then fired the ball at just the right angle to bounce it over Scott's reach. To his surprise, Scott leapt up and smacked it. John made a halfhearted attempt to return the ball and missed it.

Scott shot him a big grin. "My serve. Match point." Scott held the ball in his right hand, and squeezed it several times, like he was trying to force it to accept his will.

He looked over at John. "Man, you were something last week. Disarming that dude and saving the girl like you were some superhero." He bounced the ball on the floor. "Where did you learn to fight like that? Some karate dojo?"

John looked away from Scott and gazed at the wall in front of them. "When I was much younger I lived on an island in the Mediterranean. My friends there taught me the basics." He glanced over at Scott, then back at the wall. He crouched down, ready to return Scott's serve. "Gets me out of a jam once in a while."

Scott faced John and moved into a fighting stance. "You gotta teach me some of that. Ready for first lesson, Master Amato."

John waved him off. In his best imitation of Yoda, he said. "Ah, young Scott, for good only is the force. For your own purposes you might use it."

Scott laughed. "Good one." He served with a powerful overhand. They fought for what seemed like several minutes. Finally, John fed his neighbor an easy lob. He was ready for the game to be over, and was going to let Scott have the win. Scott took the gift and put all his muscle behind it. The ball raced straight toward John's face. He jerked his head to the left and it whizzed by his ear.

"Dude, I win." Scott ran his fingers through his sandy blond hair. He rubbed his sweaty forehead on the sleeve of his t-shirt. "That was one tough game."

John bent over, panting from the exertion. He was a good five inches shorter than the six foot three inch Scott. Keeping up with his taller friend was hard work.

Scott crossed the court and bumped fists with John. "Not bad, old man. Not bad."

They left the court and headed to the locker room. "Hey," Scott said, "I'm going to take a rain check on that beer. I'm meeting up with some buds downtown."

"No worries. I've been thinking about paying a visit to someone anyhow."

"You're still buying next time." He grabbed a towel from a rack and rubbed it over his face. "Hey, you could come tonight with us and get the tab."

John shook his head. "I'll pass. I've got an early appointment tomorrow. Besides, I can't handle staying out all night like you and your friends."

Scott laughed. "Hey, you're only about thirty, thirty-five, right? You could if you wanted to."

"If I wanted to."

"You really are one of the straightest arrows I know. You should loosen up sometime."

"Don't think I'm perfect. I've even been known to subconsciously whistle a ribald ditty popular with Napoleon's light cavalry."

Scott looked at him as if he'd beamed in from another planet. "Whaaa? Every time I think you're a normal dude you say something weird like that."

They stopped to get a drink from the cooler outside the locker room. As John sipped the chilled water from a paper cup, Scott playfully punched him in the shoulder. "Seriously, you were something with that mugger."

John drained his cup, crumpled it, and ricocheted it off the wall and into the trashcan. "Teach you I can, young Scott. But about the Force, first you must learn." He turned and entered the locker room.

After a quick shower, John pulled a bronze Greek style cross off the top shelf of his locker. For a moment he gazed at the pitted surface and corners worn nearly round. Because the symbol was heavy and awkward, he took it off when playing an active sport. He slipped it on over his head and donned his shirt.

He stepped over to the mirror and stood next to Scott. John

ran a comb through his curly black hair and his grooming was done. Meanwhile, Scott worked gel into his hair, teasing each lock into place. He combed the hair down the center of his scalp into a ridge in the fauxhawk style, trying to get just the right look. John wanted to tell him he looked like he was wearing a crested Roman Centurion's helmet. He held his tongue, but gave him a smirk.

Scott looked over at John and grinned. "Got to look good for the ladies."

John gave him a faint smile in response. "Go easy on the ladies, bud. Go easy."

He pointed down at John's ankle. "What happened to the nasty cut from that dude's knife? I thought you were going to need some serious stitches."

John glanced down at his left ankle. All that remained of the gash from the knife was a barely visible scar. Within a few days, even it would be gone.

John put his foot up on the counter and ran his finger over where the wound had been. "I heal quickly."

Scott turned back to the mirror. John slung his jacket over his shoulder and left the locker room.

As he walked through the gym, he noticed five women on treadmills. They all sported ponytails that swayed to different beats as they walked, jogged, or ran. John slowed his pace, mesmerized by the sight. For a single beat, their flaxen pendulums swung together, before separating once again into individual rhythms.

A toffee colored ponytail at the far end flicked away as the young woman turned to meet John's gaze. The athletically built woman with a small nose flashed a shy smile before averting her eyes. John responded with a look of embarrassment at being caught watching. She glanced back up at him again before returning her attention to the iPad on the stand in front of her. John picked up his pace as he headed toward the lobby of the gym. Just before he turned the corner, he glanced back over his shoulder at the row of treadmills. The toffee haired woman at the end was watching him from behind. He gave her an amused look. She blushed, and turned back to her reading.

Thirty minutes later, John sat down in a cheap plastic chair at a visitor's station in the King County jail. The clock on the wall read a quarter to six. An inch of Plexiglas separated him from the room where prisoners came and went from appointments with family members, friends or their attorneys. The seat across from John was still empty. To his right, a woman chattered away in Mexican Spanish with a man, connected by a telephone handset. From her side of the conversation, it sounded like the man had been brought in for domestic violence. She seemed to be alternating between wanting him back, and being afraid of what he would do to her if he was released. Out of the corner of his eye, John watched the man. He grunted occasionally, but said very little. John noticed he clenched and unclenched his jaw as he listened to the woman.

His observation of the drama was interrupted when a guard led an orange jump-suited inmate to the plastic chair across from John. He pushed him down into the seat and held up his right hand to John with all five digits extended and mouthed, "Five minutes." John nodded and picked up the phone.

The young man across from John squinted at him and then jerked his head back in surprise. The same look of fear John had seen through the eyeholes in the ski mask spread across his face. John smiled reassuringly, and pointed at the phone.

He finally leaned forward and picked up the phone on his side. John noticed he used his left hand to pick up the phone. His right wrist was bandaged. "Hey, you're the guy who stopped me last week."

"Yeah. That was me."

"What are you..." He left his sentence unfinished, as he stared at John.

"Seth, I'm here to give you a chance." John glanced down at some notes in front of him. "They tell me this is your first arrest." He looked up and noticed that Seth's left eye was twitching. As John watched, he wiped his nose on the sleeve of his jumpsuit. "They also tell me you're a meth user."

He glanced over John's shoulder, and then down at the desk in front of him.

"Seth, when I looked into your face last week, I saw fear. I could tell you're not some career criminal—at least you aren't yet."

Seth looked into John's eyes; he seemed to be eager for some measure of reassurance.

"I can give you a shot at getting clean if you let me."

He scowled at John. "Who says I need help?"

John shook his head. "The choice is yours." He waved at the room behind Seth. "You can live in fabulous places like this, or go straight and get your life together."

Seth scowled again. "Do you do this to everyone you beat up?

"No, just the ones I think have a chance." John leaned forward. "I'll be very honest with you. It won't be easy. The success rate for kicking a meth addiction is very slim. But otherwise you can expect to end up on the streets—dead." He leaned back, and waited.

Seth sat in silence for a few moments. "What's the deal?"

"I handle your bail, and the court releases you to a treatment program run by the local Men's Mission."

"Men's Mission? Is that like a place for homeless guys?"

"Yes, and they also run a very treatment program for drug and alcohol addicts." John leaned forward. "The director is a friend of mine. He's already agreed to take you in."

Seth wiped his nose again, then looked up at the ceiling for a few moments. Finally he said, "What about the charges against me?" He stared down at the counter in front of him.

"Most likely you'll still go to trial, or cop a plea. But things will go better for you if you're trying to get your life together."

Seth looked back up at John. "What about the girl? Is she okay?" The flash of fear on his face was replaced by a look of pleading.

"She'll be okay."

"I wouldn't have hurt her, you know."

"I hope not. I think you were so drugged up at the time that things could have gone very wrong."

Seth looked away again. "She's not from here, is she?"

"No, she's here from Rio on a fellowship program at the University of Washington. Leaves for home in a few weeks." John rapped his knuckles on the counter in front of him. "Not exactly the way to end her year in America, but she'll be okay."

Seth looked back up, relief washing across his face. John noticed the guard glance down at his watch, and then start across the room toward Seth. "What do you say, Seth? Take a shot at getting your life together, or this and worse?" He waved his hand again at their surroundings.

"I don't know. I've never been much for religion."

John nodded. "Neither am I."

Seth gave him a quizzical look. Before John could reply, the guard tapped on Seth's shoulder. He jerked his head and pulled the phone away from his face. He looked back at the guard. They had a short interchange, and Seth turned back to John. "Tell me something. Why are you doing this? Are you some kind of lawyer?"

John nodded, and smiled. "I'm in the business of helping people. I can tell you more, later."

Seth shook his head. "I don't know. I'll have to think about it. This is just too freaky." Again, he rubbed his nose on the sleeve of his orange jump suit.

John frowned. “Okay, but don’t take too long.” He pointed to Seth’s bandaged right wrist. “Sorry I hurt you. I was afraid things were getting out of hand.”

Seth looked down at the wrist, and stroked the bandage. “I’ll be okay I guess.” He looked down at the counter in front of him. “Can’t blame you for trying to protect her.”

The guard gripped Seth’s shoulder. John hung up his phone. As he turned to leave, he glanced at the woman still chattering away in Spanish to the man behind the glass. The look on his face was of barely restrained anger. He suspected that if the glass hadn’t separated them, the rage would have been released.

John stopped at the front desk where a formidable looking woman watched over the waiting room. He stopped and leaned over. “I don’t mean to meddle, but I couldn’t but overhear the couple next to me talking in Spanish and I speak the language a bit. Doesn’t ‘Me lío cuando salgo de aquí’ mean something like, ‘I will mess you up when I get out of here?’”

Anger washed over the guard’s face. “Did you hear him say that to her?”

John shook his head. “I couldn’t testify to that and I shouldn’t get involved. But maybe she should know about local shelters before he’s released.” John turned on his heel and strode out before she could question him further.

As he turned the dials on the bike lock he had an uneasy feeling that he was being watched. He slowly straightened up and then quickly turned around to look behind him. A woman, with long blonde hair and dressed in a black form fitting outfit was forty yards away, standing at the corner of the King County Administration Building.

She was looking straight at him.

She stepped to her left and was hidden by the building. John sprinted the short distance to where she had been standing and looked down the street.

Two county sheriff bicycle cops were standing on the sidewalk just around the corner, talking. When John appeared they broke off their conversation and gave him a wary look. John looked past them. No sign of the watcher.

"Excuse me officers. Did you just see a woman, dressed in black, long blonde hair come by here?"

One cop looked behind him and scanned the street. The other kept his eyes fixed on John. His companion turned back and shook his head. "No one has been by here in the last few minutes."

The other cop slowly nodded. "You okay, sir?"

John gave him a weak smile. "My mistake." He scanned the sidewalk and street beyond the pair and then said, "Sorry for bothering you." He turned away and returned to his bike.

An hour later, John pulled up to the wrought iron fence that guarded the courtyard in front of his apartment building. Before he opened the gate he looked carefully around. No sign of the mysterious figure. The encounter still had him unsettled.

He lifted his bike by the top tube, and headed up the stairs to his third story apartment, bypassing the rickety elevator in the lobby. The evening air and the breeze from the bike ride had kept him cool while he was riding. Now, perspiration broke out on his forehead. As he climbed up to his floor, sweat trickled down his back.

When he reached his floor, he dropped the bike on the carpet and wheeled it up the hall. The click, click, click from the hub echoed off the bare walls. As he passed the third apartment in his hallway he heard an animal paw at the door. He looked back over his shoulder and saw the door open a crack. A furry, dark brown cat raced past him. The feline stopped in front of John's door and looked up, purring. The door down the hall clicked as it closed.

"How's it going, Mocha?" John asked as he inserted the key in the lock. He pushed the door open and the cat raced inside, straight to the kitchen. The sound of munching soon emanated from a food dish. "Man, you'd think Sharon never feeds you the way you eat here." He parked the bike in the corner and headed to the bathroom for a quick shower.

After cleaning up, he sat down in front of the TV and picked up the remote. He turned on the ancient set, and after it warmed up, started flipping through the channels. The cat jumped up on the couch next to him and pushed its head into his lap. He started to scratch her behind the ears, and she purred so loud he could feel the vibration in his fingertips. "Good kitty, good Mocha." He set the remote down and scratched the cat on both sides of her face. She stared into his eyes for a moment, and then closed her eyes to resume her deep thrum of a purr. "Don't forget your mission, fuzz ball. Between you and me we'll get through to that wounded soul you live with." John continued to scratch her, until she pulled abruptly away, and jumped down off the sofa. She looked around the little apartment, then headed to the door, where she pawed furiously. He went over and opened the door. "That's right. Go show her some loving." He closed the door behind her and flipped the deadbolt closed.

He picked the remote up and continued scanning. He paused on different channels to catch a few local sports scores, national headlines, and then stopped when a familiar face filled the screen: Professor Wes Cavanaugh.

The camera cut to a raven haired reporter sitting on a chair opposite Cavanaugh. "We're back with Professor Wes Cavanaugh, a popular pundit on matters of religion." She turned toward him and flashed a brilliant smile. The white of her teeth contrasted with her tanned skin. "Professor, just before the break you were telling us about John's nickname, 'the Son of Thunder.' What did that mean exactly?"

"Actually, he and his brother, James, were called 'Sons of Thunder.'" He leaned forward and grinned at the anchor. "The most popular theory is he and his brother had a bit of an anger management issue—thunder referring to their hot tempers."

She raised her eyebrow. "Not exactly what you'd expect from two apostles."

"True, but remember they were human just like you and I. There are other theories about the nickname, but the Bible doesn't really explain it. Personally, I like the hot temper theory."

John gritted his teeth.

"Professor, when is your new series on the apostle John scheduled to appear?"

"I just signed a contract with this network this morning, so you get to be the one to break the news. The series is scheduled to premiere in January."

Megan flashed Cavanaugh a flirtatious grin. "I understand this is fiction, but you were telling me there are many legends that support the idea of a living apostle John."

"That's true. Many people know John was exiled to Patmos where he wrote the Book of Revelation, but most don't know why he was exiled instead of being martyred."

"Why wasn't he just killed like the other apostles?"

"The Roman Emperor Domitian did attempt to execute John for his Christian faith. Sometime around the year 95 AD, Domitian had him brought to Rome and ordered him thrown into boiling oil for refusing to renounce his faith and worship the emperor."

The reporter wrinkled her nose and grimaced.

Cavanaugh laughed, reached over, and patted her on the hand. "Not to worry, Megan. He emerged from the pot unscathed, and made many converts. But Domitian exiled him to the quarries of Patmos to keep him out of the way. After the emperor's death,

John was freed and returned to Ephesus where he lived to be an old man."

She leaned forward. "What about other legends?"

"One of the better documented ones involves Edward the Confessor, King of England, in 1042. Edward was accosted by a beggar asking for alms. The pious king took off his ring and gave it to the beggar." Cavanaugh turned to speak directly into the camera before continuing.

You shameless ham. John glanced down at the parts of a disassembled cuckoo clock on the coffee table in front of him. He picked up one of the counterweights and began to squeeze it like it was an exercise ball. "Twenty-four years later, two English pilgrims were in Jerusalem when a man gave them a ring and told them to take it to the king with a message: That Edward would be joining the Lord in six months. When they asked the man for his name, he replied, 'John the Apostle.'"

"John the Apostle?"

"Yes. The pilgrims reported back to Edward the Confessor. He recognized the ring he had given the beggar nearly a quarter century before. He prepared himself for his passing, fell sick on Christmas Eve, and died weeks later, on the feast of the three Kings."

"That is fascinating, but tell me something." She reached over and touched his forearm. "How would John have survived all these centuries? What would he be doing now?"

Cavanaugh started to open his mouth, but John had heard enough. He reared back to throw the counterweight in his hand at the screen. At the last instant, he thought better of it, and redirected his aim. The lead weight hit the wall at full force, and sunk halfway into the plaster, just above the television, one end pointing back at John. A puff of white dust emanated from the wall and settled slowly on the fake wood grain of the TV cabinet.

Chapter Five

Jesus was not a theologian. He was God who told stories.

Madeleine L'Engele

"SO OUR NEW friend, what brings you to our island on your way to Athens?" Tullius repeated the question from his position at the head of the pavilion. The villagers looked at Johanan, expectantly.

He paused. He was used to being the Beloved Disciple, the apostle and the companion of Jesus. He spoke to his audiences with the authority of one who had walked with the Christos. But he had been commanded to keep his identity a secret.

"My new friends, I travel from Asia Minor to Athens. I must admit I'm only here because my navigational skills aren't as good as I thought they were. Otherwise I would have passed far to the north of your beautiful island."

Tullius laughed loudly and stood with his cup outstretched. "To the poor navigational skills that brought our new friend to our home," he said.

The other villagers enthusiastically joined him. Some scrambled to refill their wine glasses so they could properly toast Johanan's error. It took several minutes before the hubbub died down and they again turned their attention to him.

"I travel to Athens to bring a message." He paused and slowly scanned the entire group, letting the anticipation build.

"A message of the love the true God has for all his people, including you my friends."

The villagers looked at each other and then back at Johanan. From their expressions, this was certainly not what they expected. Travelers usually brought tales of their own adventures. Most tried to impress the locals with their accomplishments—at least those travelers that weren't Roman tax collectors.

"And how do you come to bear this message?" asked Aprius, his recent opponent in the ring.

Johanan smiled at him. "I come from a community of followers of the Son of God." Again he paused for effect.

"The Son came to Earth a century ago and lived as one of us for over thirty years. Then He was sacrificed for our sins by the Romans—but rose from the dead after three days. Now He reigns in Heaven with his Father."

Aprius looked at Johanan with intensity. "Did you see this Son of God?"

How was he going to handle this question? Finally, he said, "He died and rose from the dead over seventy years ago, my friend. Do I look old enough to have walked with Him?"

"No," Aprius said. Then he pointed to Tullius, "But maybe my father…"

The villagers laughed at Tullius who raised his cup to them.

Aprius waited until the laughter died down and said, "Tell us more of the Son."

Johanan started, "In the beginning…."

Several hours later he finished with the story of the ascension. He had told of Christ's birth, ministry, and miracles. He had openly wept during his description of the crucifixion and laughed with joy when describing the resurrection. During his discourse he had seen a variety of expressions on the face of his audience. Some enraptured, some quizzical, a few disapproving. Some wept along with him.

"Remember," he concluded, "God loves the world and his people so much, that he sent his Son to live among us, to teach of his love, and to serve as a sacrifice for our sins. And then to rise again to show He is God and not even death can conquer Him. Anyone who believes in Him will join Him in Heaven where they will have everlasting life."

Side conversations began to break out among the islanders. Then questions began to pop out—some directed to him—others to the crowd in general:

"Where is he now?"

"Should we worship him?"

"But what about our gods?"

"How can we know this is true?"

The stocky, balding man with the Medusa-like beard stood. He raised his staff to gain the attention of the villagers. Johanan had noticed him during the evening. As Johanan had talked, the man's expression had progressed from quizzical to disapproving.

He waved the staff at Johanan, then addressed the villagers. "We serve the gods of our Greek ancestors. They have served our people well for untold generations." He turned his attention back to Johanan and pointed the staff to him. "When we have turned to other gods, it has been disastrous. Remember when—"

"Enough." Tullius stood up. He addressed the village in his booming voice. "Johanan has given us much to think about. But a fisherman's day begins early. Let me suggest we invite him to stay with us and tell us more of this Son of God."

The stocky man shouted. "What about—"

Tullius raised his hand to silence him. "Solon, I know what you are going to say." He lowered his hand. "But before I make a decision, I would like to hear more for myself." He looked at Johanan.

"I would be glad to stay with you and tell you of Jesus. As long as you permit me to earn my keep by letting me labor alongside you."

"We can always use another strong back on our island. You are welcome to stay as my personal guest."

Solon glared at Johanan. Then he turned abruptly and strode out of the pavilion. With each step, he thrust the end of his staff into the sand as if he were spearing a wild boar.

The islanders began to disperse. Knots of animated conversations faded into the darkness. Torches carried by individual families dimmed as they retired to their homes. Johanan followed Tullius, his wife, and children, to the largest house in the village, situated at the southernmost end of the row of huts.

Aprius walked at his side. "Johanan, is this all true?"

"Yes my friend. It is the most wonderful truth."

"You tell of it as if you were there. But you say it was seven decades ago."

Johanan measured his words carefully. "In the community where I lived, there was a man who walked with Jesus. There are many still alive today who were taught by those who walked with him. They have been taught by reliable eyewitnesses. It is all true."

Marcus said, "I don't know about this. I think there are too many gods already."

Aprius clapped him on his back. "The way you primp in that mirror, maybe you think you should be a god."

Anteia giggled. "It is his prize possession."

Johanan raised an eyebrow.

Aprius laughed. "My little brother saved his money to buy a bronze hand mirror from a passing trader. He's never far from it."

Thais said, "Aprius. Leave your brother alone."

Aprius sighed and rolled his eyes. "Of course, mother."

They reached the home and entered through a wooden gate into a small courtyard. A flock of chickens scattered as they came in. A half dozen bleating goats came up, hoping for some handouts. Two walls of the courtyard were made up of wooden poles about the height of a man. The third was the main family living quarters. Thais led Anteia into the family quarters. Tullius followed them and returned with a lamp. He led Aprius, his younger brother Marcus, and Johanan to a stable, the fourth wall of the courtyard. They went inside and were greeted by the bleating of several more goats. A medium size black dog with a gray muzzle was sleeping. He woke, looked up at them and went back to sleep. Tullius bent over and scratched him behind his ears.

"Sometimes I'm still surprised to see you are with us, Mithridates," he said to the old dog. He looked up at Johanan. In the lamplight, he could see Tullius' eyes were moist. "For many years he followed me everywhere faithfully. He waited for our boats to return from fishing at the edge of the beach. No matter how bad the weather, he was there. Now he is old and deaf and sleeps away the days." He stroked him again. "Someday I will be like him."

Aprius laughed. "Shall we make you a couch so you can wait for us on the beach, tomorrow?"

Tullius grabbed the young man around the neck. "You I will drown in the sea before I grow old and weak!"

They wrestled playfully for a few moments before Aprius graciously surrendered to his father. Tullius then picked up a blanket and a straw mat and gave them to Johanan. He led him outside to a ladder leaning up against the side of the stable. Aprius and Marcus were already climbing up to the roof. Tullius pointed up.

"There is some hay to sleep on and a tent for shelter from rains. It should be comfortable. Don't let my sons keep you awake too long."

Johanan grasped Tullius' arm. "Thank you for your hospitality. God bless you."

Tullius looked into his eyes. "I expect that with your visit, he already has."

He waited until Johanan was up the ladder and then went into the main house with his lamp.

When Johanan got to the top, he could see Marcus and Aprius in a three sided tent on the roof. Marcus had his back turned and was already asleep. Aprius was propped up on his elbow, waiting for him.

After Johanan laid out his mat and settled in for the night Aprius asked, "All you said was true? You swear by Poseidon?"

"Aprius, all I tell you is true and I will tell you more in the days to come, but I will not swear by Poseidon. I swear by the living God himself."

The next morning the sun was just up when Tullius entered the courtyard and yelled, "Up you laggards. The fish are already scheming on ways to escape our nets."

His sons tumbled out of bed and scrambled down the ladder. They knew an early start might be the difference between full nets and a meager catch. Johanan took a moment to take stock of his surroundings. Was it a dream? Wasn't he an old man? He looked over the edge of the loft and down at Tullius. It was no dream.

"Come, Johanan. You asked for a chance to earn your keep."

He climbed down the ladder, a little more cautiously than the boys who had been doing this for years.

"Sometimes we get up early and have a hot meal before setting out for the day's work." He held up a bag. "But you kept us up so late last night that you're going to sail with just dried fish and fruit."

"I hope it was worth the late night," questioned Johanan.

"I expect you'll hear much about it today. And I look forward to hearing more tonight. I must admit your tale seems incredible."

"Tullius, it is incredible. But I swear to you it's all true."

"In my youth I went to the mainland for my education. I remember meeting a group of people who reminded me of my home here on the island. They seemed to love each other and those around them very much. I found out later they were followers of your Christos."

"How did you find out?"

Tullius looked down at the sand, then back at Johanan. "They were hauled away by legionaries for refusing to worship the emperor."

Johanan nodded. "We have faced many persecutions, especially under Nero and most recently Domitian. It is not so bad nowadays under Trajan. We often worship in secret. Yet, our numbers grow because even the power of the Empire can't stop the truth."

"It does have the ring of truth to me. We stayed awake in the house for hours talking about it and have many questions. Thais fears incurring the wrath of the Romans."

They had completed the short walk to the beach. Marcus, Aprius, and another man about the age of Aprius were preparing a small boat and pushing it into the water. Tullius passed a bag to Johanan.

"Today you fish with Aprius and his crew. They'll tell me if you can really earn your keep."

"I expect they will be fair judges," He held the bag out at arm's length, "especially because I have the day's provisions." Johanan shook it and they laughed.

"By all means, come aboard, man." Marcus waved Johanan forward. "I'm ready to chew off my brother's arm if there isn't enough food in that sack."

Johanan waded through the surf and jumped aboard the boat.

He stowed the provisions in a compartment up front and grabbed an oar. Aprius sat at the stern with the steering oar in his hand. Marcus pushed the boat deeper into the surf and pulled himself deftly up and over the rail. Their companion grasped the other oar and soon he and Johanan were back paddling into deeper water. When they were deep enough, Aprius commanded them to turn starboard and Johanan switched to a forward stroke while his companion continued to back stroke. Soon they were turned into the surf and Aprius ordered them to go forward. The two were soon pulling in unison and moving the boat steadily out to sea.

Johanan glanced up at the bow and saw Marcus looking at himself in a bronze hand mirror. He was carefully grooming his beard using a wooden comb. Johanan looked back at the stern. Aprius gave him a knowing glance.

"I told you about the mirror." He smirked and yelled at Marcus. "Hey, Narcissus. How about getting the sail ready? You'll have plenty of time to make yourself pretty for the girls before we head back."

Johanan glanced back at Marcus. He gave Johanan a sheepish grin as he tucked the mirror away into a pouch.

Johanan looked back at the shore and saw several boats just hitting the water. Toward his right he saw several others in the sea, but none much farther than theirs. Evidently everyone was getting a late start this morning. He looked over at his rowing companion. Johanan recognized him as one of the young men around the fire last night. He had been sitting next to Aprius and the pair had seemed to be friends. But his expression through Johanan's discourse was more one of questioning rather than open acceptance.

His fellow oarsman looked back. "My name is Nikias. It will be good to spend the day with our honored guest."

"The honor is mine, Nikias. Your village has been very gracious." At least he was friendly.

Soon enough they were beyond the surf and Marcus set the

sail. Aprius steered them along with the rest of the fleet toward a good fishing area. Marcus fetched their breakfast and passed the bag to Johanan. He looked in and pulled out the choicest piece of dried fish and gave it to Nikias. He pulled another fish out for himself and began to chew.

The day was clear and the wind light. They were making good time.

"So, Johanan, have you spent much time fishing?" asked Marcus.

"I didn't buy the catch I brought to your village yesterday," Johanan said. "I made my living on my father's fishing boat for many years."

"Where was that?" asked Nikias.

"The Sea of Galilee. Not as big as your sea of course. But we had our struggles with storms and bad days of fishing."

"Why did you give it up?" asked Marcus.

He hesitated. He couldn't tell them Jesus himself had called him. But he could tell them part of the truth.

"I decided to become a follower of Jesus. And spread his word to all people."

Nikias interrupted. "My father is Solon."

Johanan looked into Nikias eyes, trying to divine his intentions. "Solon, the man who warned against my teachings last night?"

Nikias nodded. "He and many of the village elders teach Poseidon is our god. He rescued our ancestors from a storm on their way home from the Trojan Wars. He brought them safely to this island with their women captives and we've lived here ever since in peace."

Marcus said, "Don't forget one of the captives was the daughter of Helen of Troy which explains the beauty of our women."

Johanan thought about Marcus and Aprius' sister Anteia, and

how attractive she was. Her brilliant blue eyes were unforgettable. He could believe she was a descendant of the legendary Helen.

Aprius laughed. "Don't forget the story is also told that our ancestors were tired of fighting in the wars of the Greek kings. They just abandoned the rest of the army to find a new home and we've been hiding here ever since."

"If your father is afraid of Johanan's teachings," Marcus said, "why did he let you sail with us today?"

Nikias looked away.

"Maybe," said Aprius, "he wants his son to spy on our guest."

Nikias looked back at Aprius, a smug smile on his face. "I can't answer that, but I can say my captain is wise beyond his years."

A flash of silver off to the right, just below the surface of the water, caught Johanan's eye. He looked out to sea and saw it again.

"Over there, Aprius. I think we'll have good fishing there."

Aprius looked out to where Johanan was pointing and then back at him.

"But everyone else is heading toward our usual fishing grounds," Nikias said.

Johanan saw the sea briefly roil. "Look, a great catch waiting for us." The others looked again, but the waters were now calm.

Nikias said, "You may be the best wrestler on the island, Aprius, but you're not the best fisherman. We should follow the others."

Aprius looked between Nikias and Johanan. Then he looked back out in the direction Johanan had pointed. "We'll give our guest a chance to prove himself." He turned the steering oar. "Let's see whose gods are stronger."

Nikias shook his head, but kept silent.

"Prepare the nets. Bring down the sail."

Marcus and Nikias started to prepare the net. Johanan pulled down the sail and kept looking ahead until he saw the flash again.

"Just up there." He pointed again.

"Let's go. Cast away," Aprius shouted.

Marcus and Nikias pitched the net over the port side of the boat. Within moments a river of silvery fins and scales intercepted the net. The bounty filled it so quickly that the boat made a hard turn toward port.

"They're tunny," Marcus said over the din of thrashing fish. "These will be gold in the local market. This is a haul not even Poseidon has seen!" He looked at Johanan, suddenly embarrassed by his reference to the Greek god. Johanan just smiled back and reached over to help haul in the net.

Aprius kept on the steering oar to keep the boat steady. Johanan and Nikias held the net as the fish thrashed wildly. The four young men laughed with joy as Marcus used a gaff to hook tunny after tunny and pitch them into the bottom of the boat.

A wave sloshed over the side of the boat. "Enough," said Aprius. "If we sink the boat we'll have nothing." Marcus looked at Aprius and then gaffed one more.

"Marcus."

Johanan released his end of the net. The river of silvery fish spilled out into the open sea. As Nikias pulled the net in, Johanan scrambled over the thrashing cargo and leaned out over the starboard side to provide a counterweight. Marcus started to spread the fish over the bottom of the boat to even the load. The boat wallowed in the waves.

"Let's get to shore before we sink." Aprius said. "Man the oars and pull away!"

Johanan and Nikias each dug an oar out from under the flopping bounty on the bottom of the boat and were soon rowing steadily. Marcus busied himself by bailing out what water he could reach among the fish with a wooden bowl. Behind them, the sails of the other vessels continued out to the fishing grounds. They soon disappeared from sight.

As they approached the shore, many of the women of the village came down to shore to meet them.

"What's wrong?" one woman shouted over the noise of the waves.

The young men laughed in response.

Johanan looked over his shoulder at the gathering crowd on the beach. It must be unusual for a lone boat to return so soon. He could see the look of concern on faces. Several waded out into the surf to help the boat land.

While Johanan and Nikias continued to stroke through the shallow water, Marcus grabbed the rope tied to the bow and leapt into the surf. Soon he and several of the women were pulling the boat up into the shallows. Finally, the rest of the crew abandoned their posts, jumped into the water, and pushed the bow of the boat up onto the beach.

While Marcus and several women leaned back on the rope, Aprius, Nikias, and Johanan pushed on the stern. Despite their collective effort, they only managed to get the front half of the fully loaded vessel up on the beach.

Finally, Aprius stepped up to the side of the boat, and waved everyone over.

His mother, Thais, asked, "What's wrong. Why are you back so soon?"

Aprius pointed to the thrashing tunny in the bottom of the boat. The women gathered around to see what was causing the commotion in their peaceful village.

Marcus yelled over the noise of the crowd and the surf. "We caught all of these in one sweep of the net. Johanan called them to us."

They turned as one, and looked at Johanan. He was standing in the surf at the back of the boat. He noted Anteia in the middle of the gathering, her mouth agape.

A woman shouted out, "We have never seen so many tunny—even caught by the whole fleet in a day. He is a god."

Johanan shook his head in protest. "No, no. I'm no god." He waved his hands to the sky. "But God did bless us today."

Nikias interrupted. "Enough talk. We need to clean these before they spoil."

The women quickly mobilized. Several ran up into the village, returning quickly with large baskets. They began shuttling the fish up the beach in the baskets. Johanan heaved a basket onto his shoulder and followed them.

Thais met him and pointed to an area covered with small, rounded stones. "Put the basket there. We'll clean them."

In several hours, the best of the catch was being grilled for the midday meal. The rest was drying on racks, or being salted and set aside in casks. The fishermen of the village were used to spending their lunchtime on the water. Aprius' crew seemed to enjoy the novelty of a lunch on shore.

Exhausted and full, Johanan sat in the shade of a tree up off the beach and lay on his back. He looked up at the sky and closed his eyes. The events of the last few days and the struggle with the catch had taken their toll on him. He heard footsteps coming up the beach and sat up. It was Aprius with his seemingly ever present smile on his face. He sat down in the sand next to him and lay on his back.

"How goes it my captain?"

"A few more days like this and I'll be able to buy my father's boat and build my own house," Aprius said.

They lay on the sand in silence, savoring the quiet and their victory over the sea.

"Tell me, Johanan. Is life so easy for followers of the Son of God?"

He paused and thought over the many struggles he'd had since Jesus had called him from his fishing boat on the Sea of Galilee. He lifted himself up on his elbow and looked straight at Aprius.

"By no means. The Romans have persecuted and martyred

many of us. We grow sick and die like any man. Many followers of Jesus live in poverty. But we live as a family, as a community of believers who seek the truth. And we have solace in the fact that despite our many trials we will one day live with him in heaven." He rolled over on his back and flung his arms out to his sides. "But today, today, he has blessed us indeed!"

Aprius lay on the sand with his eyes closed. He breathed deeply for a few minutes. "My friend, will you teach me more of this Jesus? Will you teach me how to be a follower of the Son of God?"

Johanan fell back on the sand. "My captain, I will teach you all I can. Now, of you I ask a favor as well."

"Ask, and it is yours," Aprius said.

"Teach me your wrestling skills. I would like to be able to stop an attacker without hurting them, as you do."

Aprius breathed quietly for a few moments. "We will start after we nap."

Chapter Six

One sanctimonious hypocrite makes a hundred unbelievers.

Joy Davidman (Wife of C. S. Lewis)

JOHN PULLED HIS gaze away from the cuckoo clock weight buried in the wall. Professor Cavanaugh was still chattering away on the television to his new BFF, Megan the reporter.

Tap tap. That was what had pulled him out of his recollection. A soft, bird-like knock at the door.

He turned off the TV with the remote, crossed the room, and peered cautiously out the peephole. He saw the familiar figure of a woman in a skirt and jacket. It was Sharon, dressed like she was going out for a night on the town. That was unusual—Sharon going out? She was standing back from the door, fidgeting as she waited.

She gently knocked again. John opened the door. Mocha bolted from her position at Sharon's feet and zipped between John's legs into the apartment, pausing long enough to rub against his ankle. He glanced down at the cat, then looked up at Sharon.

He noticed she had curled her normally straight brown hair. The perpetual frown that usually graced her face had been replaced by a nervous smile.

"Hi. You look great," he said. "Heading out?"

"Um, yeah," she said quietly, "but I was hoping I could talk to you first."

"Come on in. Can I get you something to drink?"

"Uh, sure." She paused. "Wine would be nice."

He went into the kitchen and perused the selection in his small counter-top wine rack. *If she's going out drinking, I don't want to give her a head start.* He pulled a dusty bottle of Martinelli's sparkling apple cider out of the rack and grabbed a kitchen towel. He tossed the towel over his arm and pulled a pair of glasses out of the cupboard. He walked into the living room cradling the bottle of cider like it was a fine champagne. In his finest imitation of a snooty wine steward he said, "Mademoiselle, may I present for your approval, this fine bottle of spark-leen cider, straight from the exquisite orchards of your fair state." She giggled. "It may not have the bite of the fruit of the vine, but I assure you, it has a most piquant and fruity bouquet."

She stifled a laugh with her hand. He started to set the glasses down on the coffee table, but it was covered with newspapers, paperwork, a plate, glass, and silverware from last night's dinner, a bowl of fruit, and the rest of the partially disassembled cuckoo clock.

"John, you are such a bachelor." She folded up the newspaper and stacked it on one end, along with the loose papers. Then she piled the glass and silverware onto the plate, and took it into the kitchen. By the time she returned, he had set down the glasses and put the clock parts into a neat pile next to the stack of papers.

She took in the scene. "A cuckoo clock?"

"I've tried my hand at a number of different trades. Trying to fix this one for a neighbor."

She straightened her skirt down as she sat back down on the couch. John popped the top off with a bottle opener. It responded with a satisfying pop. "As I was saying mademoiselle, you will find this a most satisfying alternative to the wine." He started to pour the sparkling cider into her glass.

Sharon turned away, removed her jacket and put it over the back of the couch. She turned back to him. *Whoa!* With a neckline like that, she was going to draw some attention when she went out. He had never seen her dress like this.

They sat on the couch and made small talk for a few minutes. John struggled to keep his eyes on Sharon's face and away from her plunging collar.

Finally he asked, "You said you wanted to talk about something?"

She looked him straight in the eyes. Her pupils widened. She took a big swig out of her glass.

John should have known what was going to happen next. All the signals were there, but, despite his experience, he was often naive about these things. He seemed to be wired to expect all women to behave in the demure manner of those he had known in the small village of his youth.

She sat her glass down and took a deep breath. She threw herself the short distance across the couch and knocked him backward into the cushions. She lay on top of him and kissed him hard. He kissed back. Just as hard. He was surprised at how good it felt.

John put his hands on Sharon's ribs and deftly flipped her over on her back, and sat up next to her. He looked down at the surprised young woman.

"Sharon. I can't do this. This is wrong."

She blushed deeply, and looked away. She sat up and reached for her jacket. "I'm sorry. I thought you liked me."

He laughed, "I do like you. Please don't go." He grabbed her hands and held them gently in his own.

"Is it because I'm fat?"

John was surprised. He had never thought of her as fat, although she'd need to lose about ten pounds to be considered svelte. "You are *not* fat. You're very attractive. You're intelligent and funny. You would make a great partner and—you're a great kisser." He let a grin slowly, and deliberately, grow on his face. She blushed again and turned away.

"Please understand me. I really like you. You don't need to do this to get the right man."

"I'm so embarrassed," she said.

"Don't be. Under different circumstances, I would be very interested in you." He paused.

She interrupted the silence. "But?"

"I've been married before." More silence.

"And?"

"It ended badly. It was entirely my fault and the circumstances that caused the problem haven't changed."

"How long ago?"

He sighed. "It seems so long ago, but it's not long enough for me to forget the pain I caused."

Her eyes were tearing. "But you're so great. I can't believe any woman wouldn't want you."

He grasped her hands in both of his and looked her straight in the eyes.

"Thank you. That means a lot to me coming from you, but you have to understand. I'm not ready for this, even if you are."

She blushed again deeply and then stood up to go. He sensed she was working hard to stay in control.

"Please, wait. Talk to me." He looked at her and hesitated. "Why did you feel like you had to throw yourself at me?"

She choked up again. He pulled her close. She resisted briefly, and then melted into his arms. She told him how she had been active in her church youth group and had idolized her young, married, youth pastor.

"Finally, one day, I told him how I felt. We were in his office." She took a few moments to quell her sobs. "Then, he kissed me."

John waited for her to continue, although he was afraid to hear how this was going to turn out. Finally he prompted her. "And?"

"His wife walked in as we were kissing."

John sighed in relief.

"There was a big fight. She threatened divorce. In the end, she said she'd keep him if I left the church."

"What about your parents? Didn't they report him?"

"No." She stopped again to sob. "They blamed me for starting it. We fought for the next six months until I graduated from high school. Then I got my loser job and moved out." Sharon broke down crying at this point. John gave her his handkerchief and waited.

Finally he asked, "How about your parents? Do they still blame you?"

"My mom gave me the damage deposit for this place. I haven't talked much to them since then. I don't want to."

John spent the next hour listening and asking questions. When she seemed to run out of things to say he said, "Sharon. We all make mistakes, but we don't need to pay for them the rest of our lives." He paused. "You probably don't want to hear this, but God loves you."

She choked. Then in anger said, "How could he let that man—that man—ruin my life?"

"Sharon, imagine you're running a marathon." She gave him a quizzical look but nodded. "You're running the race with friends and there are people all along the route cheering you on. It's a worthy goal and you've been training for months."

She nodded again.

"But at one of the water stops along the way you grab a cup from a guy and take a quick swig, but…"

She waited, and then asked, "But what?"

"It's vinegar."

She scowled. "Vinegar? Why would he do that?"

"Exactly. Why would he do that?"

She leaned back.

"Sharon, don't mistake Christianity for Christ. The church is run by people, people who make mistakes, people who misuse their positions of authority, people who fail."

She looked into his eyes. Her own were still brimming with tears. "It still hurts. Sometimes it feels like it will never stop." She put her head on his shoulder and cried, softly.

"The whole purpose of religion is to put men and women in touch with God, to show them his love." He put his hands on her shoulders and looked her in the eyes. "Don't let flawed people get in the way of that."

She leaned against him, the tears finally subsiding. Mocha climbed up into her lap. John continued to reassure her, softly.

"Don't forget I am your friend. I'm here for you—and so is Mocha."

She laughed, and reached over to stroke the cat.

"Remember, God does love you. What you will ever find with a man here on Earth is only a pale shadow of that."

Sharon sat up, slowly. Through a teary smile she said, "You may find this hard to believe, but you're my closest friend."

John nodded, slowly. He placed his hand on her shoulder. "I'm honored."

"If you ever hurt me," she choked on her words and struggled to continue, "I don't know if I could handle it."

He reached over to the bowl of fruit on the table and picked up an apple. John held it up between them, on the tips of his fingers.

"Imagine this apple is your heart."

She smirked.

"I will always treat it with care, as if it was made of expensive, fragile, crystal."

She smiled, then reached out and took the fruit from his fingers.

"You're corny. But, I'll trust you—for now." She took a bite from the apple.

As John watched her lips close on the fruit, he realized just how attractive she was. Her slightly disheveled hair and tear stained cheeks made him want to reach out and pull the vulnerable woman into his arms. As she pulled the apple up to her lips and closed her eyes, he could imagine she was kissing him instead of biting into the fruit.

He squeezed his eyes shut and thought. *You're not some pillaging Goth, you're—*

"John, are you okay?" His eyes popped open. She was looking at him with a quizzical expression.

"Yes, I'm just, I was just…"

She interrupted his stammering and picked up her jacket from the back of the couch. "It's late. I should be going." As she stood and started to don the jacket she glanced over at the TV—and her gaze fixed on the cuckoo clock weight buried in the wall. Is that from the…" She pointed at the pile of clock parts.

He nodded. "I got a little upset at a commentator. Good thing I missed the screen."

She raised an eyebrow. "So much for your damage deposit."

At the door to his apartment, she turned to hug him. "Thank you." Mocha looked up at John and meowed. He nodded and the cat dutifully followed Sharon down the hall.

"Don't forget. You are a special woman." She turned and gave him a fragile smile.

He stood in the hallway until her door closed behind her and the cat. Then he backed into his own apartment.

John perused his email, quickly filtering out the junk from the important messages. Nothing unusual. No mission. No message. It was still time to wait.

He thought back to his encounter with Sharon earlier that evening. The feeling of her lips on his. Her body pressed up against his. He shook his head. *Why can't I have a normal life? Haven't I earned it after all these years?*

After breakfast the next morning John spent some time putting together a grocery list and a task list for the week ahead. Then he turned to the important document for the morning. After several drafts, he wrote on a note card:

Sharon,

I'd like to continue our discussion with some friends of mine. If you're interested, please be ready at 8:30 tomorrow morning. If you're not outside your door then, I'll assume you're not yet ready. Remember though, I'm here when you're ready.

Your friend,

John

He hooked his saddlebags onto the bike and wheeled it out of the apartment. He slipped the note card under Sharon's door and continued down the hall and the staircase. The fisherman had set the hook—now would she take the bait?

Chapter Seven

Learn as if you would live forever, live as if you would die tomorrow.

Mahatma Ghandi

JOHANAN SLEPT DEEPLY—A sleep interrupted by dreams of the vision of the Christos standing over his bed only weeks before. In his dreams, Anteia stood next to Jesus, looking down at him adoringly, like a loyal handmaiden.

As the sun moved, the shadow of the tree above him moved off of his face. Soon the light shone through his eyelids. He became aware of two people standing near his feet. One moved between him and the sun and cast a shadow over his eyes.

"How long has he been asleep?" one said in a whisper to the other. He couldn't tell who was speaking.

Johanan tensed his muscles and opened his eyes just a slit: Marcus and Aprius.

"Up you lazy man," Aprius said. "It's time for your first lesson."

Johanan leapt up at Aprius, who deftly sidestepped him. He

wound up on his hands and feet in the sand just beyond the two brothers. They burst out laughing, and pounded each other on the shoulders.

"I guess that will count as your first lesson. Let's go. Dinner is soon and you have much to learn."

Marcus led the way into the forest with Aprius right behind him. Johanan brought up the rear. Aprius kept looking behind them.

A few minutes into their journey Johanan asked, "What are you looking for?"

"I want to make sure we aren't followed."

"By who?"

"By those who would like to know our family secrets."

Johanan grunted. Aprius said, "When my father was a youth he was sent to Athens to live with his uncle and aunt. My grandparents wanted him to get an education."

"Do many leave the island for their education?"

"Not many. I think my grandparents were very worldly for their time." He tossed his head back to laugh. "I've also heard it said father was too much for them to handle but too young to have him conscripted into the Roman legions."

"I can imagine that. He seems to be very comfortable being in charge. I expect he chafed under the yoke of his parents."

"So I've heard." Aprius stopped to pick a handful of figs from a tree. He passed one to Johanan. Then he looked ahead to Marcus, who was trotting twenty paces ahead of them.

"Marcus!"

Marcus stopped and turned. Aprius tossed a fig at him. The younger sibling snatched it out of the air.

"Slow down, brother. You're always missing the good stuff."

Marcus bit into the fig, waved, turned, and broke into a trot.

Johanan picked up the conversation. "What did your father study in Athens?"

"The usual. Mathematics, oratory, reading. What really caught his attention though, was wrestling."

"Why that sport?"

"It turns out he had a gift for it. He's smaller than most men, but he learned moves that helped him beat larger opponents. My father is a good observer, patient, and creative. By the end of his stay, he had gained some fame in the city for his prowess."

"Why did he come back to this small place?"

Aprius turned and glowered at Johanan.

Johanan said, "I'm sorry, I didn't mean to insult your village."

Aprius turned and continued walking. "You may look at this as an unsophisticated village, but we are more than simple fisherman. We even have a school for the children on the island. We live a good life here. At least most of the time."

"Most of the time?"

"Don't expect to learn all our secrets so quickly." He bit into his own fig. "Actually, my father did consider staying in Athens and opening his own wrestling school." He broke into a jog. Johanan followed suit. In moments, he was breathing hard as he struggled to keep the pace.

Finally Aprius took up the story again. "Athens has many attractions, but he finally decided he wanted the life of the island. So he took the best of the city and returned home."

"The best of the city?"

Aprius turned, and ran backwards as easily as he had been running forward. He looked at Johanan, as if he was the stupidest man on the earth. "My mother, of course."

"How could I have missed that?"

Aprius laughed, then turned to run forward again. "I won't tell my mother you did. Marcus would have, but I won't."

He inhaled deeply to catch his breath before replying, "I'll remember that."

Just ahead of them, Marcus stepped off the trail and stood

behind a thicket of bushes, watching for spies. Aprius continued on the way and beckoned Johanan to follow. Soon they were at a clearing among the palm trees. Marcus rejoined them.

Aprius gestured to Johanan and Marcus to sit. "Johanan, you are about to learn our family secrets in the sport of wrestling. I shouldn't have promised to teach you without my father's permission. I went and asked him while you slept. He agreed because of why you asked to learn. He was impressed you wanted the skill so you could beat an opponent without harming him." Aprius smiled his big smile. "And, he knows that soon you will leave and won't oppose his position in the village."

Johanan laughed. "I would be a foolish man indeed to oppose the wise Tullius."

Aprius led Marcus and Johanan through a series of warm up exercises designed to make them limber, quick, and strong. Then he began the lesson.

First he showed Johanan how to read an opponent's intentions by reading his eyes and body movements; the way they looked, tensed their muscles, and even how their pupils changed.

"That's how I knew to avoid you when we woke you. I saw you tense your muscles. When I saw your eyes open slightly I knew you would try something."

Then he had Marcus demonstrate several holds that gave him superior leverage. Aprius let him conduct the lesson with Johanan, reinforcing what he had learned from his older brother, and building his own confidence. Plus, it kept the younger brother from getting bored. Johanan realized what was going on and was impressed with Aprius' wisdom. He would be a good leader in his own right someday.

When Johanan had successfully learned several key holds, Aprius looked up at the sun. "Time for us to be heading home. We will eat soon." They each grabbed a palm frond and swept the footprints out of the sand, so it wasn't obvious they had been practicing there.

Instead of retracing their steps, Marcus continued on their original path across the island, but this time at a run. "I warn you, Johanan. My older brother may be the better wrestler, but I am the faster runner." He left a spray of sand behind him as he broke into a sprint.

"It is true," Aprius said. "I can only beat him at short distances—or through trickery."

They picked up the pace, but not so much they couldn't continue to talk.

"You will tell us more of this Jesus tonight? My father has asked everyone to gather after the evening meal."

"I live to tell people of the Son of God and his love," Johanan said. He panted before continuing. "I am glad you want to hear more of Him."

Marcus had almost reached the beach on the other side of the island. He turned around and ran backwards so he could shout back at them. "The long, or short way?"

"Short tonight." Aprius pointed to his left. "We'll go easy on our new crewmate."

Marcus turned around and turned down a path to his left. He pulled away easily.

Aprius kept a steady pace. He clearly had no intention of trying to catch Marcus tonight.

"I want to hear more of Jesus. Your tales seem so fresh in comparison to the stale old stories about Poseidon and the other gods." He paused to take a few deep breaths and gather his thoughts. "Most in our village follow the traditional Greek gods and their ways. I must admit I only do so because it's expected."

Johanan kept quiet, in part because he was breathing hard to keep up with Aprius.

"But I'm afraid not everyone will be open to your message.

There are many who will cling to the old ways, even if your Jesus came to us himself."

"That's true. But I believe your name is written in his book, Aprius. You will become one of his followers."

Aprius looked over his shoulder at Johanan and grinned widely. "Come, we'll take a shortcut. We may still have a chance to beat Marcus."

After the evening meal the villagers gathered at the fire pit. While the men reclined most of the women were working. Some mended clothes, others weaved baskets. A group worked off at the edge mending nets. They had a night off last night for the celebration, but now life had to continue. Tullius waited until everyone seemed to be settled in and then stood to address them.

"My friends, I know some of you did not want to come tonight. I thank you for honoring my request to hear our guest out, and his story about this Son of God. I know many of you are afraid to offend Poseidon, other gods, or the emperor. In fact, I see several are not here with us tonight." He paused as those in the crowd looked around to see who was missing.

"I ask you to listen to Johanan tonight to see if his words ring true. And I also ask you to remember the amazing catch his crew made today. I have never seen so many tunny brought up in one haul. What we rarely bring home in one day his boat brought up in one sweep of the nets. Remember: a single sweep."

Many of the people in the audience looked at each other and nodded enthusiastically. Others looked straight ahead without emotion. Tullius nodded at Johanan and beckoned to him. He stood up, and walked to Tullius' side. They pounded each other's shoulders affectionately and then Tullius sat down.

"My brothers and my sisters," Johanan said. He looked around the group and made eye contact with one person after another.

Finally he continued, "As Tullius said, today we had an amazing catch. And I want you to understand that sometimes Jesus, my Lord and Savior—our Lord and Savior, blesses us in amazing ways. But those of us who follow him also experience many trials. Roman emperors have tried to silence us. They have fed us to lions, and pitted us, unarmed, against vicious gladiators. Life has not been easy for followers of the Christos." He looked around as his words sank in. "But the truth cannot be stopped. Our numbers have grown. We continue to spread the message of his love. And I would like to tell you more about our God. The God who loves all of us."

Johanan spent the next hour telling stories about Jesus. He found himself having to be cautious about how he told the story. Habit and practice dictated that he speak of these events in the first person. Now he had to tell the stories in the third person as if he had heard them from others—not as if he had lived them himself.

Finally he said, "I would like to stay with you for at least a few more days to tell you of Jesus. If you will allow me, I will work with you during the day and teach you at night."

Most of the villagers nodded, many enthusiastically. A few looked indifferent. Some frowned.

Aprius stood up and broke the silence. "I am ready to follow this Jesus. I believe you tell us the truth. I know you are a man of God and his messenger. How do I pledge my loyalty to him?" Nearly a dozen other villagers stood up as well. Johanan looked at each of them.

He looked at Tullius and said, "If you will permit me, there is a ceremony to become a follower of the Christos. Much like the baptism of Jesus himself." Johanan was aware this was a critical moment. In Greco-Roman society the heads of household spoke for all the members of the house. Over his seven decades of ministry he had been rejected many times. If things went badly, he might be setting sail tonight.

Tullius stood and looked around. "This is for each head of household to decide. As for my house, I free each adult to make their own decision." He looked at his daughter Anteia who was among those standing. "The same also goes for the women." He looked around at the crowd before saying, "I ask you all to consider this decision carefully." Tullius sat down.

Johanan breathed a sigh of relief. "Follow me." He walked down to the seashore, followed by the villagers, and removed his tunic. Still clad in his modest woolen undergarments, he waded in and beckoned to those standing on the shore alongside Aprius. Among them were Marcus and Anteia. Many other villagers, including Tullius and Thais, stood just behind them. Nikias started to step forward. His father, Solon, put his hand on his shoulder and pulled him back.

Aprius and his companions waded out into the water until they were waist deep. Johanan gestured to Aprius, who came forward. Johanan put his hand gently on his head.

He proclaimed loudly enough for all to hear, "Aprius, your sins are forgiven. I baptize you in the name of our Lord and Savior, Jesus the Christos." He gestured with his free hand and pushed down on Aprius who took the cue and ducked his head under the waves. He came up sputtering.

"My brother, remember this: love the Lord your God with all your heart, all your soul, all your mind, and all your strength. And love your neighbor as you love yourself." Johanan put his hands on the shoulders of a beaming Aprius. Then he gestured to Marcus. Aprius returned to the shore and waited. Johanan repeated the ceremony with the other new converts. Last was Anteia. When she came up from her submersion Johanan had a vision of a beautiful mermaid surfacing. He placed his hands on her wet, tunic clad shoulders. He hesitated for a moment, as he gazed at the rivulets of water flowing off of the bronzed skin of her face. He looked into her enchanting blue eyes and repeated the words with which he had charged the others: "Remember Anteia, love the Lord your God with all your heart, all your soul, all your mind, and all your strength. And love your neighbor as you love yourself."

She blushed and turned away. Together they waded to the shore where they joined the other new believers.

It was twilight when Marcus, Aprius, and Johanan retired to the stable with Tullius. They spent half an hour going through exercises together.

As they neared the end of their session Marcus asked, "Father, why didn't you and Mother come forward with us tonight?"

Tullius furrowed his brow as he gathered his thoughts. He looked at Marcus, seemingly avoiding looking at Johanan. "What Johanan says rings true—I can feel it in my heart. But I also have to consider the village. I hear murmurings about the gods of our ancestors among some. There is concern that if we turn our back on them we will face their displeasure. There is also the wrath of the Romans to fear." Then he turned to face Johanan. "I expect I will become a follower of this Jesus, even if it causes dissension in our community, but I want to choose the right time."

Johanan nodded his head slowly in understanding. "My Lord said He would bring strife and division in households and communities. Some will choose to follow him and others will violently oppose him. We see it every day. But eventually you have to choose between following the true, living, God and the old ways. I pray I will be here when you do."

"I know it my friend. I know it." Tullius stood to go. "Sleep well, men of the house of Tullius." He patted his sons on the shoulders." He put his hand on Johanan's shoulder. "I count you among us, Man of God."

Chapter Eight

God, when he makes the prophet, does not unmake the man.

John Locke

JOHN STOOD UP on the bike to stroke hard on each pedal. He was in the lowest gear but this hill still killed him every time he rode home. It didn't help to have saddlebags loaded with groceries. *You'd think five years in San Francisco would have made this easy.*

He finally reached a crosswalk near the top of the hill, only a few blocks from his Queen Anne Hill Apartment. Thankfully, the stoplight was red and he was in for a brief rest. A young woman was crossing toward him, a somewhat familiar young woman with chestnut brown hair. She was looking straight ahead, without a glance at him.

John pulled off his helmet as she came up even with him. "Hey, are you ready for that counseling session, because I sure could use some financial advice."

Startled, she stopped short and glared at him. Then with a

look of recognition she laughed. "Oh, it's Mister Going to Change the World."

"That's me, Ms.…."

"Logan. Nicole Logan. And your name was…" A car horn honked behind him. John glanced up at the light, which had just turned green. Nicole laughed. "Maybe we should continue this conversation somewhere other than the street." She stepped onto the sidewalk and John pulled his bike up next to her.

"So, how about it? I sure can use your business advice."

Nicole pursed her lips and looked at him, sizing him up. "I was hoping to go to someplace nice for dinner. But you're not exactly dressed for it." She flipped her head toward a Greek cafe' on the corner just down from the corner. Her hair swirled around her face. "This will have to do."

Minutes later they were seated across from each other at an outside table. Faint stains from previous meals spotted the red checked tablecloth. Nicole picked up the silk flower centerpiece. John could see it was overdue for a dusting. She gave John a wry smile. "Anyone who says you know how to show a girl a good time—is exaggerating."

John laughed. "Is 'a good time' about fancy places, or stimulating conversation?"

"I guess I'll withhold judgment until I see how the conversation goes."

Nicole quickly scanned the menu, and when the waiter arrived she ordered the grilled octopus. John grimaced.

She raised an eyebrow. "Not a fan of octopus? I would have thought that would be a common dish for someone who grew up near the Med."

"I'm not as adventurous as it seems—at least not gastronomically." He turned to the waiter. "No squirming sea creatures for me. I'll take the lamb gyros."

As the waiter left John turned to Nicole. "So, do we start with counseling or financial advice? When we were last together your boyfriend had just broken up with you by text message and then you used me to fend off the advances of a fellow passenger."

She looked away for a second, then back at John. "Let's start off with the financial advice. I still want to see how you're going to change the world."

He reached into his backpack and pulled out his notebook computer. In a few moments he had pulled up a schematic. He passed it over to Nicole.

She raised one eyebrow and looked back. "What the heck is this?"

"It's how we're going to change the world."

She smirked. "We?"

John tapped the screen. "One of the biggest problems in the world today is a lack of drinkable water. These are the schematics for a new filter technology that takes bad water and makes it drinkable. It even works with sea water."

"Great. So you'll be rich."

"That's not the point. We want to use this technology to purify water in third world countries where the need is critical. We want to save lives, not get rich."

"Are you part of some charity?"

"Not exactly. I told you before I was managing money for some family. I've been working with a loose network of friends to try to bring all this together. I also hired a project engineer for the technical parts." He looked down at a bread stick on his plate. "But I'm not very good at this. I'm a people person, not an organizer."

She looked back at the screen. "What's unique about it? Looks pretty normal to me."

He tapped the final tank in the diagram. "This is what's unique. It's an algae from a remote region in India. It's a highly efficient, self-replicating algae. One of the local biotech labs is making improvements to it. But it's been in use, unnoticed, by the people there for millennia."

She scowled at the computer. "Unnoticed? How did it come to your attention?"

He smiled. "I get around a lot."

Nicole gazed into his eyes as if she was trying to assess him. He looked back. Finally, she tore away from his gaze and pointed back to the screen. "So, what's the plan?"

"We create filtration systems that fit into standard forty foot long shipping containers. In each region, one location will assemble new stations and send them to other villages. Each container turns out clean water for drinking, cooking, livestock, irrigation, you name it."

She cocked an eyebrow at him. "So, you're not doing this to get rich. What are you up to?"

"Because me and my friends want to take care of God's people and teach them about Jesus Christ, the real Water of Life. One guy in our group had a mother who grew up in Africa. He suggested the best way to reach people in those countries was to provide them with water so they'd be open to our message. We started to provide money for drilling wells and other water related projects. But then one day I remembered this algae and went back to the village where I first saw it."

"Exactly where did you first see it?"

In a mock British accent he said, "All in good time, my dear Ms. Logan. All in good time." They were interrupted by their waiter, who delivered their salads. Nicole pushed aside the notebook.

As they ate she asked, "So you and your friends aren't a charity. It sounds like you should be some kind of foundation to organize and protect yourself."

"We do need some organization. I've thought of that. But we're too busy trying to save the world." He leaned over the table toward her. "But enough about my problems. How about you?"

She set her fork down. "Yes, my boyfriend dumped me." She bit her lower lip. "It turns out he was trading up for someone who could take him places I can't. At least he thinks I can't."

"I find it hard to believe he could trade up from you."

She smiled. "Very flattering, Mr. Amato. But she is beautiful, rich, and has connections he can use. I have to get by on hard work."

John reached over and tapped the notebook screen. "Maybe you should do something more important. Like help me change the world."

She picked up a forkful of salad and chewed slowly. When she finished she said, "That's pretty interesting, but I have to tell you I'm lucky to get to church on Christmas and Easter. You and your friends sound more hard core than me."

"Church attendance isn't a requirement of the job. If you believe in what we're doing and know how to pull it all together, you might be the key to helping us save the world, in our own little way."

Nicole looked down at the screen on the notebook. "Right now I'm in the middle of a big project for my company."

"Working with a guy who's better dealing you?"

"Well, yes. But I'm also part owner. It would be tough to walk away."

"Yes, but you don't come from the wrong side of Oakland and get where you are without being tough."

"But you hardly know me."

"That's true, but like I said before, I may not be good at numbers, but I do know people. I don't think it's a coincidence we ran into each other on that plane and then again just a week and a half later on the streets of Seattle."

She picked up another forkful of salad and began chewing. She glanced down at his notebook screen. "I'd want to talk to your project engineer before I'd even consider it."

"Susan Hill is our project engineer and she lives in the Bay Area. I'll have her call you to arrange a meeting."

Nicole nodded. "No promises. My personal life may stink, but my work life is pretty good." She squinted at him. "This would have to be pretty solid for me to make a move."

John grinned. "Understood." He picked up his fork. "You'd be good for us. I also think we'd be good for you."

Chapter Nine

Let us not love in word or in tongue, but in deed and in truth.

1 John 3:18

THE DAY AFTER the miraculous catch of Aprius' crew, all the fisherman of the village spent the day ashore. Some helped salt some of the fish for sale. Others worked on the boats and mended nets. After helping with the catch in the early morning, Johanan worked with Marcus, Nikias, and Aprius. While Marcus and Aprius worked on the hull, caulking leaks with bitumen and pitch, Nikias took Johanan with him to mend the nets.

"My father is afraid you'll bring ruin to our island. He believes the gods have watched out over us for ages and we have an easy life here. He thinks following your Jesus will anger them," Nikias said.

As an apostle he would normally have spoken out boldly—even in anger. Johanan sensed his tactics would need to be different here. "What do you think, Nikias?"

"I don't know. I like Aprius and Marcus. They are my friends and I think Aprius will be the headman of our island one day, a good headman, and they are both excited about following your God."

"But what do *you* think about what I am teaching?"

Nikias focused on mending the net. The silence stretched into seconds, and then minutes, before he responded. "I would like to know more before I decide for myself. But my father won't let me come to your lessons at night anymore. He doesn't want the anger of the gods against our family." He focused his eyes on the net, avoiding eye contact with Johanan.

"Then let me teach my crewmate while we work together." They continued to mend the nets over the next hour while Johanan told him stories of what had happened since the resurrection of Jesus.

Nikias proved to be a more skeptical pupil than the sons of Tullius. He asked many questions during the course of the afternoon, sometimes seeking additional detail and sometimes challenging Johanan's assertions. He had a particularly tough time with the concept of forgiveness when vengeance seemed to be the practical solution.

Johanan finally said, "God chooses to forgive us for our many sins and failings. He forgives us when we disobey his commandments. He forgives us when we fail to show love for each other. He forgives us when we willfully commit terrible deeds. As long as we seek his forgiveness, he freely gives it."

"But why?"

"Because he loves us, He created us, He wants us to be closer to him. Unlike your old gods, we're not toys or slaves to him. We're his children and he cares for us. Much as Tullius cares for Marcus, Aprius, and Anteia, and your father cares for you."

Nikias continued to work on the nets without looking up at Johanan.

Johanan said, "If he will forgive us, how can we not forgive others? That doesn't mean we have to trust those who are untrustworthy. But we must forgive them."

Aprius and Marcus chose this moment to interrupt them. "We're done with the boat for the day. And if you spend any more time on that net it will be strong enough to bind a whale," Aprius said.

Nikias and Johanan stood up. "I think we're ready for tomorrow," Nikias said. He looked at Johanan and wrinkled his forehead as if contemplating their conversation. Finally he nodded, turned and headed toward the village by himself.

Johanan and the sons of Tullius watched him go. Finally Marcus said, "Well?"

"I think he wants to believe, but he is afraid of displeasing his father."

"Yes," Aprius said. "His father is our healer and devoted to the gods of our forefathers. He will see it as a challenge to his authority."

"Yes." Marcus laughed. "Solon is so devoted to the old gods that he has even made it difficult to worship the emperor."

Johanan raised an eyebrow. "How does he do that?"

"It's not what he does, it's what he did."

Aprius interrupted. "A story for another day." He threw his arm around Marcus' neck and pulled him close.

Johanan could sense the eldest brother was trying to change the subject. He turned his attention back to their crewmate. "If we give Nikias time and support, maybe we can win his whole family," Johanan said. "It will be a task which may only be accomplished through God."

"He's our crewmate and our friend. I would like very much for him to be our brother in the Way." They continued to watch Nikias trudge up the beach. "But now, it's time for your second lesson."

They gathered up their gear and ran up the beach to the stable. After they stowed their tools they wandered out of the village with Marcus leading. When they cleared the village, Marcus took off in a slow run, fast enough to push the others but slow enough for them to keep up. After twenty minutes they reached a different clearing. Johanan stood in the center with his hands on his knees, panting. His body was young again, but he didn't have the physique of an athlete like these two brothers. After a few moments he stood up and looked across the clearing. Sitting silently in the foliage on the edge, like a neglected temple idol, was Tullius.

"How long have you been there?" Johanan continued to pant.

"Since before you came charging in like a wounded boar," Tullius said. "Aprius told me where you'd be today and I thought I'd join in the lessons. First thing, it looks like you need more work on being aware of your surroundings."

They spent the next hour working on various holds designed to bring an opponent down or hold them. For the most part Tullius let Aprius teach. He served as Johanan's partner while Aprius matched himself with Marcus. Johanan soon learned one of Tullius' strengths was his ability to confuse his opponent. He would feint a move one way. Then, when Johanan countered, he would move the other and have the advantage. Tullius patiently demonstrated how to recognize when your opponent had committed and then make your move.

"You'll notice many of our exercises are designed to make us fast. If we can wait until the last moment, our enemy in the ring can't counter our movement. Then we leverage his own movement and weight against him."

After an hour, they cleaned up the arena. Tullius complimented Aprius on his teaching and Marcus on his progress. "Soon I will be able to sit by the fire and drink wine while you two run the village."

"Why not start tonight, Father?" Aprius said.

"Besides," Marcus said, "we already have plans to put you to work cleaning fish with the women when you're too old to lead." He took off at a dead run. He looked behind him as if to dare Tullius to catch him.

Tullius laughed and then settled in next to Johanan at a slower pace. "What will you teach tonight, holy man?"

Johanan had already pondered this question. "I would like to teach about the prophecies that foretold the coming of Jesus. There are many writings that predicted his coming, his life, and his death. That may help convince some of the truth."

"Prophecies? Where were these prophecies recorded?"

"In the Torah, the Holy Book of the Jews."

Tullius was silent. Then he said, "I'm not sure why I didn't think of this before, but we should ask Simon the Jew to attend your teaching."

"Simon the Jew?" Johanan said. He thought immediately of his friend and fellow apostle, Simon Peter. But he had been crucified, upside down no less, by Emperor Nero about thirty-five years before. At least that is what had been widely reported at the time. Then again, his own death was probably now being widely reported.

"Tell me of this Simon."

"He is an old hermit who lives up toward the other end of the island. He doesn't like our food or our gods so he stays mostly to himself. He keeps a small flock of sheep and spins their wool into yarn. He trades the wool and mutton with us and ships that come to the village."

"When did he come to your island?"

"Over thirty years ago. He was the survivor of a shipwreck. He decided to stay with us rather than take passage with one of our boats or a trading vessel. We thought maybe he was fleeing from something, but he seemed a good man and no one came searching for him.

"Has he always been a hermit?"

"At first he fished with us. He had considerable skill at the craft, but his age made it difficult for him to earn his keep. And he never grew used to being around people who like pork and octopus and other foods he considers unclean. He moved to the end of the island with several sheep that he grew into his own flock. He joins us for trade or for special celebrations, but mostly he seems content to make his own way."

"May we go see him now?"

"Patience, my friend. I'll send a messenger and ask him to join us tonight. He may come just out of curiosity to hear your tales."

They continued down the path. As the village came in sight Tullius said, "Prophecies. A good topic. Prophecies are important to my people."

Thoughts of Simon Peter, his fellow apostle and his friend since boyhood, ran through Johanan's mind. Could it be he wasn't the only apostle still walking the earth?

Chapter Ten

Every twenty-four hours the world turns over on someone who was on top of it.

Sparky Anderson

PROFESSOR WES CAVANAUGH gazed down from the window of the third floor Marcher Studios waiting room to the crowd held at bay across the plaza. Several security guards stood with their arms crossed, a barrier between the picketers and the entrance. Members of the crowd waved signs such as "The Last Apostle is Heresy," "John IS dead," and "Talk about the REAL Bible."

A single handheld TV camera recorded the scene. Several times the cameraman lunged toward the protestors and jiggled the camera to make the crowd appear more agitated than it really was. For the hour he had been waiting, the crowd had marched in an orderly circle shouting words unintelligible to Cavanaugh sequestered behind the double paned glass.

Cavanaugh scratched his beard. The skin underneath was damp with nervous sweat. He glanced at the still closed door to his left. "Thomas Marcher" was emblazoned in neat gold lettering on the rich wood. No title was necessary. Anyone who counted for anything in this town knew the name of the producer.

How could everything have gone so wrong in only a week? It seemed like only yesterday that he had been chatting it up with Megan the raven-haired reporter in the kickoff appearance to what he expected would be a triumphant start to his publicity tour. Now he was being called on the carpet.

"Professor Cavanaugh." The matronly redhead behind the receptionist desk interrupted his torment. He turned his attention away from the protestors and to her. When he had first entered the room, he observed this woman wasn't the typical eye candy that adorned the outer offices of powerful Hollywood types. Then he recalled something about Thomas Marcher divorcing his wife to marry his receptionist. This replacement looked handpicked by the current Mrs. Marcher to minimize any temptation.

The matron tilted her head to the left to indicate the door. "Mr. Marcher will see you now." She smiled sadly, as if she was a field hospital nurse saying goodbye to a soldier being sent back to the front.

Cavanaugh nodded, cleared his throat, and walked across the expanse of the waiting room to the portal behind which Marcher waited. He hesitated at the door, then grasped the knob. His sweaty hand slipped as he tried to turn it. He gripped tighter and opened up the door.

When he entered, Marcher was staring out his window at the crowd below. Cavanaugh approached. "Mr. Marcher." He wiped his hand on his suit trousers and extended it. Thomas Marcher glanced over his shoulder at Cavanaugh, a grim look on his face. He glanced down at the Professor's outstretched hand and turned back to the window. Cavanaugh stepped forward to stand to Marcher's right, slightly behind him.

Finally Marcher broke the silence with his rasp of a voice. "So, what do you think about this, Professor?"

Cavanaugh inhaled deeply. "I must admit, I've been surprised by the ferocity of the attack. Who would think that speculating a bit on the fate of an apostle would raise such a storm?"

"You got that right." Marcher turned from the scene and strode toward his desk without making eye contact. Cavanaugh followed a few paces behind. Marcher shuffled a few papers on his desk and shook his head. "Those people were going to be our core audience. The people that told their friends and neighbors to tune into this feel good show." He sat down and looked up at Cavanaugh. He pursed his lips. "I figured this might be a nice little mid-rating show. Basically throwing a bone to the religious whacko demographic." He shook his head. "Now they've turned against us."

Cavanaugh responded with a weak smile. "At least I seem to have united the fundamentalists and the Catholics in a common cause."

Marcher chuckled. "You have at that. You most certainly have at that." He turned his chair toward the window. They sat in silence for a few moments before he turned to Cavanaugh and said, "You don't really believe that apostle guy is really alive."

Cavanaugh cleared his throat. "Well, it is highly unlikely that—"

"Hah. I knew it." Marcher pointed his finger at the professor. "You are a true believer."

He swallowed, but remained silent.

Marcher looked back toward the window. "Wes, you know the old adage there is no such thing as bad publicity?"

"Of course."

He picked up a thick Mont Blanc pen and pointed to the window. "From now on, I want you to arrive at the studio in a limo." He pointed toward his waiting room with the pen. "Barbara will arrange it." He pointed back to the window. "I want you to wade through the crowd with a big smile on your face. I've seen you work crowds before. I know you can handle this bunch." Marcher stood and looked across at Cavanaugh. "Engage them in friendly conversation. But don't be afraid to challenge them." He waved the pen like a conductor's baton. "Like I said, I expected this *Last Apostle* concept of yours would be just a nice little show to appease the religious conservatives. This might be an opportunity to reach for something bigger."

A broad grin spread across his face. He pulled the cap off the pen and wrote a note on the pad in front of him. "Be here tomorrow at ten. Be ready to play to the news cameras. Then you'll be meeting with your new director, Alexis Martin."

"But I thought my director was—"

"Not good enough. We're going to take a different tack with the show. Alexis is the woman for this task."

Marcher sat down and flipped up the screen to his laptop and started to type. Without looking up he said, "Remember, play to the cameras. Alexis will meet you in the lobby." He stood up and reached across the desk to shake Cavanaugh's hand. "Tell Barbara to handle the limo, and make sure it gets you here at ten sharp." He sat back down at his desk and put his fingers on the keyboard, before glancing back up at Cavanaugh. "Remember the cameras—they're your real audience." He grinned broadly and then began to type furiously.

Chapter Eleven

Do not suppose that I have come to bring peace to the earth. I did not come to bring peace, but a sword. For I have come to turn a man against his father, a daughter against her mother, a daughter-in-law against her mother-in-law. A man's enemies will be the members of his own household.

Mathew 10:34-36

THE FAMILY OF Tullius ate their dinner in the shade outside the house that evening. In traditional Greco-Roman society, the men would eat together while the women served them. Later, the women would dine alone. In the less formal world of the island, the women served, then joined the men. Johanan enjoyed the change in tradition because it gave him more opportunities to teach the women along with the men. And, he liked spending more time in the presence of Anteia.

But this night, Johanan had a hard time concentrating. He dipped his hand distractedly into one of the communal plates put out for the meal. Could this Simon the Jew be Simon Peter? He certainly fit the description of a skilled fisherman. If he was still alive he would be an old man. Could the Lord have extended his life just as he had Johanan's, albeit without restoring his youth? If Simon didn't show up that night, Johanan would have to beg off tomorrow afternoon's lesson and go visit him. He had to see if it was his old friend and fellow apostle. If Peter was still alive, what about the other apostles? Reports ranging from reliable to questionable had reported the deaths of all eleven of his compatriots. Up until this afternoon he had been sure that only he among them had survived.

He became aware Anteia was asking him a question.

"I'm sorry. What did you say?"

Marcus laughed. "Already thinking of what you'll say tonight? Your head has been elsewhere all during our meal."

"Yes. I'm afraid I have been thinking of other things." He looked at Anteia.

"I asked you how do followers of the Way pray to God?"

He looked down at the empty plates. He'd had only a few bites.

He looked up at the beautiful young woman. She was still waiting for an answer. Johanan cleared his throat. "You can just talk to him and tell him your desires and plead for the needs of others. You can just give him your thanks for blessings he has bestowed on you and your family." He thought of how Greek society valued ritual. "Also, Jesus taught us—taught his followers—a prayer that can be used in many situations. We could start with that."

"Please teach it to us," she asked.

He bowed his head, "Our Father who lives in heaven, blessed is your name. May your kingdom come and your will be done here on earth as it is now in heaven. Give us bread for today, and forgive us our wrongs, as we forgive those who wrong us. Yours is the kingdom, the power, and the glory forever and ever. Amen."

He raised his head and saw that Marcus was giving him a quizzical look. "Amen? What does that mean?"

Johanan smiled. "It's an ancient Hebrew word. Imagine someone saying, 'Truly, truly, truly' and you get the sense of amen."

He repeated each phrase several times with the group, and then the whole prayer again. Then it was time for the evening lesson.

They gathered around the village circle. Many of the faces were the same. He noticed a few new faces and could see several of the skeptics were missing. He had hoped to see Nikias and his family, but they were absent. He looked around to see if anyone fit Tullius' description of Simon the Jew, but he didn't see any unfamiliar faces.

"Tullius, what of Simon?"

"I sent Julius to fetch him, but he hasn't yet returned." He looked up the beach. "Here comes Julius, leading his donkey, and there is someone on it. Wait for our guest."

Johanan resisted the urge to race up the beach to greet him. Instead he spent the next few seemingly interminable minutes talking to individual islanders. Finally they were there and he could wait no longer. He walked out to Julius and the old man on the donkey and looked up into his face.

It was an old man with a wizened, kindly face. However—it wasn't Simon Peter.

"So you're the rabbi Julius told me about," said the old man, in a raspy croak.

"I am no rabbi, Grandfather, but let me help you down." Johanan reached up, but Simon swung his leg over and slid down to the ground on his own.

"I can still get off the donkey by myself. It's getting up where I need help." He cackled at his own joke.

As Johanan escorted him toward a seat of honor in the circle he asked, "How did you come to be here?"

"That, my son, is a long story." He patted Johanan on the shoulder. "I grew up in a small village on the coast of Judea, just north of Herod's city of Caesarea. I was born into a family of fisherman about seventy years ago."

He shuffled forward slowly.

"So, how did you come to this place?"

Simon stopped and faced Johanan. He examined his face, squinting to get a better view. Then he shook his head. "Three decades ago, probably about the time you were born, the Jews of our region rebelled against the Romans." He looked down at the sand. "Twenty thousand were massacred, including my entire family."

Johanan could sense silence around him. The villagers were listening intently.

Finally Simon continued. "I stowed away on a cargo ship bound for Corinth. It went down in a storm, and I alone washed up on this island." He looked up and waved his arm around at the gathering. "These people seemed friendly, and I figured one place was as good as another, and stayed on." A tear ran down his wrinkled cheek.

"I'm sorry to bring up bad memories, Grandfather. Please, take a seat here." He indicated a spot next to Tullius. He waited patiently while Tullius helped Simon sit down.

Johanan turned to face the gathering. "My friends, my brothers and sisters, we are fortunate to have Simon with us tonight. I plan to tell you of the prophecies concerning the Christos, the Messiah. These prophecies were written down in the Torah, the holy book of the Jewish people." He looked down at Simon, who was nodding in agreement.

"Then I will tell you of how they have been fulfilled, not just for the Jews, but for all men and women." Simon cocked his head in surprise. Johanan continued.

He picked half a dozen prophecies concerning the Messiah, ones he hoped would be familiar to Simon. He started with predictions of his birth in Bethlehem in the book of Micah and progressed through to prophecies about the nature of his death and resurrection in Isaiah. He also included several references from the books of Psalms and Daniel.

When he was done, he looked down at Simon, who was listening intently. "Grandfather, do you recall these holy writings?"

In Aramaic he responded, "Yes, yes I do. Those are all prophecies concerning the Messiah."

"What did he say?" asked one of the islanders.

Simon pulled himself up using his staff, and addressed the crowd in Greek. "All he has told you of the prophecies concerning the Messiah are true. They are all written down in the Word of God and have been taught to us since ancient times." He settled back down on his reed mat, assisted by Tullius.

Johanan said, "Now I will tell you how the Christos has fulfilled each of these prophecies." He repeated each scripture and then related how Jesus of Nazareth fulfilled each one. He concluded the lesson by saying, "There are many more ancient prophecies concerning the Messiah that have been fulfilled by Jesus. But I want you to understand these to strengthen your faith. I want you to know what I teach is true."

He answered a few questions and then said, "Enough for tonight. Tomorrow night I will teach you the prayer the Christos taught his followers—the same prayer I taught to the house of Tullius tonight."

He sat down next to Simon and asked, "What do you think of the stories of the risen Messiah, Grandfather?"

Simon breathed deeply and finally said, "I heard of this Jesus and the stories around his death and resurrection—but I also heard he was not the Messiah but only a prophet, as was Johanan the Baptist."

"He is the Messiah, Grandfather. But many of our people refused to believe it. They wanted a liberator, a king who would conquer the Romans. But God's ways are not always ours."

Simon closed his eyes and bowed his head in thought. Then he looked up and said, "I would learn more of this Messiah so I can decide for myself."

Johanan sighed. He had been afraid Simon would reject Jesus, as many of his countrymen had, and not be open to the truth.

"Gladly, Grandfather." He placed his hand on the old man's shoulder. "I will stop by on the Sabbath to teach you myself." He led him over to Julius' donkey and helped him up. "Can I walk home with you?"

"No, my son. I have borrowed this donkey many times to get home. He will spend the night with me and then come home on his own. He knows the way well."

Johanan looked over at Julius who smiled and nodded. "He'll be okay. He's fit for an old man."

"Take care of Simon," Julius said. He slapped the donkey on the rump. The beast ambled off toward the far end of the island, with the hermit astride. Johanan watched as Simon vanished into the distance.

Over the next few weeks Johanan settled into a comfortable routine. From dawn to early afternoon he and his new brothers fished, worked on the boats, hunted, or engaged in other activities required to make a living on their island. During their time on the boat, Johanan taught his crewmates passages he remembered from his own writings, as well as those of his peers. Often their discussions would be the foundation for his evening lessons.

In the late afternoon Marcus, Aprius and Johanan, and sometimes Tullius, would practice wrestling. Johanan was rapidly becoming proficient in the sport. He could beat Marcus regularly, because he had learned to exercise patience and wait for the right time to make his moves. He beat Aprius infrequently. Johanan thought even those few wins might be by design, intended to boost his confidence.

Several evenings each week he taught the villagers about the Messiah. More and more asked to be baptized until about half were now followers of the Way. About one quarter of the population, including Tullius and Thais, still attended the lessons without making a public profession of faith. The last quarter pointedly stayed away; many of them avoided eye contact with Johanan in his daily work in the village.

Johanan spent each Sabbath with Simon, even though he preferred personally to honor Sunday, the Lord's Day. They celebrated Jewish rituals and recited passages from the Torah they could remember. Johanan did his best to recall parts that dealt with the Messiah. He taught Simon about Jesus with a special emphasis on how he fulfilled prophecy. Sometimes they just talked of life in their homeland, and complained about the Roman yoke. Johanan always made sure he did a few chores that were difficult for the old man.

Nikias still seemed the skeptic, but asked many good questions in their lessons on the boat and at other quiet moments. Things were progressing well with him until one morning a few months after Johanan's arrival. Aprius, Marcus, and Johanan had finished breakfast and headed down to their boat. The sun was just coming up. Nikias was already waiting for them, sitting on the bow of the vessel. His shoulders were slumped and he was staring down at the sand.

"Why so sad, my friend?" asked Aprius.

Nikias looked up from his seat. His expression was grim. "I can no longer sail with you. My father forbids it."

The three looked at each other and then at Nikias. "But why?" Aprius said. "We are a great crew. We regularly bring back a full catch. Your father should be pleased with his share."

"Last night, I talked to him about some of the teachings of

Johanan." He looked back down at the sand. "He said further talk of this Jesus would bring ruin on our house. He fears it may already bring the wrath of the gods upon our island. He said Jesus may be a god for the Jews, but not for Greeks."

"Nikias," Johanan said, "look at me." Nikias met his gaze. "You know that's not true."

Nikias' head fell again. "It doesn't matter what I think. My father has spoken. I must obey him."

The four friends stood in silence. Finally Aprius spoke up, "Perhaps if my father spoke to him?"

"It will do no good. He can tell your father is already a follower even if he hasn't gone through the ritual. He no longer trusts him."

More silence. Finally, Nikias jumped down from the bow. "From now on I sail with my father and his crew." He turned and walked quickly up the beach.

After a few moments Aprius looked at Johanan and Marcus and said, "Today, the fisherman of the house of Tullius sail short-handed. Prepare to cast off." Together they pushed the boat into the surf.

It was a somber day. The four had grown to be a good team. One hand short meant harder work for those remaining, but more, they missed the friendly banter between their close knit crew.

The fishing was good that day, but it still failed to lift their spirits. Finally they turned for home. Aprius sat at the steering oar while Marcus and Johanan sat in the bow and started to gut their catch.

"What do you think will happen?" Marcus asked his companions.

Johanan paused and then said, "Not everyone will accept the truth of the Christos. Some will never let go of the old ways and the old gods. Ultimately we each have to seek the truth and please God. Sometimes it divides families from each other. It has already split this village."

He looked at Marcus. "My brother, lead us in a prayer for Nikias and his family."

Marcus looked at Johanan in surprise. Haltingly at first and then with more confidence, he led the three in a prayer for Nikias and his family. He concluded with, "May our crewmate and friend, his family and all the members of our village see the truth about Jesus. May they all become followers of the Christos. Amen"

"Amen," repeated Johanan and Aprius. They lifted their bowed heads and looked toward the beach. They were approaching rapidly.

"I'll bring us in." Johanan reached for the leather knife sheath on the seat next to him, but the boat was almost at the shore. He stood up and stuck the fish knife in the waistband of his garment. He grabbed the rope used to tow the boat in and tie it up. He usually swung down over the side gently into the water. This time he playfully leapt over the front, showing off one of the wrestling moves he had learned to avoid a grab for his feet.

As Johanan leapt, a wave hit the stern of the boat and pushed the bow up sharply. Just as he was about to clear the front of the boat, it hit him on the foot. Instead of landing gently on his feet, he pitched over and landed chest first in the shallow water. He managed to break the fall with his hands and even kept the rope in his grasp. He got a face full of water and felt like the wind was knocked out of him. He rolled over and away from the boat as it ground to a halt in the sand and shallow water next to him.

Aprius shouted from the stern, "Are you alright?"

He spit out seawater and coughed. "Yes, I'm okay, just embarrassed."

Marcus grasped the side of the boat and looked down at Johanan sitting in the surf. He laughed at first, then stopped. His mouth gaped.

"Johanan, your stomach."

Johanan looked down. The fish knife he had tucked into his

waistband stuck straight out from the right side of his lower abdomen. Blood gushed from a jagged wound. He started to stand up and heard a rushing in his ears as if he was on the bank of a river in full flood. He fell back into the surf, unconscious.

Chapter Twelve

Baseball is like church. Many attend, few understand.

Leo Durocher

SUNDAY MORNING AT 8:30 sharp, John was outside Sharon's apartment. As he reached over to knock on the door, it opened. Sharon flashed him a smile, then looked away as she pulled the door shut behind her.

"Is this appropriate?" She gestured at the loose, burgundy sweater and new designer jeans she wore. It was a much more modest outfit, in sharp contrast to her seductive clothing from two nights ago.

"Absolutely. Perfect."

"Are you going to tell me who we're meeting with or where we're going?" she said as they descended the stairs.

"Don't you trust me?"

"Hmm. I don't know if I should." She flashed him a wry smile, bordering on a smirk.

They walked through the gate that separated the courtyard in front of their apartment from the city outside, and caught a bus that showed up within a few minutes.

As they took a seat a few rows from the front in the sparsely populated bus, John turned to her. "Okay, enough suspense, since we're on our way. We're going to church, but this ain't your mama's church."

"Really?"

"This church meets in a converted warehouse down on the waterfront. It was founded by a pastor from Sydney, Australia. I think you're going to find the music and the message inspiring. I also find it very faithful to the truth."

She was silent.

"One of the other great things about this group is it has a wide variety of ages, including a good size twenty and thirty something population. They come here because they find the message is relevant to their lives."

"People our age?"

"You could say that."

Sharon looked out the window for a few moments, then back at John. "Okay, I'll give it a try." John sensed from the tone of her voice this was not the type of date she'd been hoping for.

Fifteen minutes of small talk later, they were at their stop. The majority of the passengers got off with them, and walked the two blocks to the plain looking warehouse with a large "Emerald Hills Church" sign on top. As they entered the cavernous lobby, they were welcomed by a young woman in her early twenties, one of many greeters talking to churchgoers entering the door.

"Welcome to Emerald Hills. Hey, John Amato, right?"

"Yes, good memory."

"I heard you talk at one of the Wednesday night services. I really like the way you make Jesus' time come alive." She turned her attention to Sharon. "Hi, I'm Bethany. Is this your first time here?"

"Yes. John dragged me down here."

"Cool." She touched Sharon on her forearm. "I bet you'll be glad he did." She pointed to a small café on their left. "Be sure to join us at the seekers' coffee hour after the service. Free latte for first timers."

"Um, thanks. Maybe I'll do that."

"See you later." She turned her attention to other people coming in as John escorted her into the lobby. They looked around the inside of the warehouse. It looked comfortable, even if it wasn't fancy. To the right was a bookstore with a steady stream of customers. In the middle of a lobby was a kiosk with flyers about activities and free pamphlets on various subjects. They stopped and circled the stand. Sharon picked up a flyer called "Emerald Hills Singles." John pulled another one and passed it to her. It was titled "The Relevance of Revelation."

"I always found the Book of Revelation to be sooooo confusing," Sharon said. She looked more closely at the flyer. Then with a start she looked up at John. "You're teaching that?"

"Yes. Maybe I can use you to test out some of my ideas."

Just then, someone yelled across the lobby. "Sharon? Sharon Gatlin?"

A tall young woman ran across the lobby and hugged Sharon, who seemed surprised and less than enthusiastic.

"It is you, Sharon. It's me, Trish, from church youth group and high school."

"Yes. I remember" John noted her aloof response to Trish.

"I haven't seen you here before." Sharon's coolness hadn't stifled Trish's enthusiasm.

"Yes, it's my first time." She looked over at John. "My neighbor brought me."

"Oohh. The famous John Amato is your neighbor?"

Sharon gave John a quizzical look. "Famous?"

He laughed. "Only in a very local sense."

"Oh, don't sell yourself short. You are." Her husband, who she introduced as Roger, joined them. Trish asked, "Why don't the two of you sit with us today?"

Sharon looked over at John. He could sense her hesitation. He suspected she was a bit uncomfortable with being reminded of her past.

"Sounds great," John said. "Lead on."

Trish took them into the main auditorium and led them toward some open seats in the middle. Along the way, she chattered to Sharon about how much she liked the church, the message, the people, and the community. She was like a telemarketer on her third quad latte of the morning. John maneuvered so he was sitting on the aisle and Sharon was sitting next to Trish.

In the back of the auditorium were two men enveloped by soundboards and video controls. An upbeat recorded song was playing through the sound system. The bass vibrated through the room and some of the people were dancing to the music:

When this world is going down
And my turn never comes around
I can make it through the day
Because you love me
Yes, you love me

Sharon looked over at John and said, "Are you sure this is a church? Sounds like a rock concert to me."

"Contemporary Christian music—one of the fastest growing music genres in America." He started to dance in place.

She laughed. "I don't think you're going to get a gig on 'Dancing with the Stars.'"

He stopped and threw up his hands in surrender.

Along either side of the stage, a video presentation showed pictures of church events and members interspersed with slides of announcements. When a slide on "The Relevance of Revelation" displayed, Sharon grabbed Trish's arm and pointed to it. "He's going to teach that," she said, and patted John on the shoulder.

Trish looked over at John. "Wow. That's always seemed too weird to me." She turned back to Sharon. "Maybe we can go together."

Sharon nodded noncommittally. "Maybe. I'd have to swap a shift at work but I might be able to swing it."

A young man and women in black worked on the stage doing last minute setup and testing of the sound system. A podium graced the left side but most of the platform was wide open.

Sharon broke away from her conversation with Trish and leaned over toward John. "What religion is this?"

"It's mainstream, non-denominational Christian faith. Don't worry, you won't be asked to give up your day job to wear robes and panhandle."

She giggled.

A dozen young men and women came up on the stage. The recorded music faded out and they began an energetic song along with a practiced dance routine. A forty-something woman led the chorus. Although the lyrics were decidedly Christian, the whole number seemed more at home in a rock concert than a church. The words to the song displayed on the video screens on either side of the stage and most of the audience joined in.

After another similar number, Pastor James Andrews took the stage. After a short introduction the events slide show that had been playing at the beginning was displayed. Andrews talked briefly about each item in his thick Australian accent, including John's Revelation series. When it came to a slide about a women's scripture study he said, "I wanted to call this 'Scripture for Sheilas' but was overruled by Mindy." He looked over at the chorus leader who put her hands on her hips and gave him a mock glare.

John leaned over to Sharon. "That's his wife."

Announcements over, Pastor Andrews then gave a short talk about the commandment to "love thy neighbor." His key point was as humans it is sometimes difficult to really feel love for those we consider difficult to love. But if we act out that love, even if we don't feel it, we are fulfilling the commandment. And the feeling would often follow.

During the talk, John stole a quick look at Sharon. The young woman at his side was intently focused on what Andrews was saying. She seemed to really be into the service. He recalled the evening two days prior and the feel of her lips on his. She really was attractive, especially when she smiled.

Focus. He kept eyes front for the remainder of the talk.

When Andrews finished, Sharon looked over at John. "That's really cool. I remember so many times thinking I just couldn't do that because I didn't like the person. I felt guilty."

"That's why I like this church. Very practical messages that help you live your life for the right purpose."

The Emerald Hills chorus followed up the talk with a ballad that left the congregation in a mellow and spiritual mood.

For God, so loved, the world
That he gave his one and only son
That who so ever believes in him
Will not perish but will have everlasting life

Sharon gave John a quizzical look. "Aren't these lyrics from the Gospel of John? John 3:16?"

"Yeah. Sounds pretty good set to music. Wish I could write like that."

Then Pastor Andrews took the stage again. "Now, I know many of you view me as just a warm up act for our second speaker this morning."

Trish elbowed Sharon. "Now you'll see." John stood up and started walking toward the front.

"One of our favorite speakers, John Amato, will talk about loving our enemies."

John took the stage to warm applause. He said, "At this point, many speakers will ask you to take out your Bibles." They tittered.

"But I'd rather you close your eyes and help you imagine what's written, so it lives within you."

John painted a picture in the minds of the audience about the adversarial relationship between the Jews and Samaritans in the time of Jesus. Then he vividly described the scene of Christ's encounter with the Samaritan woman at the well and how this violated both Jewish and Samaritan mores, all in the name of extending God's love to a people considered by many Jews to be unworthy.

He then "speculated" on how difficult it must have been for the apostles who then spent two days staying in the Samaritan village with Christ. And how this radical event must have changed their view on the depth and breadth of the love of God. He concluded by asking everyone to consider how to heal a rift with an enemy.

After a few more songs, Pastor Andrews closed the service.

John said to Sharon, "How about that latte?" She shrugged her shoulders. He turned to Trish and Roger. "Care to join us? You can tell her about Emerald Hills." They nodded and followed him up the aisle.

It took several minutes to reach the lobby because John was constantly stopped by people who wanted to thank him for his talk or to ask him questions. They had almost reached the back of the church when a tall, gray haired man stopped John and shook his hand.

"Mr. Amato, my name is Brian Leeper and I'm with LifeWater Publishers. Perhaps you've heard of us."

"Yes, yes I have." John shifted uncomfortably.

"Let's talk about you writing a book. I've heard you speak several times, and the way you help people relate to New Testament days and apply it to their lives is amazing."

Trish interrupted. "That is so exciting. What a great idea."

John held up his hand. "That's quite an honor, Mr. Leeper, but I'm not interested in doing a book."

"But you'd have a real opportunity to reach—"

John reached over and shook Brian's hand. "Thank you for the great compliment. But that's not for me."

A woman stood up from the last row of seats in the church and stepped toward John.

"Nicole?" John brushed past Brian. Sharon and the rest of his small entourage followed.

"Nice talk."

"Thanks. I assume you're spying on me."

"Well, when I Googled you, this event did show up. I was in town over the weekend and was curious."

"Does this mean you're considering my offer?"

"Considering."

"Well, why don't you join us for coffee?"

"I don't want to barge in—"

"Barge in? That's crazy talk. We'd love to have you join us, right?" He turned back to his friends. Trish and Roger agreed heartily. He noticed Sharon sported a mild frown. He took Nicole by the elbow and pointed her to the lobby café. In a few minutes they were seated cozily around a table that normally held only four.

Trish had finally slowed down, although John expected when the latte kicked in she'd be back in high gear. After John introduced Nicole to the rest and they engaged in a few minutes of small talk, Roger asked Sharon, "What do you think of our little community?"

Sharon smiled and said, "As John told me, it's not my Momma's church." She turned to John and laughed. "It was really fun. I loved the music and the message." She elbowed John. "Both speakers made a lot of sense." She looked at Nicole. "What did you think, Nicole? Is this anything like your church?"

Nicole lifted her hand. "Confession time—this is the first time

I've set foot in a church for years. Work and stuff just seems to get in the way. But I did think it was interesting."

She turned to John. "But that guy was right about you. You really should write a book. You made me feel like I was in first century Samaria."

John gave her a weak smile. "Too much going on."

Silence fell over the table. Trish finally broke it. "Sharon, they have a really great singles group here. That's how Roger and I met."

Roger laughed. "I thought we met at a club downtown."

"No, you hit on me at a club downtown. We didn't really meet until you joined the church and the singles group."

"Ouch, I do remember that blow off." He tugged on the back of his collar. "I still have scorch marks from that night."

Trish rested her hand on Roger's arm, and snuggled up to him. "You see, it worked for us."

Sharon turned to Nicole. "How about you? Are you dating?" Her tone was slightly icy.

Nicole shook her head. "I was, but that's over now."

Sharon frowned and turned her attention back to Trish and Roger.

Chapter Thirteen

Stars may be seen from the bottom of a deep well, when they cannot be discerned from the top of a mountain.

Charles Haddon Spurgeon

JOHANAN FELT A throbbing pain in his midsection. He gradually became aware he was running a high fever. His body shook with a chill that made his teeth chatter. He opened his eyes. Tightly spaced poles made a roof over him. Johanan blinked back the sweat from his eyes. Another chill swept through his body, ending again with his teeth clattering like legionaries casting dice on paving stones. He struggled to sit up.

"Uhhhhhhnn." He cried out as a sharp pain ripped through his abdomen. He fell back onto the mattress.

"Johanan." A woman's voice called from outside the room. He heard the muffled thump of footsteps in the hard packed dirt floor as someone ran toward him. He gritted his teeth to keep from crying out again. The pain subsided back to throbbing.

"Johanan, don't strain yourself," the same voice said softly.

Now it was coming from beside him. He flinched as a wet cloth was laid upon his forehead. He blinked his eyes. Anteia looked down at him with the smile of one looking at a loved one—for the last time.

"Uhhnn." The pain ripped through his side again.

"Be still, Johanan. Be still."

He felt a weight peeled off his stomach. A man's voice said in a curt manner, "Here's a fresh poultice. It's all I can do." Johanan felt a cold cloth laid across his midsection. Almost instantly it began to sting and burn. He writhed in response to the pain.

"Ahhhhh." He was too weak to fight very hard.

"That does no good. Can't you see it hurts him?" Anteia said.

"Know your place, girl. It will draw out the poison. Without it he would be dead already." Johanan recognized the voice as Solon, father of Nikias.

"I know you are the village healer, but I can see it does no good. See how the red streaks mark his stomach and his arms. The poison spreads."

"Enough." Another male voice. Tullius. Yes. Johanan realized he was in the home of his host. He remembered lying in the surf and looking down at his bloody stomach. How long ago had it been since the accident?

"Anteia, leave the poultice."

"But Father—"

"Anteia." Johanan could hear the warning in the way Tullius pronounced her name.

"Anteia," Tullius said, softly this time. "Keep Johanan comfortable, but leave the poultice. Solon's medicine has healed many."

Anteia didn't respond. Instead she pulled away the cloth on Johanan's forehead and wet it again in a clay jar. She wrung it out and gently wiped his forehead.

"Solon, come with me." Johanan could hear the men walk out.

"Anteia, how long?" He said in a rasp.

"Two weeks—two weeks, Johanan." He could hear her choke back sobs. "You must get better, you must."

The voice of the men came through the open door. "I tell you, Tullius, it is an omen. The gods are angry at the heresy he teaches. They have punished him. You see how sick he is. Next they will punish all who follow him!"

"I don't see how this could be. His words have the ring of truth about them. You see how his followers have become a changed people—and what about the success of his crew in fishing?"

"His ways are not ours, Tullius. It is an omen. Even some of his followers believe it so."

A woman's voice—Thais. "My husband, please listen to Solon. He has been your best friend since you were children. He is wise in the ways of the gods."

"Listen to your wife, Tullius. That Jew is bad for our island. He will bring down the wrath of the Romans on us. He will be our ruin."

The three voices rose in volume and pace until they became a cacophony of emotion and disparate words.

Johanan coughed to clear his throat. His voice came in a whisper. "Anteia, you must help me sit up."

"No Johanan. You are much too sick."

"You must help me." He looked her in the eyes. "You must. Or I will do it myself."

He could see her bite her lip. Her eyes watered. Then she walked across the room and retrieved a blanket. As she folded it into a thick pad she asked, "Are you sure?"

"Yes, now help me up."

She put one arm under his shoulders and reached across his chest with the other. She struggled to help him raise his torso into a sitting position. The pain caused him to draw his breath in through clenched teeth. She put one hand on his back to help him stay up. With the other she pushed the blanket behind him. Then she slowly lowered him so he was partially sitting up. She reached for the cloth again, wet it, and first wiped his brow, and then his eyes. Sweat still poured off his face.

Johanan looked over at her and smiled weakly. Then he looked down at the poultice. He grasped it with one hand and peeled it back. Underneath a seeping wound oozed blood and yellow pus.

"Uhhnnn." He resisted the urge to scream but couldn't stop a moan.

Johanan pulled the poultice off completely and flung it weakly to the floor next to his bed. His gaze rose to the open door where Tullius and Solon continued their argument. Tullius stood with his arms crossed on his chest, a stern look on his face. Solon was doing most of the talking. He gestured wildly in the face of the unusually stoic Tullius. Thais looked down at the ground and shook her head.

"Solon," Johanan said in a whisper.

"Johanan, please don't strain yourself," Anteia said.

With all the strength he could muster Johanan said, "Solon!" The plea came out short of a shout, but loud enough for the two men and Thais to hear him. Solon stopped and they all looked in at the half reclining Johanan, mouths agape. Solon and Tullius stepped over the threshold to Johanan's sick bed. Thais stayed behind in the doorway.

Solon stooped to retrieve the poultice, now covered with sand. "Leave it," Johanan said, in a soft, raspy command. He coughed again.

Solon stood up, the poultice at his feet. He looked down at Johanan, a scowl replacing his look of surprise.

"Solon," Johanan said in a voice just above a whisper. "If I die…" He paused to take several breaths. "If I die…" he inhaled again, "…your gods rule this island." Solon's scowl became a glower.

Johanan paused to gasp again. He took in one last deep breath, pointed at Solon with an outstretched arm and then with all his strength said, "But if I live, Jesus is Lord of all!"

Johanan slumped back into the blanket. His arm fell limply beside him. The room around him faded away as he slipped back into unconsciousness.

Chapter Fourteen

Conversation would be vastly improved by the constant use of four simple words: I do not know.

Andre Maurois

AS THE LIMO made its way toward the plaza in front of the studio, Wes Cavanaugh tapped nervously on the laptop bag resting on his lap. He glanced out the window to his right and noticed the In-N-Out Burger on the corner where he normally turned so he could enter at the side entrance. Only a few blocks and it would be showtime.

He consciously donned his normally engaging smile and pulled down a mirror from the ceiling. He looked as nervous as a D list actor trying out for a leading role in a Spielberg movie.

"Almost there, Professor Cavanaugh. I'll stop at the curb, then come around to let you out."

Cavanaugh looked into the rear view mirror and nodded at the driver.

"You'll do great, Professor. I caught you on Oprah once debating the people from that cult in Oklahoma. That was a tougher crowd than this one."

He smiled. "Thanks. I can use a pep talk about now."

The car slowed to a stop. He looked out at the small crowd marching in an ellipse around the front of the plaza. This time the single cameraman was supplemented by several local news crews and a camera from the studio. Evidently, the media had been alerted.

As the driver opened the door and nodded toward him, Cavanaugh grasped the handle of his laptop bag tightly and stepped out of the car into the bright sunlight. The protestors stopped their procession and turned toward him. Several studio security guards whom had been stationed on the sidewalk stepped to his side. Another waded through the crowd from the far side. "Please, ladies and gentleman. Make way for Professor Cavanaugh." With one hand, he gestured to Cavanaugh; with the other he pushed toward the studio as if he held a battering ram.

"Wait." Cavanaugh held up his free hand in protest. "This security isn't necessary. I'm fine." He strode toward the crowd. "He reached out to shake the hand of a young man holding a sign which proclaimed "John IS Dead."

"Professor Wes Cavanaugh. Good to meet you." He reached out to another who grasped his hand with reluctance. "Wes Cavanaugh, thanks for coming today." Out of the corner of his eye he saw several news cameras capturing the scene. He angled slightly toward them as he worked his way through the crowd, greeting one protestor after another.

When he reached the far side, he ascended three steps and put his laptop bag down at his side. He raised both hands into the air. "If you will allow me to make a make a brief statement, I would be glad to answer any questions you might have about my latest project, *The Last Apostle.*" With the mention of the show, the signs that had dipped as he worked his way through the crowd now sprang into action and were waved toward the professor and the cameras.

"My brothers and sisters." He beamed at the crowd. "My fellow believers." From the smirks on a few faces he knew there was some question about that. "Many of you know me as a defender of our faith, a man who stood up against the lies of *The Da Vinci Code.*" Some of the signs dipped a bit. The smirks seemed to soften a bit.

Sweat started to drip down his back—only a fraction of which was due to the hot California sun.

"I assure you I would never follow in the steps of those who would disparage our Christian faith."

"But John is dead. How could you tell a lie like that?" The young man holding the "John IS Dead" sign thrust it high as he tried to shout down Cavanaugh.

"Please, please. I'm not trying to say he is alive. I'm just trying to tell a 'what if' story that makes our faith more alive. We all know he's dead—"

"How do you know that, Professor? How do you know he's dead?"

Cavanaugh turned toward the source of the voice. A young woman dressed in a form fitting black outfit stared back at him. She shook her blonde mane to clear it from her eyes. "How do you know that, Professor?" she said in a softer voice.

He noticed the cameras maneuvering to put both the blonde and himself in their field of view. Cavanaugh took a few steps toward her along the step to make their task easier.

My God, she is stunning. I would love to put her in the show.

"Miss, uh…." He paused, waiting for her to fill in the blank. She blew a wisp of hair away from her face, and waited.

"Tradition holds that John died a very old man in Ephesus. As a scholar, I don't dispute that. My story is entirely fictional. It's pure speculation on the verse in John 21 where Jesus says to Peter about John, 'If I want him to remain until I return, what is that to you?' I'm not advocating—"

"But how do you really know?" She interrupted him in a voice that had dropped almost to a whisper. "How do you know that wasn't exactly what He meant—that John would remain until He returns?"

He stared into her ice blue eyes for a few moments. Then the normally poised professor stammered as he said, "Well, I uh, don't. But again, this is just a story. Something to entertain people. Just a tale."

Cavanaugh was startled by a tap on his shoulder. A tall young studio page in a purple blazer smiled at him. "Ms. Martin is waiting for you Professor Cavanaugh." He reached down and picked up Cavanaugh's laptop bag and turned toward the entrance.

The professor turned toward the crowd. "I'll be back tomorrow to take more questions." He glanced over to where the blonde had been standing. She had melted into the crowd. He turned to follow the page, who had paused to wait for him. He strode quickly to close the gap, glancing behind him once to see if he could spot the blonde. Some of the protestors were starting their march again. Several stood off to the side in deep conversation. The stunning young woman had vanished.

When he entered the lobby, a trim woman with a fashionably short haircut greeted him. "Professor Cavanaugh, Alexis Martin. I'm your new director." She gestured toward the security desk. "I was watching the feed from the studio camera and thought I'd send a page out to rescue you."

"Thanks, Alexis. I was a little surprised by her question." He pointed out toward the plaza. "Did you send her? I mean…"

"No, I wish I had been that smart. She just doubled our chances of making the news. But we have a lot of work to do." The page passed Cavanaugh his laptop bag. Alexis turned toward the elevators and gestured to Cavanaugh to follow. "We meet with your new creative team in five minutes."

He looked through the windows toward the crowd on the plaza, then turned to follow Alexis Martin.

Chapter Fifteen

Never let your persistence and passion turn into stubbornness and ignorance.

Anthony J. D'Angelo

JOHANAN FELT A damp cloth placed on his forehead. It traveled slowly back and forth across his brow. As it reached each end of the circuit it paused, and he felt water trickle down the side of his face. The cloth lifted up and gently blotted the moisture, first on the left side, then the right.

In the calm, a soft voice said, "Please, Jesus, make Johanan well. We need him. Please show you are the Lord of all. Please, Jesus. For me, for Johanan, for all of us. Please."

Johanan could feel the cloth wipe across his closed eyes. Then it was placed across his forehead and remained motionless.

He felt a warm hand placed on the left side of his bare upper torso. Then the soft, gentle pressure of what felt like a head, covered with thick hair, in the middle of his chest. The murmured pleading continued. He felt warm drops of moisture trickling down the middle of his stomach. Tears?

Johanan opened his eyes. He was in a semi-reclining position. Without moving, he let his eyes scan the room. He was still in the home of Tullius. His gaze fell downward. He lifted his head slightly. His eyes struggled to focus. Finally he could see the back of a head covered with long, light brown hair. He could see shimmering highlights as the light of the sun played across the beautiful mane spilled across his chest.

"Anteia?" Johanan said in a barely audible whisper.

The head whipped up off his chest as she turned to face him.

"Johanan! You are awake." She flung her head down on his chest, not so gently this time and hugged him.

He cleared his throat. "Be gentle. It hurts."

She sat back, her hands still on his upper arms. "I'm sorry. We thought you were going to die. Your fever didn't break until yesterday."

He struggled to sit up. "And what of my wound?" He could see a white bandage wound around his midsection.

"It is much better." Anteia gently unwound the bandage to expose a jagged scab in the middle of his abdomen. "The red streaks and pus are gone. It is healing quickly."

Johanan gingerly touched his midsection and winced. It was still tender, but did look much better.

"Please, something to drink."

She grabbed a clay pitcher sitting on a table next to him and poured water into a wooden cup. She brought it to his lips. He cupped her hands in his and drank deeply.

When he had finished, he kept his hands gently clasped around Anteia's. "How long since I last woke?"

She blushed and withdrew her hands from his. "Five days—five days since you challenged Solon."

He became aware of an odor in the room. He sniffed several times. "What is that smell?"

Anteia looked across the room at a shallow bowl on a table. "Solon's poultice. He brings one each day."

"But you quit using them?"

"Yes. I convinced Father we should depend on Jesus to heal you rather than Solon's gods."

Johanan smiled warmly at Anteia and placed his hand gently on her cheek. "A wise move, woman of faith. Not to mention the smell of that thing was probably making me sick."

She laughed. "Johanan, I'm so glad you are awake. I must get Father and Mother."

Anteia returned in a few moments with both Tullius and Thais. After a few questions about how he was feeling, Thais left to cook him a small fish. Tullius sat on a wooden stool and sliced a pomegranate in half. He scored the rind a half dozen times and then passed Johanan a segment. Johanan used his fingers to separate a cluster of the red seeds from the spongy membrane and dropped them into his mouth. Some of the reddish pulp dribbled down his chin.

"The village is even more divided now. Some of your followers have turned back to the old ways. Solon's argument that your injury and illness was a bad omen swayed them."

"What of my challenge? That if I recovered Jesus was Lord of all."

"News of your words spread. Not many expected you to survive. I must admit I was among them." He passed Johanan another segment of the pomegranate.

"Thais even talked me into sending for a physician trained in Athens from a neighboring island." He raised an eyebrow. "Solon was so angry at me that he didn't talk to me for most of a week—except to tell me I was not fit to be village leader if I did the bidding of my wife." He chuckled. "But the physician examined you and said Solon was doing all that could be done." Tullius passed Johanan the last section of pomegranate. "Then he advised us to prepare for your burial." Tullius smiled down at Johanan as he wiped his knife clean on his tunic. "My friend, I'm glad to see both the physician and I were wrong."

Over the next few days, Johanan gained strength. Soon he moved back into the stable, albeit on the ground level. Mithridates, the ancient dog, slept next to him, glad for the company and a warm body. The apostle was recovering quickly, miraculously so in the eyes of many. But climbing ladders and other physical activities still pained him.

The day after he moved into the stable he was walking through the village with the aid of a staff, and Anteia. They came across a partially built shelter. From an open side Johanan could see it was half filled with clay amphorae. The tall containers stood in about a dozen rows and columns. Johanan could see six empty columns. There were holes in the sand where the pointed end of amphorae had been standing not too long ago.

"What is this?" Johanan said, pointing to the shelter.

"A new era in the life of our island according to my father," Anteia said. "We are making garum to sell on the mainland."

Johanan remembered the many times he had tasted Tullius' fish sauce. Garum was a popular condiment throughout the empire. A good one could fetch a premium price.

"My father didn't tell you before, but this recipe comes from Pompeii."

Johanan raised an eyebrow. Pompeii had a reputation throughout the empire for its garum—until the city had been obliterated by Mount Vesuvius just over two decades before. "How did he come by a recipe from Pompeii?"

She smiled. "When his grandfather was a young man he ran away to make his fortune. He wound up as a laborer in a garum factory in Pompeii." She gently touched Johanan's forearm. For a second he stopped breathing. She was close enough that he could smell her sweet fragrance.

He swallowed. "And?"

"Oh." She blushed and removed her fingers. "My father tells the story that his grandfather soon decided that life back on our island wasn't so bad. He returned home without a fortune, but with the knowledge of how to make some of the finest garum in the empire."

Johanan laughed. "Smart man."

"Father has been making this recipe for a long time. It's only in the last few months that he's decided to produce enough for trade." She took Johanan's hand. Her eyes sparkled with excitement. "The whole village is involved in the plans. This will help us make up for the lean fishing months in the winter."

Johanan took in the scene. "Anteia, your father amazes me. Just when I think I've seen all he has to show."

They continued their walk through the village. Most islanders were glad to see him up and greeted him enthusiastically, but it didn't take long to notice Solon's absence.

"He went to Athens with Nikias and Dagon the morning after you woke," Anteia said. "He took some of the garum to a merchant Father knew. My father had already asked him to make the trip, but Solon moved up the date when you awoke. Many of us think he just couldn't face you. He'll come back soon enough. Then you can remind him of your challenge."

A week after awakening from fever, Johanan, woke with the sun in his eyes. He had taken to sleeping late and enjoying afternoon naps. It seemed to help with his recovery.

He heard a cough to his right and his head snapped toward it. It was Tullius, sitting on a stool next to Johanan's bed.

Tullius laughed. "You seem to have forgotten all you learned about being aware of your surroundings."

Johanan sat up slowly. "I can't wait until I can continue my lessons. I miss our time together." He smiled meekly. "And I am getting soft."

Tullius handed him a mug of water and a piece of bread. "You will rejoin us soon enough, but I came to tell you tonight is a special night."

Johanan took a bite from the bread without taking his eyes off of Tullius. He waited for him to continue.

"Solon and his sons returned late last night. Tonight we will have a celebration for his return and your recovery." Tullius paused while he took a bite out of his own hunk of bread. He chewed slowly as he pondered his next words. Finally he said, "And tonight I will remind all of your challenge, that if you lived, Jesus is Lord of all."

As the sun set, the whole village gathered to celebrate. Even Simon made the trip up from his end of the island. He greeted Johanan warmly.

"You may not know this, my friend," the old Jew said, "but Tullius had me pray over you several times while you slept through your sickness. He thought maybe one of your countrymen could do what his healers could not."

"I was not aware of that, Simon, but bless you for coming."

The old man said, "I also prepared for a Jewish burial ceremony." He patted Johanan on his shoulders. "I am glad there is no need of that, for now."

Solon and Johanan were seated on either side of Tullius in seats of honor. Solon greeted Johanan formally. Then he avoided eye contact with him through the feast.

As usual, the wine and conversation flowed freely, and by

all appearances it was a normal celebration. However, Johanan noticed people whispering to each other and looking in his direction and at Solon.

There will be a reckoning tonight. They all know it.

At first, the evening progressed routinely, including the customary footrace by the young men, and several wrestling matches. Then Tullius stood at the head of the table and raised his cup.

"Tonight we gather to celebrate the safe return of Solon from his trading voyage." He brought the cup to his lips. The other villagers raised their cups and drank as well, amid a chorus of well wishes for Solon and his sons.

"As you may have heard, Solon reports my merchant friend in Athens pronounced our garum the best he has ever tasted!" The villagers cheered this announcement, even though it was old news by now.

"Solon negotiated a premium price for our product, and he will take all we can produce."

More cheers from those present. Johanan had never seen so broad a smile on the face of the usually dour Solon.

Tullius waited several minutes for the cheers and toasts to die out.

"We also gather to celebrate the miraculous recovery of our friend Johanan from a serious injury and sickness. I, and many of you, thought we would be burying him, not celebrating with him." Tullius raised his cup again and then finished it with a long draught. The other villagers followed suit. The cheers for Johanan were loud and prolonged.

Tullius remained standing, silent. Gradually the talk died down and the crowd turned their attention to the village leader.

"Most of you know that during the depths of Johanan's illness he woke for a brief time." The villagers nodded and grunted in agreement. "And when he awoke he issued a challenge." He looked around at the crowd. They were silent.

Tullius filled his goblet with wine from a pitcher. Johanan noticed how he let the anticipation build. His skills as an orator rivaled his prowess as a wrestler.

"At a time when we fully expected Johanan to die from his injuries, he awoke from his illness and said to our good friend Solon, 'If I die, your gods rule this island.'" Tullius sipped from his goblet. He looked down at Johanan. "Then he said, 'If I live Jesus is Lord of all!'" Tullius raised his goblet and most of the villagers cheered. Solon, his family, and close friends were silent.

Tullius beckoned to Johanan. He pulled himself up and stood beside Tullius. The crowd settled down. He continued. "Many of you saw Johanan's wound and how fearsome it was." More nodding and grunting.

He turned his attention to the village healer. "You, Solon, you treated him. Only two weeks ago you saw how his wound was filled with sickness."

Solon nodded slightly in agreement.

"I call you now to examine Johanan's wound." Solon looked up at Tullius, a dispassionate look on his face. The village leader returned his gaze without flinching. Slowly, reluctantly, Solon stood and shuffled toward Johanan.

Johanan pulled the tunic over his head as Solon approached. His midriff was wrapped in a long linen bandage. Johanan reached down to untie the bandage.

Anteia stopped him. "Let me." She brushed his hands away from the wrap. Skillfully she undid the knot she had tied earlier that evening. Johanan looked down at the top of her head. When she had freed the knot, she looked up at him and smiled, her brilliant blue eyes flashing at him. Again, he had the same vision of a mermaid he had when he baptized her. He could easily imagine this young woman was a descendant of Helen of Troy.

She stood and began to unwrap the linen, passing one end around Johanan's back with one hand and bringing it around with the other. She was so near she almost embraced him each time the cloth changed hands behind his back. Johanan was aware of how close she was to him.

"Careful, Anteia, Father is watching," Marcus said in a mock warning tone. The villagers laughed.

Anteia blushed. Johanan looked up at Tullius, who was indeed gazing intently at his daughter, an uncharacteristic scowl in his face.

Finally, Anteia stepped back with the bandage cradled in one arm. Johanan stood with his arms outstretched, waiting for Solon's inspection.

Solon stepped forward to examine the site of the wound. He glowered.

"Nikias, bring me a lamp." He beckoned to his son. Nikias fetched one of the oil lamps illuminating the feast. Solon held it up to Johanan's stomach. After examining the site of the wound with the lamp and his fingers, he looked up at Johanan's face as if he was confirming it really was his former patient.

He stepped back and said, "Impossible. There's not even a scar."

"What was that, Solon?" asked Tullius.

"Impossible. There is no scar. There should be some sign of the wound."

Other villagers rushed forward to see for themselves. Johanan stood with arms raised as he was inspected by more than a few doubters. When half a dozen villagers had examined Johanan and pronounced the same results as had Solon, Tullius clapped his hands to get everyone's attention.

When the crowd had settled down Tullius said, "Johanan's recovery is a miracle. Even the healer can't believe it." He looked over at Solon who had returned to his seat and was avoiding Tullius' gaze.

"Many of you have noted that before tonight, my wife and I did not come forward to be baptized even though our children did." He looked down at Thais who was reclining behind him.

"But tonight we ask to become followers of the Way, Christians, like many of you already have."

Most of the villagers greeted this news enthusiastically. Choruses of, "Me too," "My family too," and other shouts of agreement could be heard. Tullius raised his hand and signaled for silence.

Then Tullius again turned his attention to the healer. "Solon, we have been friends since we were but little boys running naked in the sand. I ask you and your family to join us in this journey. After this miracle, I think it is clear Jesus *is* Lord of all. It is time to leave the old gods behind."

The crowd erupted in cheers. Even Nikias joined in. Solon glowered at his eldest, who looked back at his father and fell silent.

Solon stood and looked around at the villagers. When they had fallen quiet he shouted, "It is sorcery I tell you. It is an affront to the gods. We will never follow that Jew, Jesus." He beckoned to his family and started to walk out. A few other villagers stood to follow.

"Wait," Aprius said. Solon stopped and glared at him. Then he turned away as if to continue his departure.

"Before anyone leaves or is baptized, there is something you should all know," Aprius said. Solon stood and faced him. The healer still looked as if he would stalk out at any second.

Aprius slowly and patiently scanned the crowd until the only sound was the pop from the flames of the oil lamps and the lapping of waves on the shore.

"Johanan didn't just recover from a knife wound." Then he turned and looked at the apostle. "Our friend's recovery was even more miraculous, because during his illness—he was being poisoned."

Chapter Sixteen

It is the nature of man to rise to greatness if greatness is expected of him.

John Steinbeck

NICOLE RUSHED INTO her office and closed the door behind her. Her lunchtime meeting with Susan Hill, John Amato's project engineer, had gone deep into her afternoon and she only had thirty minutes before her next appointment. Nicole had only grasped about fifty percent of the technical details about the filtration technology that Susan had disgorged during their meeting, but she had grasped a few key facts: this could be world changing technology and they needed someone to organize the effort. The question was, could she trust John Amato?

On her computer screen, the Intelius report on John Amato stared back at her. Born as Giovanni Amato in Kosovo, of Italian lineage. Emigrated from there in 1999 and Americanized his first name to John. Became a citizen in 2003. The background report had only recently added his move from San Francisco to Seattle. No criminal record. Licensed counselor.

The Google search wasn't much more enlightening. It mentioned some of John's charity work with a homeless shelter in San Francisco. A number of writers had quoted him in blogs and even local newspapers. Apparently, his talks at the churches he attended were quite popular. That was a bit odd—he seemed to attend several different area churches. But no bylines or articles he'd written himself. To her, it seemed like such a popular speaker would also do at least a little writing of his own.

"How are things going?" Startled, Nicole almost dropped the coffee cup she was bringing to her lips. Dan's Armani-clad frame filled her doorway.

She set the cup down. "Just fine. All my reports are up to date if you have questions."

"No, I meant with you." He stepped into her office and gestured at the open chair in front of her desk. "May I?"

She looked back at her computer screen. "I'd rather you not. I'm trying to get a few things done."

"Look, Nicole. We can't keep on like this."

Her glare was a lightning bolt right between his eyes. "Yes we can, Dan. I've been nothing but professional in public with you. I'm doing my job just as well as ever. Maybe even better without personal distractions. You just do your job and we'll be fine." She turned back to the screen.

"But we used to be such a great team. It was so much fun. But now, the tension—"

"Is your fault. Live with it. If you can't, just buy me out." She kept her eyes on the screen, blinking rapidly.

"You know we need you. For this project and for the team."

"I'm really busy. Please close the door on your way out."

He paused, turned, and closed the door a bit too firmly.

Nicole tried to read the screen through her wet eyes. She

reached over to the tissue box on her desk and pulled one out. She gently blotted away the tears. She turned back to the monitor and clicked on a link to an article in the *Seattle Times* from seven months ago. She scanned through it until she found John's name highlighted:

John Amato, recent appointee to the advisory board of the Seattle Men's Mission said, "I was pleased to join the board because I fully support the philosophy of the shelter. We're here to help people get their lives together and lead productive lives. We do that by sharing the love of Christ…"

She looked up a contact in Outlook and dialed it. A familiar voice, coarsened by a lifetime of unfiltered cigarettes, answered.

"Well hello, Baby Girl."

"Chuck, you know I hate that name."

"Can't help it. When I see your name on caller ID I think of when I used to bounce you on my knee after me and your pop pulled a long shift."

"Maybe that explains why I loved the trampoline in gym class."

He chuckled, a long low laugh. Then his tone became serious. "Ya know, your dad was the best partner I ever had. He was a great cop."

She choked—her dad, gone nearly a decade from cirrhosis of the liver. She swallowed before responding weakly. "I bet you say that to all the kids of your ex-partners on the force."

"Nah. He was the best. You know that, Baby Girl. And you were the daughter I never had."

She paused. "I was calling about that job I asked you to do…"

"That John Amato fella? Now, he's an unusual one."

She leaned forward. "Tell me."

"Like ya know, escaped from the war in Kosovo. Wandered a bit. Now a do gooder in our parts."

"But what about the money?"

"That part is true. He is rich."

"How do you know?"

"Easy. I can't give away all my secrets of the trade."

She sighed. Chuck liked to draw out the drama. No use rushing him.

"Let's just say I managed to find out who was managing his account in his Cayman Island bank."

"And?"

"Special clients, those with lots of money, rate a senior account manager. Small fry get junior guys."

"I hope you didn't break any laws to get that info."

"You might say laws are different in other countries, and the cost of doing business will show up in your bill."

She sighed again.

"Anyways, my guess is this John Amato guy is worth ten to twenty mil."

She whistled. "Not bad for a guy with a beat up laptop."

"Huh?"

"Never mind." She drummed her fingers on the desktop. "So, where do you think it came from?"

"Can't tell. I do know lots of cash vanished from Kosovo during the civil war. But he don't seem like the type. Someone who robbed for a living would be living large—not living in a dumpy little place. Maybe his story about getting it from friends is true." He chuckled. "Now, I wish I had friends like *that.*"

"Pension isn't doing it for you?" She knew his pension was adequate—it was how he blew it that caused issues.

"Me? I'm just waiting till you hit it big and decide to take care of your old Uncle Chuck."

She hesitated, thinking of her just finished encounter with Dan. "Doesn't look like that will happen soon. Better keep your private eye shingle out." She tapped her fingernails on her desk. "What else were you able to find out?"

"Not much. Banks there don't ask too many questions—and they don't share information too easy. Bad for business, you know."

"Do you think he's hiding something?"

"Who knows. Maybe he's a straight shooter; maybe he's covering his tracks. But if I find out something else, I'll call ya."

"Thanks Chuck. I knew I could count on you."

"Take care, Baby Girl." She put the receiver back in the cradle.

Nicole leaned back in her chair. *Enough.* She picked up her mobile phone from the desk and selected a contact from her list. Her thumb hovered over the send button for a moment. Finally she stabbed it and put the phone to her ear. It rang once. Twice. On the third ring a voice answered.

"John Amato."

"John, this is Nicole Logan. I'm going to be in Seattle for the next few weeks. Let's talk."

Chapter Seventeen

In this world you will have trouble. But take heart! I have overcome the world.

John 16:33

"POISONED? JOHANAN WAS poisoned?" Aprius' pronouncement echoed through the crowd. Finally the din died down as they waited to hear more.

"How do you know this?" asked Tullius.

"The day that Johanan issued his challenge, I stumbled across a henbane bush on the other side of the island."

"Henbane? That is a poisonous plant," Nikias said.

"Yes. Years ago my father once showed a bush to me and warned us to stay away. He burned that bush so it wouldn't hurt anyone."

Johanan saw Tullius nod in agreement.

"When I came across this bush, I noticed it because of the unpleasant smell. I remembered it from my father's warning. Then I saw two things that made me think."

He paused and looked around at his fellow villagers.

"Even though the bush was in a remote location, there were footprints around it. I looked closer and noticed some of the branches had been cut."

The murmur began to build as villagers began to piece together Aprius' clues. After a few moments they turned their attention back to Aprius.

"Finally I figured out what had attracted my attention. The smell reminded me of something." He directed his attention to the head of the hall.

"It smelled just like the poultice used on Johanan's wound. The poultice made by—Solon!"

Now everyone's attention turned toward the village healer. He stared back at Aprius.

After a moment of silence Solon said, "That is a serious accusation, young man."

"Yes it is," Aprius said in a barely audible voice. "One I was reluctant to make."

"Speak up," shouted several villagers.

"I wasn't ready to make this charge until I examined the poultice and found several crushed henbane seeds in the paste."

Solon scowled and looked at the ground.

In a soft voice, Tullius asked, "Friend of my youth, what do you say of this?"

He looked up at Tullius, his brow creased as he pondered his thoughts.

"There are many potions a healer may use. Sometimes you need to use a poison to draw out a poison. I may have used henbane in the poultice."

Shouting and arguments erupted in the gathering place as villagers questioned and defended Solon. He stood in silence, frowning at the ground in front of him. Tullius let the din go on for several minutes before raising his hands to signal for silence.

"We are not going to settle this tonight. The village elders will meet tomorrow to discuss this."

"But Father—"

"Enough," said Tullius. "Tomorrow will be soon enough."

Aprius nodded, and stepped back. A look of disappointment flashed across his face.

Tullius turned to Johanan. "Teacher, tonight is a night for celebration. I ask you to baptize my wife and myself so we may become followers of the Christos."

Johanan embraced Tullius. "Gladly. I have waited long for this moment." He turned and walked toward the shore. The crowd parted as he passed through. Some touched him as he went by as if they wanted to feel the power of the holy man. Some dropped to one knee, others bowed. Johanan could feel pride swell within him. Then he stopped and thought to himself, *Remember, this isn't about me, it's about Him.*

He turned to the villagers. "Come with me and become followers of the Christos. It is Him you seek, not me. I am only an emissary."

He turned and continued the short walk to the shore. Already stripped to the waist for the examination of his wound, Johanan removed his sandals and waded in until he was waist deep. Most of the village was gathered on the shore. Tullius and Thais were first to follow him into the water. Johanan began with the village leader.

"Tullius, my friend and protector, I baptize you in the name of our Lord and Savior, Jesus the Christos." He gently pushed him under and then lifted his hand. The big man stayed under, as if he wanted to prolong the moment. Then he came up slowly. A look of intense joy was on the face of the village leader.

"Remember Tullius, to love the Lord your God with all your heart, all your soul, all your mind, and all your strength. And love your neighbor as you love yourself."

Johanan placed his hands on Tullius' shoulders, who responded in kind.

"Thank you Johanan. Thank you, my son."

Tullius turned to face the crowd on the shore, stretched his arms out, and shouted, "Behold, a new man." They broke out in cheers.

Johanan turned his attention to Thais. Tullius stood by as Johanan repeated the ceremony. Thais came up sputtering. When Johanan was done, she embraced both Johanan and her husband.

A handful of other villagers came out to be baptized. Then out waded Anteia and Marcus, one on either side of a wrinkled old man. They held his arms to keep him steady in the rising surf.

"We bring a distinguished guest," Marcus said.

"Simon, it brings me great joy to see you here."

"After hearing your fantastic tales of the Nazarene and witnessing his miraculous healing of my friend, who am I to deny our Messiah?" Simon said.

Johanan struggled to complete the baptism of Simon as he choked on his words several times. When he finished he said, "We were countrymen, now we are brothers."

In the dark, one more islander waited to be baptized. Johanan could see it was a man standing knee deep in the water, but he couldn't see his face. He waved for him to come forward. The villager waded out.

Johanan drew his breath in sharply in surprise. Then he exhaled and said quietly, "I didn't expect to see you here. Please, come forward."

When Nikias stepped forward to be baptized, Johanan reached out and put his hands on his shoulders.

"I've looked forward to this for many months, but are you sure you're ready for it?"

Nikias looked down at the water then back up at Johanan. "I have to. I can't deny the truth, even though I must deny my father."

"Then come forward." Johanan placed his hand on Nikias' shoulder. "I baptize you in the name of our Lord and Savior, Jesus the Christos." Before Johanan could place his hand on Nikias' head, he ducked under on his own. He came up by himself within a few seconds. Water streamed down his face. Johanan suspected it wasn't all seawater.

"My brother, my crewmate, remember to love the Lord your God with all your heart, all your soul, all your mind, and all your strength. And love your neighbor as you love yourself."

"I will, always."

"You must also remember to honor your father and mother."

"But he is not one of us—they are not of our community."

"They are still your parents, and worthy of your honor."

Johanan and Nikias waded back to the beach where they were met by the family of Tullius, as well as many other villagers.

Aprius was the first to speak. "What of your father, Nikias?"

Nikias looked at the sand and swallowed. "When we returned to our home I tried to convince him it was time to turn our back on the old gods and follow Jesus. He would have none of it."

He looked down at the sand again.

"Finally I said, 'Even if you won't follow him, I must." Nikias swallowed as he struggled to keep his composure.

"He said, 'If you do, you are no son of mine." Then I gathered my belongings and left. He spat at the ground as I left."

Tullius stepped forward and put his arm around the young man. "Stay with us tonight. I will talk to your father tomorrow."

Early the next morning, Johanan heard Tullius outside at the foot of the ladder. "Up you laggards, the fish are swimming into the nets of other men already." Johanan pushed Mithridates gently aside and quickly dressed. By the time he met Tullius at the door Nikias, Aprius, and Marcus were climbing down the ladder.

"Johanan, you are up. You must be feeling better," exclaimed Tullius.

"Yes, it is time Mithridates guarded the stable by himself. I think today I will rejoin my crewmates."

Aprius patted Johanan on the back. "I will give you light duty today. You may steer the boat while we haul in all the fish you are going to call for us."

"Gladly, my captain. Gladly."

They followed the rest of the fleet to the fishing grounds. It was good to be back as a crew together. They joked and bantered throughout the day. Johanan noticed periodically throughout the day that Nikias would at times grow quiet. Soon enough Marcus or Aprius would draw him back into the conversation or give him some task to take his mind off his situation. Johanan noticed Solon at the helm of his own boat on the far side of the fleet. Throughout the morning, he kept his boat at a distance.

Their ship paired with another boat to drag a set of nets between them. Aprius, Marcus, Nikias, and the crew of the other boat kept busy pulling in full nets and both vessels quickly neared their capacity. Aprius gave orders to turn back.

"Wait," Johanan said. "Maybe we should help fill the other boats. We will all need a large catch to make enough garum to supply all of the Empire."

Aprius thought for a moment. "A fine idea. Then we will all spend the winter reclining on soft couches and eating. Maybe I will buy a slave to feed me fine delicacies."

Nikias said, "Let me start feeding you fine delicacies, even though I'm not your slave." Aprius glanced over just in time to see a whole fish flung at him. He jerked his head back, just in time to avoid the projectile.

Aprius looked sheepish. "Maybe—maybe I'll just feed myself."

They spent a few more hours helping fill other boats and soon the fleet returned to the island, every vessel riding low in the water.

As they pulled up on the beach Tullius walked down to meet them. "Aprius, I have need of you now. Come."

He continued down the shore, stopping at several other boats and calling on one or more of the men. Finally he reached the boat of Solon at the far end of the beach with an entourage of six men, in addition to himself and Aprius. Johanan could see him talking to Solon. The village healer nodded and then left his boat in the hands of his crew. He headed up the beach with Tullius and the rest.

"The village elders," Marcus said. "They meet to discuss Aprius' accusation." Johanan and Marcus looked over at Nikias who was putting away the nets, ignoring the drama on the far side of the beach.

"Come," Marcus said. "We have much work to do today and we are shorthanded."

Anteia and her mother brought several carts down to their boat. Marcus and Nikias began separating the fish into the carts. Nikias explained, "These type of fish are good for our garum. We will take them up to where the vats are kept. The other fish will be used for salting and drying as normal." Johanan soon caught onto how the kinds were divided and helped complete the sort.

"Nikias, you take Johanan up to our garum vats. I'll take the rest of the fish to be cleaned."

Nikias and Johanan each pushed a cart across the sand, to the head of a trail that led toward the east end of the island. He had not traveled this path since recovering from his illness. He noticed it had grown from a footpath to a deeply rutted cart trail. They had traveled only a short distance when they turned off onto a new path. Almost immediately he noticed a pungent odor. They were soon in a large clearing with a dozen wooden vats lined up in rows. Each was about the diameter of a man's outstretched arms and up to Johanan's hip in height. The nearest one was stained on the outside with the briny fish sauce and looked many years old.

The others looked much newer—only a few had garum stains on them. On the far side of the clearing two men were assembling yet another vat.

Thais waved to them. "Bring it over here." She looked over the carts of fish. "A good selection. Take them over there and cut them up."

Nikias and Johanan wheeled their loads over to a large plank where Nikias began cutting the larger fish into chunks and tossing them into several large reed baskets. The smaller fish he tossed in whole.

"Don't you remove the bones?" asked Johanan.

"No, by the time we're done the bones will be left behind. I'll show you."

When the baskets were full, Thais directed them to an open vat. On the bottom was a layer of a variety of herbs. Johanan recognized some such as dill and coriander, but others were unfamiliar.

"We trade for some of these herbs, but others are grown on our island," Nikias said. "In fact, Simon the Jew collects some on his end of the island. Even he is part of this enterprise."

Johanan picked up a small handful of herbs from the vat and let it run through his fingers back onto the bottom.

"Don't worry, Johanan, there's no henbane in that mixture."

Johanan's head jerked up to look at Nikias. "I wasn't thinking that. I was just—"

"No matter." He rested the basket on the edge of the vat. "Johanan, if my father did try to poison you, I am sorry." He started to pitch fish by the handful over the herb layer. "He is so afraid of the anger of the old gods that I fear he did something unwise."

Johanan reached into the other basket and started to toss fish into the vat. "No matter, brother. I'm still alive. Hopefully it will help your father see the truth."

They emptied the containers into the vats, and spread them in an even layer over the herbs. Then a boy came over with wooden buckets of salt, which he poured in a layer over the fish. Johanan and Nikias returned to the cutting board to fill their baskets again. While they were engaged in their work, Thais and Leonisis began to spread another layer of herbs over the salt in the container.

By this time, several other fishermen had joined them with their own carts. Within an hour, two vats were filled with alternating layers of herbs, fish, and salt. When each was full, the men put on a heavy cover to seal the concoction.

Nikias led Johanan over to a stack of crude wooden bowls next to the cutting board and handed him two. "Fill each of these two bowls with eight seashells." He pointed to a stack of small seashells. Next to it was a pile of small stones.

Johanan counted out the seashells into the containers and followed Nikias back to the vats they had just sealed. Nikias took them and put one bowl on each.

"The vats now sit for eight days to cook in the sun. Each day Thais will take a shell out until the bowl is empty. That means it's ready for the next stage."

"Now, it's time to see—and smell, the next step," Nikias said. Thais gave Johanan a wooden rake, stained dark by garum, and directed them to three vats in the second row. They took a bowl filled with small stones off the top of the first vat and removed the lid. The smell of decomposing fish was strong. Nikias took the rake and mixed the concoction thoroughly before they replaced the lid and put the bowl back on top.

He removed a stone from the bowl. "They start off with twenty-three stones. The vat is stirred each day for each of those stones." Nikias pointed to the nearly full bowl. "This one is only ten days old."

Johanan readied himself for the stench and was not disappointed. This batch was much more liquid. He kept the rake and stirred the contents.

"This next one is nearly ready." Only two stones were in the bowl on top. When they removed the lid the smell was not nearly so overpowering. Johanan could see fish bones and other parts on the bottom of the vat. He ran the rake through the amber colored mixture. When he pulled the rake out, the garum dripped off of it like warm honey.

"In two days we'll pour the garum off of the top of that vat into amphorae and seal them. Then we'll discard the remnants in the sea.

"And sell it in Athens?"

The smile faded from Nikias' face, and he stared at the grass at his feet. Johanan suspected he was recalling the expedition to the ancient city with his father.

Johanan interrupted his thoughts. "Come, let's go back to the beach. We still have to take care of our boat."

Nikias, Marcus, and Johanan were just finishing up the maintenance when Aprius arrived.

"What happened?" asked Marcus, casting a sidelong glance at Nikias.

"They asked me many questions and had me take them to the henbane bush I found."

"Then?" Nikias said.

"They told me to leave. They were still discussing the situation when I left."

"What of my father?"

"Solon is still with them."

Chapter Eighteen

You can tell whether a man is clever by his answers.
You can tell whether a man is wise by his questions.

Naguib Mahfouz
Egyptian Novelist

CAVANAUGH WORKED HIS way through the crowd of protestors in front of the studio offices. By now he knew a number of them by name. He also knew which ones he could engage in friendly banter and which ones were best avoided. The one he hadn't seen since his first day was the stunning blonde with the ice blue eyes. He had asked a few of the organizers about her, but none had seen her before that day or since.

"Professor, is there an announcement today?" Cavanaugh looked at the young man who had asked the question and reached out to shake his hand.

"Announcement? Not that I know of." He struggled for the young man's name. "Barry, isn't it?" He nodded in the affirmative. "Why do you ask about an announcement?"

Barry pointed to the area in front of the studio doors. A podium was set up with a microphone. Several news cameras were setting up. Cavanaugh scratched his beard as he took in the scene. "I haven't the faintest, Barry."

He strode toward the front door. As he passed several members of the news crews asked, "What can you tell us about the big announcement, Professor Cavanaugh?"

He stopped to talk to them, greeting several by name and gave them the same answer as he had given Barry: "I haven't the faintest."

Finally he skirted the podium and entered the front door. His director, Alexis Martin, and several other studio types were gathered in the center of the lobby, waiting for him.

"Alexis, what is this—"

She thrust a sheet of paper in his hands. "Read this. When you're ready, we'll go out and you take the stage."

He studied the paper in front of him for a moment, then looked up at Alexis. "You know there is no way to prove this either way."

"Then the studio's money will be quite safe."

"But…" His voice faded as he grasped what was happening. He looked down at the paper again. Read through it a few times, then looked back at Alexis. A bold grin replaced the puzzled look on his face. "I'm ready. I am very ready."

Flanked by Alexis and several others, he strode out into the sunlit plaza and approached the podium. He laid the paper down on top then scratched the mike with a fingernail. The sound came through loud and clear from the speakers set up on either side. The cameras positioned themselves and the protestors pushed forward.

After he had made everyone wait a few moments, he rustled the single sheet of paper and held it up before placing it flat on the podium. "My name is Professor Wes Cavanaugh. I am the creator of the new Marcher Studios television series *The Last Apostle.* I am pleased to announce that in connection with the series, Marcher Studios is making a most unusual offer." He smiled, and gazed around at the cameras and at individual members of the crowd before continuing.

"As many of you know, several weeks ago a young woman in the crowd assembled here asked a very provocative question. 'How do I know the apostle John is really dead?' " Many in the crowd nodded. Cavanaugh glanced down at the paper. "I am pleased to announce that Marcher Studios will offer a prize for the person who can answer that question." At this point he picked up the paper and waved it in the air. "Marcher Studios will pay one million dollars to the person who can prove the apostle John is dead, or, Ladies and Gentlemen, prove he is *alive.*" He slammed the paper down on the podium. The sound reverberated across the plaza like a thunderclap.

Chapter Nineteen

He who has a why can bear almost any how.

Friedrich Nietzsche

THAIS WAS JUST finishing preparations for dinner when Tullius returned home. He called the whole family together, including Nikias.

"The elders have met to discuss Aprius' accusations." He paused and looked at Nikias. "Solon has admitted to using henbane but denies he was trying to poison Johanan."

"But how could that be?" Aprius interrupted.

Tullius held up his hand to silence his eldest.

"We offered him a one year exile from the island. He turned us down and demanded a trial by the Roman magistrate."

Johanan's throat went dry. Unpleasant memories of Roman justice flooded his mind.

"The village elders have agreed to contact the Roman authorities. In the meantime, Solon has consented to remain in the village until the matter is resolved."

Aprius gave voice to Johanan's thoughts. "Won't the Romans discover many of us are Christians? We may be in great danger."

"Yes, the elders discussed that risk." Tullius sighed. "Solon may have demanded a trial in the belief we would be afraid of calling in the authorities. We decided we could not let this go. Otherwise we would never be able to administer justice again. The elders prayed together," he looked at Johanan. "We decided if the Christos could heal Johanan, He can protect us."

Tullius stood and let the implications of this decision sink in.

Nikias broke the silence, "What of me? Did you discuss my decision of last night with him?"

"Yes, I did talk to your father of you." Tullius placed his hand firmly on Nikias' shoulder and squeezed. "For now, you are my son."

Chapter Twenty

If success attend me, grant me humility.
If failure, resignation to thy will.

David Livingstone
Scottish Missionary and Explorer

"DON'T TRY SO hard. Let your body do the work, like I showed you on the dock."

Nicole turned her head to look behind her at the curly haired man. John was ensconced behind her in the rear cockpit of a tandem kayak. He flashed his brilliant smile, like it had been reserved for her since the beginning of time. The sun rising behind him created a halo effect around his head as she squinted at him. She scanned the brightly colored shirt that stuck out from under his life vest. He may have a halo like a saint, but she doubted a saint would wear a Hawaiian shirt covered with sea turtles.

She turned back to face the front. Her sudden movement made them rock side to side. She held the paddle still to try to quell the motion.

"Don't worry, I've got it." The boat continued to glide forward. She could hear the waters of Lake Union slurp at John's paddle as his smooth, powerful strokes cut neatly into the water behind her.

She reached forward and dipped the right hand of her paddle into the gray green water. She pulled it toward her then repeated the motion with her left. The glacier blue kayak glided through the water with a slight bobbing motion as it cut through the wake from a cabin cruiser that had passed through a minute earlier.

"That's more like it. Keep it up and it will soon feel natural."

She glanced down at her reflection in the glassy surface of Lake Union. It almost did look like she knew what she was doing. As she dipped her paddle, it broke the illusion of a mirror. She turned her head forward and watched as the point of the boat cut through the water.

"How do I know I'm in synch with you?"

"Don't worry—I'll follow your lead. Just keep it smooth and steady."

"That could be dangerous. I told you I'm a klutz. That's why I avoid sports like golf."

"I thought all business gurus loved golf."

"Not me. I have to bypass schmoozing on the course."

They continued to glide through the waters toward the Lake Washington Ship Canal.

"Well, Mr. Amato, I have to say this is the most unusual job interview I've ever had."

"Some say I'm an unusual guy."

"Can't argue with that." She looked up at the span high above the mouth of the canal. The sound of traffic drifted down from the roadway on the top of the graceful arch. "What bridge is that?"

"Aurora."

"It's no Golden Gate Bridge, but it's still pretty."

"And second only to the Golden Gate Bridge in the number of suicide jumpers."

Nicole rested the paddle across the kayak and gazed up. As they passed under the span she picked it up and started to stroke again. They cruised on in silence until they were clear of the shadow.

"For someone who claims to be a klutz, you seem to be pretty graceful for a rookie kayaker."

She turned back and shot him a warm smile, then returned to her smooth strokes. "When I was a kid I had Coke bottle thick glasses. Didn't help me much in developing hand-eye coordination. Also had its drawbacks in the social development department."

"You wear contacts?"

"No, the modern miracle of Lasik." A fish broke the surface of the water in the canal ahead of them. It left an eddy that quickly faded.

"Listen to me complaining about wearing glasses to a guy who had to live through a civil war. I must sound like such a whiner."

They padded on for a few more moments before John resumed the languid pace of their conversation. "You might say I've seen many lifetimes of trouble. But I've also seen my fair share of happiness and miracles."

She had led many negotiations in her time, but for some reason this one made her nervous. Finally she broke the silence. "So, Mr. Amato, you wanted to talk to me about helping you change the world."

"I did. We need your help."

"So what are the terms of your offer?"

"Offer?"

She looked over her shoulder, maintaining the rhythm of her stroke. John looked back into her eyes. She thought she caught a flash of a look like that of an adoring puppy. Maybe it was wishful thinking. She finally broke away from his gaze. "I mean are you offering me a job?"

"I'm hoping you can help me with that. What do we need?"

She continued to paddle. "This really is the most unusual interview I've ever had."

"Seriously. You know what our problems are. I've told you what me and my friends have done already. If you were me, what would you do?"

Nicole took a deep breath, then launched into a pitch about how she would incorporate the group as a charitable foundation. John would serve as the chairman of the board of directors. The close advisors he had would serve as board members. Other members would be recruited based on the needs of the foundation. The board would help establish ties with influential leaders who could help them. When she was done, she waited. They glided on, the silence broken only by the paddles cutting into the waters of the canal.

When she couldn't wait anymore, she looked over her shoulder and broke the silence. "Well?"

As she looked into his eyes they suddenly widened. He let go of the paddle with one hand and pointed in front of the boat. "Shark!"

She swiveled her head around and scanned the water in front of her. Her breathing picked up. "Where?"

"Just ahead to the right. See it?"

Only a gray seagull bobbed on the water in that area. No dorsal fin in sight.

"Do you mean that seagull, smart alec?"

"Oh. Sometimes I have a tough time telling them apart."

"There are no sharks in this canal—it's fresh water."

Nicole grasped her paddle firmly and dipped the right blade into the water. She jerked back and up, hard. Then turned around just in time to see John spluttering from a face full of water. He used what was obviously a bad word in an unfamiliar language.

She laughed. "Are you swearing at me in Serbian?"

"Something like that. Sorry." He shook his head and then

grinned. "Nice shot for someone with lousy hand-eye coordination." Nicole turned around and began to paddle again.

After several strokes John asked, "In this new foundation, what would your job be?"

She swallowed. "President. I run the operations, handle the project, manage finances. All that stuff." When he didn't respond she added, "Under your guidance of course."

Two crews on training runs from the University of Washington interrupted their conversation. They waited for the two shells to pass by, coxswains calling out, "Stroke, stroke, stroke." Eventually they faded into the distance.

John still didn't respond. Finally she said, "If you'd rather, you could be president and I could be vice president."

"No, I like your first idea better. I'm better with people. You should handle the rest."

She smiled. This was certainly an unusual interview, but it was going her way. "Okay, we're agreed on that. So what are the terms of your offer?"

"I thought we just worked that out. You're going to set us up as a foundation, get us organized so we can save the world, and you'll be the president."

"No, I mean salary, benefits, stuff like that."

"You're the president. You figure it out."

She twisted in her seat to look back at him, setting the kayak wobbling. "You want me to set my own salary?"

"That's part of 'stuff like that,' isn't it?"

She gave him a quizzical look. "This isn't how it's supposed to work. You're supposed to make me an offer and then I negotiate for more."

He smiled. "I told you I'm not good at this stuff—and some consider me unusual."

She turned back to face the front and resumed stroking. "I

have to warn you. I'm making good money at my current company and my value on the open market is pretty high."

They glided on in silence for a few minutes before John said, "As a young man I pursued ambition before I realized what I really needed to pursue was affection."

A seagull flew low over their kayak and pulled up a dozen yards in front of them. It did a clumsy imitation of a hummingbird, trying to hover just in front of them. After a moment it realized they wouldn't be tossing it any scraps. It turned and flapped down the canal toward the Puget Sound, squawking in indignation. John turned them around and they headed back toward Lake Union.

"If it was all about money, I don't think you'd be talking to me. I believe you want to be happy. And until you decide to serve God and his creation, you will never be truly happy."

She let the paddle rest on the kayak and let John push them forward. On the bike path to the left of them, an elderly couple sat on a bench. They waved as John and Nicole glided past. She smiled and nodded, not confident enough to release the paddle for a return wave.

She turned the situation over in her mind. Best case, she'd love doing this. Worst case, she'd make a clean break from Dan and add the title of president to her resume. She dipped her paddle in the water and began stroking again. "I do have a question about the source of the money in your accounts."

"Sure. Fire away."

"I confess I hired a private detective to check up on you."

"Oh."

"I like to know about the people I work with. Been burned at least once, you know."

He paused for an uncomfortably long period of time. "So, what did your detective friend uncover?"

"He raised a concern about your money."

"I told you it was entrusted to me by friends. I can't tell you much more."

She spit it out. "This detective mentioned that during the civil war in Kosovo a lot of money went missing. Not that I believe you would—"

John interrupted. "I understand how someone could come to that conclusion. But you've seen how I live. It's hardly the lifestyle of a refugee that looted the treasury."

She turned back to look in his eyes; those deep, sincere brown orbs.

"Nicole. I lived in a small village. As you know, there was a lot of ethnic cleansing in that civil war. About a million people displaced. Nothing is left from my life there. Nothing I want to remember—or talk about."

She nodded. "I can imagine this is tough. I just need to know I'm making the right decision."

Their conversation was interrupted by the roar of a seaplane. They paused to watch as it circled the Space Needle and descended steeply. When the pontoons settled into the waters of Lake Union, the momentum of the plane died rapidly. The rudder on the tail flipped hard to the left and the plane turned away from them. The engine thrummed as the plane taxied toward the seaplane terminal on the far side of the waters.

John said, "de Havilland Otter. Probably coming from the San Juan Islands or Victoria."

"Seaplane service in the heart of downtown." She turned toward John and smiled. "I could fall in love with this city."

He picked up the earlier conversation. "As the president of the foundation, you'll manage the money. But you'll just have to take my word that there's nothing illegal about the source."

She looked back into his eyes. He was either being honest or he was the greatest liar in the world. She turned away and started to paddle again.

"Okay, I'll believe you. I just didn't want there to be any surprises."

"Don't worry. Nobody is going to be hauled away and have to wear an orange jumpsuit."

"Too bad. I bet I'd look good in one."

He chuckled softly. "I'll take your word for it."

"Okay, what's the next step?"

"We're meeting a friend for lunch."

John turned the kayak toward a collection of yachts moored at the south end of the lake. Gently, he pulled up next to a low dock with a yellow and black sign: "Transient Moorage 3 Hours Max."

"My, my. Lunch on the lake. Maybe you do know how to show a girl a good time."

John held firmly onto a dock cleat while Nicole gingerly lifted herself onto the wooden deck. She held the boat as John exited the craft. Under his guidance, they lifted the kayak onto the dock. John secured it to the cleat with a cable lock.

The hostess at Duke's Chowder House on the pier was watching something intently when John and Nicole walked in. They were almost at her station before she noticed them.

She blushed and pointed at the wall on the far side of the bar. "Sorry, good game on. M's 5, Yankees 3, top of the ninth."

Nicole noticed a large, black man sitting in a booth on the right. He looked up from his newspaper at them. As he smiled his shining white teeth split his ebony face like a jack-o' -lantern with a thousand watt bulb inside.

He unfolded his tremendous frame from the bench seat and stepped forward to embrace John. Nicole noted John's head only reached his shoulder. Then the big man stepped back and pointed at John's chest. "Does Jimmy Buffet know you raided his closet?"

John glanced down at the Hawaiian shirt, peppered with sea turtles. Then he reached out and pushed the black man's hand away. "Since you gave me this, it must have been you that raided his closet."

The man laughed and clapped John on the shoulder. He stepped forward to greet Nicole. To her relief, he didn't hug her as well. But his massive paws engulfed her outstretched hand.

"So this is the woman who's supposed to help us change the world?" His warm hands grasped hers firmly for a moment.

John nodded. "Nicole Logan, meet David Freeman."

She looked up at David. "Your name is familiar."

He smiled and gestured toward the booth. "I played a little ball in college."

John interrupted. "Don't be fooled by his modesty. All PAC 10 for the Huskies, drafted by Atlanta in the third round. Turned it down to work overseas in the mission field."

"Must be where I heard your name. I don't follow football much, but my ex-boyfriend is a rabid Stanford fan." She rolled her eyes. "He dragged me to more than one game."

Nicole slid into one side of the booth. John and David took seats on the other side facing her.

"Nicole, I wanted you to meet David because he's one of my closest friends and advisors. He's also the visionary behind the 'Water of Life' project."

She said, "We should have rented a triple kayak instead of a tandem. Then you both could have grilled me while we were paddling."

David laughed, a booming laugh that seemed to echo in his frame. "Do I look like I could get into one of those itty bitty boats without snapping it in half?"

She gave him a shy smile. "I guess not."

John pointed to David. "He's the one who suggested if we wanted to teach people about Christ, the Water of Life, we needed to provide them with water *for* life."

David nodded. "My mom came here from Africa when she was a kid. I grew up hearing stories about how her family walked miles every day to get drinkable water. And about the missionaries that helped them immigrate to this country where her family never had to worry about it."

He elbowed John. "But this is the guy who made it possible. His little magic algae makes the system really work."

"Just stumbled across it."

Nicole looked David in the eye. This was the kind of guy who would walk into a room and naturally command attention. "You turned down the NFL to work overseas as a missionary? Are you still doing that?"

He shook his head and responded with a quiet voice, "No. I came back a few years ago because my parents aren't aging well. Right now I'm the director for a drug and alcohol counseling program at the local men's mission. But enough about me, let's talk about you. Where do you worship, Nicole?"

She was saved by the waitress who arrived with their dishes. David worked his way through one deep batter fried hunk of cod before he repeated his question. "You were about to tell us where you worship."

She chewed her mouthful slowly before answering. "I don't actually go to church much. I mean I believe in God and everything. But my career keeps me pretty busy."

"Then why would you want to hang with a bunch of holy rollers like us?" David gave her an earnest look. She couldn't tell if he was challenging her or just being forthright.

"First of all, it's a worthwhile cause. I know that around 3.4 million people die a year due to water related illnesses."

"That's right, and every ninety seconds—"

"A child under five dies of causes related to unclean water or poor sanitation," Nicole said.

David grinned. "I see you've done your homework."

She returned the smile. "From a personal standpoint, it's a way to grow." She shot him a confident look. "And I'm good at making things happen. That's what you need right now."

He smiled and answered with a half chewed mouthful of food. "Agreed." He swallowed before continuing. "You gonna move up here?" Without waiting for an answer, he dove back into the fries as if he was at a training table where the meek went hungry.

She scowled. "Not now. I think I can run it from my place back in San Francisco and just come up here every few weeks."

David had just stuffed another handful of fries into his mouth. He nodded and grunted. Then he elbowed John and pointed to the TV at the end of the bar. Nicole looked over her shoulder. The game was over and a clip of Professor Wes Cavanaugh addressing a crowd of reporters was playing.

David said, "There's the guy with the reward for the person who can prove the apostle John is dead or alive."

Nicole looked up at the TV. The scene had changed to a figure in a crowd—a slender blonde woman dressed in a form fitting black outfit. She was saying something, but the sound on the TV was off. As the camera zoomed in on her she blew a wisp of hair away from her face.

Nicole turned toward John. He was staring at the screen, mouth agape. She turned back to the TV. It had cut away from the wispy haired blonde and back to Cavanaugh.

"Are you okay, John?"

He blinked his eyes and turned back to her. "I'm good. Why do you ask?"

"You looked like you'd just seen a ghost."

He shook his head. "Just can't believe the fuss people are making about that show."

She sat in silence for a moment and then said, "I read an article in the paper this morning about Cavanaugh and his reward and thought of you."

John's eyes widened. He had a piece of salmon on the tines of his fork and was about to insert it into his mouth. He stopped and it dropped onto his plate. "Thought about me?"

"Yeah. You're an expert on biblical times. You should go for that reward."

"I met Professor Cavanaugh last month at a lecture and heard about his challenge. It's a stupid stunt to promote his TV show."

"It may be a stunt, but there are some pretty interesting legends he talked about in the article. Like the fact that the apostle's grave is empty—"

"How realistic is it that a two thousand year old man is wandering the earth and no one has figured out his identity? Cavanaugh knows nobody will ever claim that reward."

David put his arm around John. "I have a better idea. You should pretend to be the apostle John. With your brains and murky personal history, you could pull it off."

John snapped, "Forget about it. We have more serious things to do."

"Easy there, bud. Just joking." David withdrew his arm, turned back to his plate and scooped up the last of his fries. With a half full mouth he said, "Besides, Cavanaugh is on the wrong track. It's not John that's alive, it's Lazarus."

Nicole sat back in her chair. "What?"

John elbowed David and said, "The whole concept of the apostle John still being alive is based on the Gospel of John. You know throughout the whole book of John it refers to the 'Beloved Disciple' but never says John is the Beloved Disciple."

She nodded. "I vaguely remember."

David said, "After Jesus' resurrection, he's walking with Peter on the shore of the Sea of Galilee and the Beloved Disciple is following them. Jesus is telling Peter what a horrible fate awaits him. Then Pete looks back at the Beloved Disciple and asks about *his* fate."

John picked the story up. "Jesus said, 'What do you care if he stays alive until I return. We're talking about you.' But it never says John is the Beloved Disciple."

David laughed. "The Bible doesn't say Jesus said, 'We're talking about you.' Most translations of the Bible say He said, 'You must follow me.'"

"Were you there? There wasn't exactly a court reporter taking down the dialogue."

"Yeah, right. But the main point is it never says that the Beloved Disciple, the guy who was going to remain alive until Jesus returned, was John." He waved a batter fried chunk of cod at John. "Some people think it was Lazarus."

Nicole scowled at the two. "I feel like I'm sitting around with a couple of geeks—but in this case, Bible geeks."

David's laugh boomed across Duke's. "Now *that's* a new one. But you're on the right track. The only guy who knows more about the Bible than me is John. But in this case he's wrong."

John shook his head. "I'll give you that Vernard Eller wrote a very compelling argument that the Beloved Disciple is really Lazarus, but most people who lived near the time the Gospel of John was written identify the Beloved Disciple as John himself."

"Yeah, but those people thought the earth was flat."

John pointed at the TV screen with his fork. "Why don't you call Cavanaugh up and tell him to bag the title *The Last Apostle*. He needs to call his show *Lazarus Lives*."

Nicole sat back in her chair. "You two are totally over my heads. Maybe we could go back to talking about how we're all going to save the world?"

Fifteen minutes later, David, unsatisfied with one plate of fish and chips, had ordered another and was partway through it. Nicole stood up. "I'm going to use the ladies room before we paddle back." She strode away.

John moved around to where Nicole had been sitting so he could face David. He waited until the big man had finished chewing a mouthful of food. "So, what do you think? Is she the one?"

David shook his head slowly. "I don't know, bro. Wondering if she's in this for the right reason." He waved a fry at John. "If you ask me, she's on the rebound. Just looking for a way to get away from the guy who burned her and make a name for herself. President is a much more impressive title than consultant."

John nodded, almost imperceptibly. "I've had the same thoughts myself." He reached across and grabbed one of David's fries. "Then again, it's not like I haven't had my own periods of weak faith."

Freeman scowled. "You? You're Mr. Faith himself." He reached across the table and plucked the fry out of John's fingers and popped it into his own mouth. "On the other hand, I've never heard you give me your testimony. I've told you how I became a Christian but I've never heard your story."

"I'm sure you've heard my story, but that's not important now." He pointed toward the entrance. "What about Nicole?"

David grinned. "Maybe you've developed a soft spot for her. Who wouldn't want to hang out with a smart and pretty girl like her?"

John grinned. "There is that, but I'm not in the market for a girlfriend. This is really about how we save the world."

David picked up another chunk of cod but paused before shoveling it into his mouth. "You're the boss. If you think she's the one, I'm with you." He bit off half of the fish and said, while still chewing, "But you're still wrong. Lazarus is the dude who's still wandering the earth—not John."

John smiled and turned his attention to the TV at the end of the bar. The segment about the Cavanaugh news conference was long over but he was still unnerved by the image of the blonde on the screen. There was no doubt in his mind. It was the same woman who had been watching him after his visit to Seth in the King County Jail—the mysterious figure dressed in black who had vanished down a sidewalk past two bicycle cops.

Chapter Twenty-One

Pray as if everything depended on God and work as if everything depended on you.

Saint Ignatius of Loyola

JOHANAN RUBBED HIS sleepy eyes with the sleeve of his robe. His other hand steadied the ladder leading down from the rooftop sleeping quarters as Marcus scampered down. Aprius was already heading toward the beach, the supply bag with their breakfast slung over his shoulder.

He looked out toward the sea and noticed the sail of a lone vessel already close to the horizon. The rest of the fleet was still on the beach. Only a few of the fisherman were yet tending to their boats. When Johanan reached the foot of the ladder, he pointed to the horizon and asked Tullius, "Who's getting an early start?"

"No fishing for them today. I've sent them to ask the provincial governor for a magistrate to hear the case of Solon." Tullius sighed.

Johanan put his hand on Tullius' shoulder. "How likely is it he'll do that?"

Tullius shook his head. "I think he'll refuse our request. He's unlikely to send someone on the three to five day journey to hear an accusation brought by some plebs on an unimportant island. He's more likely to tell us to bring Solon and the witnesses to the capital in Corinth."

Johanan stood in silence.

Tullius looked over at Johanan. "We rarely get the Romans involved in our affairs. They stop by to collect their taxes, but mostly let us go our own way."

"How do you usually administer justice?"

"On the rare occasions when we do need to punish someone, our elders prescribe hard labor or a short period of banishment. The guilty accept that, because Roman justice would rarely be as lenient."

Tullius sighed again and patted Johanan on the shoulder. "It's in God's hands now." He gave him a gentle nudge toward the beach. "Good fishing today, my son."

Several days after the elders had left for the capital, Johanan called together all the baptized to the courtyard of the house of Tullius. They gathered for the private meeting after the evening meal in a somber mood. Persecution of the followers of the Christos was old news. Some had even witnessed it in their travels. But while Johanan had mentioned the suffering of the faithful, the villagers hadn't really dwelt on it. Their island was peaceful and the idea of being tortured for their faith was far from their minds when they waded into the surf with Johanan to become followers of the Christos.

Johanan waited until the chatter had died down. "My friends, my brothers, my sisters, I have called you together to discuss the danger we face." He now had their undivided attention. "I have told you before of the persecution at the hands of the Romans. Tonight I want to tell you more of the courage of our brothers and sisters in the faith."

He spent the next half hour recalling stories of how compatriots had bravely suffered and died rather than deny Jesus. He concluded the vignettes with his own experience of being boiled alive in oil by the Emperor Domitian, and surviving, although he relayed the tale in the third person. "Although the Lord chose to save the apostle Johanan, the Beloved Disciple, from death in that instance, He often brings his faithful home to live in Paradise with Him." He paused to let the concept sink in. "I myself yearn for that day, but I know it must be in God's time, not mine."

As he looked around, he wondered if the people in this courtyard would beat him to that reward, even though he had nearly six decades on the oldest of them.

They waited in silence for his next words. "While we may never deny our Lord, it serves no purpose to call the attention of the authorities to ourselves. We often worship in secret, spreading the word as best we can."

Marcus said, "You mean we can't be a Simon Peter, and deny our Lord?"

The rest of those present nodded. They all recalled the story of Simon denying Jesus three times before the cock crowed. Johanan was pleased at how they had learned.

"Yes Marcus, but like Simon Peter, if we are called to martyrdom, so be it. Otherwise we are called to make disciples of all men and spread the faith."

Johanan picked up a walking stick and pointed it toward the sky. "I don't know what the trial of Solon will bring. We may be persecuted, we may have to flee from this beautiful island, or, we may be delivered from the hands of our oppressors." More nods from the somber gathering. "However, if any of you do flee the island, I want you to know of a secret sign by which you can identify other believers."

He gestured for those close by to step back and clear a space in front of him. Then he used the stick to draw a curved line in the sand. Nikias held up a torch to illuminate the sand in front of Johanan. The crowd jostled to get a look at what he had drawn.

"This line is one half of the ichthys, the Greek sign for a fish, one with which you are all familiar. It is also a symbol many followers of the Way use for the Christos." He took the stick and drew another line, curving the opposite way of the first. It started at the same point as the other but crossed over two thirds of the way down. "If you draw the first arc and a stranger completes the ichthys for you, it is an indication they are a fellow believer."

On the evening of the tenth day after they departed, the boat of the village elders returned. They reported the provincial governor had agreed to send his youngest brother as magistrate to judge the case.

"The governor didn't want to deal with the case at all," one elder said. "His brother spoke up and agreed to serve in his place. He has a farm on a neighboring island he wants to visit." He smirked. "And maybe he just likes the idea of pretending he's the governor himself."

Late the next afternoon, a moderate sized sailing vessel was sighted approaching. The representative of the Roman Empire had arrived.

Fabius Lupus, the youngest brother of the provincial governor, or propraetor, was accompanied by two legionaries and four sailors. They brought tents to house the representative and his guard. The sailors would sleep on board.

That evening the village held a feast to honor the arrival of the magistrate. Their visitor had brought an amphora of wine ashore to be shared at the celebration. Soon goblets of it were being passed around. Johanan noticed it was much stronger than the vintage usually served on the island. He also noticed the soldiers and sailors whom accompanied Lupus were helping themselves to plenty of the fermented drink.

As the food was passed around, the magistrate sampled some of the local fish sauce. He said to Tullius, "This is excellent garum. What is your source?"

Johanan could almost see Tullius' chest swell with pride. "We make it ourselves from an old recipe of my family. I will arrange to have an amphora delivered to you as a gift."

"I must have at least six amphorae to share with my brother and friends. What is your price for five more?"

Tullius named the cost that had been negotiated with the merchant.

"Done." He pulled a purse out of his belt and counted out the coins into Tullius' hand. "Have them delivered to my ship in the morning."

"As you wish." Tullius stood there with a silly grin, but said nothing further. Johanan smiled at seeing Tullius dumbfounded—an unusual situation.

The magistrate took another swig from his goblet. "My brother the propraetor will be pleased with this delicacy. Your garum will be known throughout the province."

The evening passed pleasantly enough until Anteia, carrying a full tray of baked fish, walked past one of the legionaries. He reached out, grabbed her and pulled her into his lap.

"How about a kiss from the most beautiful maiden on the island?" the drunken legionary said. She dropped the platter onto the sand.

"Let me go." She tried to push away from him. He put his arm around her and pulled the young woman closer.

Aprius rushed forward. "That's my sister. Release her!"

The other soldier stepped toward Aprius. "She's your sister, not your wife. Let him have his fun." He pulled out his gladius, pointed it at Aprius, and waggled the short sword like a scolding finger.

Aprius reached into his belt and drew a knife. He held it in front of him, tip pointed at the Roman. Other villagers grabbed knives or pulled them out of their belts. The first legionary stood, pulled Anteia close to him, and pulled out his gladius. Two sailors grabbed knives and fell in next to the legionaries. The other two sailors dropped their wine goblets and took off at a dead run down the beach.

The Romans were well trained and well-armed. The villagers were lightly armed, but numerous. Fabius Lupus, his wits dulled by the wine, watched everything unfold from his reclining position, as if he were watching a spectacle in the coliseum.

"Centurion!" said Johanan in a commanding voice. He used a title many levels above the legionary's true rank. He stood up and faced the Roman, who held Anteia close to his side. Johanan's hands were open, palms toward the soldier, slightly out from his side. His gesture showed he was unarmed.

The legionaries and villagers turned toward Johanan, and hesitated. The bloodbath was delayed, for at least a moment.

"Centurion," Johanan said in a quieter voice. "You may be willing to kiss a beautiful young woman in front of her brother, but surely an honorable legionary in the service of the mighty Roman Empire would not dishonor a maiden—in front of her betrothed."

The soldier hesitated, then loosened his grip. In a low tone he said, "Well, no one said she was promised to anyone." Anteia pulled away and ran out of the shelter towards her home. Her mother followed.

The magistrate finally roused himself from his stupor. "Enough!" He clapped his hands. "We have a busy day tomorrow." He looked at the two legionaries and waved toward the tent. "Go prepare my quarters." They placed their swords back in their scabbards and walked unsteadily down the beach. He turned to the sailors and ordered, "Return to the ship." They nodded and headed down toward their boat.

He faced the villagers and waved toward the legionaries. "I regret the indiscretion of my men. They are used to being garrisoned in areas where the women are a bit less, may I say, innocent." He looked at Johanan and nodded. "My apologies for offending your betrothed."

Johanan returned the nod. "Apology accepted, Citizen."

The magistrate waved his arm in dismissal. "The trial begins in the morning." He turned and headed toward his tent, using the slow and purposeful gait of a man who is compensating for having had too much to drink.

The islanders watched him go, still in shock at what had almost happened.

Finally, Tullius walked over to Johanan and slapped his hand on his shoulder. "You, my son, saved our honor, and I'm sure, many lives." He placed his hand on Aprius' chest. "You should take a lesson from him in cool thinking."

Aprius gave a perfunctory nod and then turned his attention to Johanan. "Betrothed? Is there something you're hiding from us, or did you lie to that Roman to save our skins?"

"Neither. I didn't say she was betrothed." A sly grin crossed his face. "I just implied an honorable Roman legionary wouldn't dishonor a maiden in front of her betrothed. I neither said she was engaged or that I was her promised one. They chose to make that conclusion. Under the circumstances I decided it was best to not correct that misconception."

Aprius clapped him on the shoulder. "You fox. This is a part of you I haven't seen before. I'm glad you're on our side."

As the gathering broke up, Tullius told Johanan and his family to go ahead without him. "I am going to pay a visit to Solon.

He may have committed a crime, but he has been my friend since we were still suckling children." The next words obviously pained him. "I don't know what will happen tomorrow, but if this is his last evening with us, I will spend it with him."

The next morning Tullius, Nikias, Johanan, and Aprius waited on the shore with six amphorae of fish sauce sticking upright in the sand. They had to roust Tullius, who had returned home from his visit with Solon only a few hours before sunrise. He had little to say about his time with his friend. Based on his bloodshot eyes and sluggish demeanor, he had enjoyed himself too much.

They watched as the sailors struggled to lower an ornate chair from the ship at anchor onto a small boat. Fabius Lupus evidently wanted at least some element of officialdom for the trial. After the cargo was loaded, two of the men rowed the vessel toward shore. The small boat pitched back and forth during the short journey through the surf, almost tipping the cargo and crew into the water several times.

When the boat finally reached the beach, the four islanders pulled it up onto the sand and helped steady it. The sailors jumped into the surf, lifted out the chair, and carried it up onto the beach. They politely greeted the four waiting villagers. After they deposited the chair on the sand, they carried each amphora down to the boat and carefully laid it on the bottom. The villagers pushed the small vessel back out into the surf, and the sailors climbed in and turned it back toward the ship. One pulled steadily on the oars while the other kept the amphora steady.

When they were out of earshot, Aprius said, "Not a mention of last night."

"Not a proud moment for the magistrate," Tullius said. "Nor for those two. They were the ones who abandoned their comrades when everyone else was drawing weapons."

Johanan said, "There were times in my homeland when they would not have hesitated to take the woman and butcher those who tried to stop them."

Tullius looked at Johanan and nodded before turning back to watch the sailors. "Yes, but Judea was a colony in rebellion. This is a peaceful province." He spat into the surf and looked back at Johanan "And Rome favors keeping the peace."

The men continued to watch as the boat wallowed through the surf, in danger of swamping at any moment. They finally reached the ship and carefully passed each amphora up to the two waiting crewmen. The villagers watched the whole operation, expecting at any moment the cargo would drop into the surf and sink to the bottom.

When the last amphora had been safely transferred, Tullius turned and walked up to the chair. Nikias and Aprius picked it up, and Tullius led them up the beach to the pavilion. They placed the chair at one end of the shelter. Johanan looked toward the tent of Fabius Lupus. The Roman was walking toward them, wearing a ceremonial toga. The legionaries followed a few paces behind, fully dressed in their armor. Many of the villagers were starting toward the pavilion as well. Johanan looked toward Solon's house. The village healer and his family were on their way toward Solon's rendezvous with his fate.

If Roman justice followed its normal course, in a few hours the trial would be over. The peaceful island would likely be changed forever.

Chapter Twenty-Two

Nothing is permanent but change.

Heraclitus

NICOLE SAT DOWN in a chair in front of Dan's desk and folded her arms. He gestured toward the small refrigerator against the wall. "Do you want a coke or something?"

"No, let's just get this over with."

His mouth dropped open. He pursed his lips. "Get what over with?"

She uncrossed her arms and leaned forward. "I'm quitting. This is my two weeks' notice."

He leaned back in his chair and exhaled. "Now let's not be hasty. I know things have been tense since we broke up, but we can—"

"We didn't break up, Dan. You dumped me for Penny Walker."

"Now wait a minute. That shouldn't affect our business relationship. We're still partners and you're in the middle of an important project."

"Yes I am, and now you're going to have to deal with it." She sat back in her chair and folded her arms again. "All my reports and plans for the Neely Seafoods project are up to date. I'll be glad to provide a detailed briefing so the handoff is as smooth as possible."

"But we don't have anyone of your caliber on staff. That's a complex project and it's going to take time to find someone. And Neely is an important customer. This will make us look bad—very bad."

"That's your problem. Maybe you'll have to roll up your sleeves rather than spending your time running around town with Penny Walker on your arm."

His face reddened, but he held his tongue. "You have a year to go on this project. You can't just dump it on us."

"I can't? Guess what—I am."

"But what are you going to do? You're still a partner in this company."

"So buy me out."

"We don't have the cash right now."

"Borrow it from Penny's mommy and daddy. Or let me keep my shares. But if I do, I *will* be watching the financials closely as part owner."

"Are you going to work for a competitor?"

"No." She relaxed and let her hands slip into her lap. "I'm going to be the executive director of a charitable foundation. One that's going to change the world."

Dan's jaw dropped again. "A charitable foundation? That's *so* not you."

Her tone was now calm. "You'd be surprised."

Dan leaned back in his chair and held a handmade oak pen between his thumb and forefinger. Nicole recognized it as the one she had bought for him at the Pike Place market in Seattle—a pen she had carefully selected to match the oak desk handed down to

Dan by his great grandfather. He began to tap it on that same desk.

Dan had engaged in this nervous habit fairly often in the two months since their breakup. At this point in their relationship, he was as open to her as a paperback romance.

He put the pen down and placed his hands flat on the desk. "Setting up a charitable foundation and running it could be seen as a violation of your non-compete agreement. We could prevent you from doing that."

"You would do that to me? After all I've done for you?"

"I have to look out for the best interests of DANISoft."

She leaned forward and grabbed the front edge of his desk. "You don't care about DANISoft—you care about Danny."

"All I'm saying is that—"

"Just try it—you sue me and I'll bury you and your company."

His eyes narrowed. "Forget the two weeks notice. You can get out now."

She pushed back her chair and stood up. She smiled. "Gladly. And good luck with Neely."

Chapter Twenty-Three

Many receive advice, few profit by it.

Publilius Syrus, 42 B.C.

JOHN'S PHONE CHIRPED. He picked it up off of his desk and glanced at the text message. It was from Scott: *Game at four?*

That was unusual. He and Scott usually planned matches days ahead of time. Four o'clock was only forty-five minutes away. He looked around the desk in his office. Nothing that couldn't wait. John texted back: *On my way.*

He wheeled his bike up to the rack in front of the gym, just in time to see Scott pull his Mustang into the parking garage.

John caught up to him in the locker room. "Ready to get your butt kicked, old man?" Scott said.

"Loser buys?"

"You're on, bro, best of three."

Scott quickly ran up the score. John's mind was elsewhere:

Sharon, Nicole, the Water for Life project, anything else but this game with Scott.

"Are you in this game or not?" Scott said. "You really don't suck this bad."

John pulled himself out of mental reverie. "Just making sure you're overconfident so I can bury you."

John battled back but lost the first game 13-15. He reminded himself he needed to be present to the people he was with, and right now, that person was Scott.

As Scott bounced the ball off the floor, getting ready to serve, John asked, "So why the late notice for a game?"

Scott glanced over at him, then turned away. "I was going out of town this weekend with a girl I've been dating. Reservations at a B&B up in Victoria and everything." He bounced the ball again. "She cancelled on me last minute."

He tossed the ball up in the air, used an unkind word to describe her, and drilled the ball into the wall. John suppressed a grin and returned the serve.

John ran up the score in the next game. The banter picked up now that he had his head in the game. With years of experience, training, and muscle memory, John was a threat in almost any sport that involved skill and coordination. An impetuous young man like Scott was like a canary in the mouth of a cat. But John was a playful cat with ulterior motives; in this case motives in the best interest of the canary. John ran up the score 14-5 and then let Scott come back. When John scored the winning point, Scott swore up a storm.

"Man, do you talk around your mother like that?"

"Dude, she was a Marine. Where do you think I learned how to swear?"

John waited a moment. Then asked, "What about your father?"

Scott glanced at him and shot him a quick glare before turning away. "What father?"

"Sore subject?" John bounced the ball on the floor of the court.

Scott huffed. "He bailed on us when I was a kid. Left my mom and his partner to run his business." He pounded the edge of his racket into his open palm. "Last I heard he was a drunk on the streets of some city in California."

John bounced the ball once, twice. "You ever want to meet up with your dad again? Maybe you could connect. Help him out." He bounced the ball again.

Scott shook his head. "Why should I care about him?" He glared at John. "You gonna serve, or not?"

John held the ball between his thumb and forefinger. "So, bud, how about a different bet?"

"Like?"

"Loser buys breakfast tomorrow. Winner gets to pick the place."

Scott frowned.

"Unless you can't beat an old man like me."

Scott smirked. "You're on." John flipped him the ball.

John kept it close to keep it interesting, but twenty minutes later he put away the winning shot.

Scott swore again. "So, where am I taking you to breakfast?"

"I'll tell you tomorrow morning. Be ready to go at seven thirty."

"Seven thirty? I'm still in bed then."

"That was the deal. I win and I pick." He shoved Scott on the shoulder. "But don't worry, I won't break the bank. I know you have payments to make on your fancy 'stang."

As they left the court, they picked up towels at the front desk. "Hi, John," said the slender redhead attendant.

"Hi Laurel," John said. They exchanged pleasantries and then John and Scott withdrew to the locker room.

"What is it about you?" Scott asked. "She obviously has the hots for you, but she totally ignored me."

"That's because I treat her like a person, with respect. She feels safe with me. With you, she probably feels like she's being stalked." John whacked Scott playfully with his towel. "Imagine how you'd feel in her position."

"Man, I *wish* she would stalk me. I could live with that."

"Breakfast, seven thirty. Don't make me wait."

Chapter Twenty-Four

We often critically judge others by the law… while for ourselves we want God to grant us abundant grace.

Mark Hall of Casting Crowns

CITIZEN FABIUS LUPUS took his seat in the ceremonial chair and carefully rearranged his white toga as the villagers gathered. The legionaries each took a position on either side of Lupus. The two sailors who had not fled the fight the night before stood on the outside of the crowd, observing the spectacle.

Johanan looked around the pavilion. Most of the village was here. He did notice Anteia was missing from the observers. Considering the events of last night, it was probably best if she remained out of sight. Even though she had been involved in the case, as a woman, her testimony would not be accepted in a Roman court.

When the villagers had settled down Lupus said, "Bring forth the accused." Solon stepped forward and stood in the opening before the ceremonial chair. Lupus looked at Solon. He scanned him from his feet to his head. Then he looked over at Tullius. "Why is this man not bound?"

Tullius stepped forward. "He is bound by his word to appear before you. I trust him to honor that word."

Fabius Lupus cleared his throat. "Very well, who accuses this man?"

Aprius stepped forward. "I accuse him."

"Why do you call upon the representative of the Roman Empire to judge this man?"

Aprius launched into a lengthy explanation of Johanan's injury, treatment by Solon, and Johanan's recovery after they ceased using the poultice. He concluded with his discovery of the henbane bush and his connection of the poultice smell with that of the poison. Lupus interrupted Aprius periodically with questions or asked him to repeat statements.

When Aprius had finished, Lupus said in a booming voice, "Bring forth the injured man." Aprius stepped aside as Johanan moved forward.

"You have recovered from your wound?"

"Yes, your Excellency, I have."

Fabius Lupus looked at Solon who had faded away into the edge of the crowd. "Come forward." Solon stepped into the sandy arena again. Aprius and Johanan stepped back into the crowd.

"What do you have to say about these accusations?"

Solon bowed his head slightly. Johanan's mind, and heart, began to race. He had been in this situation many times, often with dire consequences. If Solon brought up Johanan's conversion of many villagers to the Way, Fabius Lupus could hardly ignore it. He would force the islanders to swear to the divinity of the emperor. Those who refused would likely be imprisoned, tortured, and executed.

Solon fell forward on his knees. "Yes, I did try to poison him. I beg for forgiveness."

Lupus leaned toward the bent over figure. "Why did you try to poison him?"

The crowd held its collective breath. Johanan could see some praying silently.

"I was jealous."

"Jealous? Did he seduce your wife?"

"No. It is my son." Solon's confession was muffled by the sand as he cried out. "I was jealous of how my son listened to him more than me."

"Your son? Listened to him? About what?"

"The world. Johanan is a traveler and his tales attracted my son, Nikias. He found this stranger more interesting than me, his father."

Johanan was shocked. No denial? Not a word about Johanan's preaching of the Christos? The magistrate might have sympathized with someone who tried to eliminate a follower of the Way. But this pathetic confession would not help his case. Where was the defiant Solon who had demanded a Roman trial?

Lupus said, "That is what all this is about? The poisoning and demand for a trial was about your jealousy over the attention paid by your son to a stranger?"

"Yes, Citizen, I was foolish. I beg your forgiveness." Solon was prostrate in the sand now.

Lupus sat back in his seat. The crowd began to murmur as he considered the situation before him. Finally he said, "Given your confession and the fact your victim has recovered...." he paused. The villagers waited in utter silence. Only the sound of the ocean and seabirds broke the stillness. "I sentence you to be scourged."

The crowd gasped. He could have sentenced Solon to death for attempted murder, but based on how vigorously the punishment was carried out, scourging might still be a death sentence. Men had died from blood loss or shock from this form of justice. It was often used as a prelude to an execution. Even if he survived, he might die later if his wounds themselves became sick, much as Johanan's had.

Solon rose and stood, shoulders slumped, resigned to his fate. His wife, Perpetua, screamed and threw herself at the feet of Fabius Lupus, begging for mercy. He waved her away. One legionary stepped forward and jerked her to her feet and pushed her into the crowd. The other grabbed the village healer by the arm and led him a short way down the beach toward a large boulder. He went obediently. The legionary pushed him down to his knees in front of the large rock and roughly pulled Solon's tunic off.

Many times Johanan had seen the island children compete to be "King of the Rock" on this boulder. He imagined that in their youth, Tullius and Solon had played the same game right here on this stone. Now it would be the scene of the healer's sentence.

Most of the villagers watched as the Roman tied a rope to Solon's right wrist and threw it over the rock. He pulled Solon to his feet and pushed him against the boulder. He pulled the rope tightly so Solon was held firmly against the rough stone. He tied the loose end around Solon's other wrist. One side of his bearded face was pressed against the rock. In large towns, the crowd would have gathered for the spectacle but here, the victim was their friend and neighbor. Several of the villagers left, likely because they couldn't stomach what was coming. A number of mothers gathered up their children and scurried away.

Perpetua screamed. Tullius stood on one side of her with Nikias on the other. They each held her tightly to prevent her from rushing forward. She lunged toward Fabius Lupus crying "No," over, and over again.

The second soldier brought a small trunk forward and opened it. He removed his armor and tunic and set it aside. The first pulled a whip out of the trunk and uncoiled it. He passed it to the other, who was now stripped to the waist. The sweat running down his heavily muscled back glowed in the morning sun.

Johanan pushed his way to the leading edge of the crowd until he had a front row view.

The legionary felt the tip of the whip. It was barbed with small metal spikes. He dropped the tip into the sand and began to coil the leather up into a large loop. He positioned himself closer to Solon so his whip would be at just the right distance as he began the scourging. Perpetua continued to sob and beg for mercy.

"Honored Citizen!" Johanan said in a firm voice that cut through the bedlam. He strode into the gap between the Roman and Solon. He faced Fabius Lupus, who was still seated. "Honored Citizen," he said, more softly, but still loud enough to be heard over the cries of Perpetua.

The soldier next to Lupus began to move toward Johanan. Lupus raised his hand and gestured him to stop. "Speak," he said, a faint smile of amusement on his face.

"Your Excellency," Johanan said, bowing slightly. "I was the party injured by this man. By all rights I should be ready to see justice carried out."

Perpetua broke out in a fresh chorus of sobbing. She collapsed to her knees between Tullius and Nikias.

"But rather than ask for justice for Solon, I choose to forgive him. I ask you, as the representative of the empire, to lift the sentence against him and set him free."

"You want me to set him free? The man who tried to kill you?"

"Yes, your Excellency. I forgive this man and ask you to set him free."

The magistrate leaned back in his chair and stroked his chin. Finally he said, "A most generous action for a man who has been wronged. However, it still doesn't change that he committed a crime and deserves punishment."

Johanan nodded in acknowledgement. "I understand, Honored Citizen. In that case, I ask to help him bear his punishment." Without waiting for a response, he strode over to Solon and put one arm around the rock and the other around the village healer's neck. Johanan's face was next to Solon's, his back shielding half of the islander's body.

"What are you doing?" Solon said.

Johanan whispered, "My Lord commands me to forgive those who have wronged me. Even though I couldn't spare him his own sacrifice, I can help you bear your punishment."

"This is madness," Solon said.

"As you wish," Lupus said. "Carry out the sentence." Johanan braced himself for the pain of the lash.

"Honored Citizen." Johanan turned his head to see who had called out. Aprius was sprinting toward them. He stopped where the apostle had made his plea and turned toward the magistrate.

"I am the accuser in this case. I too forgive Solon and ask to help him bear his punishment." He bowed toward the judgment seat, and without waiting for a response, strode to the boulder. He stood on the other side of Solon and grasped his neck.

"What is this? Are you both mad?" Solon asked.

"No, I am just showing love to my neighbor, as the Christos commands," Aprius whispered. "But be honest, uncle, you've wanted to flog me yourself since I let all your chickens loose and blamed it on your son."

"I knew that was you! You have blamed Dagon for most of a decade and he has denied it." Solon struggled to turn his face toward Aprius.

"Yes, I confess I did it and lied. I ask for your forgiveness."

Johanan almost smiled. The whip was about to cross all their backs and they were squabbling about a boyhood prank. Then he felt an arm around his neck as someone else joined their trio. He looked into the face of Nikias who was now standing behind his father with an arm around Aprius and Johanan.

"How could I let my crewmates and brothers share my father's punishment by themselves?"

Solon said, "Nikias, Aprius just confessed to being the one who released all our chickens when he was a boy, just as I have always suspected. Did you know he was the one?"

"He would never answer me, Father, but I thought it was him."

Solon had not shared a word with Nikias in weeks, and now it was about this? Johanan felt another arm around his neck as a new body pressed against his left side. "We will all share in the punishment," Marcus said. Johanan felt Nikias push up harder against him. He looked back. There was another row of men behind him, now two rows, now he couldn't see through all the faces. They were pressed up hard against the rock by the pressure of those who had followed Johanan's lead.

"See what you've done, Johanan?" Solon said. "Before I just had to endure a scourging, now I will be crushed to death."

Aprius let out a breathless laugh.

"Enough," They could hear Fabius Lupus shout over the bedlam. "You petition me to come to your miserable little island to administer justice, then you deny the justice that should be administered. What kind of place is this?"

Johanan struggled to turn his head toward the Roman. He couldn't see through all the bodies surrounding him. The voices around him had gone silent.

"Optio, bring me the prisoner."

The men around him began to shuffle. "What should we do?" Aprius said.

"Move back," Johanan said. "Give us some space." The crowd started to back away from the rock.

He heard the clang of steel on stone. The rope holding Solon in place went slack. Within a few seconds, the legionary was pushing Marcus and Johanan aside and tugging on the rope in an effort to extricate Solon from the mass of men. He pulled him free from the pack and shoved him roughly toward the magistrate. The soldier pushed him down on his knees in front of the angry Roman.

Fabius Lupus stood and looked down on Solon's bowed head. "I should take you back to the capital and sell you into slavery. He looked up at Johanan and then scanned the crowd. "I should sell you all into slavery for attempting to make a farce of Roman justice."

"Your Excellency," Johanan said, "that was not our intention."

Fabius Lupus looked back down at Solon. "If you are ever reported for anything else, I will bring you back to the mainland for your trial and then put your head on a pike outside my home—and maybe not in that order."

"I understand, Citizen," Solon said. "I will cause no more trouble." He fell forward on his hands in front of Fabius Lupus.

"Guards, gather up my belongings. We depart immediately."

Shortly, Fabius Lupus and his escorts were down on the shore. A boat from the village was pressed into service to help haul their supplies back out to the boat. The entire village, except for Solon and his family, had gathered on the beach. Tullius had told Nikias to take his father, mother and brother back to their home.

Aprius and Marcus arrived on the beach with another amphora of garum. They pushed the base into the sand. Tullius addressed the waiting magistrate. "Your Excellency, please accept this gift in honor of your visit." He pointed to the clay container of fish sauce. "The tale of your compassion will be told on our island for generations."

"Yes, of course," Fabius Lupus said. Then he looked over at Johanan, who was standing on the edge of the beach. "You, come with me."

Lupus began to stride up the beach. Johanan turned to follow, as did one of the legionaries. Lupus turned to the soldier and said, "Stay here and make sure everything is loaded onto my ship, including that." He pointed to the amphora. Lupus stood a head taller than Johanan. He continued up the beach at such a pace that Johanan almost had to break into a run.

When they were out of earshot of the crowd, he stopped and turned so quickly that Johanan nearly ran into him. He stood for a moment, looking out at the sea. Then he faced Johanan.

"I have witnessed something like this only a few times before in my life." He looked directly into Johanan's eyes and paused. "In each case it involved followers of Jesus of Galilee—Christians."

Johanan hesitated and then nodded. "Yes, Citizen, I am a Christian."

Chapter Twenty-Five

Everyone thinks forgiveness is a lovely idea until they have something to forgive.

C.S. Lewis

AT SEVEN THIRTY sharp, John rapped his knuckles on Scott's door. To his surprise, his friend opened the door almost immediately.

"You ready?"

"Yeah, you got me curious with this mystery breakfast. So, where are we going? Do you want me to drive?"

"No, I'll handle the transportation." They walked out the front door and down the sidewalk.

"I've seen your car, man. You sure it will make it to where we're going?"

By this time they had reached the bus stop. John asked, "Who said we were taking my car?"

Scott looked up and down at the bus stop schedule. "Where we going anyway?"

"All in good time, bud." John looked up at the approaching bus. "I hope you brought your wallet."

Thirty minutes later, after making one transfer, they got out at John's regular stop down by the mission. The bus pulled away leaving Scott and John on the sidewalk. Scott looked around at the dirty buildings, a panhandler on the sidewalk, and a cluster of men loitering around the mission across the street. "Where in the hell are we eating anyways?"

"Winner's choice, right?"

"Yeah?" Scott's tone was concerned.

"Well then, follow me." John stepped off of the curb into the crosswalk and headed across the street. He glanced over his shoulder at Scott who was still standing on the sidewalk, looking around at his surroundings. Finally he followed in John's wake.

John introduced Scott to David Freeman and some of the other staff.

David's hand engulfed Scott's as he shook it. "Here to help?"

"I lost a bet."

David laughed and slapped Scott on the back. "We'll take volunteers anyway we can." He put his arms around the pair and guided them behind the serving counter. After giving each a pair of plastic gloves, he pulled a scoop out of the battered warming dish full of scrambled eggs and handed it to Scott. "Everyone who eats here earns his meal." John took a position just after Scott in the line and started serving up home fries.

John greeted each person and exchanged light banter with each as they came through the line. Finally he spied the man he had been waiting for in line. The pea green fatigue jacket he wore was dotted with faded Marine Corps patches. His leathery face looked a generation older than his true age. When he reached John's station, John gave him a generous portion of fries.

"Be careful about those eggs." He pointed to Scott's serving tray. "My friend cooked them himself and he's a bachelor."

"Hey," Scott said, "nine of ten of my dinner guests live to see the next day."

"But what about the day after that?" the man in the fatigue jacket asked.

"I only offer a twenty-four hour warranty on my cooking. After that, you're on your own."

"I'll try a serving anyway. I don't have much to live for."

"We'll see about that," John said. "But even so, I'd try em. Somebody needs to be the brave man to test them for the rest of us."

The next guest was Seth. John didn't recognize him at first. When he had faced him nearly a month before at the jail, he had been dressed in an orange jumpsuit. Now he was dressed in worn but neat street clothes and had shaved off the scraggly beard and had a close cropped haircut.

"Seth, good to see you here."

Seth's gaze had been focused on the eggs that Scott was ladling onto his plate. His chin jerked upward at his name. "Um. Yeah. Uh, John Amato, right?" He stepped in front of John and nodded at the scoop of home fries John was offering.

"Save us two seats next to my friend in the fatigue jacket and you can tell me how things are going."

Seth gave him a weak smile and nodded, before shuffling to the next position.

After fifteen minutes of this, they were replaced by two others and joined the line to get their own meals. John spied Seth at a table with the man in the fatigue jacket who had ventured to try the eggs because he didn't "have much to live for."

The man looked up and then went back to his almost finished meal. John turned his attention to Seth. "They treating you okay here?"

He nodded. "I'm doing alright. Was tough at first, but I feel like I'm on the right track."

John elbowed Scott, who was sitting right next to him, and just across from the man in the fatigue jacket. "You should get to know my friend here. Eventually they'll want you to get a part time job and his company uses a lot of temp workers."

Scott nodded. "We do a lot of document scanning for local businesses. Always looking for reliable people to fill positions." He paused. "Reliable people."

The man in the fatigue jacket looked up from his now empty plate. "Big scanners that take in stacks of paper and put it all on computers?"

"Yeah, you know anything about it?"

He grunted. "I used to have a company like that." He dropped his fork on the fiberglass tray. "Until my wife shacked up with my partner and pushed me out."

Scott had a forkful of home fries ready to enter his mouth. He paused. "What was the name of your company?"

The man looked at Scott. "Adlersoft. You heard of it?"

Scott dropped his forkful of fries and gave John a long, hard glare. Then he turned back to the man and stood up. "You weren't pushed out. You ran out on me and mom. And then your partner croaked and the place went under."

A look of recognition washed across the leathery face of the old man. In a voice just above a whisper he asked, "Scottie?"

Scott put his fingers under the edge of his tray and flipped it up. What was left of his meal splattered across the table and the front of the man's fatigue jacket. "The name is Scott—not Scottie."

Scott turned and stalked out. John jumped up to follow him. He met up with him on the sidewalk. Scott turned to face him. "Did you know that was my father?"

John nodded. "I knew him from a mission where I helped out in San Francisco." He looked down at the ground. "I had hoped that would go better."

Scott practically spit out his words. "That bastard abandoned my family when I was just a kid. Did you just think we were going to hug and make up?"

"Don't you think before you write him off that you should hear his side of the story?"

Scott turned away. "He's had twenty years to tell his story. Never bothered to take the time." He turned and stalked up the street.

The phone rang four, five, six times. Nicole scowled at the paper in front of her. The account numbers and phone number for the Cayman Islands bank where John kept his money were printed on the letter prepared by his former financial advisor. John had passed the unopened envelope to Nicole along with the password that she'd need.

Finally, on the eighth ring, a male voice answered in a clipped British accent. "Royal Caribbean Bank. How may I help you?"

Nicole explained who she was and provided the account numbers and password. The man at the other end asked a few questions and then said, "Ms. Logan, I'm afraid that there is an unfortunate situation here. I am actually from the government."

"Oh?"

"Yes. There have been some discrepancies with the bank here and all accounts have been frozen for the time being."

Nicole's mouth went dry. Had John lied? Was he hiding something?

He continued. "We tried to contact you, but the phone number listed on the account has been disconnected."

Nicole could hear her heart beating as the man went on.

"Unfortunately, I cannot tell you how long our investigation will take."

All her plans for making a name were evaporating. She had signed on to a sinking ship. She clicked the off button on her phone and put it on the table.

Chapter Twenty-Six

When the student is ready, the teacher will appear

Buddhist Proverb

JOHANAN WAITED IN silence as Fabius Lupus looked out to sea and pondered the revelation that many of the islanders were Christians. Finally, he turned back to Johanan and said, "Every time I have witnessed the execution of followers of this Jesus of Galilee, I have been amazed at how willingly they went to their deaths. How they refused to turn in their brethren to save their own skin. I have wondered about the faith that would give men and women such courage." He paused and looked back down the beach where the islanders were gathered, watching the boats ferry the last of his belongings to the ship.

"As a young man I witnessed the attempted execution of the last living member of the inner circle of this Jesus. The emperor attempted to boil the man in oil. I watched as the condemned emerged from the boiling cauldron unscathed." He squinted at

Johanan. "He was also named Johanan. He was much older than you, but there is some likeness."

Johanan suppressed a smile. "I know of this man, the apostle Johanan. He and I are both from the same region. Perhaps a tribal resemblance?"

"Maybe, but it is of little matter at the present." He paused again. Then he put his hand on Johanan's shoulder. "I would learn more of this Jesus and his ways. After I visit my nearby farm, I am returning to my estate in Athens. Will you come with me and be my teacher?"

Johanan smiled. "Citizen, I would be honored to teach you, but I don't know if that is the path the Lord has chosen for me."

"I don't understand."

"I am currently discerning what he has in mind for me next. But I can make sure someone does come to teach you about our Lord and his ways."

"Tell me more."

Johanan pondered the request. "I do know there are Christians in Athens where you have your residence. In fact, I was on my way there when I stopped here for supplies." He looked down at the sand, then back up at the Magistrate. "This was supposed to be a short stopover, but I have been here for months."

Lupus laughed. "I can imagine why you would be tempted to remain here in this beautiful place rather than continue on to Athens." He removed his hand from Johanan's shoulder. "Do this for me—within three months send a messenger with another amphora of garum to my storekeeper. I will tell him to be on the lookout for it. That messenger will be my teacher, whether it is you or another."

With a wry smile, Johanan said, "Are you sure, your Excellency, this is not just a ploy to supply yourself with free fish sauce?"

Lupus threw his head back and laughed loudly. Johanan looked back down the shoreline at the waiting villagers and entourage. They were all looking intently in their direction.

"I will gladly pay double for the shipment—but I must have a teacher."

"You shall have one, Citizen. I will see to it personally."

An hour later the ship pulled up its anchor and set sail, Fabius Lupus stood at the stern and waved goodbye to the village. His anger over the events of the morning had obviously evaporated. Johanan waved back along with many of the other villagers.

Tullius walked to the edge of the water and looked down at his feet, then slowly out toward the departing ship. He repeated the motion several times. Finally Marcus asked, "What are you doing, Father?"

Tullius looked up and smiled. "I will tell you, but you must first come with me." He walked up the beach a short distance followed by his sons, Johanan, and several other curious villagers. He stopped at a pile of rocks.

"Pick up the largest one you can carry, and come with me," he said. Each of them picked up a rock, trying to outdo each other by selecting the biggest one they could carry. They grunted as they waddled back down to where they had started. Tullius dropped his on the sand at the high tide mark and motioned the others to do the same.

When they had all deposited their load, he waved out at the departing ship. "I was looking out at the water, trying to decide how long the dock will need to be for our new port. We will need one to handle all the trading vessels that will stop here." Then he waved at the pile of rocks at his feet. "You have just helped lay the foundation."

When they had all enjoyed a good laugh, the other islanders dispersed to their homes. Tullius then turned to Johanan and said, "Holy man, tell us what the magistrate wanted from you. He certainly seemed to be amused by what you had to say."

"I may tell you of that later. But right now I want to know

what happened today. What led to Solon's change of heart? He kept the secret of our faith when it might have saved his hide."

Now it was Tullius' turn to laugh. "I suspect my visit last night may have played a part in that."

"Tell us, Father," Marcus said. "What did you say to him?"

Tullius crossed his arms and gazed out at the sail of the magistrate's ship, now vanishing over the horizon. He smiled a self-satisfied smile. "We spent most of the evening talking of old times and the many games we played in our youth. We talked all night as we have not done for many years. And we drank enough wine for ten men I'm afraid." He slapped the side of his head. "I think a demon has taken up residence in there."

Then Tullius looked at Johanan and his sons with a wide grin. "Toward the morning when I was preparing to leave I said to him, 'Don't forget the story of the emperor that sends us our catch.'"

Aprius and Marcus burst out laughing. They pounded each other on the back, both of them bent over, momentarily unable to regain their composure. Johanan looked dumbfounded at the two brothers, then back at their father. "I am missing part of this tale."

Marcus managed to recover his voice first. "Do you remember when I said something about Solon making it difficult to worship the emperor? It was soon after you got to the island and we were talking about how he was strongly loyal to the gods."

Johanan wrinkled his brow. "Yes, I vaguely recall it. Aprius changed the subject quickly, as if there was something to be hidden from me."

Aprius broke in. "Yes, at that time we still didn't know you well enough to trust you with all of our secrets."

"May I continue the story, my sons?"

"Yes, Father, of course," Aprius said. Then he and Marcus burst out laughing again. They finally quieted down enough for their father to continue.

"As I was saying," Tullius said, "I reminded Solon about the emperor who sends us fish. Years ago, when my sons were just boys, we had a famine. The catch dried up. We would spend all day fishing and come home with only enough to feed a handful of our people. This went on for months. Several families that had been here for generations moved to the mainland or to other islands to feed themselves."

Marcus interrupted. "This is the best part."

Tullius grabbed his son around the neck and pulled him close. "You talk enough for two old women." Marcus squirmed away.

"I'm sorry, Father. Please continue."

"As I was saying, the emperor at that time was Domitian. We had a small bust of him so we could worship him according to his decree. Solon worshiped him as well, but his real loyalties were to the old gods. During this period of famine, we burned even more incense to the emperor asking for the fish to return. We still had no relief."

"One morning Solon loaded up his boat as usual. Then he did a strange thing. He tied the idol of the emperor in the bow of his boat along with a bowl for burning incense. All that day he burned incense and prayed to the idol while we cast our nets alongside his. As the day went on, he begged and pleaded more and more frantically for the emperor to bring us fish. We thought he was going mad."

Marcus started to speak again. Aprius placed his own hand over his younger brother's mouth.

"The catch that day was no better than those of the recent months. Finally I called for us to return home." Tullius smiled as he looked at Johanan and his sons.

"Then, Solon cut the idol loose, picked it up, and held it above his head. He yelled loud enough for the whole fleet to hear, 'If you won't bring us fish, Domitian, then you can send us fish.'" Tullius paused.

Johanan finally asked, "And?"

"Then he threw the bust into the sea. We were all shocked.

Defiling the idol was a sure death sentence for him. We returned home and didn't say anything about it."

"What happened after that?"

"Two days later the fish runs returned to their normal strength. Within months, some of the families had returned. Since then we have not paid much attention to emperor worship. If visitors notice the absence of an idol to the emperor, we tell them it was stolen and a new one is coming."

Johanan looked at Marcus with a growing smile. "That does indeed explain your comment on how Solon made worship of the emperor difficult."

Tullius said, "When I reminded Solon of that story last night, he turned as pale as the moon. He had not thought about the incident in years, but he knew if the authorities heard of it, he would grace a Roman cross, or worse."

"So you bought his silence about our worship of the Christos?"

"No. Solon may be a stubborn man but he is also a smart man. He knew a discussion of religion would bring up that part of his past. He decided that a confession and a motive that didn't pit us against him was his best option."

Tullius slapped Johanan on the shoulder. "But none of us expected you to forgive him and earn his freedom."

"I fully expected to be punished with Solon." Johanan looked at the two brothers. "It was only because of the love of your sons and other believers that we were spared scourging."

Tullius gestured his sons toward him and put one arm around each. Then they pulled Johanan in, completing the circle. Tullius began to pray, "Lord Jesus, thank you for saving our village today. Thank you for sparing my friend, Solon."

When Tullius completed his prayer of thanksgiving minutes later Johanan said. "Spread the word to all the believers: Tonight is a special night. We will celebrate the Lord's Supper.

Chapter Twenty-Seven

When the gods decide to destroy someone they usually get them to dig their own hole.

Andrew Greeley in *The Priestly Sins*

ALEXIS MARTIN CLEARED her throat. Instantly the chatter in the conference room died down. Professor Cavanaugh turned away from his conversation with a fresh faced intern and turned his attention to the director. He had noticed when Ms. Martin wanted the attention of her crew she got it. Underneath her friendly exterior lurked a shark that reacted to any challenge to her authority like blood in the water. He'd seen one staffer push his opinion a bit too hard—and be conspicuously absent at the next meeting.

Coffee cups, power drink cans and half eaten bagels littered the main table. Cavanaugh had arrived just a few minutes ago, but evidently the three writers had been there for hours. He couldn't tell if Derek, the senior writer, had slept in his clothes or just neglected to iron them. Then again, he doubted if Derek owned an iron.

"I have an important announcement—a very exciting one." She scanned the room, letting the suspense build. Cavanaugh admired how she played her small group like he played a lecture hall.

"*The Last Apostle* is going to take a change in direction." She gazed directly into Professor Cavanaugh's eyes, her thin lips in a smile that bordered on a grimace. She turned away.

"This show is going to be much more edgy than our original concept. The idea of having John roam the world acting like a secret angel or an undercover Oprah is just not going to work."

Cavanaugh swallowed. He waited to hear her out.

Alexis glanced at Cavanaugh, She turned her attention to the three writers, all sitting in a group across from her. "Think of John as—the James Bond for Jesus." She stared at them, as if daring them to challenge her. Their eyes widened, and they nodded slowly in unison. The professor wondered if their cautious support was driven by a lack of enthusiasm for the change in direction or the realization that their workload had just increased exponentially.

Martin stood and started to gesture wildly. "Imagine John is the defender of the faith, charged with intervening on God's behalf." She placed her hands, palm down on the table and leaned forward. "God said 'Vengeance is mine,' and sometimes John, The Last Apostle, is his instrument of vengeance."

Cavanaugh's throat grew dry.

Martin aimed her index finger, first at the group of writers, then she swept the room. "And because we know John was a man of passion as Professor Cavanaugh has taught us, a man with a temper. He will on occasion give way to those passions, like any man."

Cavanaugh raised his hand timidly, like a nervous schoolboy. "Ms. Martin?"

Alexis Martin sat down. "Yes, Professor. You don't approve?" The challenge was thinly, very thinly, veiled.

He lowered his hand. "What is driving this change, if I may ask?"

She smiled that barracuda smile. "I've been unhappy with the original concept since the beginning, but did my best to make it work." She leaned back in her chair. "However, the trend for the coming season appears to be suspense. Spy thriller series are the coming trend."

"But, John is known as the Apostle of Love—"

Martin rolled her eyes. "I know that. But I had a series of focus groups commissioned. We ran this concept by them and they ate it up. We may lose the fundamentalists, but we'll pick up mainstream America. I believe we'll strike gold with this change."

Cavanaugh was speechless. This was the first he had heard of these focus groups. This was far from his original idea. "Ms. Martin, you know I have the greatest respect for your reputation—"

"Good. Then you'll fully support my judgment in this matter."

The room contained nearly a dozen staffers, but it was as if Cavanaugh was the lone student looking across the desk of Martin, the school principal.

"As the executive producer of *The Last Apostle*—"

"As the executive producer, Professor Cavanaugh, you serve in primarily an advisory role." She stared him down. Cavanaugh swallowed.

She continued in a syrupy, sweet tone. "If you check your contract, Professor, you'll see I have full creative control of the show. I *insist* on that in all of my contracts." She leaned back and folded her arms. "That's one of the reasons why I have a track record of success in an industry littered with failures."

"But—"

"But you have a choice. You can remain involved with the show, provide us with historical and character background on John, and influence it within the bounds of the new vision." She placed her hand palm down on the polished table in front of her.

"Or..." she paused. Only the breathing of the staffers broke the silence. "Or, you can watch from the sidelines as an uninvolved bystander." She smiled that barracuda smile again.

Cavanaugh inhaled deeply before responding; willing his voice to sound confident. He was worried it would crack like a boy going through puberty. "Well, why don't we just all hear more about this new concept?"

Chapter Twenty-Eight

To the person who does not know where he wants to go, there is no favorable wind.

Seneca

SETH SAT ON a waterfront bench, soaking up the early afternoon June sun. The morning had been spent with the mission director and four other members of his rehab group, visiting the aquarium and doing other touristy stuff; a reward for three weeks of satisfactory progress in the program. The others were standing at a railing, tossing popcorn in the air to seagulls, which darted and wheeled through the air as they competed for the morsels.

They squawked in anger at each other for stealing the food, and at the men who were not doling out the food fast enough. Seth had joined in the fun for a few minutes and then sat down to rest. He noticed David Freeman, his counselor, glance over his shoulder periodically at him.

He slouched back against the hard wood of the bench, hoping

to catch at least a quick nap before they headed back to the mission for work duty and more classes.

"Mind if I sit here?" Seth looked up to see a stunning blonde wearing a black tank top smiling down at him. He looked her up and down, and then remembered she had just asked him a question.

"Sure." He sat up and self-consciously straightened his rumpled windbreaker.

"I haven't seen you down here before, but you don't look like a tourist."

He glanced over at the blonde. Her ice blue eyes were riveting. What was her angle? She was too clean looking to be a hooker, not to mention it was a bit early in the day to be plying that trade.

"No, I live around here." He stole another glance. God, she was amazing, almost as if she had been designed by an artist, rather than born of a woman. He noticed David glance back at him. He didn't seem to react to the blonde next to him. Was he blind or something?

"Are you with them?" She pointed at the group at the railing.

"Yeah, I guess I am."

"Friends? Family?"

"Kind of." He swallowed. "I'm in a rehab program down at the men's mission. The big guy in the brown leather jacket is the director. The other guys are in the program with me." There. It was out.

"I see." She sat in silence for a few moments. "How is that going?"

He sniffled, and almost rubbed his nose on his sleeve. He pulled his handkerchief out of his pocket, turned his head away, and wiped his nose. He stuffed the handkerchief back in his pocket before turning back to her. "It's going okay, I guess. The people at the mission are nice, and I'm feeling better."

"I see." She looked away from Seth, and to the group feeding the seagulls. "Don't they talk about God a lot down there?"

"Well, yeah. I mean, it is a mission you know."

She nodded. "I guess I never had much use for God. I mean, he takes credit for beauty like this..." She paused and waved her hand at the scene before him. Then she leaned toward him.

Seth glanced down to where her form fitting shirt met the curves of her body. Man, she was something.

"I mean, he takes credit for the great things, but ducks responsibility for the terrible things in the world: innocent babies being killed in disasters, rape, the holocaust." She turned away and sat back against the bench.

Seth sat silently.

"I mean, he could stop the wars in the Middle East if he wanted to, but he doesn't."

He nodded.

She turned her face toward him. "Do you miss the meth?" She smiled sweetly.

He turned away from her and inhaled deeply. He knew it was bad for him, but he still craved the rush. David glanced back at him. Their eyes met. David gave him a broad smile and nodded slightly. Seth gave him a weak grin. David turned back to the action at the railing.

"I know I'm better off without it, but I do miss it."

"Seth, I've seen you before. I watched you shoot up once, at a place over in West Seattle."

He turned toward her, and squinted. She didn't look familiar. How could he have missed her? A breeze off the waterfront blew her wispy hair in front of her face. She brushed it back with her delicate hand.

"I'm living alone right now, and I need someone to help protect me." She looked at him, and flashed that sweet smile again. "Someone I can trust."

He could hear his heart beating in his chest.

She reached her hand out to hold his. He hesitated, then

reached out and grasped it. The dream didn't evaporate at his touch. Her hand was warm, deliciously so.

"My name is Thea." She squeezed his hand. "Seth, do you know what an anagram is?"

"Uh, yeah. Isn't that where you take a word, mix up the letters, and come up with a new word?"

"Smart man." She reached out with her other hand, and grasped his in both of hers. "My name is an anagram—an anagram, for heat." She almost hissed the last word. Thea released him, and leaned back. She spread her arms across the back of the bench, just touching his shoulder with her left hand.

"You know, I don't have any money or nothing. I'm just a druggie in rehab."

"That's okay, Seth. I can take care of the money and other things." She gave him that syrupy smile, then pointed to the street behind them. "In about a minute, a Metro bus will pull up to the stop right there. You'll see it coming from a block away. Don't get up until it's almost here." She turned toward him, and looked straight into his eyes. This time, the smile was seductive. "Get off at the Safeco Field stop, and wait there for me."

Seth looked at David and the others. "But what about them? He'll see me go."

"Don't worry, I'll take care of them." She leaned toward him. "I need you, Seth. Don't let me down."

She stood up and pulled the hem of her tank top down. It now fit even more snugly than before. She strode toward the men at the railing. Seth's jaw dropped. From behind, she looked like a model strutting down a catwalk. His mouth went dry.

Thea reached the group and took up a position on the railing just to the left of David. She leaned up against the barrier and turned to the men. Seth saw her flash her brilliant smile at David, and ask a question. She pointed out over the water. Maybe to the Olympic Mountains? Bainbridge Island? Or something else.

David and the others all looked at her, and then out to where she was pointing.

Out of the corner of his eye, Seth saw the bus pulling up to the stop. He looked over, then back at the group at the railing. The seagulls still wheeled over them, squawking more loudly then before, as they protested this interruption to their meal. Thea was still gesturing toward the horizon, and they were looking off at something in the distance. Seth stood up and strode toward the bus.

Chapter Twenty-Nine

I am always ready to learn, but I do not always like being taught.

Sir Winston Churchill

THE EVENING OF Solon's trial, the believers on the island gathered at the pavilion for dinner. When everyone had settled down, Johanan stood and addressed them.

"I've told you before of the last supper of our Lord. I must confess that despite hearing and reading of the event many times, much of it still remains a mystery to me. Tonight we will follow his instruction on remembering Him through the bread and wine."

Johanan picked up a loaf of bread from the table in front of him and raised it up. "Lord, we share this bread in memory of you. This is his body." He broke off a small piece and bowed his head in silent prayer as he ate it. Then he broke the loaf in half and passed one part to Tullius on his left, the other to Simon on his right. In turn they followed his lead, each breaking off a piece and passing it on. They each prayed silently as they consumed it.

Johanan waited until everyone had finished the ritual and then lifted a jug of wine. "Lord, we share this wine in memory of you. This is his blood." He poured a small amount into his goblet, raised it, and then drank it. He prayed silently as he swallowed. Then he put his goblet down and picked up the jug of wine. He carried the container around, pouring a splash into the outstretched cups of the faithful. As he reached Anteia, he noticed Solon, Perpetua, Nikias, and Dagon waiting a dozen paces outside the pavilion. The four were dressed in clean himations over their tunics, not their everyday clothing but rather the more formal Greek-style mantle.

"Please serve the rest of our brothers and sisters, Anteia." He passed the jug to the young woman. She smiled back at him and took the container from him.

Johanan beckoned to Solon's family. He walked up to the head of the table and said to Tullius, "Please make room for our honored guests." Tullius scooted those near him down enough to make room for his old friend and his family.

Johanan retrieved the remnant of the loaf he had broken earlier and broke off a piece. "This is his body," he said to Nikias, holding it aloft. Nikias nodded and took it, bowing his head in prayer as he slowly ate it.

Anteia arrived with the jug of wine and hesitated. She gave Johanan a quizzical look. He pointed to Nikias' goblet. Then he waved his hand over those of Solon and the rest of his family, while shaking his head. She poured and he repeated the ritual he had observed being carried out.

Johanan looked at the village leader. "Tullius, would you please lead us in the Lord's Prayer?"

Tullius nodded and stood. He waited until he had everyone's attention and then led the community in a recitation. When he finished, he bowed to Johanan and sat back down.

Johanan gestured to those gathered in the pavilion. "My brothers and sisters," he paused and looked at Solon, Perpetua, and Dagon, "and our honored guests—let us eat." The solemnity of the reenactment of the last supper gave way to jovial feasting.

As the meal was drawing to a close Solon stood and cleared his throat. He gestured to Perpetua and Dagon to stand. Then he addressed the reclining Johanan. "We are ready."

Johanan stood to face the family. "Why do you make this choice?"

"Tullius is fond of saying I am a stubborn but smart man."

Tullius interrupted. "That is why I sent you to negotiate our contract for the garum. I knew you'd be smart enough to find out what the value should be, and too stubborn to give in to the buyer's demands." The other villagers joined in the laughter. Tullius raised his goblet. "To Solon."

Solon waited until the tribute was over. "Despite the evidence and Nikias' persuasive arguments, I resisted your Christos. But it wasn't until today, when the one I had harmed," he looked at Johanan, "and the one who accused me," he nodded to Aprius, "were willing to forgive me and stand by me, that I could no longer resist the truth." He paused and looked around at his fellow villagers. "The time for the old gods is past. We wish to worship the true God with you."

Johanan led them down to the shore where he removed his tunic. He said to Nikias, "You too, my brother." The five of them waded out until they were waist deep. He gestured for Perpetua and Nikias to come out into deeper water with him.

"Perpetua, in the name of our Lord and Savior, Jesus the Christos, I baptize you." He gently pushed down on the woman, who stayed under only briefly and then came up gasping.

"Thank you, for saving my husband today." She embraced Johanan.

He said, "My sister, your sins are forgiven. Love the Lord your

God with all of your heart, all of your soul, all of your mind, and all of your strength. And love your neighbor as you love yourself." He kissed her on each cheek. "Now go forth and show the love of the Christos as we did for your husband."

She held her son in her arms briefly and then waded back to the shore. Johanan waved Dagon out. They repeated the ritual with Nikias' brother. As he waded back to his mother, Solon came out to stand before Johanan.

"Solon, Jesus said the good shepherd would leave ninety-nine sheep to find the precious one that was lost. All that has unfolded here has helped you find the voice of your true master. Today is a great day in Heaven and in this village."

Solon nodded. "You are the one who didn't give up on me, holy man."

When they had completed his baptism, the village healer threw one arm around his son's neck and the other around Johanan's. Together they walked side by side back up to the beach.

Tullius met them and escorted them back to the pavilion where they dried off and put their himations back on. As some of the villagers started to get ready to return to their homes, Tullius announced, "Please, before you go, we must share another goblet of wine, because I have important news for us all. On a day like this it is too early to end the feast."

The community settled back in for more festivities. After Tullius had waited long enough to pique their interest, he stood in his accustomed spot at the head of the pavilion.

"My brothers and sisters, today has indeed been an auspicious one. Our friend Solon was shown mercy by the empire, thanks to the example of Johanan, Aprius, Nikias, and all of us who are learning to live as the Christos would have us." He raised his goblet and took a long draught.

"We were once united as a community. Now that Solon and

his family have joined us as believers, we are united as brothers and sisters in the Way." Again he raised his goblet in tribute.

He stood in silence until he had everyone's attention. Finally, he said, "I have two important announcements to share with you tonight. As you know, we have successfully launched our trade in garum. If the reaction of the brother of the propraetor is any indication, we will soon be famous throughout the empire and will sell all we can make." Nods of agreement rippled through the crowd.

"To service our trade we will need a proper dock. Today, several of you laid the footing for the pier to help us to transfer our goods to the ships that will call on our humble island." Tullius pointed to the small mound of rocks down the beach from their pavilion. "Building a suitable port will not be easy or fast. I ask each of you for your help." Johanan could see most of the villagers had a quizzical look on their faces.

"Beginning tomorrow each able bodied man should carry one cart load of stone for himself and each member of his family every day." He looked over at Johanan. "Except of course, for the Lord's Day. We want the blessing of the Christos on this plan." He turned his attention back to the gathered crowd. "You will notice of course, there seems to be plenty of rock available on our island." The villagers laughed.

"As we deposit our loads from the foundation out into the harbor, our pier will begin to grow. We will also have help from ships that deposit their ballast rock so they can take on our garum. It will take much time." He looked around at his fellow villagers, nodding in agreement. "But we have been here for centuries, and will be here for many, many more."

Solon stood and raised his goblet. "To the pier, and the wisdom of our leader." Tullius nodded in acknowledgement as the villagers drank in honor of his idea.

When they were finished, he waited again for their attention.

"I now have an even more important announcement." He

looked at Johanan, who was reclining next to Marcus. "Many, many months ago a stranger with bad navigational skills found his way to our island." The islanders chortled at this reminder of Johanan's admission of how he had wound up among them.

"During that time he has taught us of the one true God through his words and deeds, been miraculously healed from a grievous wound, and become our true friend." Murmurs of agreement interrupted Tullius. Those close to Johanan clapped him on the shoulder and on his back.

"While our community has always been a close and peaceful one, we have now become brothers and sisters in the Way. We are united in life and beyond, thanks to Johanan."

Johanan felt uncomfortable at all this attention. He shifted nervously as he sensed Tullius was building to something.

Tullius breathed deeply and smiled at the holy man. "Although Johanan is not from our land, he has become one of us. I would like to make those ties even stronger." He scanned the crowd, making them wait. Finally, he returned his gaze to the apostle. "Tonight, Johanan, I offer you one of my greatest treasures." He paused and tipped his goblet toward him. "I offer you a most precious possession—the hand of my daughter, Anteia."

Chapter Thirty

Bad news goes about in clogs, good news in stockinged feet.

Welsh Proverb

"JOHN, I AM sorry. Seth was there one minute, and then he was gone. He never gave me a hint he might try to escape."

John inhaled deeply, exhaled slowly. He leaned back in his chair and looked up at David, who was standing in the doorway to John's office. In very even tones he said, "Do you have any idea where he might have gone?"

"No, he could have run off into the crowd, ducked into a shop, or even jumped on a ferry or bus. It happened so quickly."

"Have you notified the police yet?"

"Not yet. I was hoping he'd turn up." David sighed. "I should have known better."

"Better call them now."

John's phone rang. He looked at the display and nodded at David. "Let me take this. It's Nicole."

David stepped out into the hallway to make his own call.

"Hi, Nicole."

"John. Where are you?" Her voice was cold, icy cold.

"In my office down at the mission. What's—"

"Don't move. I'll be there in ten minutes." She hung up.

John stared at the phone. In the month since she had taken over the foundation, she had brought order out of chaos and brought them closer to being ready to deploy their clean water technology to Africa. He had learned to trust her and even turned over the information for the Cayman accounts to her.

On a personal basis, she had warmed to him quickly and he found himself drawn to her. She was beautiful, smart, and funny. He had struggled to keep his personal distance—to make sure she didn't think that their relationship could go beyond just friendship. But the tone in her voice just now was that of a mother ready to scold a child.

Out in the hall he could hear David reporting Seth's disappearance.

Nicole ran up the steps to John's office on the third floor. David was standing in the hallway, just putting his phone away. He smiled as he saw her.

She brushed past him.

She inhaled in an effort to catch her breath before speaking. She glared at John. He gave her a quizzical look.

She waved the envelope containing the Royal Caribbean bank account information at him. "I just got off the phone with the bank. Do you know what they told me?"

He shook his head slowly.

"There have been some *discrepancies* at the bank and your account is frozen. Did you know about this when you asked me to take on this job?"

John looked at her wide-eyed, then shook his head. "No. It can't be. Everything is in order."

"Can I see that?" David was standing next to her, hand held out for the envelope.

She slapped it into his hand.

She leaned forward on the desk. "You promise me that you knew nothing about this? I was warned that your finances were fishy and now this happens."

"Nicole, last I checked everything was fine. I haven't even looked at the account since my advisor passed away."

Nicole stood up and crossed her arms across her chest. She looked at the ceiling in an effort to keep tears from spilling out of her eyes. Wouldn't Dan like to see her now.

"Look at this." David waved his phone. "Royal Caribbean Bank is being investigated by Cayman Island authorities. It happened just a few days ago."

"Let me see that." Nicole snatched the phone out of David's hands and scanned the article he had retrieved. *Royal Caribbean Bank under investigation…all accounts frozen…Bank President missing and believed to have fled the country…*

She sank down into the chair across from John. "I'm sorry I got mad at you. This was such a shock." She sighed deeply.

"I had such big plans." She looked up at him. From his blank stare he was still taking it all in. She imagined what Dan would say. Could see him smirking at her predicament. Her voice cracked as she said, "Now, I'm not sure what to do."

Chapter Thirty-One

Make your life a mission—not an intermission.

Arnold Glasgow

ON SATURDAY EVENING, Nicole sat in an overstuffed chair in the lobby of the Lake Union Marriott Courtyard, scrolling through email on her phone. Out of the corner of her eye she saw a car pull in and looked up. It was a dark green, Jetta—long overdue for a wash. John smiled at her from the driver's seat. Nicole gave him a sad smile, as if she was looking at a man heading to the gallows. She slipped the phone into her purse and stood up. As she strode toward the door, John came around to the passenger door and opened it for her.

John gave her a wry smile. He bowed ceremoniously and, like the coachman of a princess, waved her toward her seat.

As John slid into the driver's seat, Nicole said, "On the 'good news' front I just got an email from Susan in West Ghana. She's been set up with a good village to be the first site for making filter plants. I just gave our supplier orders to ship the goods."

"You sure that's a good idea—given the situation with the bank?"

"I'm working on ways to bring in money. And the bills won't come due for a month."

John exhaled sharply. "Talk about walking in faith."

She nodded. "I'm sorry that I accused you of hiding the problems with the bank from me. It was just such a surprise."

"My fault." He ground the gears as he downshifted to head up a hill. "I should have paid more attention to what was going on."

She reached over and touched his forearm. "It would really help if you could open up with me about the source of the money. Especially after this incident."

John looked her in the eye, briefly. "I wish I could, but I made a solemn pledge. All I can tell you is it has nothing to do with why the bank is under investigation."

"I guess I should be happy knowing that you can keep a secret. Although I pride myself on being able to pry them out of almost anybody."

Nicole reached up and tucked a loose section of the headliner back under the loose trim.

"I've never been in your car before. It's, uh, nice."

"You don't have to be polite. It's basic transportation. What I like to call 'two keys and a heater,' and sometimes the heater conks out."

As they chugged up the incline he said, "The church is only a few miles away, but the hill is a killer. You might want to pray the Jetta makes it."

She laughed.

They rode in silence for a moment. Then John asked, "What do you drive?"

"Beamer. Bought it with my first big bonus check. Spends most its time garaged."

He grunted in acknowledgement.

The car stalled once on an uphill section, but just a few minutes later they pulled into an open spot on a side street a few blocks from St. Anne's. As they walked toward the entrance of the century-old Catholic church, Nicole grabbed his arm for comfort and pulled him close, much as she had nearly four months ago on a jetway at the San Francisco airport. He glanced down at her in surprise, but didn't pull away.

"I don't understand this. I thought you were a Protestant. This is a Catholic church."

He shook his head. "I'm not a Catholic, nor a Protestant. I don't worship Christianity. I worship Christ."

"I should have figured you'd be a radical." She released him and cocked one eye. "What church did you go to when you were growing up?"

John smiled. "It was very different."

As they entered, she noticed that the altar that graced the center of the church sat on a raised, round platform. The two steps leading up to the dais were made of a light colored limestone. The floors throughout the church were a polished concrete. No money wasted here on a carpet. The space echoed with voices talking in quiet whispers and the sound of shoes on the hard floor.

John led her into one of the pews furthest from the altar. As they took their seats, Nicole rapped on the wooden seat with her knuckles. "Would be nice if they could invest in some padding."

He grunted and opened up the hymnal.

The children's choir, outfitted in red and white robes, traipsed in and started to set up. Each was carrying a folding wooden chair, except for the smallest girl, a redhead with a liberal smattering of freckles. A boy next to her, who had a strong family resemblance, was carrying two chairs.

Nicole elbowed John. "They're so cute, just like a herd of puppies." He turned to her and gave her a weak smile.

As they stood for the opening music, she looked over her

shoulder at the priest and his small retinue processing up the aisle. He had bronzed skin and jet black hair.

She leaned over and whispered to John. "Hispanic?"

He nodded and whispered back. "Mexican. Moved here from Cozumel as a kid."

As the priest took his position at the altar, she leaned over again. "He's kind of cute."

John smirked. "He's not available." He pointed to the words in the hymnal. They both joined in the opening song.

When the priest began the mass, his lightly accented English enchanted Nicole. As he made his opening remarks his bright white smile and gaze washed over the entire congregation as if he was a loving shepherd who had been reunited with his flock.

He introduced himself as Father Domingo Da'Silva but said everyone called him "Father D." When he mentioned the topic of his homily that night would be on Padre Pio, a Capuchin priest and mystic who had passed away in 1968, John elbowed Nicole. "This is quite the coincidence."

She whispered. "How's that?"

"It just is."

She pushed him away. "Enough with the riddles. I'm getting annoyed with you." She glanced up at him. A self-satisfied smirk graced his face.

As Father D began his homily, he wandered around the altar in the center of the church, first talking to one section then the other. He spoke without notes, waving his arms in wider arcs as he grew more passionate. Several times he came dangerously close to knocking over the candle stands. Nicole leaned over to John and said, "They should take away his wireless mike. He really needs to be chained to the podium." John chuckled but quickly turned his attention back to the talk.

Father D had just finished giving some background on Padre

Pio and how he had exhibited the stigmata, the wounds of Christ, from 1918 until shortly before his death.

"When Padre Pio first began bleeding from his hands, his feet, and his side, just as the crucified Christ did, it was investigated as a fraud." Father D reverently pointed to his own hand, feet, and side. To make sure he made his point he stepped around to the other side of the altar and repeated the gesture.

"Soon enough the Padre began to exhibit other signs he might be a modern day prophet." Father D told of how Padre Pio had identified Polish Bishop Karol Wojtyla as a future Pope. Sure enough, in 1978 the bishop was elected Pope John Paul II.

It was a chilly day in May, 1952 and John was standing in line for the early morning service at the church in San Giovanni Rotondo. He had read a newspaper account of the controversial Padre Pio, who was building a hospital in a small Italian town located in rolling hills above the Adriatic. The Capuchin priest had supposedly suffered from the stigmata since the waning days of World War I. The article detailed miracles and prophecies attributed to the padre, as well as comments from his legion of detractors. Archbishops, theologians, and doctors had declared him a fraud.

Over the millennia, John had exposed more than one charlatan who abused their position as a leader of the faithful for their own gain. He thought it was time to check out the padre.

The line for the five a.m. service began to assemble around four in the morning. Even though it was a weekday, John was surrounded by a large crowd of pilgrims there to see the mystic. When the massive doors finally creaked open, he seated himself in one of the back pews of the crowded church.

The mass seemed to flow normally with nothing out of sorts except for the density of the crowd. When time came for communion, John joined the line inching forward to receive the Eucharist. As each participant reached the head of the line, they took the next available spot to kneel at the rail surrounding the altar.

When John himself reached the head of the line he knelt at an empty place along the rail. The padre was working his way up and down the railing intoning in a regular cadence, "Corpus Christi," Latin for "Body of Christ" as he gave communion to the faithful.

When the padre reached John's spot on the rail, he lifted up the host to present it—and the cadence stopped. He looked straight into John's eyes with his mouth frozen open. John sat there with his mouth open and tongue extended to receive the Eucharist. The people on either side of John looked over to see what had caused the halt in the ritual. John remained in position, mouth open like a baby robin waiting to be fed.

The gray bearded priest seemed to regain his composure. He started to say, "Corpus—" halted again, and finally completed the ritual. "Corpus Christi."

John responded in Latin with, "My Lord and my God." The padre slowly and deliberately placed the Eucharist on John's tongue, paused, and then finally moved on to the next person on the rail. John stood, crossed himself, and returned to his seat.

When the padre had finished communion he beckoned to a brown robed friar in one of the front rows. John could see the padre gesturing in John's direction. The friar looked back toward John and nodded. John slouched down in the pew so he would be harder to see. The mass continued.

At the end of the service, John suddenly found the friar at his elbow. "Signor," he said in Italian, "Padre Pio would like to hear your confession."

John looked back at the brother with a wide-eyed look on his face. "Sprechen Sie Deutsche, Padre?"

The friar repeated his request in passable German. John nodded. The monk beckoned and headed off to the confessional. John stood up and froze. He wanted to flee out the main doors, but felt like a moth dashing into a candle flame. He sensed danger, but couldn't tear himself away. He followed the brown robed brother.

The friar led him to a booth like confessional. "You are very fortunate, mein Herr. People usually wait two weeks to be able to give their confessions to Padre Pio." When the door opened he waved John forward.

John kneeled and closed the door. He was separated from the padre by a screen and thin panel. When the divider slid aside, John began with the traditional, "Bless me, Father, for I have sinned—"

The priest interrupted him in whispered Italian, "Johanan, Apostle, Beloved Disciple, it is you!"

John was stunned. He hesitated for a moment and then protested, in German, "In Deutsche, bitte."

Silence from the other side of the divider.

John broke the silence. "I am Johannes Fischer from Germany. I just—"

The padre interrupted him. "Enough. I *know* who you are, *Johanan son of Zebedee*."

John sat, dumbfounded.

After a few moments the padre stated, "You must accumulate a large fortune because He has need of it. Save money for a great purpose. Do you understand, his Beloved Disciple?"

John almost protested, then stopped. The padre had given these instructions not in Italian—but in ancient Aramaic.

"But I am not skilled in the ways of money. I never have been."

Again, in Aramaic: "He has need of a fortune and has chosen you to accumulate it. You will be the steward of these riches. Do you understand?"

"I understand, brother, but—"

Pio interrupted, "Our Lord is pleased with you and your work. You will reach even more people for Him when you are ready. Now go." He slid the divider shut to signal the session was ended.

"But Padre," John protested.

Padre Pio switched to Italian. "Brother Garrido." John could hear the divider on the other side of the confessional open. The pilgrim on that side began the ritual with, "Bless me, Father, for..."

The friar who had escorted John earlier pulled the door open and beckoned to him. "Come young man, others wait their turn."

John spent half an hour walking through the village while he waited for the hour-long bus ride to Foggia where he would catch the train. He passed the construction site of the hospital. The planned "Home to Relieve Suffering" was still several years away from opening. John himself had been behind more than one such institution, but had always depended on others, or divine intervention, to provide the funds. Now it looked like he was being called to provide the money for a future mission.

On the homeward bound train John sat down in an empty compartment. As the train was pulling out, a neatly dressed man with a well-used trunk and leather valise rushed in. He nodded at John and hung his jacket on a hook. The afternoon was already warm and the man had loosened the sleeves of his shirt. As he pushed his trunk onto the overhead rack, John noticed his bared arm. It sported a six-digit tattoo with a triangle. He sat down and opened the leather valise and pulled out a ledger. He was soon engrossed in work.

As the train picked up speed the clack of the train wheels on the tracks settled into a soothing rhythm. John watched his companion tally figures. After a few minutes, he glanced up at John.

John asked, "Auschwitz?"

He nodded slowly.

"I was there too."

The two looked at each other across the compartment like brothers who shared a horrible secret that could never be spoken of. John reached out his hand and said in German, "Johannes Fischer."

"Franz. Franz Wallenberg."

"Herr Wallenberg." John nodded at the ledger in Franz's hands. "You work with money?"

"*Ja*. I am a banker in Geneva."

"Do you help people accumulate wealth?"

Wallenberg's eyes grew wide as if he had been wrongly accused of giving a nun a black eye. "Why do you ask?"

John nodded and smiled. "*Mein Freund*, it is no mistake you sat in my car."

He flashed forward to the night in early May when Franz's daughter Greta had called from San Francisco to tell him of his old friend's death. He recalled meeting Nicole on the flight down to meet with Greta. He smiled as he remembered some of the stories he had shared with Greta. But of course he had never told Franz, nor Greta, how they had come to be seated in the same train compartment. Many things had transpired between "Johannes" and Franz since that afternoon on a northbound Italian train, but it was only a microscopic slice out of the life of the Last Apostle.

John was snapped out of his reminiscence by a collective gasp from the congregation. Father D had indeed finally given a candle stand a glancing blow. A quick thinking altar server stepped forward and grabbed it as it tottered.

Father D helped the acolyte reposition the candle and then turned around to face everyone. With a sheepish expression on his face he said, "Maybe I should tie myself down and conclude this homily." The audience chuckled.

He walked to the podium that stood on the opposite side of the altar from where Nicole and John sat. He stepped behind it, stretched his arms wide, and then with great drama, firmly grasped it with both hands. "There, how's that."

A ripple of chuckles rolled through the congregation.

"In conclusion, when someone tells you Christianity is a dying religion, you can tell them about people who live our faith and make the world better. People like the Reverend Martin Luther King, who was Reverend King before he was Doctor King. A man who championed the cause of racial justice in our country. Mother Theresa, who cared for the poor in the face of tremendous odds in India."

Father D had started to gesture again. He stopped and placed both hands firmly on the podium again and made a great production of gripping it firmly. He looked over at the pair of altar servers. "Don't worry, you're safe." The congregation broke out in laughter.

"Also remember Padre Pio—a spiritual man who experienced the stigmata, built a hospital to ease the suffering of others, and was named a saint in 2002. A simple man from simple beginnings who chose to share the love of Jesus Christ and make the world better."

John muttered, "Amen to that."

Nicole leaned over. "What did you say?"

"Just agreeing with Father D."

Chapter Thirty-Two

I don't know what the future may hold, but I know who holds the future.

Ralph Abernathy

THE WEDDING FEAST of Anteia, daughter of Tullius and Thais, and Johanan of Galilee was a joyous affair. It combined the local customs of the island, traditions brought from the Jewish culture of the groom, and emerging rituals of the early Christian church. The feasting and tributes extended far into the evening with no sign that they would let up before the sun rose.

Anteia was dressed in a himation woven of fine wool and dyed a light violet. Johanan noted it was pinned at her shoulders using two polished bronze brooches in such a way as to leave her shoulders bare. As she moved, the gown flowed easily around her well-formed figure. Her hair was braided and coiled into an elaborate knot on the back of her head. A loose strand teased the back of her bare neck. She laughed easily and displayed a confidence Johanan had never seen in her before. He spent the evening stealing glances at the young woman he had married earlier that day.

Finally, Johanan decided he'd had enough of the celebration. He caught the eye of his new bride. She met his gaze for a moment, then blushed and turned away. Then she smiled shyly back at him, without flinching, the depths of her love evident in her glistening blue eyes.

Johanan gestured with his chin in the direction of the beach. She nodded slowly. He quietly stood and stepped outside the pavilion, not noticed by the revelers. She waited a few moments, and then joined him just outside the range of the torchlight. He took her hand in his and led her up the beach to the head of a trail leading to the honeymoon tent set up for them the day before.

The moon was bright enough that he could follow the sandy path without a torch. From the voices he could still hear emanating from the pavilion, their absence hadn't been noticed.

Ten minutes later, they reached the tent that had been pitched, appropriately, on the site of one of her father's secret spots for wrestling training. Johanan pulled back the flap and tied it open. He took Anteia's hand again and entered. The moonlight from outside lit the interior only dimly. Johanan sat on a stool and used a flint and steel to light a small pile of tinder on a clay plate. The nervous groom took several minutes to complete a routine task that should have taken only a moment. His bride stood next to the door and nervously giggled.

Finally the tinder was burning and he lit several clay oil lamps. He untied the door flap and let it close. The interior of the tent was now dimly lit, with shadows from the light of lamps flickering on the woolen fabric walls.

Johanan stepped up to Anteia, who looked down at the sandy floor. She turned her face up to meet his gaze. He put his hands gently on her shoulders and then softly kissed her.

"Anteia, my darling, I never thought I would marry, and I certainly never expected it to be someone of such rare beauty."

"I never expected to have such a prize in a husband. It was worth waiting for you."

He kissed her softly again. Then she stepped back and said. "Turn around." He turned, the vision of her sly smile burned into his mind.

He could hear the rustling of her garments as she removed them. He was tempted to turn but resisted. Instead he closed his eyes and gave silent thanks of praise for this day. He couldn't believe that he was going to be a first time bridegroom at one hundred years of age.

He heard the sound of blankets being pulled back and the creaking of the wedding bed as his new bride lay down; then the rustling of bedding.

"You may turn around now."

Slowly he turned to face her. She lay in the bed with blankets up around her bare shoulders. Her hair was now loose and cascaded across the side of her face and across her throat. Anteia's clothing was laid neatly across a stool at the foot of the bed. Johanan stepped slowly across the tent and sat down on the edge of the bed. He stroked her bare shoulder.

"Shouldn't you put out the lamps, Johanan?"

He smiled. "And deprive myself of such a lovely sight?"

She blushed again.

He pulled the blankets down slowly until they were just above her hips. Her right arm was across her breasts, covering them to preserve a modicum of her modesty for another moment. Her blush deepened as her husband's gaze took in her face and then her body. Johanan slowly stroked her arm from the shoulder down to her elbow, repeatedly, as he prolonged the moment. He leaned over to kiss her.

"JOHANAN," a voice commanded. It echoed around him as if from a large chamber. He looked up, to the roof of the tent.

"JOHANAN!" It was behind him. He turned in the direction of the voice. The wall of the tent was gone. Instead he saw the opening of the empty tomb of Jesus, just as he had seen it that Sunday morning seven decades ago. The stone that had sealed the door was to the side. Now it was bathed in moonlight instead of the light of the morning sun.

"Johanan, my Beloved Disciple," the familiar voice echoed from the tomb. "Someday, yes, but not here, not now."

Johanan sat bolt upright in bed, panting heavily. The moonlight lit the roof of Tullius' stable where he had been sleeping.

"Bad dream?" Marcus said in a sleepy voice.

Johanan looked around. His breathing slowed. "A dream, yes."

Aprius turned over to face Johanan. "Was it about our sister?"

He paused. "Yes, some of it."

Aprius pulled himself up on one elbow. "Before long, you will be her husband, and she will turn into yet another nagging wife. Then your real nightmares will start. Remember my words, brother."

Marcus chuckled. Then he asked, "Johanan, did you have any idea my father would make that offer to you tonight, about Anteia?"

Johanan settled back down on his bedding between the two brothers. "Not in a hundred years."

Chapter Thirty-Three

The mind is not a vessel to be filled but a fire to be kindled.

Plutarch

JOHN GRIPPED THE door handle of the Mekong Noodle Palace. He hesitated and turned to Nicole, who was towing a burgundy colored suitcase.

"You sure we should be eating out given the situation with the bank?"

She nodded. "We're not at the point where we need to live under a bridge and dine on squirrel." She flashed a confident smile. "And, I have a solution to discuss with you."

He pulled the door open. As they entered, the hostess greeted John warmly and escorted them to a table of honor. In the few seconds it took to seat them, she chatted with Nicole. "You with very special person."

"Kim, that's enough."

"John, you always so modest. I have to do all bragging for

you." She escorted them to a booth in back and headed off to her next customer.

John pushed his menu aside. "You said you have a plan?"

Nicole pointed to the menu. "You're the regular here. What do you recommend? And don't forget I have to catch my flight."

"The pho with local Dungeness crab is the house specialty."

"Hmmm. Noodle soup. Sounds a little messy for someone wearing a white blouse."

When Kim returned John ordered the fried rice with pork. Nicole selected spring rolls. When Kim had poured tea for them and headed back to the kitchen Nicole said, "I did say I have a plan."

"You mean beyond keeping your blouse clean?"

She smirked. "Funny guy." She tapped her fingers on the table. "We need to go public."

John raised an eyebrow.

"We don't know how long our Cayman money is going to be locked up. I've looked into loans, venture capital—all of those will take too long. We need money fast, and more than we can raise off of credit cards."

"And of course drug deals are also off the table."

She poked him in the forearm. "Of course." Then she leaned forward. "But if we go public with our cause in a dramatic manner, we can raise the money we need through donations on our website."

John looked intently at his tea and took a sip, as if she wasn't there.

Finally she broke the silence. "Look, John, I know you're a private person, but this is about our cause and the foundation, not about you. And right now we need a quick infusion of capital to get us through this crisis."

He looked away from his tea and returned her gaze. She stopped for a second, gazing into his deep brown eyes. She marshaled her argument. "We have some real breakthrough technology that can make a huge difference. But we need money and we need it fast."

He nodded, and took another sip of his tea.

"Who knows how long it will be before the problem with the Royal Caribbean Bank is sorted out. If we go public, we can get more people, money, and countries behind us."

He nodded. "I get it, but I'm not sure we're ready."

"Look, millions of men, women and children die each year because they don't have access to clean water. Every day we delay means more people lost—including a lot of children."

Kim arrived with their orders. She fussed over John and extracted a promise to visit her brother Matt before he left. Their conversation interrupted, Nicole inhaled the aroma of her spring rolls.

"This smells heavenly."

"Play your cards right and I'll introduce you to the cook after we eat."

Nicole looked across the table at John. He was the type of guy you might, or might not, look back at if you passed him on the street. But she found herself drawn to him.

She said, "I notice you're very good with your chopsticks."

"Good for a guy from the Mediterranean you mean?"

"Good for a native even. I've traveled to Japan for work but never got the hang of them. Have you spent much time in Asia?"

"Among other places."

She dug her fork into her dish, and paused. "Back to my proposal."

John nodded. He lifted his chopsticks back to his mouth.

Nicole bit her lower lip. His silence infuriated her. "I know you don't like this, but part of the story is you."

He raised an eyebrow.

"Your refugee to riches background is a great human element which could really help us break the story."

His eyes flared with anger. "Absolutely not." He dropped his chopsticks. Nicole sat back in her seat, surprised at his reaction. The anger faded from his face.

"I'm sorry, but if we do this, I can't be part of the story." He picked up his chopsticks.

What is this guy hiding? She leaned forward. "Can I ask why?"

He finished chewing his mouthful of pork. "Look, you know there's a lot of pain in my past. I don't want to relive that—especially in the press. That part of my life must remain private." He gave her a pleading look. "Please, respect that."

She nodded slowly. "Okay, I get it. But what about the idea of the foundation going public?"

He frowned. "I need to think about it."

In an alley a block away, Seth adjusted his fake beard using a small hand mirror.

"Hurry," Thea said. "He went in there nearly half an hour ago. You'll miss out on this chance if you take too long."

"I'm hurrying, I'm hurrying." He pulled the watch cap down over his head and put on a pair of battered sunglasses. He pulled the pistol out of his pocket and pulled back the action like Thea had shown him. It was now loaded and ready to fire.

"Take the safety off." Seth clicked it. The gun was ready to bark death.

They walked down the street toward the Mekong Noodle Palace.

"Remember, if you pull the gun on the hostess, John will move to protect her. If you shoot him, it will look like a botched robbery. No one will pin it on you."

"How do you know all these things, Thea? You seem to know a lot."

Thea looked back at Seth. Her perfect teeth and smile looked like they'd be more at home on a supermodel than on a fellow meth addict. The blonde hair and high cheekbones completed the picture of a woman who should be in magazine advertisements, rather than planning a crime.

"I just observe things. Then I use them to take care of my friends." She looked ahead and pointed to the restaurant just a half block away.

"There it is. You can't miss it. Remember, the hostess station is straight ahead. John will be seated to your right. When you pull the gun he'll move and you empty the whole clip into him."

Seth shuddered at the scene running through his mind. He shook his head, "No, this is a bad idea."

She grabbed him by the front of his shirt and pulled his face close for a passionate kiss. Then she stepped back. "It's the only way to keep you out of jail. He's the only witness available. The girl won't come back from Brazil just for the trial."

Seth looked at the ground. She lifted his chin so he looked directly into her eyes.

"I'll wait for you back in the alley. Then we'll make our getaway to my father's house."

He stared into her icy blue eyes for a long moment. "Why don't you come with me?"

"John will recognize me. He'll know something is up. Besides," she stroked Seth's beard, "you're the only one with a disguise."

Thea pointed to the Noodle Palace and gave Seth a kiss on the cheek. "You can do this. It will be over in a few minutes. Then your troubles will be gone."

She gently pushed Seth toward his quarry. The meth head trudged toward the restaurant. He fingered the trigger of the gun in his pocket and looked over his shoulder at Thea. She was already heading down the street toward the alley at a fast trot with her blonde mane whipping behind her.

Nicole opened her fortune cookie and pulled out the slip of paper. "Oh, listen to this: it says 'Remember three months from this date. Good things are in store for you.'" She waved it at him. "As if I believe in this junk." She ate half the cookie and put the rest back on the plate. "What does yours say?"

John tore open the plastic bag, pulled out the cookie and cracked it open. As he read the slip. the smile faded from his face. Printed in red block letters was "GO SEE MATT NOW." John flipped over the paper. On the back in the same typeface was, "NOW!"

Was this a gag by Kim? But the cookie was one of those that came in a sealed plastic bag.

He slipped the fortune into his pocket, pulled out his wallet, and laid cash on top of the bill. "You said you'd like to meet the cook?" Nicole was dusting crumbs off of her jacket.

"Maybe it would be better some other time." She picked up the napkin and touched it to the corner of her mouth. John reached over and firmly grabbed her hand.

"We have time if we go quickly." He grabbed her carry on suitcase and yanked her up to her feet. She barely had time to grab her purse as John pulled her toward the kitchen doors.

Seth hesitated on the sidewalk in front of the Noodle Palace. His heart started to race. Thea was right. He needed to do this. Otherwise he'd be going to jail. He couldn't handle that. If John was dead, there would be no witnesses.

He adjusted his sunglasses and the watch cap. He fingered the gun in his right pocket. He walked up to the door and pulled it open.

John pushed his way through the kitchen door with Nicole behind him. A big Vietnamese man in his mid-twenties looked up from behind the prep table. His muscular body looked like it would be more at home in a gym than in a kitchen.

"John, Kim tell me you here."

John released Nicole's hand. She moved from her trailing position to stand beside him.

"Matt, I only have a few minutes. I wanted to introduce you to a new friend, Nicole Logan."

Matt wiped his hands on a towel and came out from behind the prep table to shake her hand. "Welcome to my kitchen. John's friend is my friend."

Then he turned to John, embraced him in a big bear hug and lifted him off the ground with a grunt.

"You need come by more often. We miss you." He dropped John to the ground.

John gestured to Nicole after Matt released him. "Nicole is working with me on the Water of Life project."

Matt turned his attention to Nicole. "Are you scientist?"

She laughed. "No, I'm a project manager. I'm just good at bringing order out of chaos. I leave the science to the smart people."

John put his hand on Nicole's shoulder. "We've created a foundation to manage the project. Nicole is the president."

Matt grasped Nicole's hand in both of his. "What John is doing very important. He need someone like you to help." He waved at John. "He no good with numbers. He always leave too big a tip."

Nicole smiled warmly at the affable cook. "Tell me, Matt, how did you come to be John's friend?"

Matt's laughter filled the noisy kitchen. "I try to rob him one night. He take my gun and turn me in to the police. Then next day he bail me out of jail."

She raised her eyebrow at Matt, and then turned to John. "Really? I never knew about this side of you."

John gave her a distracted smile.

"Of course, he bail me out on condition I get a job and become good citizen."

Nicole looked at the muscular cook and then back at the slightly built John. "How did *you* disarm *this* man?"

Matt said, "John master of Kung Fu. One time he joke with me and tell me he the one who first teach Chinese martial arts."

John smiled at Nicole. "Both Matt and I have been known to tell tall tales."

Matt walked over and put his arm around John. "He like my big brother, help me go to culinary art school, and never give up on me."

John said, "It won't help to put Nicole in tears with your sappy story, Matt. She has to catch a flight."

The big cook walked back over to Nicole, "You help John change the world. He need someone like you."

Nicole reached out to shake Matt's hand. "Enough of this mutual admiration society. I need to get to the airport or I'll miss my flight."

Matt beckoned to Nicole and John and opened the back door.

"Go to end of alley and then right on the street. Light rail station just two block down." Again he took Nicole's hands in both of his. "Remember. John need you."

Seth walked into the restaurant. The hostess looked up with a smile. Her friendly expression quickly faded and was replaced with a look of concern.

"One for lunch?" she asked.

Seth ignored her question and looked over to his right, his finger nervously stroking the trigger of the gun in his pocket. That side of the restaurant looked almost full. He slowly scanned the tables. No John. He looked again. Thea said he would be there. She was rarely wrong about anything. He pulled his sunglasses down to get a better look.

"Would you like a seat, sir?" the hostess asked. Her polite tone had been replaced by a chilly one.

He glanced at her quickly, then over to the left side. No John there either. He looked back at the hostess. He could feel sweat running down his forehead and into his eyes. The fake beard itched.

"Mister?"

Seth breathed deeply, a sigh of relief. "No. I was just looking for someone." He drew his hand quickly out of his pocket. He could see the hostess gasp and look down at his side. She let her breath out and looked up at him. Seth looked down at his empty palm. He had been grasping the gun so tightly he could still feel the steel in his hand. He looked back at her. A drop of sweat fell off the tip of his nose. Seth turned and rushed out.

The alley in back of the Mekong Noodle Palace stank of day old garbage but the distance to the nearby street was mercifully short. A small flock of seagulls was tearing at a blue trash bag that had burst open. They squawked indignantly when John and Nicole approached and flew off. When the pair had passed the bag, they circled back and resumed their attack.

When they reached the sidewalk near the cabstand Nicole grabbed John's arm. He turned to look at her. "Before I go I want to talk about the publicity campaign."

"I'd like to think about it for—"

"Look, I've moved heaven and earth in a very short while to get us this far—"

"I'll admit you have moved earth."

She smiled. How could she remain mad at this guy? Finally she asked, "Am I the president of this foundation or not?"

"It's just that—"

"I'll keep your personal story out of it. But if you want me to lead this organization you need to trust me."

He looked up toward the sky. *Was he thinking, or asking for divine guidance.* He finally looked back into her eyes and nodded. "Okay. We'll do it your way."

She smiled, leaned over, and kissed him lightly on the lips. "Thank you."

John touched his lips, where Nicole had just kissed him. As if he didn't believe what had just happened.

Nicole blushed. "I'm sorry. That was totally inappropriate." *Or was it?*

He smiled shyly. "No worries. Just unexpected." He turned and waved over an oncoming cab.

She took his right hand in both of hers. "In any event, thanks for trusting me. I won't let you down." Nicole released his hand and grasped the handle of her suitcase. But as she headed toward the waiting cab, she noticed that the sensation of John's lips on hers lingered.

Chapter Thirty-Four

To the world you may be one person, but to one person you may be the world.

Heather Cortez

AFTER JOHANAN'S VISION of his wedding night with Anteia, he slept fitfully—his mind racing between memories of the joy of the wedding and the command: "Not here, not now." When he heard a banging on the ladder and the voice of Tullius, it was a relief from his torture. "Up, sons of mine. We have orders of garum to fill, and no fish to fill them."

The lethargic trio roused themselves from their beds and scrambled down the ladder, Johanan descending last. Tullius met them at the bottom with a bag containing their breakfast. Aprius and Marcus ran down to the shore. Tullius walked down with Johanan.

"Thais acted angry that I didn't consult her before making my offer to you last night." He put his arm around Johanan's shoulders as they walked. "But I know that secretly she was pleased. She has often said she wished you would stay here."

"What about Anteia?" asked Johanan. "How do you think she feels?"

"That one is easy. I watched her when I made the announcement. At first, she was as surprised as everyone else." Tullius clapped him on the back and laughed loudly. "But then—I have never seen such a smile on her face."

Tullius stopped with Johanan at the water's edge. "I could also see she was disappointed when you said you were greatly honored at the prospect, but would need to pray about it."

"I need to seek guidance. If it was my choice it would be easy. She would be a wonderful catch for a lowly fisherman like me."

"You are far more than a fisherman, but keep thinking like that." Tullius passed him the sack of food. "She won't wait forever."

Nikias arrived and started to push the boat out into the surf. "Let's go. We have rocks to haul for the pier once we've brought back our catch and processed our garum. Before long I will yearn for the easy life of a Roman galley slave."

They spent the day fishing with the rest of their small fleet. As they worked, Nikias, Marcus, and Aprius recited stories and passages of holy writings Johanan had taught them. Their minds were well trained in memorization and he rarely had to correct them. As usual Nikias, asked questions that got them into lengthy discussions. Johanan noticed that more and more often Tullius' sons would address the subject matter without needing his guidance. They were all learning quickly, and eagerly. He was impressed by their enthusiasm and love for learning about the Christos.

Using the tactics the fleet had learned to work together, they quickly filled all their craft. As they sailed home, Johanan noted that not once had anyone brought up the subject of Anteia. They seemed to recognize his need for privacy as he pondered his future.

He would need to announce it soon though, out of respect for his hosts.

As they approached the shore, Marcus interrupted a discussion of the nature of heaven. "It would be good if we could have a copy for our island of at least some of the sacred writings. You've said yourself, Johanan, there is much missing from your memory."

"Yes," he responded, "that is true. I can only give you a sampling of the more important ones."

"Where could we find copies?" asked Nikias.

Johanan thought. There were certainly copies available in Ephesus where the community had a number of faithful scribes working, but he couldn't go back there. There were too many there who had known the younger Johanan and would ask difficult questions if he appeared.

"I'll have to think about it. There are several places we might go. We just have to avoid the Roman authorities."

When they arrived back on the island, Johanan volunteered for the duty to take the load from their catch to the garum factory. The others worked on boat repairs and cleaned the rest of their haul. As he wheeled the cart loaded with fish into the clearing, he saw Anteia on the far side working with her mother. She looked up and smiled as she saw him and then averted her gaze.

Johanan cut up the fish and took it to the next open vat. A layer of herbs had already been laid out on the bottom. As he was spreading his fish out, Anteia appeared silently by his side with a bucket of salt.

"Were you surprised by your father's announcement last night?" he asked, still looking down at the bottom of the vat.

"Yes, very." He looked up and took the bucket of salt from her. For a moment, his hand rested on hers. She looked away and gently moved her hand away.

As he slowly poured the salt over the fish, he thought back to his dream and the sight of Anteia waiting for him in their bed.

"Johanan, I was surprised, but also pleased. I would be honored to be your wife."

He continued pouring the salt. "I would like nothing better for myself, Anteia." The memory of his vision persisted. "When I am finished with my work, please walk with me."

With the help of his prospective betrothed, Johanan finished his work in short order. Anteia talked briefly to her mother and followed him out of the clearing. Rather than taking the return path to the village, he turned right and pushed the cart toward the beach. He left it next to a mound of stone suitable for pier construction. Then he continued down to the shore with Anteia at his side.

They stood there for a few minutes and watched the sail of a merchant ship traverse the horizon. Finally, Johanan looked into her eyes and spoke.

"Anteia, last night I dreamt of our wedding, and wedding night." The young woman turned away.

"Johanan," she said in protest.

Now it was his turn to blush. The man who spoke with an air of authority to thousands was now on unfamiliar ground.

"I—I didn't mean it like—like that." He fumbled his words.

She looked back at him with a sly smile, evidently enjoying his discomfort.

He took both her hands in his. The best way to handle this was quickly. "Anteia, in my dream, Jesus told me I couldn't marry here, or now."

"Oh." She looked away. He kept her hands in his.

"Please understand. I don't know if this means not with you—but it does mean now is not the time."

"Are you sure it wasn't only a dream and not a vision?"

He released her hands and looked back out to sea. The sail of the merchant ship had vanished.

"I wish it were only a dream, but it was so vivid and lasted so long. It could only be a vision." He sighed. "Rarely does He communicate his intentions so clearly. I can't go against this message."

Anteia turned her face away from him. He gazed at the back of her head. Her long hair flowed in the soft breeze. *What a prize this woman would be.*

She turned back to him. Her eyes were brimming with tears. "Oh, Johanan…"

At that moment, he wanted to embrace her; to kiss away her tears, to tell her she would be his. *Lord, I have been a faithful servant. How can you deprive me of this?*

"Oh, Johanan." She sobbed.

He took one half step forward, then stepped back.

She clenched her fists at her side. "Johanan." Anger swept aside the look of grief on her face. "How could you do this to me?" She turned, and ran down the beach toward the village.

Johanan stood, rooted to the spot. He knew if he pursued Anteia he wouldn't be able to resist her. He would defy his Lord. He clenched his eyelids, squeezing the tears out. His fists shook in anger, and he drew in his breath sharply. After a few moments he opened his eyes and blinked away the salty water. She was gone.

He turned back to his cart. It waited next to the mound of stone. He grasped a rock off the pile, lifted it up and into the cart, then turned to get another. When it was full, he pushed it slowly down the path to the foundation of the new pier. There, one by one, he set each stone carefully into its place.

When the family gathered for dinner that night, Anteia was absent.

Johanan cleared his throat. "Where—"

"She will not see you or speak of you, Johanan," said Thais.

"She is staying with the family of Leonisis." Thais glowered at Johanan. "She told us to ask you about what happened. She would tell me nothing."

Johanan told them of his vision, culling the more graphic parts, and concluding with where Jesus had instructed him, "… not here, not now." They were all disappointed.

"I would like nothing more than to stay here, to marry Anteia…" He choked, and had to swallow hard before continuing. "To marry Anteia, and be part of your family." He looked down at the hard packed floor. "But I cannot deny my Lord. I cannot deny *our* Lord."

After a few moments of silence Tullius asked in a gentle voice, "What now, Johanan? What now?"

He nodded and looked around the room at the people who had become his family. "Athens." He choked, swallowed hard, then continued. "I must go to Athens."

Chapter Thirty-Five

Sometimes I would like to ask God why he allows poverty, suffering, and injustice when He could do something about it. [But] I'm afraid He would ask me the same question.

Anonymous

NICOLE SCANNED THE room of reporters. The turnout for the press conference had been less than she hoped for, but was still respectable. *USA Today* had sent a young reporter who looked as if he had just started shaving. But at least one national science magazine had sent a correspondent with some expertise in the field. The only broadcast media were two local television stations. But she had her own camera crew ready so they could post the event on YouTube.

Nicole had picked out her clothing carefully and spent two hours at a local salon in an attempt to project a highly professional, but feminine and appealing image. As she chatted it up with several of the local broadcast reporters before the presentation, she got the impression she had hit the mark. One of the local

TV reporters seemed more interested in her than in the topic of the conference. Hopefully it would pay off with appreciable screen time on the news. Maybe even result in getting picked up by national affiliates.

At each seat was a press kit and a sealed cardboard container about the size of a shoebox. Pitchers of ice water were scattered throughout the room. Many in the audience were munching on the oversized Costco muffins she had brought in. The initial part of the event had been fairly normal, but she was about to shake things up.

David sat to her right behind a pitcher of cloudy looking water that rested on a table up on the dais. To her left was Susan Hill, nose buried in an iPad. Nicole tapped on the microphone to get their attention. "As promised, I have Susan Hill, our project engineer, to answer any technical questions that I can't answer—which will be most of them." The crowd tittered. Susan gave a nervous wave and closed her iPad.

Nicole turned to her right. "I'm sure many of you locals know my handsome assistant, David Freeman, former University of Washington football star and a board member of the Galilean Foundation."

David waved to the crowd. A reporter sitting on the front row asked, "David, how do you think the Huskies will do this year?"

The big man laughed. "Save those questions for after the presentation, Rubart. I hate to say it, but this will be even more interesting than football."

Nicole nodded to David. He picked up the pitcher of murky water and started to pour it into a large funnel sitting on top of an empty pitcher. She could smell the dirty sample from here. She wrinkled her nose. The water coming out looked like something from a mountain spring. She straightened her blouse and smiled at the crowd. *This was her moment.* "As you can see, it goes in looking like used dishwater—and I assure you, it's much worse than that—and comes out looking like expensive bottled Italian water."

The smallish crowd nodded as if they were the audience at an infomercial going into its second hour.

"But I have two surprises for you." David held up a box that looked like the ones in front of each reporter. "Go ahead and open up your boxes and you can try for yourself." They perked up a bit as they broke the seals on the box. Each pulled out a wide bottomed lab beaker, a small funnel equipped with a filter, and a jar of water that matched the dirty sample on the dais.

"Before you open your jars and repeat the experiment, I have to warn you it smells even worse than it looks."

Several reporters cracked the jars open and winced. One yelled out, "Sheesh. This stinks like Rubart's socks."

"Hey, how do you know what my socks smell like? You been digging through my laundry?"

The crowd chuckled. Nicole waited for the laughter to die down. "Next time we'll let Mr. Rubart contribute his socks to the test, but this time we just pulled it from a local sewage lagoon." A grimace ran across the face of the audience. Several sealed up their jars and took a drink from one of the pitchers of clean ice water spread throughout the room.

On the dais, David was holding up his beaker and pouring the dirty sample into his own funnel. Several of the more game participants repeated the experiment at their tables.

"As I mentioned earlier, this filter material has been bred from a very unique algae from a remote village in India. Some genetic engineering has made it even more efficient. It's the miracle ingredient of a highly effective system that turns even salt water into clean, drinkable, water."

Rubart interrupted her. "How did you find out about this algae filter stuff?"

Nicole looked at John, standing in the back of the room.

Without thinking she said, "Mr. John Amato, our founder, discovered it."

John winced as the audience turned to face him.

Rubart asked, "How did you hear about it, Mr. Amato?"

He smiled weakly. "I just ran across the rumor in my travels and decided to check it out. Turned out to be true."

Another reporter asked, "Are you from Seattle, Mr. Amato?"

Nicole rescued him. "This is about what our foundation is doing, not about Mr. Amato. And I did promise you two surprises this morning."

They turned away from John and back to her, begrudgingly. David dropped a few ice cubes into his now filtered beaker of water. "Mr. Freeman will now demonstrate that the water is safe to drink."

Rubart said, "Don't try to pull a fast one on me, Freeman. I've been watching you."

David drained the beaker and then beamed down at Rubart. "Would I try to pull a fast one on a sharp fellow like you?"

The man behind him laughed. "You're talking about Rubart. He's a sports reporter, not a science reporter."

Rubart turned to his antagonist. "Hey, hey. You ain't exactly writing for *The Smithsonian*, if you know what I mean."

"Gentleman and Ladies," Nicole said. "Don't take our word for it. You can test the results for yourselves." They looked at the beakers in front of them. Several raised their now clean samples and held it up the light.

Rubart said, "Looks good, but I ain't trying it." Everyone else nodded in agreement.

Nicole held up a pitcher of ice cubes. "How about if I let you sample it on the rocks?" They all shook their heads.

She smiled her most engaging smile. Now it was time to reel them in. "I did promise you two surprises." She picked up the pitcher of ice water sitting on the table to her left. It looked just like the pitchers on the tables in front of the reporters throughout the room. Pitchers now close to empty in most cases.

"The second surprise is you've probably already tried it. The ice water in your pitchers came from the very same water as our sample. We filtered it this morning."

Rubart jumped up and raced out the back door, in a frantic race for the bathroom. After their looks of surprise had passed, several of the other reporters held their beakers up and examined them more closely.

Chuck Boyd set his empty beer glass down on the battered wooden table. Through the window he could see that the infamous Bay Area fog still engulfed the airport. Another thirty minute delay of his flight to Denver had just been announced. Most likely it would eventually be cancelled. He debated calling it a day and driving home. Instead, he signaled the server for another beer.

"Excuse me, would you mind if I took this seat?" Chuck looked up to see a thin man dressed in wrinkled khaki as if he had just returned from a safari. "It's a bit crowded here."

Chuck nodded and gestured at the open seat in front of him. He brushed aside the empty plastic basket that had contained a bacon burger, but now only sported a grease stain on the paper liner. "I hear ya. My flight's been grounded for two hours."

He nodded at the stranger who was perusing the menu. "Coming back from vacation?"

The stranger gave him the weak smile of one who was desperately tired but wanted to be gracious. "Actually, I'm a reporter. I'm just returning from an assignment in the Balkans." He turned his attention back to his menu. "I had hoped to be in my bed now sleeping off jet lag."

A familiar face on the television over the bar caught Boyd's attention. He pointed to the monitor. "Will you look at that. See that pretty girl—she's the daughter of my ex-partner on the force." Nicole was speaking into a microphone and gesturing to a large black man who was pouring murky looking water into a filter resting on top of a lab style beaker. The scene changed to the audience as half a dozen leaped to their feet and raced out of the room, several holding their hands over their mouth. In the background he could see Nicole still standing at the lectern with a triumphant smile on her face.

Boyd's companion nodded at the TV and then turned back to his menu. Boyd glanced at the closed caption running across the bottom of the screen as it cut back to the news anchor. Something about a dramatic display of some new type of water filter. *Man, it must be a slow news day.* The scene cut to a man in his mid-thirties with dark, curly hair. He was nodding at the camera. The caption underneath said, "John Amato, Foundation Chairman."

Chuck reached across the table and touched the reporter's forearm. "You said you just got back from the Balkans?"

The reporter nodded.

"That guy there came from that area—from Kosovo. Now *he* has an interesting story."

His companion raised an eyebrow. Boyd could see a look of skepticism on his face. With his professional discretion weakened by exhaustion and a series of beers, he launched into everything he knew about John Amato.

Chapter Thirty-Six

In youth we learn, in old age we understand.

Marie Von Eschenback

A WEEK AFTER JOHANAN was forced to spurn Anteia, he prepared to set sail for Athens with Tullius, Marcus, and Aprius. As they loaded their boat with a dozen amphorae of garum in the breaking moments of dawn, the other men of the village stopped by to wish them well on their journey before setting sail for their day of fishing.

Thais, Perpetua, and many of the other women came to bid them a safe journey. As the sun rose, Johanan saw two figures coming from a house at the far end of the village. The hair of the two swirled behind them in the morning breeze. One head was enveloped in the ebony mane of Leonisis; the other was the light brown hair of Anteia.

Johanan jumped off the bow of the boat and strode toward them. He met the pair before they had reached the crowd. Anteia stopped and looked down at the sand. Leonisis hugged her around the shoulders and glared at Johanan.

Anteia looked at her friend and hugged her back. "I will be fine. You may go." Leonisis released her, shot Johanan an angry glance, and stalked up the beach to the crowd of well wishers.

"Anteia, I'm so sorry—"

She held up her hand to stop him. They stood there for a few moments. Finally she broke the silence. "Johanan, when I first came to you to be baptized, I must admit it was because I liked the handsome, interesting stranger who had come to our village." She looked up at him, her eyes glistening with moisture.

Johanan smiled at her. He wanted to reply, but he was too choked up.

She smiled back. "Since then I have come to love Jesus as Lord, and not just because you are his emissary among us. She choked back a sob. "Last night Aprius came to visit me."

"Anteia—"

She shook her head and smiled. "The men of my family have a reputation for making persuasive arguments when they make visits in the night." A tear rolled down her cheek. "Aprius was wise enough that he didn't even have to resort to wine to convince me of my folly."

Johanan stood silent.

"He asked me if I was a follower of the Christos or a follower of my own pride."

Johanan took a step forward.

She looked into his eyes through water filled eyes. "I'm here to say I accept his message, and his will, as well. I regret my anger toward you. Forgiveness is what the Christos taught, and I would not wish you to think I had not paid heed to your lessons."

He willed himself to stand there, only one pace apart from her. What he wanted to do was stride forward and envelope this remarkable girl in his arms. Finally, he said, "Anteia, your beauty runs deep."

She looked away and held her hand out, palm down. He stepped forward and grasped it in his hands and brought it gently to his lips. She looked up at him. Now his own eyes were brimming with water. "Anteia, I hope someday he will tell us here, and now, and together."

She blushed, and nodded. "Do you think it will happen, Johanan?"

"I don't know, but I will pray every day we are apart."

"As will I." She swallowed hard before continuing. "Every hour of every day."

He nodded, and looked down at his feet. He dug in the sand with his sandal, like a lovesick boy.

"Johanan—I promise to wait for you."

He shook his head. "Don't make that promise. I'm not sure what the future holds for me. You must do what you think is his will."

Finally he looked back at the boat being loaded on the beach. Everyone was standing, staring at the unfolding drama. When they saw Johanan turn to look at them, they rushed back to their activity.

Johanan released her hand and gestured to the crowd. "We've put on enough of a show. I have a long journey ahead of me."

They returned to the boat, walking side by side, a respectful distance from each other, but their hands held lightly together. When they reached the gathering Johanan released her and helped finish loading the boat. He saw Anteia whispering in the ear of Leonisis. The two giggled.

They quickly completed preparing the vessel for the journey. After a final round of farewells, Tullius said, "Come, we must sail while the weather is good. We have a long day ahead." They pushed the heavily laden boat into the surf. Johanan was the last to clamber aboard. As he looked back from the bow at the receding shoreline, he saw a familiar figure hobble down to the shoreline and sit apart from the gathered women.

"Tullius, didn't you say Mithridates used to wait for you down at the shore?"

Tullius leaned out over the side of the boat, and looked back at the village. He sat back down and said, "Yes, but it has been many years."

Johanan watched as they pulled away from the shore. One by one, those on the beach turned away from the sea and went about their daily chores. Eventually, only Mithridates and Anteia remained on the shore. As the village faded from sight, Johanan saw Anteia squat next to the old dog, put her arms around him, and bury her face in his neck. Her light brown hair flowed over his neck like a scarf of fine silk.

Late that afternoon they passed a big island with a moderate sized port. Several larger ships could be seen tied up in the harbor. Tullius said, "That's where we usually take our salted and smoked fish. Enough ships call there that we can usually make a quick sale and return home before nightfall."

"Why don't you sell the garum there?" asked Johanan.

"We can make a much better profit in Athens, even with the additional time. Plus, it is a good opportunity for our young men to see the city." He smiled at his sons, who were snoozing in the bow. "Someday, when we have a proper dock for larger ships, they will come to us and we won't have to make this trip."

They passed the days of the journey fishing, learning from Johanan of their faith, and napping. Most nights they pulled up on the shore of a small island rather than risk running into something in the dark. They spent one night at sea when the charts showed a large gap between islands.

With only a few days left on their journey, they pushed off from a beach where they had spent the night. They had only been underway for a short time and the morning sun was still low in the sky when Marcus pointed in the direction of the rising sun and said, "Father, look."

They all peered in the direction of the breaking dawn, shielding their eyes from the sun with their hands. Johanan noticed a single-masted vessel with six oars in the water. It was at least three times the size of their small boat and was bearing down on them—fast.

Tullius grunted. Then he said, "Pirates. Not everyone respects the Pax Romana. Aprius, Johanan, man the oars." He gave Marcus directions on adjusting the sails, and used the steering oar to steer a course straight downwind.

Aprius and Johanan dug in deeply with their oars, and the boat responded. But the larger boat, with three pair of oars, was gaining quickly. Johanan watched as a man stood in the bow of the pirate ship and raised his right hand. A grappling hook on a rope dangled from it. He swung it back and forth in a half arc, and flashed them a gap toothed grin.

Tullius looked forward to Johanan and Aprius. "Faster. You must go faster." Johanan was astonished to see the look of fear on his face. Aprius began to call out a faster cadence, and they stroked faster. The ship behind continued to gain.

Johanan felt a gust of wind on the back of his neck, and looked over his shoulder. Their sails had gone slack. "Keep rowing," said Tullius. The look of fear on Tullius' face was even more intense. He turned the steering oar hard to the left.

As they turned, Johanan could see a dark line of clouds rapidly approaching from his right. That's what had caused the change in the wind. He looked to his left. The sails of the ship pursuing them had filled with wind from the oncoming squall, slowing them down. But their momentum and the quick turn had brought them close enough for Johanan to be able to count the number of teeth missing in the grin of the man on the bow.

The pirate pulled his lips back in a fierce grimace, and swung the grappling hook around several times before he released it to fly over their boat. Johanan's eyes followed its path over his head and he watched it splash into the water on the other side of their boat. The rope fell, slack, across their ship.

"Pull, pull fast." The gap toothed man yelled at the men behind him.

"Aprius, Johanan, grab the rope. Don't let the hook set," Tullius said. He abandoned the steering oar as the two, grappled for the rope now snaking across their deck as the pirates pulled on it.

As Johanan braced his feet against the rail and pulled hard on the rope, he felt heavy drops of rain on his neck. The wind gusted, and rocked the boat wildly. By now Marcus had scrambled aft and all four men pulled back on the taut rope. It only seemed to serve to bring them toward the pirates faster. The gap toothed man looked down on them. His grin broadened as they reeled in their prey.

Tullius yelled over the sound of the wind and shouts from the other boat. "Pull the rope toward the back. We must keep the hook from catching."

The four lunged as one a single step to their right. They stumbled as they struggled to keep their balance in this seaborne tug of war. Johanan was braced against the hull, while the others scrambled to find a grip against other surfaces. Johanan glanced up at the gap toothed man. His look of triumph had been replaced by fear. He was looking over their heads toward the horizon.

"One more step," said Tullius. They lunged again, and the rope was lined up next to the stern. "Push it over the back, now." With a heave they lifted the rope over the stern until it was clear of the hull.

Tension released, the rope traveled quickly toward the bow of the other ship for a moment, then caught on something. Johanan looked behind him just in time to see the steering oar whip back and catch Tullius in the chest. It knocked him backward, over the side of the boat, and into the sea. As Tullius vanished beneath the waves, Johanan's attention was torn upward to the roiling black clouds of the squall bearing down on them. It was the mouth of Gehenna, and it was about to devour them.

Chapter Thirty-Seven

Everyone has a plan, 'til they get hit.

Mike Tyson

JOHN HAD JUST finished the eighty-eighth pushup in his morning routine when the phone on the coffee table in his living room started to play "Amazing Grace." He wiped the sweat off his forehead with the sleeve of his t-shirt and picked up the phone. The display read, "Unknown Name and Number." Probably a telemarketer, but he clicked on the ANSWER button.

"John Amato."

"Mr. Amato, this is Alex Silva from *News World Magazine*."

He paused before responding. He wanted to be polite but really didn't want to talk to reporters. "Uh huh."

"I understand you emigrated to the states from Kosovo?"

"That's true."

"I caught your appearance on TV the other day and had a few questions."

John breathed in slowly. He was still winded from the workout that had been interrupted. "Mister…Silva was it? I like to have our foundation president handle all inquiries about the Galilean Foundation and the great work we're doing."

"But I don't want to talk about the foundation. I want to talk about you."

John felt a noose being pulled snug around his neck. He sensed the hangman was ready to pull the lever to the trapdoor. "I'm not important, the foundation is. You're obviously aware of part of my past and can probably understand it unearths painful memories—"

His phone rang. He glanced at the display and saw it was Nicole. He clicked on the IGNORE button and returned to his dance with Silva.

The reporter said, "I understand it might be painful, but the public deserves a few answers, don't you agree?"

"Answers? Answers about what?"

John waited. Silva was making him wait. He resisted the urge to ask the question. Instead he gritted his teeth.

"Specifically about the source of the foundation's money."

"Mr. Silva, it would really be best if you talked to Nicole Logan, our president—"

"Oh, I already have and she was helpful. But she wasn't able to explain where the money you used to start your charity came from in the first place. Some vague story about three friends gave it to you—"

"Look—do you think I'd be living in a little apartment in Seattle and working as a counselor if I was in this for myself?"

"I'm not sure about your motivations, my friend. I just know lots of money went missing around the time you left the Balkans and most of your money is kept in an offshore account."

"How do you know where my money is?"

"I'm a reporter. It's my business to find the facts. And of course, I can't reveal my sources."

John breathed deeply to calm himself. He closed his eyes for a few moments before continuing. "Mr. Silva, I understand your suspicion. All I can tell you is the money was given to me by friends in trust and in confidence. So in this case I can't share any details. Since you've done your research, you know I'm using it for noble purposes."

"Maybe you're feeling guilty about something in your past and are trying to make amends for your sins. If you tell me more, maybe I can help clear your name."

John gripped the phone so hard he thought the case would crack. Finally he said, "I don't think there's a story in clearing my name. Please take all future inquires to Ms. Logan."

He pressed the END button and noticed Nicole had left a message. Without listening to it, he called her back.

"John—did you just get a call from a reporter?"

"Yes." He was seething but spoke calmly. "He seems to know a lot about me."

"I'm afraid it's my fault—"

"Did you tell him?"

"No, but…"

"Please, just tell me."

"Remember I told you I had a private detective do a background check on you?"

"Yes."

"The questions he asked sounded like he had read the report from my detective friend. If that's the case *I'll* kill him."

John breathed deeply. "Don't worry. I've done nothing wrong—*we've* done nothing wrong. We need to stick with your plan."

"Oh, John. I'm so worried. What if my plans to go public destroy the foundation?"

"Nicole, in the end, God is with us. Just remember that."

They spent several minutes talking about how to respond to

the smear piece Alex Silva seemed to be assembling. Nicole committed to crafting a press release to be ready by tomorrow morning. When they were ready to wrap up the conversation John said, "Don't worry about this, Nicole. It will work out in the end. Prayer, persistence, patience."

He hit the END button and gripped the phone tightly. He had a strong urge to slam it down onto the floor. Instead, he took several deep belly breaths and placed it gently on the coffee table. He stood up, peeled off his sweat soaked t-shirt and headed to the bathroom for a shower.

The article that Alex Silva published was as bad as John and Nicole had feared. Over the next several days, John found himself cornered by reporters, with and without camera crews, more than once. He gave them succinct and clear responses to the accusations. But he noticed the only sound bite that seemed to make the news was his closing comment, "Please contact the president of the foundation for more information." It made it seem as if he had dodged the questions posed to him.

He felt as if half the city was looking at him with suspicion, or was it just his imagination? Friday morning as he watched yet another unflattering clip of himself on TV he gritted his teeth. This was just a passing crisis; he'd certainly weathered much worse. He shouldn't care—but he did.

Chapter Thirty-Eight

God, your sea is so great and my boat is so small.

Prayer of the Breton fisherman

AS THE FIRST wave crashed over them, Johanan heard the sound of wood ripping. He looked back in time to see the grappling hook flying through the air back toward the pirates, the wide end of the steering oar impaled on two of its hooks. The handle of the oar flopped back and smacked him on the shoulder. He fell face down on the deck, now awash in seawater. The ship rocked back, and he managed to grab the railing, rising above the sea. He coughed out a mouthful of salt water. *The steering oar! It's gone.*

"Father!" Johanan turned toward the sound of Aprius' voice. Aprius held tight to the stern, bracing himself against the hull. Marcus had his arms around the mast. They both looked into the vicious sea, empty of any sign of their father. The next wave crashed against them. The boat rocked wildly. Johanan looked up into the sail, whipping savagely in the wind. The rope connecting the sail to the starboard side had torn free. The wind filled the canvas. It was going to pull them over.

He lunged across the deck, and grabbed onto the mast, just above Marcus' head. He pulled his knife out of its sheath.

"Father," said Marcus weakly.

"Marcus." Johanan tapped him on the head with the butt of his knife to get his attention. "Help me free the sail or we all die."

As the ship lurched, Johanan fell toward the railing and grabbed the rope where it was secured to the gunwale. He looked up at Marcus, who was still holding onto the base of the mast. Marcus looked back at Johanan, despair in his eyes.

Another wave washed over them. Johanan held tight to the railing, bracing himself against the slippery deck. As the boat heeled over, he looked down at the sea, only inches from his face. The side of the hull dipped under the water, then rose slowly, like a drowning man surfacing for the final time.

Johanan grabbed the rope and sawed furiously. He looked down at Marcus, who was hugging the mast with both arms. Johanan could hear him plea, "Jesus, save us from this storm."

At that moment, a gust of wind filled the sail. The rope was pulled taut and parted with the next swipe of Johanan's knife.

The base of the sail flew free. Still tethered to the spar at the top of the mast, it flopped wildly in the breath of the squall and started to pull the ship over. Johanan leapt to the mast and slashed wildly at the rope that secured the spar to the top of the mast. The wind shifted, and he slipped on the deck as it rocked. He grabbed at the railing with his free hand as he fell toward the side of the ship. The vessel rocked violently toward him and his chest crashed into the gunwale. His knife hand slammed into the railing with the ferocity of a mule's kick. The blow knocked the knife out of Johanan's hand. He watched it fly toward the sea, and disappear blade first into the thrashing water. He closed his eyes. *God save us, please my Lord, save us.*

He looked up at the top of the mast. It had dipped toward the sea, nearly touching a rising wave. But now the rope holding the spar to the top of the mast was unreeling like a loose thread pulled by a playful boy. The spar and sail flew free, releasing their ship. They rolled upright, just as another wave blasted salt water into Johanan's face and under his tightly closed eyelids.

When the wave cleared, he opened his eyes and blinked to clear them from the sting of the seawater. Marcus was looking back at Johanan, a silly grin on his face. He brandished his own knife in his right hand and held the other end of the rope he had just severed in his left hand. "You need to keep your blade sharper, Johanan."

"Good man." Johanan reached over and slapped him playfully on the side of his head.

Aprius was suddenly at their side. He grabbed onto Johanan's shoulder and shouted into his ear. "We're still not safe. Start bailing." Johanan looked down at the deck. It was awash in water and garum. Several of the amphorae had broken and their contents mixed with the seawater filling their vessel. Even as he took in the sight, another wave broke over the sides and threatened to swamp them.

The two brothers grabbed wooden buckets tethered to the side, and Johanan picked up the base of one of the broken amphora. They slashed frantically at the water with their bailing instruments and flung it over the side, only to have it replaced with each crashing wave.

"We must lighten the load," Johanan said. He pointed to the remaining amphora strapped to the bottom of the boat. Aprius nodded and pulled out his knife.

As he grasped the rope securing the garum, a voice came from the rear of the boat. "No, not the garum." They looked back to see Tullius hanging on the stern—only his head, arms, and shoulders visible. Seawater was dripping down from his hair and soaked beard. Tullius pointed to his left with his chin and said, "Look."

Through the pouring rain, they could see the sun shining on the water only two stone's throw off their port side. It swept toward them, like a wave rushing up a beach. When the trailing edge of the squall passed over them, they were bathed in sunlight. The tossing sea began to subside.

"Father," said Aprius. He dropped his knife next to the garum and rushed to the stern. Marcus and Johanan followed him.

"Careful," said Tullius. "You'll swamp us." As he spoke, a wave splashed over his head. He sputtered. With all four men at the back of the boat, it was dangerously low. Johanan rushed forward to the bow, leaving the two brothers to pull their father in over the stern.

With a heave and help from a wave, Tullius was deposited in a heap on the bottom of the boat. He lay there for a moment like a great fish landed. Then he sat up. "Bail, we could still sink."

Johanan and the two brothers took up the task again, this time making quick headway. Soon, most of the bottom of the boat was clear and the immediate danger of sinking was past.

Johanan slumped against the stern of the boat, exhausted from the battle and the emotion of losing, and recovering, Tullius.

As Marcus bailed one last bucket of water, he stood up, and looked toward the horizon. "The pirates—where did they go?"

Johanan looked out across the water as well. There was no sight of the ship that had been pursuing them.

Tullius waved toward the waters on his right. "You won't see them again. As I was clinging to what was left of our steering oar, I saw them capsize. They went down like a stone."

Aprius gazed over the sea, in the direction of the retreating squall. "The storm almost destroyed us, then delivered us."

Johanan laughed weakly. "Remember, I didn't promise you life as a Christian would be easy."

One oar, in addition to the steering oar, had been lost in the storm. Johanan created a makeshift replacement out of two planks that floated near them. By rowing in shifts, they managed to reach one of the larger islands in the area by nightfall. They beached the boat on a sandy shore and built a fire to dry off and cook their dinner. As they ate, they recounted the story of their narrow escape from death, giving thanks to God many times. Finally, they drifted off to sleep around the fire.

As Johanan lay by the fire, he looked up at the brilliant field of stars. *Lord, if I can't die, what would have happened if our boat sank? Would I be delivered by a great fish like Jonah? Would I have floated to the shore on a passing piece of timber? Would I have died and been resurrected like Lazarus? Or did you deliver my friends just to save me?* Finally, he slipped off into a deep sleep.

In the morning Tullius shook Johanan. "Up, holy man. Time to get to work."

Johanan sat up. The sun was already above the horizon.

He squatted next to Johanan and passed him a hunk of salted fish. "No bread this morning, it was all soaked in the storm."

Johanan chewed the morsel slowly, delaying the act of getting out of bed. He looked across the fire. Marcus was still rolled up in his blanket on the other side. Aprius was stoking the fire with a few more pieces of wood he had scavenged.

"I need you and Marcus to rig the spare sail and patch the boat. Aprius and I will check the shoreline to see what washed up. We're short several oars."

Johanan nodded toward Marcus. "I'll wake him."

By late morning Marcus and Johanan had patched a number of leaks, and replaced the sail and rigging. They were cleaning the last amphora shards out of the bottom of the hull, when Tullius and Aprius returned, carrying several oars between them across their shoulders.

They dropped them in the sand just above the boat. "We found them washed up on the far end of the island, along with a half dozen bodies." Tullius kicked at the oars. "We can cut one down to replace our missing oar. The other will make a fine steering oar as it is."

They departed within the hour, propelled by their spare sail and a fair wind.

Chapter Thirty-Nine

For life's adventure, Lord, I ask
Courage and faith for every task;
A heart kept clean by high desire,
A conscience purged by holy fire.

McDermand

FROM THE ENTRANCE of the Starbucks, Nicole spotted John near the back. He had his nose buried in the newspaper. He was sporting a vintage Hawaiian shirt emblazoned with parrots she had bought him in a second hand store. Now that she saw him wearing it, she realized it was way too loud.

She glided quietly across the space and slid into the chair across from him. He looked up at Nicole and flashed a tired smile. She reached across the table and put her fingertips on the back of his forearm. He looked down at where she touched him. She pulled her hand back. "Sorry, it just looked like you could use a friend."

He gave her a weak smile. "I could. Seems like every other person I see on the street is giving me a dirty look." He put his hand on the newspaper. "Doesn't help that my photo is splashed on the front page of the local section again."

"Then again, it could be that shirt I gave you offends their fashion sense."

He looked down at his chest and then back at her. "It is a bit attention getting."

She put her palm over the back of his hand. He glanced down. She kept it there. "They don't matter. What we're doing does." She gazed into his deep brown eyes. For a long moment she stopped breathing. Then his cell phone chirped. He ignored it.

Nicole pulled back her hand and nodded toward his phone. "Don't you want to get that?"

"Oh. I guess." He picked it up, stared at the screen, and raised an eyebrow.

"Hate text?"

"No, it's Scott. He wants to meet at the Greek café near our apartment building." He scowled at the phone, then looked back at Nicole. "This is my neighbor that's been dodging me since I sprung his dad on him."

She laughed. "That wasn't your most brilliant move." She nodded at the phone. "You should see him."

He nodded and slid the phone into his pocket. As he stood he asked, "Want to come?"

Fifteen minutes later Nicole and John were in the entrance of the café. He scanned the patrons looking for Scott. Nobody looked familiar—and then he spotted two men sitting in the far back, both wearing baseball caps and Groucho Marx glasses. One beckoned toward John.

John and Nicole took the two open seats across from the pair. Their faces were each obscured by the large plastic nose over a fuzzy mustache. Bushy eyebrows on the top of the glasses frames completed the goofy disguise. One of them held up another set of the glasses and offered it to John. "Here, put these on," he said in a serious tone of voice. He looked at Nicole. "Sorry. Didn't know he'd bring a date. You're on your own."

Nicole blushed. "I'm not his date. I work with him."

John laughed. "Scott, Walt, what's going on?"

"Just put them on." Scott said. "We don't want to be seen with such a shady dude."

John smiled and obeyed.

Scott pointed to a large pizza topped with what looked like every ingredient imaginable in the middle of the table. "Help yourself."

As they ate, Scott recounted how he had asked his mother about the split with his father. "She admitted that what he told me was true." He gave Walt a sidelong glance. "She did cheat on him with his partner and they forced him out."

Walt looked down at the tablecloth. "Still doesn't excuse me for running out on my boy." He looked over at Scott.

Scott choked out a response. "S'over." He picked up a slice of pizza and bit into it.

Walt put down his fork. "We've been hanging out a lot in the last few days. Catching up a lot. Wanted to thank you."

John took in the scene before him, then pulled the glasses off. "I want to talk to you about what you've been hearing in the news."

Scott held up his hand, "No need, dude. I've seen that junker you drive and you live in the same ancient apartment house as me. If you're making off with millions, you have a really weird way of doing it." He pulled down his glasses and looked over the eyebrows. "And, you are the straightest guy I know."

Scott glanced at his father. "I've also learned not to believe every story you hear."

Walt responded with a weak smile.

"However," Scott said, "we will let you pick up the tab since you're filthy rich."

"That's another misleading story." John pulled out his wallet and dropped a few bills on the table. "But I will cover the tab this time."

After he'd settled up, John and Nicole stepped out on the street. He nodded in the direction of her hotel. "It's about a mile to your place. You up for a walk?"

She nodded and they set off. They'd only gone about six blocks when John heard an odd noise from an alley. It was still bright on the streets but the angle of the setting sun made the space between the two brick buildings very dark. He squinted and looked into the shadows.

"Help, please help," a soft voice said. He couldn't tell if it was male or female, adult or child. He stepped into the shadows. Something didn't feel right.

He looked at Nicole "Call 9-1-1. I'm going to check this out."

She arched an eyebrow. "Shouldn't we wait?"

"Please, help me." The call from between the buildings was louder this time. He motioned for Nicole to stay where she was and stepped into the alley. His eyes adjusted to the darkness and he could see movement deep in the shadows. Behind him he could hear Nicole talking in a muted voice.

A woman stepped out from behind a large dumpster. Even in the dim light he could see that her all black form fitting clothing contrasted sharply with her whitish, blonde hair. She grinned at him.

It was the mysterious woman who had been watching him and had vanished—the same woman who had been on the news clip with Cavanaugh.

She opened her mouth. "Seth." Although her lips moved, the voice didn't fit the figure standing before him. It was a croaking that sounded more like the voice from a tracheotomy patient. A chill ran deep in John's bones.

"Seth," the incongruous voice repeated.

Another figure moved into sight from behind another dumpster, this time about twenty feet ahead to his left. As his eyes rapidly adjusted he could see it was Seth—looking much worse than when John had seen him last at the mission. His eyes were red rimmed and he sported several days' worth of stubble on his gaunt face.

In a fraction of a second John processed the situation.

He glanced over his shoulder and yelled at Nicole, "Run!"

He turned back toward Seth and held his hands outward, just like the first time they'd met in an alley. "Seth—"

A flash came from near Seth's waist. A force slammed into the middle of John's chest. He staggered backward. Another flash and this time the blow was just under his collarbone. It spun him around so he was facing the exit to the alley, still on his feet.

Nicole! She had entered the alley behind him and stood at the entrance, mouth agape. She took a step toward him. He looked into her eyes and held out his hand to stop her. In a breathless voice he commanded, "Run."

He heard a bullet whiz by his ear, then a second. He felt a pain in his back as another round pushed him forward. He staggered for a few seconds before falling forward on his face.

The apostle looked down at the scene about ten feet below him. The body of John Amato lay on the floor of the alley, dark blood spreading out from below. Three crimson stains grew on his back as well. He noted, dispassionately, that the entrance wound on his back could be distinguished from the two exit wounds from the bullets that had hit him in front. The entrance hole was small and neat as opposed to the two vicious looking craters which were surrounded by ripped fabric.

He looked toward the alley entrance where Nicole had stood. She was laying flat on the ground. Blood pooled to one side of her. He knew he should be afraid, upset, or something. But in his disembodied state there was no emotion, only reason.

John looked over and down at Seth. He was still standing in

the same place, gun raised. John looked where the woman had been. She had been replaced by a figure about the size and shape of the blonde, but which seemed to be made of thick, greasy, smoke. Streaks of red lightning flashed through the woman-shaped form.

John noted the reflection of lights flashing off the walls of the alley. He rotated slowly from his position above his own body, to see the source. A patrol car had pulled up to block the entrance of the alley. He assumed the siren was running but could hear nothing. Several police officers jumped out and positioned themselves behind the vehicle. They drew their weapons and aimed them into the alley. He could see the lips of one of them moving as he barked orders.

John looked down at himself. He appeared to have stopped breathing. With the same lack of surprise as a man who noticed that the rain falling from the sky was, once again, wet, the two thousand year old companion of Jesus Christ realized he was, once again, dead.

He looked up at the blue sky above the alley. Each time this happened he hoped he would see the light that beckoned him home to his Lord and Savior. Today he only saw a few clouds against the deep blue background.

He turned around and looked back down the alley. Seth had ducked down behind the dumpster. The smoky being was moving toward Seth, red lightning still flashing throughout the form. For a microsecond, like the effect of a strobe light in a darkened room, the figure was replaced by that of the woman.

"Seth," Thea said as she stepped toward him.

"The cops are here. I'm hosed."

"Yes, my love. I wanted to save you and take you to my father's house. Now it looks like you will spend the rest of your life in prison."

"I can't do that," he sobbed.

"You'll be without me, without your meth. It will be a miserable existence. I am sooooo sorry for you."

From the alley entrance the police officer barked at him, "Put down your weapon, NOW!"

"Seth, my love, there is one way out..."

John watched as the smoky figure approached Seth. The red lightning flashed more rapidly. Twice in rapid succession he saw it replaced by the facade of the blonde woman again. There was something fluid and seductive about it. He could see Seth speaking but could still hear nothing. Seth was holding the gun in his right hand, waving it around as he talked to the being.

Then Seth stopped and stood up straight. The red lightning in the sinister form flashed more rapidly and brightly until the form was a flickering neon red. Seth raised the gun and aimed it at his head.

John wanted to shout, "No," but he had no vocal cords with which to yell.

The muzzle flashed.

The smoky form shrank to a bright red pinpoint in an instant, then vanished in an explosion of light.

Seth stayed upright for a moment as his body resisted the inevitable, then collapsed in an untidy heap.

Chapter Forty

The nations which have put mankind and posterity most in their debt have been small states—Israel, Athens, Florence, Elizabethan England.

Dr. William Ralph Inge

FOUR DAYS AFTER their narrow escape from the pirates, Johanan, Tullius, Aprius, and Marcus reached the Greek mainland and sailed up the western shore of the peninsula until they reached Piraeus, the port city of Athens.

They tied up at a spot assigned to them by the harbormaster and hired a donkey drawn cart and driver. At the local waterfront market they managed to sell the fish they had caught and salted on their journey. Soon they were on their way to the fish sauce dealer.

As they followed behind the cart, Johanan put his hand on Tullius' shoulder. Johanan said, "I wonder if I might be able to buy an amphora from our shipment from you."

"No, you may not." A grin spread across his face. "I will gladly give you one, if you tell me your purpose."

Johanan looked around at his companions and beckoned them to fall behind out of earshot of their cart driver. "This must remain in strict confidence." He waited until they each nodded in agreement. "I didn't tell you this beforehand, but Fabius Lupus asked me to provide him a teacher."

Marcus said, "The magistrate wants a teacher of the Way?"

"Yes. He has been intrigued by our faith because of the courage he has witnessed in our brothers and sisters and—a miracle he saw decades ago. I confessed to him our island was mostly Christian. He asked me to send him a teacher."

"But what of the garum?" Aprius said.

"The bearer of the amphora is to be his teacher."

"You?"

"I don't yet know, but the garum delivery was the agreed upon sign."

Shortly, they were at the dealer of fine foods. Tullius directed Aprius and Marcus to wait outside with the cart driver. He and Johanan stepped inside the building. It took a few moments for their eyes to adjust to the dimly lit room. Johanan looked around at shelves of wrapped goods and racks of amphorae. Tullius called out, "Aristedes?"

A pudgy hand pulled aside a curtain hiding a back room. "Tullius?" A rotund man stepped into the front room and pounded Tullius on the shoulder. "Old friend, it has been too long."

"Yes, it has been much too long."

Within a quarter of an hour their amphorae were unloaded and the cart driver on his way.

The five men sat around a low table drinking watered down wine and sampling delicacies provided by their host.

"Has your father told you tales of our youth and how I bested him at the gymnasium?" Aristedes asked Marcus and Aprius, "or did he lie and tell you he was the better athlete?"

Marcus and Aprius laughed. Marcus replied, "Most of father's tales of his friend Aristedes involve how you both romanced the women of Athens. He never seems to talk of your studies together."

Aristedes patted his ample belly. "Thanks to my trade, those days are long gone. Fortunately for your father, he took back the best of the women we wooed."

"And what of your wrestling matches?" Aprius said.

"Both were true. When we first met, I easily won. As he became a student of the sport, and wilier, he was one of the best in the city."

They traded tales until the late afternoon. Finally Aristedes stood and walked over to the amphorae of garum sitting in a rack. He pulled a small knife out of a sheath hanging from his leather belt. The merchant pried out the wooden plug at the top of one of the amphora, and then took several long and noisy sniffs at the opening. "Ahhh, just as good as the last shipment."

He pounded the plug back in place with the butt of his knife and turned to Tullius. "I have buyers for all of your garum. Several men of noble families came back and asked when I would have the next shipment from you."

Tullius said, "Then of course you will be able to charge a premium."

"Yes my friend." Aristedes sighed, and shook his head. "And you shall share in the additional profits. All I ask is you keep it coming."

They discussed where they might be able to purchase extra wooden vats so they could increase production. Aristedes promised to introduce them to the cooper in the morning. Finally he named a new, higher price for each amphora.

"A fair amount," said Tullius, "but only nine are for sale this trip. We lost two in a storm, and one is promised to another buyer."

"It will do." Aristedes retreated to the back room and returned with a small leather bag. "Here it is. Bring more back next time, and there will be more coin for all of us."

Johanan noted Tullius put the bag away without counting the money.

"I can offer you space to sleep on the floor of my shop for the night if you'd like."

"I may have a place for us to sleep with friends in the city," Johanan said. "If I can't locate them, can we come back?"

"Of course, and if I don't see you tonight, we will visit the cooper together tomorrow."

They took their leave of Aristedes and ventured out into the street. As they worked their way toward the ancient and enduring Greek city, Tullius pointed out a pile of overgrown stone that had once been a proud building. Gnarled olive trees clawed at the foundation. "Some of these ruins date back two or more centuries, when the city was crushed by the Macedonians or Romans. My uncle told me that hundreds of years ago, in the glory days of the city, Athens was ten times its current size."

They reached a square where a large marble pedestal stood. Lead pipe jutted out of the empty foundation. "My uncle said when he was a boy, an elaborate fountain once stood here. After Rome burned, Emperor Nero raided the city for art for his new palace, including this fountain."

As they came closer to the city, they noticed a number of building projects in progress. Tullius said, "The emperors have been more kind to the city in recent years. It may be a backwater city in the mighty empire, but it is respected for its cultural and intellectual history."

Finally they came in sight of the Parthenon on top of the Acropolis. Tullius gestured toward the majestic building with its high marble columns and brightly painted friezes around the top. "Someday we will have even greater buildings to glorify the Christos."

Aprius laughed. "My father and his grand visions of the future."

Johanan made several inquiries of passersby and soon they

were outside a large residence just inside the city. Johanan knocked on the substantial door. After a few moments, it swung open. Based on his plain, short, tunic the young man who answered it was a house servant, or even a slave.

"What is your business?" he asked Johanan.

"I seek Strabo, the master of this house."

"Who seeks Strabo?"

Johanan took his staff and drew a curved line in the dust on the street in front of the doorway. When he had finished, he looked up at the young man and said, "A friend."

The young man took the staff out of Johanan's hand and completed the fish symbol. Then he returned the staff to the man from Galilee. Johanan drew an eye on the ichthys, then used his sandal to erase the drawing.

The young man looked up and down the street, then said to the four, "Please, come in."

In only a few minutes another man, only a few years older than Aprius but a good hand taller, greeted them in the entrance hall. His straight, brownish hair reminded Johanan of the winter pelt of a donkey. "Welcome brothers, I am Gaius, the scribe. What brings you to the house of Strabo?"

"My name is Johanan of Galilee. These are friends from an island of your province."

"You are from the homeland of the Christos? Welcome to our small band of followers."

Gaius explained that Strabo, the master of the house, was out of the city tending to the business of his farm, but would return the next day.

"Tomorrow evening our church gathers here for supper and for worship. We have a room where you may stay if you wish."

He led them to a chamber where he provided them with a basin of water and towels so they could clean up. They stowed their remaining amphora of garum in a corner. They learned from

Gaius he had been born in Macedonia and sold into slavery as a young boy. He learned his trade as a scribe, and for many years tended to the business of his owner, a trader in spices. When his master became a Christian, he had freed Gaius and all the slaves in his household.

"I learned from his example and became a follower of the Christos as well. I remained in his employ until his death. Since then I have worked for Strabo." After some more small talk he took his leave. "I will see you tomorrow evening, but for now I must go do the work of my master."

When they were alone Aprius said, "How did you know of this place?"

"I've never been here, but I have heard the name of Strabo. He is a wealthy landowner who was known as a leader of a house church in Athens." He sat down on a short stool, exhausted. "Maybe someday the name of Tullius will provide safe haven to traveling believers."

The next morning they went back to Aristedes' shop, loaded with bread and cheese they had bought at the market. They shared breakfast before he escorted them to the cooper. Tullius settled on a price for four with the merchant and arranged to have them delivered to their boat the morning after next.

The islanders spent the rest of the day touring the city on foot. Tullius led them to the Gymnasium where he and Aristedes had learned the skill of wrestling. They watched the men engage in sport for an hour and then walked to the market. Tullius walked down a street crowded with stalls and finally stopped in front of a merchant's stall.

"When I first saw your mother, it was here. She was tending to her parents' pottery business. From that moment on, she was the only woman in Athens I wanted to pursue."

They pondered the sight for a few moments. Then Marcus asked, "How long have Grandmother and Grandfather been gone?"

"Over twenty years." He turned to Johanan. "We received word that a plague had swept the city. When it was over we came back and found the families of my wife and uncle had all perished. If she had stayed here, she might have as well."

They let Tullius indulge in his memories for a few more minutes. Then he led them through the crowded streets back to the house.

That night several dozen believers gathered in the house of Strabo. They shared the bread and wine of the last supper ritual, much as they had on the island. Johanan noticed that Strabo pronounced a blessing upon the bread and wine before sharing them, a local variation of the ritual. Gaius read several passages from writings, including some from Johanan's own.

Then Strabo introduced their visitors. "Tonight we are joined by Johanan of Galilee and his companions from an island in our province. Johanan has established a new community of believers there. They come to our city for trade."

Johanan stood and introduced his companions. Then he announced, "We also come here for another, greater purpose." He looked around the dimly lit room at the small community. "I have been asked by a Roman official to provide him with a teacher. He wishes to learn about our faith." Murmurs and questions interrupted his announcement, as he had expected. The empire was the major threat to their growing faith. Although persecution had been mild under Trajan, the brutality of Nero and Domitian were still recent history.

"I believe he is sincere about his desire to learn about our faith. If we provide him with a proper teacher he will become one of us, and we will have a powerful patron in this province to protect us."

"Why should we believe him?" said a man in the back of the

room. "The Romans have used ruses in the past to deliver believers to their deaths."

Johanan nodded and waited until the conversation sparked by the challenge died down. "Yes, you are correct. However, I believe this is no trick. He spared one of our villagers, whom he could have easily executed. When he asked me for a teacher, he cited the bravery he had witnessed among the persecuted members of our faith." Johanan paused. "He also told me of being witness to a miracle. He was there when the apostle Johanan, the last living disciple of Jesus, was boiled in oil and survived. That is why he wants to learn more about our Lord and Savior."

"That's it!" An ancient man in the back struggled to his feet, steadying himself with a gnarled staff. "Now I remember where I've heard your voice and seen your face before. You *are* the apostle Johanan. You *are* Johanan bar-Zebedee. The Beloved Disciple has been resurrected, like our Savior before him."

Chapter Forty-One

...the LORD your God goes with you; he will never leave you nor forsake you.

Deuteronomy 31:6

JOHN'S EYES OPENED wide. He gasped and inhaled sharply. He was looking into the face of what appeared to be an Emergency Medical Technician holding a long needle. Clear fluid was dripping from the tip.

"Yo, he's back with us. I don't believe it," the EMT said.

Another EMT looked down at John. "I told you not to give up, kid. You stick with this job long enough and you'll see lots of miracles." He turned away. "Put that away and help me hook this up." The voices faded as John slipped into unconsciousness.

John felt a warm hand holding his. He opened his eyes. Anteia looked down upon him. Her mane of deep brown hair was framed by a deep blue Mediterranean sky. Tears streamed down her face. "You can't leave me. I love you."

He gripped her hand. Her name escaped his lips in a soft whisper. "Anteia." He struggled to stay, but faded back into oblivion.

Voices shouting. "Can you hear us, Mr. Amato?" He opened his eyes briefly. He was being moved quickly through narrow halls. He could hear wheels squeaking rapidly under him. Medical equipment was beeping in the background. More voices talking rapidly. Sound fading away…

Blackness.

Two voices nearby, one unfamiliar, the other familiar:

"He's recuperating incredibly fast, Mr. Freeman. Usually in a case like this we'd be discussing whether or not your friend is an organ donor. However, I still don't think it's a good idea to have people in his room, despite his amazing recovery."

David's voice: "You can use the word, Doc, it's not just amazing—it's a miracle.

"Okay, Mr. Freeman, it's a miracle.

Nicole's voice: "Doctor, you say he's in a coma but you don't know why. I think it would help to have people who care about him around him."

Nicole. Nicole was alive. A wave of relief washed over John.

Blackness.

Disparate voices speaking to each other, talking to him, reading bible verses. Voices intruding into his consciousness. Old Testament readings, New Testament sections written by his friends, some written by himself.

The steady beep, beep, beep of a medical monitor.

Blackness.

Two familiar voices, both young women:

Nicole's voice: "They say he's recovering quickly but don't understand why he hasn't come out of the coma."

Sharon's voice: "I'm just glad he's off the critical list."

Nicole's voice: "Do you want to read some more?"

"Sure" *The rustling of pages.*

> *"Peter turned and saw that the disciple whom Jesus loved was following them. This was the one who had leaned back against Jesus at the supper and had said, 'Lord, who is going to betray you?' When Peter saw him, he asked, 'Lord, what about him?'*
>
> *Jesus answered, 'If I want him to remain alive until I return, what is that to you? You must follow me.' Because of this, the rumor spread among the brothers that this disciple would not die. But Jesus did not say that he would not die; he only said, 'If I want him to remain alive until I return, what is that to you?'"*

Nicole's voice: "I'm not sure we should read that passage. John gets worked up anytime the topic of Cavanaugh or his show comes up."

A laugh. "Exactly. I figured it might get through to him."

"Girlfriend, I like the way you think."

"I saw Cavanaugh on *The View* the other day. He was saying they added that last part after he died."

"Really?

"Makes sense. Sounds like someone trying to explain after the fact why John could be dead but Jesus hadn't yet returned."

"Yeah. I get it."

"Nicole, can I ask you a personal question?"

A pause. "Okay, shoot."

"Are you and John—together?"

Soft laughter—nervous, soft laughter.

Blackness.

A voice muttering something rapidly in Vietnamese.

A young woman's voice, unfamiliar: "Matt, please, in English. Nicole says he may be able to hear us."

Matt's voice: "Sorry, I forget."

Voices praying quietly next to his bed.

Matt: “He can’t die. He made me man I am.”

“He won’t die. Have faith.”

More prayer, softly muttered.

The young woman in a stern tone, like that of a mother scolding a child: “Matt.”

“Yes?”

She switched to Vietnamese. “Get your hand off of my butt.”

Blackness.

The feeling of a damp cloth wiping his brow, gently, slowly; a hand holding his. Was that a warm head of hair on his chest? “Anteia, Anteia.”

Blackness.

Scott’s voice: “I don’t know what it is about you, dude, seems like there’s always people here visiting you and reading. This is the first time I’ve been alone with you. Nicole said I should come even though you’re out. She asks me to read but I think I’ll just talk. She’s staying in your guest room, you know. She’s pretty frosty to me, but hot in a way. I wonder if there’s something going on between the two of you.

“I wish you were awake so I could tell you about my dad. He did awesome in his interview. My boss told him if he stuck with his temp job in the warehouse for another month and got a good reference he’d put him in our sales training program. He’s afraid he’s just another drunk. Me, I think he’ll come through.

“I keep running into that Sharon chick here in the hospital and in our building. There’s something different about her. She’s lost weight and is looking pretty good. I asked her out a couple of times but she just says she’ll think about it.”

John struggled to speak—to protest.

Blackness.

Two familiar voices:

Nicole: “He would be so proud of what you’ve done, David. I’m sure he’d be pleased at how you handled things.

David: "He will be proud of what we've done, Nicole. He'll be back with us. I have faith."

"But the doctor said he could stay like this for years."

"Have faith." Silence for a long moment. Then the rustling of pages. "My turn to read. In Hebrews it says, 'Keep your lives free from the love of money and be content with what you have, because God has said, Never will I leave you; never will I forsake you.'"

John was laying in his bed—in Ephesus. He looked up, and there stood Jesus, in brilliant white, just like he had seen him nineteen centuries ago.

"Remember, Johanan, know I am with you always." The Lord extended his hand. The apostle reached out and took it. It was warm. It was surprisingly soft—not the hand of a carpenter.

As David read, Nicole held John's hand gently, as she had been doing so often over the last few weeks. She missed his gentle way with the people around him, his humble attitude. She knew their relationship should be strictly business, but it was rapidly becoming more than that.

She was about to release his hand and head down to the lobby to do a little work when she noticed his eyelids begin to flutter. Finally they opened wide. He turned to look at her. He seemed to be having trouble focusing.

Softly she said, "Good morning, sleepyhead. We missed you."

David looked up from his bible and came over to stand by John's bed. "I knew you'd be back, bro."

John tried to croak out a question. He stopped and cleared his throat. "How long have I been out?"

Nicole said, "Two weeks, John." Her voice broke as she continued. "Two very long weeks." She smiled down at him and laughed with joy, tears rolled down her cheeks. She turned toward the open doorway and yelled, "Nurse! Please get the doctor."

The doctor arrived quickly and examined John. "You're a very lucky man, Mr. Amato. I told your friends here that normally we should be making plans for your memorial service."

John smiled and rasped, "You can use the word miracle, Doctor."

He chuckled. "I've been reminded of that a few times. How do you feel?"

"Like I've been slugged in the chest by Joe Louis."

"Joe Louis?" The doctor wrinkled his brow.

"Oh, he was a heavyweight champ in the 30's and 40's. I'm a bit of a history buff. Think Mike Tyson."

"That I understand."

Nicole said, "Here's another miracle." She pulled a small plastic bag out of her purse and held it in front of John's eyes. He reached up and took it from her. It was the Greek style bronze cross he wore around his neck. It was severely dented as if something sharp had struck it dead center.

Nicole pointed to her chest. "The first bullet hit the cross and was deflected. Otherwise it would have gone right through your heart."

John glanced down at her arm. A bandage covered the front of her bicep. "What about you?"

She grinned. "Just a flesh wound." She raised her arm as if it flex. "It will be awhile before I paddle a kayak again, but I'll be okay."

"But I saw you lying on the ground. I thought you were dead."

She furrowed her brow. "You saw me lying on the ground? But you went down before the shot that got me."

He nodded. "Out of body experience. I watched everything like it was on stage."

She frowned. "They say one of the bullets that missed you hit me. I passed out like a teenage girl at a Justin Bieber concert." She gave him a weak grin. "So much for the tough cop's daughter from Oakland."

He looked directly into her eyes. "Why did you follow me into the alley?"

She blushed. "I don't know." She shook her head. "I couldn't leave you there on your own."

John cleared his throat and handed the bag containing the cross to Nicole. She held it up to the light. "Looks really worn. Have you had it long?"

He nodded. "It should be in a museum."

She put it in her purse. "Maybe we can get it fixed."

"I'd be happy if you'd just get a jeweler to take the dent out."

Nicole held up another plastic bag. This contained the Hawaiian shirt John had been wearing. The parrot pattern was interrupted by blood stains and shredded fabric. "This didn't survive—but that's probably a good thing."

John smiled.

The doctor, who had finished his examination and was making notes on a tablet PC said, "The other, uh, miracle, is your recovery. I've never seen wounds heal so fast."

John asked, "Does that mean I can go home now?"

"Not so fast. We need to keep an eye on you for a while." He cleared his throat. "In fact, I mentioned you to a few of my colleagues at the university medical center. Your case is unusual enough that they'd like to do a little research on you. I'm sure they'd be interested in hearing about your out of body experience as well."

John shook his head. "Sorry, Doc, not interested in being a lab rat."

The doctor nodded slowly. "If you change your mind…"

He smiled. "Anything else?"

"I'd like you to get a little rest now. Your friends can bring you up to date on all the excitement in a few hours."

Chapter Forty-Two

A man who misses his opportunity, and a monkey who misses his branch, cannot be saved.

Hindu Proverb

WHEN THE OLD man announced to Strabo's house church that Johanan was the apostle himself, resurrected, the gathering erupted:

"Could it be?"

"The prophecy is true. The writings of the apostle do not lie."

"Praise the Christos."

Johanan sat in shock for a few moments. He looked over at Tullius and his sons. They stared at him in awe, as if they had found that Jesus himself had been dwelling among them for the past year.

He stood and gestured everyone to be quiet. It wasn't an easy task to quell the excitement caused by the pronouncement.

"My brothers and sisters, I wish I *could* tell you I was the Beloved Disciple resurrected, but that is not the case." He could see disappointment on the faces of congregants. "I do come from the same region of Galilee as the apostle Johanan. He and I probably have relatives in common. That would explain the resemblance, wouldn't it?"

Several nodded.

Gaius stood up. "You must forgive our community, my friend. It is only a few weeks since the news of the apostle's death reached us here. It has led some to question our faith."

Johanan feigned surprise at the news. "The Beloved Disciple is gone? How did it happen?"

Strabo responded, "The man who brought us the news did not know. Given that he was over a century old, we assume it was of natural causes. It appears he is the only one of the twelve to not die a martyr."

Johanan raised an eyebrow. He was not surprised to hear there were few details surrounding his "death." His companions at Ephesus were probably not eager to announce they had let a century old apostle wander away in the middle of the night—at least that's what they thought they had done.

"And what of this crisis of faith?" Johanan said.

Gaius said, "You are familiar with the Gospel written by the Beloved Disciple himself?"

Johanan only partially suppressed a smile. "I am."

"Then you are familiar with the passage where Peter is walking with the risen Lord and is warned of his own fate. When he turns around and sees Johanan he asks what will become of the younger disciple. Jesus tells Peter, 'If it is my will that he remain until I come, what is that to you?'"

"Yes, I remember that part."

"My brother, as Johanan grew more and more advanced in years, the word spread he would remain alive until Jesus returned. It gave us great hope the Lord would be returning soon." Gaius shook his head slowly. "But now, the last apostle is gone and the Lord has not come for us."

Strabo interjected. "Some believe the prophecy was false. They now question other prophecies, and the writings as well."

Johanan nodded. "I can understand why you would interpret the writings this way, but consider this: Jesus did not say the apostle would live until he returned, he only said '*If it is my will that he remain until I come, what is that to you?*' His intention was to tell Peter to worry about his own fate, not that of Johanan, the Beloved Disciple."

Most of the assembled faithful nodded as they pondered his statement. He decided to emphasize the point. "If our Lord had said, '*It is my will that he remain until I come…*' then there would be cause to question the prophecy, but that's not what he said. He said, "*IF it is my will…*" This time there seemed to be more enthusiastic agreement.

Gaius the scribe said, "Perhaps I should add a note to this passage explaining this?"

Johanan nodded. "I think the apostle would approve, if you made it clear the note was not part of the original writing."

The ancient man in the back spoke up, "I've been telling you that for a week, but you ignore me. A stranger comes in and says the same thing and you accept it. Bahhh! A prophet is not honored in his own home town."

Strabo chuckled. "Josephus, you are right in that you have been arguing that interpretation, but you are no prophet, and this is not your hometown."

Josephus waved his staff at the crowd in the basement. "You all want the Lord to come back tomorrow. You're sorry that the prophecy isn't as you wished. You want out of this desperate life because you yearn for the glory of the Kingdom of Heaven." He paused and stamped his staff on the ground. "But what of his command to go and make disciples of all nations? Would He come back before we had done that?"

Gaius said, "But Rabbi, the word about the Christos has been taken to many nations of the world. Thomas has been to India, Mark to Alexandria, and Paul to many nations. We have been faithful to that command."

Josephus shook his head, as if he was talking to a little child. "Gaius, Gaius, Gaius. He said make disciples of all nations. You are thinking only of the Roman world." He swept his hand across the room and looked into the distance, as if he was staring at the horizon and not the dank wall of their meeting place. "Has one of you met a man who has looked over the edge of the earth and returned? Have you?" He waited, but no one responded.

"But many of us have met traders who have been to distant lands, and returned with tales of yet more unexplored territory." Again he stamped his staff into the dirt floor for emphasis. "What about the people of those nations? What about the people of my own nation, Palestine—the people of the Lord himself? Do you think he will return before we've had time to fulfill that commandment?"

A chill ran through Johanan as he recalled the words of his Lord from a year ago: "All my sheep are precious to me. You must save many before I return."

The basement in front of his eyes faded away. It was replaced by the vision of the great multitude dressed in white robes that he had seen on the island of Patmos decades before. But this time Johanan noticed the individuals in the crowd rather than just the crowd.

A small cluster of people near him came up only to the level of his chest. Their skin was blacker than the darkest Ethiopian he had ever seen. Just to their right were people from a race that stood two heads above his own. Their flesh was so pale that the contrast between their skin and robes was barely noticeable. Their hair was wispy; the color of sun-bleached wheat. A man and women with skin the shade of red clay, flat noses, and coarse black hair stood next to them. All held palm branches and cried out, "Salvation belongs to our God, who sits on the throne, and to the Lamb."

Johanan scanned the assembly. It stretched to the horizon. He noticed more unfamiliar skin tones and facial features in the eyelids, noses, and brows of those nearby. It might be centuries before the church reached all these people from these far off nations. Were there even that many people in the world today?

He heard the voice of Jesus as if he was standing right behind him. "When the world learns who you are, I will return."

Instantly the vision of multitudes dressed in robes of white was replaced by one of devastation. Decaying corpses dotted a barren landscape covered with acrid smoke. Johanan heard the wailing of countless souls in the depths of grief. Then on the horizon he saw four men on horseback. As they drew near he could see that one rode on a white mount, the second on a red one, the third was on a black horse, and the fourth on a pale steed. The man on the red horse waved an enormous sword and pointed it at Johanan.

Johanan looked back toward where he had heard the voice of Jesus. Nobody behind him—only more devastation. He turned forward. The scene had been replaced by the multitude in white robes. All these people still to be gathered?

He felt an elbow in his ribs and the vision vanished. He was back in the basement. Aprius asked, "Are you well?"

Johanan stared at Aprius in shock. The vision had been so real and the warning clear. All those people depending on him to keep his identity a secret. Otherwise the end times would descend upon the earth—and many in the multitudes would never know of Christ.

Aprius put his arm on Johanan's back and shot him a concerned look.

Johanan shook his head and inhaled deeply. "Just remembering something I'd once seen." He nodded toward Josephus who had just sat down on his bench. "I believe our brother grasps the truth of the situation."

"What of the news our guest brings about the Roman official?" said a woman sitting next to Gaius.

Gaius stood, "I will teach him."

Several voiced their agreement. Others nodded in support of the idea.

Strabo stood. "My young friend, you would be a worthy teacher, and with the Lord's help you would win his soul to our cause. But we cannot spare you from the important work of copying the sacred writings. And if this would prove to be a trap, we could lose you forever."

Gaius sat down, a disappointed look on his face. Then Josephus pulled himself to his feet, using his staff. "I am the logical choice. Plus none of you listen to me." The congregation laughed gently.

"I think you may be right, brother Josephus." Strabo furrowed his brow and looked at the old man in the corner. "Your memory of the new and old scriptures is better than any save Gaius'. As a rabbi, you might be able to pass yourself off as a teacher of a religion still tolerated in the empire. That would draw less attention, and give our potential patron some concealment of his true interest."

"Finally," Josephus said, "you listen to me." He sat down, this time with a look of satisfaction.

Strabo looked at Johanan. "It is settled then: Josephus will be the teacher for this citizen." Then he turned his attention to Gaius.

"There is another threat to our community. Twice, in recent months, the local authorities have almost captured our scribe and his work. We must find a place where Gaius may conduct his work in peace. We need more copies of the sacred writings so we may spread the good news."

General discussion broke out as several threw out suggestions about where he might hide. Then from Johanan's right came a familiar voice: Tullius'.

"I may have a solution."

Chapter Forty-Three

While introducing the song [Jesus]Bring the Rain at a concert, the lead singer of the band MercyMe talked about the problems that he and his family had recently faced.
He said, "I'm not sure what God has in mind with these challenges."
A woman in the audience shouted out, "He's using you to change my life."
His response: "Then it's all been worth it."

KIRKLAND, WASHINGTON, MARCH 2007

THAT EVENING NICOLE and David sat down in John's hospital room as he slowly ate his dinner.

John said to them, "So I understand I should be proud of what has gone on in my absence."

David looked at Nicole, then back at John. "How do you know that?"

"During my coma I could hear parts of conversations, including something the two of you said about me being proud of how David handled things."

She patted David on the shoulder. "True. You picked a fine time to be out of commission. The feeding frenzy over your murky past got worse after that meth head shot you. Then Mister-Acting Chairman of the Board here did several interviews defending your honor."

John raised an eyebrow. "A dumb jock like you defended my honor?"

David put up his fists to prepare for mock battle. "Last time I stand up for you." He laughed his booming laugh and engulfed John's hand in his. He nodded to Nicole. "It was really her brilliant strategy. She hired an outside auditor and opened up our books to a local business columnist. Paper trail shows nothing is fishy about how the money is used."

Nicole brushed a lock of curly hair back from John's face. "But my friend, Chuck Boyd, helped really fix things."

John furrowed his brow. "Boyd? The guy who leaked the story in the first place?"

She gave a weak smile. "The same. He managed to get a copy of records that showed the account was opened in 1978—over twenty years before you left Kosovo."

John frowned. "Isn't that kind of information supposed to be confidential?"

"Chuck has his ways. The less I know about it, the better."

David said, "1978—you were like still in diapers, right?"

John grunted.

Nicole pulled a piece of paper out of her notebook and held it up. "He also found out it was opened by a Johannes Fischer and transferred to you in 2003." She looked over the page at John. "Did you know him?"

John looked away. "Johannes Fischer?" He paused a long while. Finally he said, "I know of him, but I've never seen him face-to-face." He held his fist up to his mouth and gave a weak cough. "He's gone now."

Nicole put her hand on John's forearm. "Oh, I'm sorry. You're still recovering and we're cross examining you."

John shook his head. "It's okay."

He looked over at David. "So a few interviews by a football star and a little detective work got us out of the woods."

Nicole shook her head. "It also helped one of our local congressmen got caught in a compromising position with his housekeeper. Much more salacious and newsworthy than a money paper trail from an old war."

David said, "In one respect it was a real blessing. Kind of along the lines of 'no publicity is bad publicity.' We managed to raise money through donations and have an offer to license the technology for commercial use. We have enough to move forward with our first site in Africa, even without the money in the Cayman Islands bank."

Nicole nodded at David. "And speaking of the Cayman bank." She paused a long while.

John finally interrupted the silence. "Yes?"

She smiled. "News reports are that the investigation should be done this week, and we'll have access to that money as well."

John grinned. "I should get shot more often if this is what happens while I'm out."

Nicole put her hand on John's arm. "Let's not resort to that." She adjusted the pillow behind his head. "I do have a question for you."

"What's that?"

"Who is Anteia?"

"Who?"

"In the ambulance you called me Anteia. And several times when your forehead was being sponged by a nurse, or one of your friends—or me—you said the name Anteia. At least that's what it sounded like."

John remembered being in the ambulance, seeing Anteia looking down at him, her saying, "You can't leave me. I love you." He remembered holding her hand.

He looked Nicole in the eye. "Were you holding my hand in the ambulance when I said Anteia?"

Nicole flushed, and turned away. "Yes, with my good arm. I was so afraid for you."

John looked up at the ceiling. "Anteia was a friend who took care of me during an illness years ago. This probably brought back those memories. I haven't heard her name in a long time."

The next morning John woke up to find Scott sitting in his room playing a handheld computer game. When he noticed John was awake he pulled out his earpiece and greeted him. "Hey, man, I heard you were back with us."

"So, do we have a game this afternoon?"

"Doc said it will be awhile for that. Maybe by the time you've recovered, my dad will be ready to make it a triple."

Scott filled him in on what had been going on. John vaguely remembered hearing some of this during his coma, but he let his neighbor continue, paying half attention until Scott said, "I finally got Sharon to agree to a date."

"Sharon?"

"You know, the hot looking girl that lives two doors down from you."

"I know who you're talking about."

"There's nothing going on between the two of you, is there?"

"No, that's not it." He practically squeaked out his reply.

"Anyhow, I've been asking her out since I ran into her here

at the hospital. She finally said, yes but she was going to pick the time and place."

John scowled. "Tell me more."

"She must be taking lessons from you. She told me to meet her on the sidewalk at 8:30 in the morning this Sunday. She's not taking me to the mission, is she?"

John chuckled. "Just dress neatly." He pointed to a cane sitting in the corner. "Can you pass that to me?"

Scott picked it up and handed it to him.

John sat up in bed and pointed the tip of the cane at Scott and said sternly, "Scott, if you hurt that girl I will replace this cane with a real sword and gut you like a salmon."

Scott looked at him in surprise.

"She's a special girl, not another notch on your bedpost." He cleared his throat. "Not that you should be collecting any notches."

"Okay dude, I hear you."

John put the cane down and asked, "I was wondering what you'd heard about my shooting. Do you know if they found a woman, a blonde woman?"

A quizzical look crossed Scott's face. "I didn't hear anything about a woman, but in case you care, that Seth dude ain't dead. He's one floor up."

Chapter Forty-Four

We can do no great things, only small things with great love.

Mother Teresa

THEY MANAGED TO sneak past the nurse's station with Scott pushing John's wheelchair. When they reached Seth's room, there was a police officer outside in a chair. He looked up in recognition. "John Amato?"

"Yes, I've seen you at church, haven't I?"

"Yeah, and I've heard you speak. Great to see you recovering so fast."

"Thanks, I'm glad you remember me." He looked past the officer into the room. "I was wondering if I could talk to the patient."

The officer looked over his shoulder. "You mean the guy who tried to kill you?"

"Allegedly?"

"Nah, he confessed. Not like he could pass it off as self defense."

"Yes." John looked back at the officer. "You're welcome to sit in if you'd like—just to make sure I don't strangle him. I just want to talk."

The officer looked into John's eyes. "This is kind of unusual."

"Please, it's important."

He hesitated, and then shook his head. "Well, he'll certainly be no danger to you. I'll just watch from out here."

Scott wheeled John into the room and parked the wheelchair an arm's length from the bed. Scott sat down in a chair next to the other bed, which was empty.

Seth's head was heavily bandaged. He was hooked up to an IV and had an oxygen line going into his nostrils. When they came in he was sleeping. Within a few minutes he looked up to see John at his bedside.

"Amato. They told me you survived." His words were slurred, either from the head wound or the medication. "Glad I didn't kill you."

"I'm glad to see you alive too."

They sat there in silence for a few moments.

John finally said softly, "Seth, I tried to help you go straight. I got you set up with a place to stay. I offered to ask the judge to go easy on you if you completed rehab. But you tried to kill me?"

Seth looked away. "Thea said you were just saying that to make sure I showed up for the trial. She said they'd put me away for a long time."

"Is Thea the blonde who was in the alley with you?"

Seth looked over at him, a surprised look on his face. "You saw her? The police said there was no one with me. Said I must have been hallucinating."

"I saw her. Pale complexion, whitish blonde hair, dressed in black."

"That's her. Must have slipped out somehow after I shot myself. Anyways, the cops didn't see her."

"Tell me about Thea. How did you meet her?"

"She just showed up one day on the waterfront when I was out with David and some of the guys. She told me to leave the mission, helped me score meth, find places to sleep. Told me if you were gone the case against me would fall apart." Seth paused to catch his breath. "She said afterwards we could go stay at her father's place and be together."

"What else can you tell me about Thea?"

"She was hot. She told me her name was an anagram—you know, where you mix up the letters to form a new word—for heat."

Seth looked at John "Why am I telling you all this?"

"I think you understand I'm here to help you, and Thea was using you to get to me."

"What did she have against you anyways?"

"It was really more about an old friend of mine. Her father hates him."

Seth looked away, deep in thought. Finally he said, "Being here in the hospital has actually helped clear my head. He laughed a nervous laugh. "Good thing for both of us that I'm a bad shot."

Scott interrupted. "Bad shot, right. Now even the army won't take you."

Both John and Seth looked at Scott as if he was the best man passing gas during a wedding ceremony.

"Sorry. Just trying to lighten things up."

Finally John said, "Seth, you're probably going to jail for a long time. But I'll do my best to see you get into a rehab program with a lighter sentence."

Seth sat in silence for a few moments. "I guess I blew my chances for 'Student of the Month' at the Men's Mission. Maybe I'll have a better shot in prison." They chuckled lightly at his joke.

"Good. I'll come back to see you." John beckoned to Scott.

As Scott started to push him out John said, "Seth."

"Yeah?"

"Thea isn't just an anagram for Heat."

He could see the wheels turning in Seth's head. "Yeah, I guess so."

When they returned to John's room, David and Nicole were waiting. They didn't seem to be surprised that their friend had snuck out, but they both still looked worried. They helped John get back into his bed and made small talk with Scott for a few minutes.

After John's neighbor departed Nicole said, "It looks like we have another crisis. West Ghana is threatening to pull the plug on the Water for Life project."

"What?"

Nicole gave him a grim look. "We got a call from the office of the Prime Minister. He said if you don't meet with him he'll evict our team from the country. I can't get anyone to explain the purpose of the meeting."

David shook his head. "I've spent time in that region on mission trips. Sometimes people don't get the help they need because of government corruption or power struggles." He hung his head in despair. "I can tell you of plenty of cases where aid was available, but was withheld by factions fighting for power."

Nicole asked, "What do you think is going on here? When I asked for the purpose of the meeting, they refused to give me details."

David sighed. "I'm afraid they heard about the wealth behind the Galilean Foundation." He shook his head. "They might be planning to extort a bribe. It wouldn't be the first time that's happened to an organization like ours."

Chapter Forty-Five

The better part of one's life consists of his friendships.

Abraham Lincoln

THE CONGREGATION OF the house church led by Strabo turned as one to face Tullius. He stood up and cleared his throat. "As I said, I may have a solution to the problem of protecting your scribe, Gaius, from Roman authorities." Johanan smiled as he anticipated Tullius' next words. His friend knew how to work an audience, whether it was on his own small island or in the heart of Athens.

By the end of the evening it was agreed: Gaius would return to the island with a copy of some of the scriptures and supplies for writing. The trips to bring garum shipments to the mainland would serve as cover for the transfer of new copies of the holy writings and as an opportunity to replenish supplies for the scribe. Gaius would be ready to set sail in two days.

In the morning, Johanan and Aprius escorted Josephus to the house of Fabius Lupus. The old rabbi led the way, while the other two carried the amphora on poles slung through the handles of the container. The wooden rods rested on their shoulders and the clay container of garum swung gently back and forth as they made the short journey.

When they arrived at the large home, a neatly dressed slave at the front entrance directed them to a side door. When Josephus knocked, another servant squinted at them through a small window in the door. His crooked nose appeared to have been broken—more than once.

"What business do you have with my master?"

Johanan bowed his head. "We have a delivery of the finest garum, at the request of Citizen Fabius. He gave special instructions to bring it to his storekeeper."

"Oh." The man looked them all over suspiciously, and then opened the door. "And who brings this order?"

Johanan patted the old rabbi on the shoulder. He took the cue. "I, Josephus, a resident of Athens, fulfill the citizen's request." He leaned on his staff as he bowed.

"I am the storekeeper. He has given me instructions." The storekeeper pulled out a leather pouch and counted out several coins into Josephus' hand. Johanan watched and noted; it was twice the agreed to amount.

Josephus turned to Johanan and extended his hand with the coins. Johanan placed his hand over the old man's.

"It is yours to keep, grandfather."

The storekeeper looked over his shoulder into the dark room behind him. "Boy, hurry up. There's work to be done."

The sound of wooden stool legs scraping a stone floor emerged from the darkness. A muscular youth came out through the doorway. He grasped the amphora, and with a grunt, lifted it by himself. He carried it back into the room.

Josephus reached his gnarled hand out to Johanan and gently grabbed his chin. He stepped so close that Johanan could smell the olives he had eaten on bread for breakfast. Josephus looked Johanan in the eye and turned his face to the left, and then to the right, as if he was examining a colt he planned to buy.

Finally he released Johanan and stepped back. He squinted. "If you are not he, you must be in his family line. You are his twin in appearance and voice."

Johanan smiled. "As I said Rabbi, we are from the same region. We may be closely related."

The old man waved at Johanan and Aprius. "Your work here is done. You are dismissed."

The storekeeper beckoned to Josephus. "Come. We can't keep my master waiting." The rabbi followed him into the room and the door closed behind them.

Johanan turned to Aprius. "You heard him, we are dismissed." He patted his companion on the back. "It's in the Lord's hands now."

By the time they returned to the house of Strabo, Gaius, with the help of Marcus, had completed packing his belongings. Johanan watched as Marcus and Gaius engaged in an energetic conversation that alternated between life on the island and the mysteries of their faith. Aprius joined in the discussion and Johanan smiled at the developing bond.

Only a few moments later Tullius returned from Aristedes' shop in Piraeus where he had spent the morning. He took in the sight of the three young men talking and looked over at Johanan. "I think he will fit in just fine with the young men of our village." Then he turned and interrupted the conversation. "My sons, my brothers, I have a request of you."

They returned to the gymnasium, this time with Gaius. For a

while they sat on the benches on the perimeter and watched the men who were engaged in wrestling. Several matches went on at one time in a large, sand filled arena.

Finally, one of the men who had just won a match came over to them. As he toweled the sweat off of his forehead, he asked them, "Where are you from, strangers?"

Tullius laughed. "Our beards must give us away as visitors."

"Yes, we follow the fashion of the emperor."

"We come from a small island in the Aegean. I'm afraid we tend to follow the fashions of old."

"I see you are watching our sport. Would you care to join in?"

Tullius stroked his beard. "It looks a little strenuous for an old man like me. Perhaps one of my sons would be interested?"

The Athenian turned his attention to Aprius. "I can see from your scar that you aren't afraid of a fight. Care to give it a try?"

Aprius traced the line across his face with a forefinger. "Knives and fisherman are sometimes a dangerous combination." He leaned forward and wrinkled his brow. "What is the objective of the sport?"

"You earn a point by throwing your opponent so that his back touches the ground. We play to three points."

Aprius looked over at his father and shrugged his shoulders. "It sounds simple enough. I'll try it."

The local smiled in anticipation. "Don't worry, I'll go easy on you."

Aprius dispatched him quickly, three points to none. He did the same to the next challenger. A larger man was then matched to him and he edged out a three to two victory.

Johanan could hear comments of the watching crowd.

"Look at how fast he moves. He has the speed of Mercury."

"Did you see how the stranger knew the moves of his opponent before he even made it? He is a wizard."

"He was not even familiar with this sport. How does he do it?"

After the third match, Aprius begged off. "This is indeed a strenuous activity. Perhaps my little brother could participate in my stead?"

Marcus had similar success, winning his first two matches three to zero and three to one. By now a crowd had gathered to see the strangers with their unique style and skill best the locals. After beating his third opponent three to one, he yielded the arena to Johanan.

Johanan had to work harder than his two young friends but still won each of his first two matches, three to one. Then the local champion took his place in the ring opposite Johanan. He was nearly half a cubit taller, and likely a good third heavier—and it was muscle, not fat.

It soon became clear the giant opposite him was used to winning using his size and brute strength. He charged Johanan twice. Both times, Johanan managed to use his weight and speed against him to flip him and gain a point. On the third charge the Athenian managed to get an arm under his leg. Johanan found himself being held up in the air for a few moments. His captor bellowed before throwing him down forcefully on the sand. As he glared down at Johanan lying on his back, the other Athenians and the islanders laughed loudly.

Johanan gritted his teeth and clenched his fists. Then he told himself, *It's only a game.* A sheepish smile replaced the look of anger on his face.

He took a few moments to catch his breath before getting up. *I really am too old to be doing this.* He slowly got back on his feet.

The giant taunted him. "You can yield now, and save yourself from further pain."

Johanan shook his head. "And dishonor my brothers? I may not be worthy to face you, but I can't surrender in front of them."

His opponent rushed him, more cautiously than the first time, but with renewed confidence now that he had demonstrated his physical strength over the visitor. Johanan faked as if he was going to step to the right then at the last minute went to the left. The giant was on his back in the sand before he knew it.

Johanan was panting from the exertion of the match. He looked down at the man, who was staring back at him in shock. He reached down with both hands. The giant reached up with one massive paw. Johanan grunted as he helped him to his feet.

He clapped Johanan on the shoulder, "Well done, little man." The rest of the spectators and the islanders then surrounded him and joined in the congratulations.

Finally Tullius interrupted, "This has indeed been entertaining, but we must prepare for a voyage."

As they departed, the friendly local who had first invited them to join in the sport asked, "Where did you learn to wrestle like that?"

Johanan grinned widely and looked at Tullius before responding. "Right here, my friend. Our skills have their foundation right here."

Chapter Forty-Six

Water is life, and because we have no water, life is miserable.

A voice from Kenya
Rich Stearns in The Hole in our Gospel

TWO WEEKS AFTER John woke from his coma, and over the protests of his doctor, David, Nicole, and John were on a flight to West Ghana. Nicole had managed to delay the meeting due to John's condition, but could not get the government representative to explain the need for the face to face session.

When they entered the main terminal at the airport in the capital city, the three looked around to see if someone had been sent to pick them up. None of the signs being held up by drivers were for them. John looked over to his left at two soldiers dressed in the khaki uniform of the West Ghanan Army. One of them looked down at a picture in his hand, and then up at the three of them. He stepped toward them and waved at his companion to follow him.

"Mr. Amato?" the soldier said to John in a voice that contained strong strains of a British colonial accent.

"Yes, that's me."

"Please, you and your companions will come with me." He turned and strode toward the exit of the terminal.

"What about our bags?" asked Nicole.

He looked over his shoulder without slowing his stride. "They will be delivered to your hotel."

David, Nicole, and John looked at each other. David shrugged his shoulders and rushed to catch up to the first soldier. Nicole and John followed in his wake.

After a twenty minute jeep ride through the city, they were led into the lobby of the trade ministry building. Their escort said, "You will wait here," and turned to go.

"We were told we'd be meeting with the prime minister," Nicole said.

He ignored her protest. "You will wait here," and left without further explanation.

They sat for two hours. Civil servants traversed the lobby on their way into or out of the building. A few gave them sidelong glances. Finally, a well-dressed woman stepped out of the bank of elevators and made her way to them. She nodded to them and said, "The minister will see you now."

They stood to follow her. She nodded to the security guard who waved them through. A man held the elevator open for them.

"Are we going to meet with the prime minister?" asked Nicole as they rode up in the elevator.

David put his forefinger to his lips to signal silence.

"You will be meeting with the minister." The elegant woman offered no further explanation; she just smiled.

They disembarked at the top floor. A disinterested soldier, equipped with a semiautomatic rifle, glanced up from a magazine, nodded, and then went back to his reading. The woman led them to large, copper clad double doors. She opened both wide and then stood to the side. She gestured for them to enter.

Behind an ornate desk sat a dark skinned man dressed neatly in a cobalt blue suit. He looked to be in his early fifties and wore thin, wire rimmed spectacles. He stood as they entered and gestured to a small table with four chairs at the side of the room.

"Please, Mr. Amato, Mr. Freeman, and Miss Logan, have a seat."

He joined them at the table and took the fourth seat. "I am Abram Mutato, the minister of trade. I must confess that your invitation to our country was not entirely, shall I say, forthright. The prime minister issued the message to your organization on my behalf. You will not be meeting with him."

John thought, *Here it comes. Rather than dirty his own hands, the prime minister is delegating extortion to one of his underlings.*

David said, "We're glad to be here so we can answer any questions you have."

The woman who had brought them up returned with a tray with four small cups and two pots. She addressed the group. "We have both coffee and tea for you. What would you care for, Miss Logan?"

"Please, I'll take coffee."

Minister Mutato warned, "The coffee is good, but is much stronger than your American version. That is why the cups are so small."

"I'd still like to try it. I enjoy a good espresso."

The assistant served the four of them in turn. When she was finished, the minister addressed her, "Thank you Miss Abeba. Please close the doors behind you." She nodded and departed.

When the doors were closed he continued. "I have called you here because I want to meet the leaders of the organization that is raising the hopes of my people. I have met your woman who is setting up the filter plant and believe her to be sincere, but she does not make the decisions for this Galilean Foundation."

The three of them nodded but kept their silence. David had coached them to let their host take the lead in the meeting.

"You see, many people have come here to help before. The United Nations, Christian organizations, and others think they know what is best for my people. Some of them are honest, but some are more interested in lining their own pockets." He waved his hand, as if dismissing their predecessors. "They consider us to be backward, and gullible."

He stopped to noisily slurp his own coffee. "The situation here is not always stable. Muslims and Christians battle each other. Ancient tribal disputes frequently erupt. Not everyone has the fortitude to persevere in this situation."

He took another sip of coffee and then looked at each of his guests. "This Water for Life project brings great promise, but I will not have the hearts of my people broken yet again."

David responded. "Minister Mutato, we are here because we want to help your people. We will not break their hearts."

The minister looked at David. "Tell me, Mr. Freeman, from what tribe are your ancestors?"

"My mother was from the Tsonga tribe in South Africa. She took the name of the missionary who helped her family immigrate to the United States." David shrugged. "My father traces his family to slaves in the South. He doesn't know about his African origins."

The minister looked at Nicole. "And you, Miss Logan?"

"Oh, uh—I guess I'd say mostly Irish and Norwegian. I'm pretty much a typical American mutt."

Then he looked at John. "From the news reports, your people are of the Balkan nations."

John dodged the implied question. "I see you are well informed."

The minister set down his coffee and reached behind his neck.

He pulled a thin gold chain over his head and palmed the pendant as it came clear of his collar. He held the hidden object over the middle of the table, the chain dangling down. Then he turned his hand over and slowly opened his fist to reveal a small gold cross.

"You see, in the end, we are all from the same tribe."

The next morning, John, Nicole, David, and minister Mutato were on a Huey flying to the site of the filter assembly village. Mutato had traded in his suit for olive colored slacks and shirt. The members of the foundation were also dressed in casual attire suitable for an expedition. Along the way, the minister talked to them on the headsets they wore to cover the din of the turbine motor. He pointed out herds of wildlife, thriving villages, and abandoned ones.

"Many of the people here must lead a nomadic life because of lack of clean water. It is a source of much conflict and poverty here. If you can provide good water, you will help to make a more stable and peaceful life."

John noticed several metal patches on the control console. Two had been painted over, but one was bare metal. When he had Mutato's attention, he pointed at them and raised an eyebrow in question.

Mutato pointed to the two painted patches. "Vietnam. This is a surplus American helicopter." Then he pointed to the fresh repair job. "Rebels."

When they arrived at their destination, they saw ten forty-foot shipping containers lined up on the edge of the field which served as a landing zone. Six of the containers stood alone, but workmen were clustered around and in the openings of the other four. John could see the flame from a torch cutting an almost complete circle in the end of one. A small crowd assembled in front of the structures. Most of them were ebony skinned. A woman deeply tanned, but still obviously Caucasian, stood out in the group.

The helicopter settled on the earth and John, David, Nicole, and Minister Mutato jumped onto the grass, flanked by two soldiers. When they had cleared the still turning rotor, the white woman broke from the crowd and practically tackled John.

"Easy there, I'm still a bit fragile."

Tears streamed down Susan Hill's face. "I'm so glad to see you here. I heard you died."

He put his arm around her shoulders as they walked away from the helicopter. "As Mark Twain once said, 'The reports of my death have been greatly exaggerated.'"

When the helicopter had departed, leaving the minister, two soldiers, and the three Americans, Abram Mutato gave them a tour of the plant and the village. He had taken a personal interest in this project, to the point of locating it with one of his tribal families. Mutato was obviously revered in this village as a local boy who had made good, and honored his roots.

The village chief introduced them to a team of locals working inside one of the containers. They were assembling a series of troughs and connecting PVC pipes. He used a wooden staff to point out how the water would flow through the container. "In each of these big tubs the heavy sediment falls out and is drained." He tapped his staff on the final trough. "And here, the miracle muck filters out everything else."

He turned to Susan who stood right behind him. "Did I get that right, Miss Hill?"

She laughed. "Miracle muck? Perfect. My work here is done."

That night they gathered in an open sided pavilion for supper, where the village leader, dressed in his formal tribal dress, made an articulate speech thanking the visitors for entrusting the Water of

Life project to his tribe. He talked at length about how this would not only build stability for his tribe, but would bring a more lasting peace to his nation.

"We take this moment in the history of our tribe most seriously. Not only will we share water for good, we will also use it to tell others of the true Water of Life."

John turned to Nicole. "You have done an amazing job pulling this all together. If it wasn't for you we'd still be talking about it."

She gave him a wry smile. "You were the guys with the vision and the secret ingredient. I'm just the person who brings order out of chaos."

The chief beckoned to his wife sitting at his side. She passed him up a loaf of bread. He raised it over his head and said, "In the name of Jesus Christ, we bless this bread." He brought it down and cradled it against his chest and broke off a small piece. He closed his eyes and ate it. Then he broke the loaf in half and handed each portion to the person sitting to his right and left.

"This is his body. We eat this in memory of Him."

As the loaf halves made their way around the pavilion, David kneeled behind Nicole and John and put his arms around them. "This is what it's all about. This is why we are here."

Nicole looked over at John. "I see I'm not the only one crying here."

He smiled back through eyes welling with tears. "Just having a déjà vu moment—one of too many to count."

The next day Minister Mutato returned to the capital city. David, Nicole, and John spent the next five days working with the people of the village and visiting nearby locations. On the morning of the sixth day a helicopter took them directly to the airport.

Mutato met them in the lobby of the terminal where he bade them farewell. "You have seen that my tribe—your tribe—are a hardworking people. They will not let you down. You must not let them down."

Nicole hugged him. "We won't. We're here for the long haul."

John hugged him as well. "We're here until He returns. We won't break their hearts."

When David hugged him Mutato said, "Your ancestors will be proud of you. You have not forgotten your people."

After the minister left them John turned to his companions. "Our connecting flight back home goes through Athens. I'd like to extend our layover there a day so we can take a side trip. If you're too tired I understand, but I would appreciate your company."

Nicole and David looked at each other and nodded. David responded. "Sure, we're game."

"Great. I'll make arrangements."

Chapter Forty-Seven

The wise man in the storm prays to God, not for safety from danger, but for deliverance from fear.

Ralph Waldo Emerson

GAIUS WAS FASCINATED by the islander's success in the ring against the local athletes. As a slave he had been given little time for recreational physical activity. As they walked back to the house of Strabo, Tullius explained how he had come to be a local champion in Athens and then taught his sons, and then Johanan, the sport.

Gaius asked, "What about me? Could you teach me to wrestle like that?"

Tullius smiled benignly. "Perhaps, just perhaps, we will take another into our inner circle."

The next morning they said their farewells to Strabo and his household.

"Take good care of our scribe," Strabo instructed Tullius. "We need his work to spread the good news."

"I will. He will have a home with us as long as it is safe."

The four men set off on foot to the port, following a donkey drawn cart led by one of Strabo's servants. It was loaded with the boxes containing the precious scrolls and supplies of the scribe and their personal gear.

When they reached their boat, the cooper was already there with the promised vessels. They had been disassembled so they could be stowed in the hull for the journey. The men arranged the parts of the vat and the chests with the scrolls. They secured them tightly with ropes so they wouldn't shift during the crossing. The merchant and Strabo's servant left them to their work.

As they began to load their personal gear, Aprius reached for the bag containing Johanan's belongings. The apostle placed his foot on his luggage and said, "I won't be coming with you."

Everyone stopped what they were doing and looked at Johanan. Finally, Marcus broke the silence. "Where will you go? What will we do without you?

Johanan looked around at his friends. He swallowed hard before he answered. "I don't know where I will go. I just know it is time for me to move on. I must obey his call."

"Did you have another vision?" Marcus asked.

"No, little brother, true visions are rare. Many go their whole life without one. In this case it is just a feeling my time with you is at an end, at least for now."

Marcus said, "But what will we do without you? You are our teacher."

Johanan looked down at Gaius who was sitting on the chest containing the scrolls. "You have a new teacher who will be faithful to the truth. You also have a wealth of knowledge in the writings." He choked up. "I must spread the word to other people now."

Marcus started to speak, but couldn't get the words out. He looked down at the pouch at his waist and pulled out his bronze hand mirror. He extended it to Johanan.

"Here. My gift to you."

Johanan shook his head. "If you really want to give me a gift, live for others."

Marcus looked down at the mirror in his hand and threw it over his shoulder without looking back. Johanan watched it slice into the water of the bay and vanish. Marcus nodded. "I will."

They made many promises in their parting. Johanan promised to return to the island someday. Tullius agreed to explain Johanan's decision to Anteia, and Gaius pledged to be a faithful teacher. Finally the scribe and the men of the house of Tullius untied their boat from the dock and began their journey back to their small paradise.

Johanan stood on the dock and watched. He waved one last time and waited there until they passed out of sight. By that time, he could barely see through the tears welling up in his eyes.

He rubbed his eyes with the sleeve of his tunic and turned back to the port city. As he strolled he lamented silently. *Oh, Lord, what would you have me do? What would you have me do?*

One of the first merchants he saw as he stepped off the dock was a barbershop. Only one of the two chairs was occupied. A barber sat on a stool next to the other chair, sharpening his shaving knife as he chatted with his coworker and customer. Johanan paused. He didn't want to take a chance at being identified as the Beloved Disciple again. A new hairstyle would help.

Johanan stepped inside and placed his bag on the floor. The idle barber greeted him and gestured toward the open chair. "It looks like a long while since you have been to an establishment such as ours."

"Yes, I have been away a long while on my master's business."

"Shall I cut your hair and shave your beard in the modern style?"

"That would be fine."

He pondered his next move as he sat. The barber chattered

away about news in the city and empire as he worked on Johanan's hair and beard. Greek barbershops were well known for being sources of news, but the apostle wasn't paying attention.

Johanan thought back to Josephus' proclamation that the Beloved Disciple was among them, resurrected. As long as he traveled in the Mediterranean there was a danger that elderly people who had known him in his youth might come to the same conclusion. It would take another generation until those compatriots had passed from the earth. At that thought, he felt a twinge of envy. He didn't understand why he had been called to do the Lord's work past a man's usual span of years instead of joining him in heaven.

Perhaps he should follow in the footsteps of his fellow apostle, Thomas. Years after their Master's resurrection, Judas Thomas Didymus had traveled to Syria and Persia to spread the good news before ending up in India. Word had come several decades ago that Thomas had died a martyr's death there, but not before founding several churches. Johanan had heard nothing about those fledgling communities for many years.

Johanan remembered the nickname for his fellow disciple among many believers: Doubting Thomas. He recalled well the incident which had given birth to that name. Thomas alone among the remaining disciples had missed the resurrected Lord's first appearance in the upper room. He insisted that he wouldn't believe the others until he could put his hand in the wounds of the risen Jesus. Johanan smiled as he remembered Judas Thomas Didymus' reaction upon being invited to do so by the Messiah when he next appeared to them: "My Lord, and my God."

Johanan preferred his own nickname: Thomas the Brave. When Jesus had announced he intended to return to Judea where Lazarus had "fallen asleep," fear had overcome the disciples. They tried to talk their teacher out of returning to the area where they had narrowly avoided being stoned on their previous visit.

They reasoned if Lazarus had fallen asleep that he would get well soon. The twelve did their best to talk Jesus out of returning to that region.

As the barber shaved Johanan's face, he recalled Jesus finally announcing, "Lazarus is dead, and for your sake I am glad I was not there, so that you may believe. But let us go to him."

The disciples continued to murmur about the foolhardiness of such a decision until Thomas stood up and announced, "Let us also go, that we may die with him."

Johanan couldn't ignore that challenge and appear to be less courageous than Thomas Didymus. He had stood up as well and agreed. One by one the other apostles had acquiesced. They returned to Bethany where they witnessed Jesus raise Lazarus from the dead, and learned to trust even more in their Master. He had become Doubting Thomas in the end, but to Johanan, he would always be Thomas the Brave.

He had been ignoring the nattering of his barber, responding only periodically with a grunt of agreement. But about this time the conversation of the pair next to him caught his attention.

"So what do you trade for in India?" the other barber said.

"Spikenard and other precious oils and spices."

Spikenard. Johanan recalled Mary, the sister of Lazarus, pouring a bottle of the precious oil on the feet of Jesus and then wiping His feet with her hair. He listened closely.

"A valuable cargo. And when do you leave?"

"As soon as I find a replacement for my scribe," his customer said. "He ran away when I told him about this voyage."

The barber chuckled. "You may have a difficult time with your search. There are scribes about but I fear they will be reluctant to leave a comfortable life here, even for the possibility of riches in the spice trade. You may have to buy a slave."

"That would be difficult. I have invested in supplies and passage for my crew to Antioch. I have only enough to hire a caravan to traverse the road to India. I would rather not make this journey without someone to help me maintain records of my trade." His grooming completed, he stood and paid the barber out of a small leather pouch of coins.

"The ship will leave for Antioch on the high tide in two hours, with or without me. I fear I will have to find someone along the way."

"May the gods be with you on your journey," said the barber. The merchant nodded and turned to go.

Johanan cleared his throat, loudly. "Pardon me."

The merchant stopped and turned toward him. "Yes?"

"I couldn't help but overhear of your dilemma. As it happens I am well-traveled and not afraid of a long journey to the east."

"Yes?"

"I also have experience as a scribe."

Chapter Forty-Eight

. . . you can't go home again.

Thomas Wolfe

THE MORNING AFTER leaving West Ghana, Nicole, David, and John boarded a twin-engine turboprop at the Athens airport. The plane climbed quickly to the low altitude airway for the short flight. From their height, John could see ferries and other boats dotting the Aegean waters below. The color of the sea varied from deep blue to turquoise depending on the depth. A multitude of rocky islands with white sandy beaches broke the surface of the sea. The stark white plaster of the buildings on each island was broken up by red and blue domes.

"What an incredible view," remarked Nicole as she peered out the window next to John.

From the seat behind them, David shouted so he could be overhead above the engine noise, "Imagine what it was like when the apostles and early Christians lived here."

"Sailing ships, Roman galleys, and lots of fish," responded John.

Within minutes they were descending to an airport on an island to the southeast of Athens. They walked from the small terminal down to the ferry landing. They waited only twenty minutes before they were able to catch one of the passenger vessels that connected the local islands.

The three of them stood on the bow of the boat and enjoyed the sun and sea breeze as the small ferry chugged its way to their destination. John noticed Nicole was wearing a black, Greek style blouse embroidered with gold. She must have picked it up in the hotel gift shop the night before.

She leaned against the railing, closed her eyes and turned her face toward the sun. John watched her hair swirl around her face in the wind. After a minute she opened her eyes to see him watching her. She smiled at him.

"You fit in well here."

She smiled, closed her eyes, and turned back to the sun.

John looked over at David who responded with a smirk, then turned to look over the railing at the sea below.

After several stops they pulled up to a wooden wharf located on a small island. A number of boats were tied up on the other side of the dock, many of them fishing vessels. An old man with white hair and beard was painting the trim on one of them. He nodded to the three as they walked up to the beach.

John looked to his left where an ancient stone jetty jutted out into the sea. It was a mixture of different types of stone, topped by a crumbling concrete surface. Sand had built up along one side.

When they reached the road that fronted the bay, John turned left and led them to the foot of the jetty.

"I wonder how old this is," commented David.

"It dates from the time of the Romans—I would expect," John said. He reached down and affectionately patted a worn stone as if he was greeting an old friend. "Let me show you something else that dates nearly to the time of Christ."

They continued along the road a few hundred yards until they reached a little used trail that headed inland. Shortly they were in a clearing where large, rectangular, stone tubs were lined up in rows. Many of them were overgrown with vegetation and others were falling apart.

John waved at the clearing. "This is where they made garum, a fish sauce popular in the empire." He led them over to a tub that was relatively intact. "They chopped up whole fish, layered them with spices and salt and let them ferment. After about a month they'd draw the liquid off and ship it to buyers."

Nicole wrinkled her nose. "Sounds putrid."

John chuckled. "It was at first, but it was pretty good after the fermentation process. This island was well known for their quality garum."

"Your knowledge of things never seems to amaze me, John," David said. "Who else would know about this site on a little tiny island in the middle of the Mediterranean?"

"I was blessed with a good memory and a desire to learn. However, this is not the real reason I brought you here. Before I show you that, let's get lunch."

They quickly found what appeared to be the only taverna in the small town. Four men, two older and two that could have been their sons, sat at a table on the sidewalk. The two elders were playing backgammon while the younger pair watched. One sported a worn tan cap and the other an equally aged blue cap. Both wore the stubble of a day old beard. The younger ones had deeply tanned faces and the same stubble as their elders. One of the younger men smoked a hand-rolled cigarette. As the trio passed by, the two older men tipped their weathered caps. They all nodded at John, Nicole, and then David. After they passed, the four started chattering rapidly in Greek and then burst out laughing. Nicole looked back at them and caught them watching the trio, still laughing. They sheepishly averted their eyes and went back to focusing on their game.

She said to John and David, "I wonder what that was all about."

John replied, "They were talking about us of course. The one with the cigarette said, 'I wonder if they got off the boat at the wrong stop.' The one with the tan cap said, 'Maybe they came to our island to rob our store and get rich.' Then the man against the wall said, 'Either way, they are very bad navigators.' That's when they all lost it."

"Man, how many languages do you know?" David asked.

"When you grow up in this region of the world, you pick up a few."

Nicole looked back at the men, who were looking at the three visitors again. "I was afraid they were saying something crude." She flashed them a coquettish smile. This time they grinned, nodding and tipping caps as if in apology.

As John pulled open the torn screen door to the taverna, the rusty hinges squealed in protest. He held it for his friends and entered after them. The inside of the café was clean, but worn. The dated Formica counters and table tops made John think it looked like the whole place had been dumped off on the island in the '50's, with an occasional coat of paint the only attempt at remodeling.

Behind the counter a stout old woman with wavy hair looked up as they entered. A young woman in her mid-twenties was seated at one of the tables typing away on a MacBook Air. She looked up, and greeted them in heavily accented English, "Good morning, would you like to sit inside or outside?"

David laughed, "Do we look that much like foreigners?"

She smiled and said, "From your clothes, you are American."

John said, "Let's sit inside. It's a little warm outside for me."

She directed them to a table and brought them menus. John noticed her long dark hair, artificially streaked. From the back she could have been Anteia's twin in size and shape. But where Anteia's facial features were rounded, this woman's were more angular. When she handed John his menu she looked directly at him and smiled. She had a small gap in between her front teeth that was rather cute.

When his gaze locked with hers, he felt like he was looking through her blue eyes into a time nineteen centuries before. He knew he was being rude but continued to look directly into her eyes, without blinking. She stared back.

Finally she said, "Do I know you?"

"I visited here about twenty years ago," he said softly.

"I would have been five. Must be someone else I remember." She broke away from his gaze and pointed at the menu in front of him. "Do you need me to interpret for you?"

The menu was in Greek.

John shook his head. "No, I can read it."

He recited the list of dishes. When he read the one for grilled octopus, he grimaced. Nicole laughed. "Don't worry, I'll skip that this time."

They settled on freshly caught tuna and several pasta dishes. Nicole commented after their plates had been served, "None of that smelly fish sauce, I see."

John laughed. "They haven't made that here for a long time. Your nostrils are safe."

When they had finished a leisurely lunch, John led them out of town. The cobblestone street that led inland was worn but in good repair.

Finally they came in sight of a building set alone in a clearing. The front part of the building was white, plastered stone, in the classic style of the Greek isles. The back section was three times the size of the front and consisted of bare cinder block walls with tile roofing. John led them into the front entrance.

A young man with curly dark hair was seated at a desk behind a short counter. On the walls were a variety of framed icons of what appeared to be apostles or saints, interspersed with photos of families, couples, and distinguished looking individuals. The photos included black and white, faded color, and newer portraits. The men in the photos all had bushy mustaches that threatened to swallow their mouths. The young women were singularly beautiful. The older women retained their looks, if not their figures.

The man behind the desk looked up and greeted them in Greek.

John responded in the same language, "Good morning, I am John Amato from the United States. Do you speak English?"

"My name is Panos," he said in English with a minimal accent, "but your Greek is excellent."

John gestured to Nicole and David. "My friends don't speak the language."

"Of course, welcome to our island. We don't get many visitors." Then he looked back at John. "John Amato. You are from San Francisco?"

"I was, but now I live in Seattle."

"You have bought from us before on our website."

"Yes, that's me."

He turned and yelled through the open doorway behind him, "Angelos, prepare coffee. We have friends here from America."

As John sat sipping gritty Greek coffee with Angelos, Panos, David, and Nicole, he recalled another visit to a building once located where he now sat. In 190 AD, nearly a century after he had parted from the islanders, Johanan had kept the promise made to Tullius on the dock in Piraeus and returned to the island. The garum industry was thriving and a sturdy stone pier serviced the ships that called on the village. Although the people he had known were gone, he could see his former friends in the faces of their descendants.

The Christian community there was vibrant and had managed

to avoid the ire of the authorities. Once Johanan had professed his faith and earned their trust as a fellow believer, they took him into their confidence on another element of their village.

An elderly man had led him to a secluded stone building, located down a secret trail. Inside were rows of benches and tables where half a dozen scribes worked away at copying scriptures.

"Nearly a century ago a Christian scribe from Athens fled to our remote island to hide from the Roman authorities. Athens was not safe for followers of the Way—especially for those who made copies of holy writings."

Johanan nodded. "The Roman emperors still swing between tolerance and persecution."

"Yes. And that's why we have kept our little scriptorium a secret from the earliest days."

"And that scribe was named..."

"Gaius."

Of course. Gaius the former Macedonian slave.

Using his cane, the elderly man pulled himself to his full height and puffed out his chest. "That scribe was my grandfather." He leaned toward Johanan. "Today my sons and brothers, continue the work he started." With a smile in his eyes he told Johanan, "When I was a child he would tell me the story of how he came to be here. The man who brought him was the legendary Tullius, the founder of the garum industry on the island."

As Johanan took in the sight of the hard working scribes, the grandson of Gaius added, "I never knew him, but Tullius was my great grandfather."

Johanan looked at the master scribe. At first he choked on his words, then said softly, "Then your grandmother must have been—Anteia."

"Yes, a wise and beautiful woman, even in her old age. Her faith in the Christos inspired me as a young man." He leaned forward on his cane. "But how did you know of my grandmother, my friend?"

Johanan nodded and then put his arm around the stooped shoulders of his companion. "The Lord has revealed many things to me my brother, many wonderful and mysterious things."

"What brings you to our island, Mr. Amato?" Panos' question interrupted John's reminiscence.

"Please, it's John." He gestured at the building around him. "We were returning from a trip to Africa and were passing through Athens. I wanted to see the place that makes such beautiful Bibles."

Angelos said, "Would you like a tour of our shop?"

They led him through the building where a number of old style letter press printers were turning out large sheets of paper that were cut into individual pages. Angelos said to the trio, "Most of our business is in Greek, but we do publish other editions, including English, as John knows."

He led them to another room where craftsman were embossing pictures with gold leaf accents. "Each one of our Bibles contains twenty four different icons. We have pictures of apostles, old testament prophets, the virgin mother, and the Lord." He picked up a beautifully decorated picture of an old man in a robe holding two tablets. "Moses, of course."

"These are amazing," Nicole said. "You could frame any of these and put them in a museum."

Angelos beamed at the compliment. "My brother would like to replace all this with digital printing presses. It would be more cost effective, of course, but you could never get the same craftsmanship as we have here."

He reached for two other pages. He passed the first to David. "This one is of your namesake, King David." The icon showed a shepherd with a sheep over his shoulders and a staff in his hand.

The second page he passed to John. "This one is of your namesake, the apostle John." John looked at the picture of the serene young man who stared back at him. The halo around his head was in gold leaf. A bird of prey was in the background over his right shoulder. In his hand he held a rolled up scroll.

Nicole pointed to the icon. "Why the bird?"

John answered. "It's an eagle, the symbol of the evangelist." Angelos and Panos nodded.

"It's so beautiful," remarked Nicole.

John turned toward his companions and gingerly held the picture up next to his face, "Beautiful yes, but not a good likeness." They chuckled at his joke.

Angelos laughed. "Next time, we use you as model." He passed Nicole a third page. "I'm afraid we have none that would match your name, but this one is of the Holy Family." Gold leaf also provided the precious glow of the halos for Mary, Joseph, and the Christ Child. "Please accept these as our gift."

He led them to the next room where a different group of craftsmen were creating covers for the bound volumes. Although the smell of fresh leather filled the room, the finished product looked like it had spent centuries on a shelf. A large gold cross surrounded by four smaller gold crosses graced each cover.

John picked up two of the finished Bibles and passed one to each of his companions. "I would like to buy each of you a copy for your faithful service to the Galilean Foundation."

David thumbed through the treasure in his hand and cocked his head at Panos. "How much do each of these cost?"

"Four hundred dollars, US."

"Wow," he looked at John. "That would feed a lot of poor people."

Nicole said, "These are amazing, but this is a Greek Orthodox version."

John nodded at their protests. "Yes, they are expensive, but as Jesus said, 'The poor will always be with us.' Besides, I want you to have something to remind you of the beauty and breadth of our faith." He looked at their hosts. "Not to mention this provides a good living for the faithful people of this island."

The two brothers grinned.

As John led the way back to town, Nicole watched him from behind. Angelos walked by his side and the two chatted as if John had grown up with him on the island. David was just behind her and Panos walked beside her, flirting shamelessly.

"If I know that American women were so pretty I would visit your country long ago."

She laughed, then deflected his attentions by asking questions about the history of the island. She listened half-heartedly but her attention was on the familiar head of curly hair ahead of her. She had never seen him so emotional. Several times in the Bible printing plant he had seemed close to tears, especially when he held up the icon of the apostle John. *What is his connection to this place?*

In ten minutes they reached the outskirts of the village and its worn cobblestone streets. When they came upon the backgammon players near the taverna, they stopped. Angelos put his hand on the shoulder of the older man in the tan cap and chattered to him rapidly in Greek. The man nodded and looked at John and his companions. Then Angelos turned to the Americans and said, "You have two hours before your ferry arrives. Share some wine with us and meet the rest of our family."

He stepped inside and the sound of an animated conversation could be heard. He returned in a moment with a bottle and led them to a gate next to the building. They passed through it into a courtyard shaded by large trees. The man in the tan cap whom Angelos had accosted earlier joined them.

"My friends, this is my father, Nikodemos. Father, this is Mr. Amato from America. He has bought many of our Bibles."

Nikodemos reached out to shake his hand. In a thick Greek accent he said, "A pleasure to meet you, Mr. Amato."

"Johanan, please."

"Oh, like the apostle."

"Yes, like him."

They sat at the table. In moments the young woman from the taverna who had served them and the old woman who had been behind the counter joined them. They carried wine glasses and a plate of cut goat cheese and hard crusted bread. As Angelos poured from the bottle. he said to John, "This is my mother, Petra, and sister, Sarah." He switched to Greek to address his mother.

His sister interrupted. "We have met them already. They had lunch here."

"Yes," John said, "and she pegged us for Americans right away. She is more perceptive than her brother." He smiled at Panos. Nicole noticed that Sarah smiled at John's compliment. No shy smile this one, rather that of a confident young woman.

The family and the three visitors chattered for an hour and broke open another bottle of wine before David asked, "How old is the Bible printing business on your island?"

Angelos said, "We can't prove it, but stories say we have had scribes making copies of scriptures here since the second or third century. We do know we have had a Bible printing business on the island since the 1600's. Our first press was a Gutenberg press."

Nicole stammered, "You have a Gutenberg press on this island?"

Panos laughed. "No, one of our ancestors dumped it in the sea years ago. Today we could sell it and be rich."

Nikodemos elbowed his wife. "We curse his name every day."

David cocked his head. "Really?"

Angelos chimed in. "No, only on days when the bills come due."

Nicole asked, "How long has your family been on this island?"

Nikodemos leaned back in his chair and smiled broadly. Only his lower teeth peeked out from his bushy mustache. In his thick Greek accent he said, "Legend is our village was founded by the crew of a vessel shipwrecked on their way home from the Trojan wars." He beamed at his wife and daughter. "And one of their captives was the daughter of Helen of Troy. That explains the beauty of our women." Sarah blushed.

Panos laughed. "Don't forget the other legend, Father. Some say our ancestors just grew tired of fighting the wars of the Greek kings and fled to this island for a peaceful life." They all joined in the laughter.

John raised his glass. "A toast." Nicole saw tears welling up in his eyes. "To a village and family that has been a steward of our faith since the days of its infancy."

They raised their glasses, to the island, and islanders.

Chapter Forty-Nine

There are some people who live in a dream world, and there are some who face reality; and then there are those who turn one into the other.

Douglas Everett

NICOLE POPPED THE DVD in the player and turned to John. "This will not be what you expect."

From his seat on the couch he raised one eyebrow. He reached into the bowl of popcorn on his lap. "But you did promise me a movie night?"

"Yep. A very special one. Maybe the most important one you've ever had." She sat down next to him and pressed the menu button to skip past the previews. The opening screen for the movie *Iron Man* popped up.

John looked over at Nicole. "I guess I should have expected you weren't the chick-flick type. But how is *Iron Man* a special movie?"

She flicked a piece of popcorn at him from off of her finger tip. He snagged it with a quick move of his hand and popped it in his mouth.

She turned to the screen. "Just watch."

Nearly two hours later the movie was winding down. Nicole elbowed John. "Pay attention to this scene."

"Yes ma'am." He straightened up in his seat.

On the screen, Tony Stark, played by Robert Downey Jr., was holding a press conference where he denied being the super hero Iron Man. As the alibi he had been provided by a secret government agency began to unravel, he finally confessed to the gathered reporters, "The truth is—I *am* Iron Man." The conference erupted as reporters jumped to their feet and started firing questions.

Nicole reached over and picked up the remote. She pressed the pause button and turned to face John.

"John. I want to take our relationship to the next level. Do you feel that way about me?"

John nodded, almost imperceptibly. "On a personal level, I'd like that very much. But I don't think that's a good idea." His voice trailed off, and he looked away.

"I think I understand why you feel that way and I think I can solve that problem. But I need to know something." She pointed at the screen. "Are you Iron Man?"

John laughed, a nervous little laugh. "That's a comic book. You know there is no Iron Man."

"Not *that* Iron Man. I mean, are you John, the Last Apostle?"

His mouth gaped. "What? What makes you think that? I mean, even the idea he's alive is crazy."

Nicole put down the remote and sat back, folding her arms. "Hearing about Cavanaugh's challenge and all the facts and legends behind it have made me think: maybe it's not such a crazy idea after all. Even in the first century they thought he'd live until the return of Christ."

She turned toward John and pointed her finger at him. "And then there's you. You seem to be fluent in a dozen languages."

He leaned back, hesitating before he responded. "I tell you, I've traveled a lot."

"Yes, I can tell. We visit a remote Greek isle and you act like you lived there before. You know details about a backwater place that barely shows up on a map."

"I told you—"

"You talk about biblical days as if you lived there. But you refuse to consider writing a book. And your own past history is a total mystery. It seems like you popped up a dozen years ago and stay on the move." She looked into his eyes. "If I didn't know your warm heart so well, I'd think you were some kind of spy or hit man.

John started to open his mouth. She put her finger to his lips to silence him.

"Then there's the matter of your miraculous recovery from a shooting that should have killed you. You healed so fast the docs wanted to study you. But you said no, and acted like it was just another day in the life." She pulled her finger away.

"You don't make sense the way you explain yourself. But it makes a lot more sense if you're a guy who has been around for two thousand years."

John looked away.

"Then there's your name: John Amato. I looked it up. Amato is Italian for love. John the Apostle was known as the Apostle of Love."

He looked back at her, wide eyed.

"And speaking of 'Johns' there was Johannes Fischer—the man who opened up your offshore bank accounts." John looked like he wanted to tear away his gaze, but couldn't.

"I don't remember much of what I learned living as a kid in Germany, but it doesn't take a genius to know Johannes is the German form of 'John' and that Fischer is German for…" Her voice trailed off.

She looked at him expectantly—daring him to deny he knew the answer. Finally, he finished her sentence. "Fisherman."

"And of course, the apostle John was by trade…"

He paused for a moment. "A fisherman."

At first she smiled at him like she had just come from behind in a marathon to beat him at the tape. Then her expression softened. "John. I fought this. I was afraid it was a rebound romance. But I can't deny I'm in love with you. But I need to know the truth about you."

She watched his face as he took it in. After a long pause, he said in a measured tone, "Nicole, I think I love you as well. But I don't think our relationship is a good idea. And the whole idea of John being alive is—"

She held up her hand. "Enough. You are also the most evasive person I've ever known. But I've never caught you lying and I'm betting a real apostle would not tell a direct lie." She put her hand gently on his shoulder. "John, the next word out of your mouth had better be either 'yes' or 'no' in response to my question. If it isn't, I will walk away from you and the Galilean Foundation forever." She gripped his shoulder tightly. "No more dodging, no more evasive answers."

She inhaled, as if she was trying to get up her courage, then blurted out. "Are you John, son of Zebedee, the two thousand year old apostle of Jesus Christ?"

John started to speak, then firmly closed his mouth.

She pulled her hand away from his shoulder and folded her arms. For a moment she stared at the frozen image of *Iron Man* on the TV screen. Finally she broke the silence. "I can't go on like this." She snatched her purse off of the coffee table and strode to the door. She jerked it open and turned back to look at John. He was frozen in place, a look of desperation on his face. He stood.

She held up her hand. "Don't follow me unless you're willing to answer the question." She stepped through the door and slammed it behind her. She started to race down the stairs and had to slow part way down because tears were blurring her vision. She stopped at the landing and waited, listened for the sound of footsteps or a door opening behind her. Nothing. She sobbed once, got a tighter grip on her vanishing composure and then walked slowly down the stairs.

Halfway down the front walk she stopped, turned around, and looked up at John's second story window. It was open and he was sitting on the sill; one leg hanging out. He had a pleading look, like a high school boy who has just asked a cheerleader to the prom and is waiting for her answer.

She yelled up at him, "All I want is your answer: yes or no."

He stared down at her. It looked to her like he had moved his lips slightly, then pursed them tight. From this distance, it was hard to tell.

She turned and in three strides was at the gate. She grasped the handle, pulled the gate toward her, and stopped, still standing in the courtyard of the apartment building. When she looked back at John he was still sitting half in, half out of his window. She waited for what seemed like an eternity. Her fist clenched the handle of her purse and she squeezed her eyes tight to clear out the tears. *All I want is an answer—just a simple yes or no.*

She released the handle of the gate. The spring loaded hinges pulled it shut and it clanged like the door to a prison cell behind her. She stalked back up the sidewalk, through the entrance of the apartment building, and back up to the second floor. When she arrived on the landing John was standing in the hall outside his door. She pushed past him and into his apartment without looking him in the eye. She took her place on the couch. Tony "Iron Man" Stark was still frozen on the screen of the TV. John followed her in and sat down next to her, still mute.

She picked up the remote and turned off the television. The picture was replaced by a blank screen, showing a thin coating of dust. Still staring at the TV, she said, "I think I get it. You can't say 'no' because it's true and you won't lie. You can't say 'yes' because for some reason you're forbidden to." She wrinkled her brow.

She looked back at John. He sat, unflinching. He looked like he was holding a winning hand in a poker game and doing his best to mask his emotions.

"If I'm right about this, someday I'll be an old crone but you'll look like you do now." She smirked. "If that's true, I'm getting the better end of this. I can live with this. I can." She placed her hand on his. "You can trust me with your secret."

She waited for a response and finally asked, "Well?"

John put his fingers to his lips.

"Oh, I forgot." She waved her hand. "I release you from my command that your next word must be either yes or no."

John breathed a sigh of relief. "For a minute I thought you were just coming back to get your DVD."

She laughed. He grasped her hands and enclosed them with his. "Nicole Logan—you are a formidable woman."

She gave him a wry smile. "Not bad for a girl from the wrong side of Oakland, you mean."

He shook his head. "Not bad—period."

She paused before asking, "John, have you been married before?"

His eyes widened. "What makes you think that?"

"Sharon said you told her you'd been married once before, and it ended badly."

John sat, stone faced.

"Let me make another educated guess. You've been married, probably many times. And there are generations of your descendants running around the world."

John pursed his lips. "I've been given a line that I can't cross. You have to respect that."

She nodded. "Then let me speculate, but you don't respond." She pointed to the door of his apartment. "Your friend, Scott. His last name is Adler."

A sly smile crossed John's face momentarily before he suppressed it.

"And of course Adler is German for eagle, the symbol of the apostle John." She shot him a coy smile. "I bet if I go far enough back in Scott and Ben Adler's family tree I'll find a forefather who either vanished or died under mysterious circumstances. That's why you're so patient with that idiot."

"Idiot?"

"He hit on me several times while you were in the hospital. When he wasn't busy hitting on Sharon."

John shook his head. "Scott is kind of a project for me."

"And you never explained why you moved to Seattle. I expect you followed his dad in order to bring them together."

John looked away, at the bright day just through the open window. "There's a bigger issue here."

"Bigger? Isn't this enough for one day?"

"Afraid not." He picked up her hand and held it between his. "I love you, but I can't protect you. What would have happened in that alley if Seth had gunned for you instead of me? There are those who will try to get at me by hurting you."

She gazed into his deep brown eyes. She knew she wanted to spend the rest of her life looking into those eyes. "So, what do we do?"

He sighed. "There's only one choice."

"Which is?"

"We disappear."

Chapter Fifty

Be self-controlled and alert. Your enemy the devil prowls around like a roaring lion looking for someone to devour.

1 Peter 5:8

PROFESSOR WES CAVANAUGH was seated in front of his TV, paging through a copy of the latest script revision for the pilot of *The Last Apostle*. He shook his head. He couldn't believe the direction the show was taking.

He sipped from a glass of Warre's Vintage port—a recent gift from his agent. As he read through the handwritten notes on the script, a news story caught his attention:

"Last week, three members of the Galilean Foundation returned from their visit to the African nation of West Ghana. The foundation is the mysterious organization behind the new water purification technology in the news recently. John Amato, the founder of the group, and the only connection to the unnamed trustees, declined comment. Nicole Logan, the president of the foundation did offer this statement."

The camera zoomed in on Nicole. Two men, identified by subtitles as John Amato and David Freeman, stood behind her. Nicole spoke into a microphone shoved into her face by a reporter. "We're glad to report our meeting with the government of West Ghana was successful. Our operations to manufacture and distribute water purification systems in that country will go ahead as planned."

She reached back and grabbed the hands of Freeman and Amato before continuing. "Jesus' first miracle was to turn water into wine. In his name we are turning sludge into water."

The three turned to go and waved off further questions. The camera focused on the departing John Amato. The reporter commented, "Just a month ago, Mr. Amato was shot multiple times in a Seattle alley and was expected to die. Some say it was a miraculous recovery."

Cavanaugh froze the picture on the screen. He had heard about the shooting and the Galilean Foundation in passing. For some reason Amato had seemed familiar but he couldn't remember why. But now as he looked at John Amato, the encounter during his lecture in Seattle came flooding back; the provocative questions of a true scholar during the lecture and the confrontation afterwards.

Cavanaugh muted the television and looked up a contact on his cell phone and selected the mobile number. In a moment his phone was dialing.

A woman answered, "Professor Cavanaugh, good to hear from you."

"Yes, Ms. Christopher, it has been awhile."

"I take it this isn't just a social call?"

"No it isn't." He cleared his throat. "Michelle, you are familiar with the John Amato and Galilean Foundation story up in Seattle?"

"Professor, I make it my business to be familiar with what's going on in the world."

"I met the man briefly after a lecture in June. For some reason he struck me as a very unusual person then."

"You usually have good instincts about things."

"Yes, thank you. In any event I would like to know more about Mr. Amato."

"What would you like to know about him, Professor?"

He sipped his port before answering. "Everything, Michelle. Everything."

Coming soon

THOMAS THE BRAVE

JOHN THE IMMORTAL SERIES-BOOK II

CHAPTER 1

JOHN BIKED PAST the entrance to his apartment building, glancing furtively to either side, scanning for people who didn't belong there. There had been no sign of Thea since he had been shot up in the alley, but he didn't feel like he could rest easy.

Half a block on he saw Dorothy from apartment 303, out walking her pug, Enzo. He had just done his business and was enthusiastically scratching up a patch of grass with his hind legs. Dorothy pulled a baggie out of a pocket on her floral print dress and leaned over to clean up after him. He considered stopping to talk to her, but knew that she found her present task slightly embarrassing—as if a proper pug would use the toilet.

Having confirmed the front was clear, he circled the block and entered the alley, coasting silently toward the back of the building. Nobody appeared to be secluded among the usual assortment of dumpsters. John unbuckled his helmet, opened the back door with his key, and gave one final glance around before entering.

Once inside he breathed a quiet sigh of relief. In the months since he'd been shot in the alley, he'd been on high alert. This vigilance was wearing on him. He hoisted the bike onto his shoulder and carried it so the hub wouldn't make its steady click, click, click as it rolled.

When he reached the lobby he ignored the elevator and hesitated on the stairs leading up to the first floor. Voices drifted in the hallway above him—familiar voices.

He recognized Scott's voice first. The quieter one was Sharon. From what he could hear of the conversation, the young man was putting the moves on John's next door neighbor. He was tempted to listen more but knew Scott well and could anticipate the direction this was going. He started up the stairs but stepped carefully, passing over the creaky third riser, keeping his breath even and quiet.

When his head reached the level of the second floor hallway, he could see Sharon leaning against the wall, one foot on the floor, the other against the wall. Her knee was pointing outward at Scott who was standing so close that he could have leaned over and kissed her. One of his hands was on the wall next to Sharon's head.

The darkness of the stairwell concealed John's presence for a few moments and he could hear Scott press Sharon, "You know you want to go with me. It's one of the best B&Bs in Victoria."

John gritted his teeth. Even though the kid was a direct descendant, he wanted to gut him right there.

At this point, Sharon turned her head toward John. She dropped her foot to the floor and gently pushed Scott back. He stood up straight.

"Hi. We were just talking about you." She dropped her eyes to the floor momentarily before returning her gaze to him.

A puzzled look flashed across Scott's face and he cocked his head at Sharon.

"We were thinking you and Nicole might want to join us for dinner tonight at Doyle's—if she's in town."

Scott scowled slightly, then his expression softened. "Right, that's if you're not too busy." John suppressed a smile. He figured a double date was the last thing Scott wanted right now.

John pulled the bike off his shoulder and dropped it to the floor. It bounced and settled on the carpet. "She's in town. In fact we just finished looking at condos."

Sharon frowned.

Scott chimed in. "She sold her place in San Francisco already?"

"Yep. Good market and she got several above asking offers. She expects to be here permanently by the end of the month."

Sharon asked, "Are you planning on moving in with her?" Her tone was sharp—more accusation than question.

He shook his head. "No." He understood her anger. Months before he had gently rebuffed Sharon when she came on to him, explaining he had been married before and it had ended badly. Now, it probably seemed like a brush off since he and Nicole started dating soon after.

John was rescued by the sound of scratching behind the door next to Sharon. She opened it and a cat darted out. It rubbed briefly against her legs and made a beeline for John, weaving in and out of his feet and purring like an Indy Car on the starting line.

He reached down and scratched Mocha on the side of his face. He pushed against John's hand.

John looked up at Sharon. She was sporting a slight smile.

"Don't listen to that cat. I already fed him."

He grinned and stood up. Mocha dashed past Scott—ignoring

him—to John's door where he stood expectantly and yowled in as demanding a tone as he could muster.

"Maybe I can find him at least a snack." He looked at Scott, then at Sharon. Last thing he wanted to do was leave Scott alone with this woman. "I'll call Nicole to see if she's available. Even if she isn't, I'll join you."

Scott responded with an unenthusiastic, "Sure thing."

Mocha yowled again. John smiled and pushed his bike to his own door.

Inside his apartment he picked up The Seattle Times that he had set aside that morning and flipped through it. The Seahawks were gearing up for their first preseason game and the Mariners were still on the bubble for the playoffs. An item in the entertainment section caught his eye: Million Dollar Last Apostle Challenge Brings out Crackpots and Scholars.

"The producers of The Last Apostle television series have made a million dollar offer to the person who can prove that the apostle John is still alive or truly dead. The potential reward has brought out a cast of cranks and academics. A number of people have claimed to be the apostle himself, including one Utah woman who claims to be the reincarnated John.

"According to Professor Wes Cavanaugh, the executive producer of the show, 'All serious claims are being reviewed by a team of respected archeologists and biblical scholars. Some view this as a publicity stunt, but this is a legitimate offer'."

John shook his head. He went on to read that proving the fate of the last living disciple of Christ was problematic at best, and the studio's money was safe. But the offer, along with the protests by religious groups, had created a buzz around the show. It was now one of the most anticipated shows of the season.

John rolled up the newspaper and threw it down on the coffee table. He had hoped the series would live a short and unremarkable life. He had protected his identity for over nineteen centuries. Could the apocalypse be brought on by the fallout from a TV show?

He picked up his cell phone and selected Nicole's number from the favorites. She picked up almost immediately.

"How's my guy?"

His mouth went dry. He should be used to the sensation of a new love by this time, but it was still as fresh as the first time.

"Life has all kinds of possibilities—thanks to you."

"Glad to be of service."

He cleared his throat. "I know it's been a long day and you were going to take it easy, but we've been invited to Doyle's by Sharon and Scott."

After a moment of silence she replied, "I know Scott may be—"

"Don't say it."

"Sorry. It's just that I'd rather scrub my toilet with a toothbrush than spend time with him."

"I know. But I don't want to leave the two of them together."

She sighed. "The things we have to do."

"I'll make it up to you, somehow." He glanced at his watch. "If you're there at 5:00 we can have half an hour alone before they show."

"That's a good start—wait a minute. I have an incoming call. Hold on for a sec."

John glanced at the newspaper on the table. On top of his worries about Professor Cavanaugh's show, he had another problem—how was he going to protect Nicole?

She came back on the line.

"John, you'll never believe who just called."

Her tone of fear made his throat go dry. "Who?"

"Professor Cavanaugh. Wes Cavanaugh."

"What did he want?"

"He wants to meet with you. Wouldn't tell me why."

John swallowed. Life was about to get very complicated.

Authors Note: Writing is a Team Sport

One thing that I've learned in my journey as a writer is that it is not a solitary profession—it is truly a team sport. This book was born of my question: What if Jesus really did mean that John would remain alive until he returned? I always thought it would make a great television series.

The spark of the idea was first nurtured when I found out Mike Maples, the husband of a co-worker, was a professional screen writer. He liked the idea and pitched it to several industry professionals. Unfortunately, they were looking for more edgy concepts at the time. Mike suggested: Write it as a book.

I had always enjoyed writing and his enthusiasm for the project encouraged me to give it a shot. About a year later I was done—at least I thought so. Along the way my wife, Laurie, had read it countless times and given me sound advice. I had also accumulated a number of readers who provided encouragement and feedback, and in some cases connected me to industry professionals. Buzz Leonard, David Leeper, Sr. Shirley Mallory, Francis Moses, Sue Bregel, Andrew James, Alex Bruski, Crystal Warren, John Adamski, Robert Gartner, Woody and Donna Gatlin, Patti Scarrah, Jacques and Valeria Musafir, Mike and Kathy Evans, Ruth Mercado, Helm Lehman, Tom Howorth, Michael Kostov, and Robert Coronado were all important members of my team as I labored in the minor leagues of writing.

I then joined the Northwest Christian Writers Association (NCWA) sure that my book was ready and I'd be able to quit my day job any moment. I learned quickly that:

1. My book was not ready;
2. Most authors have one thing in common—a day job; but
3. I was now part of a supportive group that could teach me the craft and the path to publication.

Through NCWA and the American Christian Fiction Writers (ACFW) I was blessed to work with countless mentors, supporters, and critique partners like James Rubart, Kathleen Freeman, Amy Letinsky, Randy Ingermanson, Kim Vandel, Loree Cameron, Steve Brock, Pat Schantz, Connie Mace, Dennis "Doc" Hensley, Gigi Murfitt, Mindy Peltier, Sarah Moser, Austin Boyd, Les Stobbe, Karen Higgins, Lori Reichel Howe, Michael Duncan, Michelle Holloman, Janalyn Voigt, and Lynnette Bonner.

I also connected with two editors who gave me important guidance. Jeff Gerke coached me on the basics of the craft early in my journey. And his innovative on-line Marcher Lord Select contest exposed *The Last Apostle* to the world. It led every round until the final. It was a thrilling ride for this novice.

Mick Silva reviewed the entire manuscript, gave me some great direction, and also validated the strength of the tale. He also said I had what it took to become a career writer. That means a lot coming from someone who learned his craft at a major publishing house.

The team at Made for Grace Publishing fell in love with my concept and helped take it over the finish line. The great cover art and layout work by DeeDee Heathman, marketing planning and advice by Bryan Heathman, Catherine Barrack's copy editing, and audio version work by Kathy Knox turned a dream into reality. You exceeded my expectations.

John Harten, my editor, gave me some great ways to strengthen the story and provided some essential encouragement. And his knowledge of ancient times helped correct factual flaws. It helps to have an editor who was an archeology major.

The major credit has to go to Jesus, the Author of all. He planted the idea in the first place, put the right people next to me on the journey, inspired me in innumerable ways, and even used writing as a form of therapy during difficult periods in my life. I once gave up on Him, but He never gave up on me.

If I've forgotten names blame it on this long journey, my imperfect memory, and the fact that we needed to save room for the story.

Dennis Brooke

WATER FOR LIFE

The lack of clean water is a world wide crisis that costs many lives. Some estimates say that 1600 children under five die each day due to lack of clean water, sanitation, and hygiene. Unfortunately there is no Galilean Foundation with ground breaking technology to help provide drinkable water.

Fortunately there are real life organizations that are making a difference in this crisis. I support World Vision and their clean water initiatives.

As the World Vision website says:
Clean water frees children from deadly water-related diseases. It liberates women and children from a life spent gathering dirty water. It restores health and opens the door to education, a promising future, and a full life—the kind of life God intends.

Go to www.worldvision.org and search for "clean water" to find out they help and how you can be part of the solution.

Discussion Questions

1. The character of Johanan/John walks the line of being less than honest without lying:
   a. In what situations do you think it's appropriate to be less than open and honest?
   b. In what situations are you less than honest—but it's really not appropriate?

2. The modern John uses a clean water initiative to reach people for Christ:
   a. What are your personal efforts to spread the good news?
   b. Is there something that you—or even your book club—should start doing?

3. Themes:
   a. What do you think is the central theme of this book?
   b. What scene best illustrates this?

4. Longevity:
   a. If you were going to live a long life in a youthful body, what would you do different?
   b. Are there any of those things you should do even though you don't expect to live for two thousand years?

5. Johanan/John has to give up personal desires for a greater good.
   a. What is a personal situation where you had to make the same type of choice?

b. What were the results?

6. John goes to churches for several different denominations.
    a. If you go to church, how did you choose your church?
    b. If you don't go to church, how would you choose one?

7. If you send an email to John Amato what response do you get?

Have your own discussion question? Post them on the group Facebook page at www.facebook.com/groups/TheLastApostle or at www.TheLastApostle.com

CPSIA information can be obtained at www.ICGtesting.com
Printed in the USA
BVOW08s1211190116

433426BV00001B/1/P

9 781613 398395